GIRL DINNER

BY OLIVIE BLAKE

THE ATLAS TRILOGY
The Atlas Six
The Atlas Paradox
The Atlas Complex

Alone With You in the Ether
Masters of Death
One For My Enemy
Gifted & Talented
Girl Dinner

Januaries

AS ALEXENE FAROL FOLLMUTH
My Mechanical Romance
Twelfth Knight

GIRL DINNER

OLIVIE BLAKE

MANTLE

First published 2025 by Tom Doherty Associates / Tor Publishing Group

First published in the UK 2025 by Mantle
an imprint of Pan Macmillan
The Smithson, 6 Briset Street, London EC1M 5NR
EU representative: Macmillan Publishers Ireland Ltd, 1st Floor,
The Liffey Trust Centre, 117–126 Sheriff Street Upper,
Dublin 1 D01 YC43
Associated companies throughout the world

ISBN 978-1-0350-1142-1 HB
ISBN 978-1-0350-1143-8 TPB

Copyright © Alexene Farol Follmuth 2025

The right of Alexene Farol Follmuth to be identified as the
author of this work has been asserted in accordance with
the Copyright, Designs and Patents Act 1988.

All rights reserved. No part of this publication may be reproduced,
stored in a retrieval system, or transmitted, in any form, or by any means
(including, without limitation, electronic, mechanical, photocopying, recording or
otherwise) without the prior written permission of the publisher.

Pan Macmillan does not have any control over, or any responsibility for,
any author or third-party websites (including, without limitation, URLs,
emails and QR codes) referred to in or on this book.

1 3 5 7 9 8 6 4 2

A CIP catalogue record for this book is available from the British Library.

Endpaper art by Little Chmura

Typeset by
Printed and bound in the UK using 100% Renewable Electricity by CPI Group (UK) Ltd

This book is sold subject to the condition that it shall not, by way of
trade or otherwise, be lent, hired out, or otherwise circulated without
the publisher's prior consent in any form of binding or cover other than
that in which it is published and without a similar condition including
this condition being imposed on the subsequent purchaser.

Visit **www.panmacmillan.com** to read more about all our books
and to buy them.

For my sisters, eternal friends

I. RECRUITMENT

II. EDUCATION

III. INITIATION

IV. INVITATION

V. DINNER

PART I

RECUITMENT

Women only want one thing . . . a forehead kiss from a handsome man who brings home the bacon for her to make tartiflette from scratch.

—Transcript from a VidStar by
@TheCountryWife

SEVEN

WEEKS

TO

INITIATION.

1

The clatter of dinner that evening was familiar, monotonous, like the pain in her low back that never really went away. For some months Sloane had also been desperate to become unaware of her perineum. Not even for it to feel normal or even comfortable—that felt too high an ask. To simply forget she had a perineal region would be bliss itself within the context of her daily aspirations. Gradually she had been able to go minutes, then hours, then days and even weeks, and on the whole it felt as if she had impressively willed her way to nirvana. But with the euphoria of forgetting her pelvic floor came the reminder that thirty-three years of bipedalism and gravity could never really be thwarted; that if it wasn't one thing, it would be another. If it wasn't the third-degree perineal tear that had taken four months of woo-woo meditation and therapeutic fingering to heal, it was run-of-the-mill mortality—the helpless slip of a vertebral disc. In these moments Sloane became overwhelmed by a rush of disappointment in herself. She was ordinariness incarnate.

Behind her, Isla, apple of her eye, object of a love so richly milk-sweet and cream-fat it sometimes felt erotic, banged on the tray of her high chair, not for the first time that evening and, with the way things were going, also not the last.

Bang. "Max," said Sloane. Bang bang bang. "Max, she's trying to get your attention."

"Hm?" Max looked up from his phone. (His phone! His pressing emails! His fucking emails! His precious fucking news headlines!)

"Sweetie," Max cooed to Isla, "don't bang your cup." Then he returned to his phone.

Bang. "Max." A deep, steadying sigh. "She wants more juice." Bang.

"Did you see this about the new humanities dean?"

Bang. Bang. "What?" Sloane sampled the spaghetti from the pot of boiling water, gauging it not for the perfect degree of chewy al dente perfection as she had during her peak hostessing years, but for the slight quality of mush, for ease of chewing. Fucking Christ, another bowl of spaghetti Bolognese felt like it might kill her in some unmistakably spiritual way, but it was the only thing Isla would deign to eat—the only thing Isla would even *consider* broaching the sanctity of her mouth. Her sweet darling mouth, which was iron deficient. A sweet innocent deficiency that was likely causing Isla's poor sleep, her inability to stay down on her own, through the night, so that Sloane could do the same. Bang!

"The new dean. I told you, right? Crawford got MeToo'd."

Briefly, Sloane considered saying aloud to her husband that no, Crawford didn't *get MeToo'd,* he got the consequences of his own actions—or so Sloane had discovered months ago, back when Max insisted they have the entire department over in thanks for solving their little two-body problem (two academics in need of two jobs, with Sloane being the extra, undecorated body and therefore the problem; thus, the humanities department had strung her up to their chariot to be dragged through the city of Troy, or so it felt to Sloane on the scale of domestic humiliations). Victoria Ellsworth hadn't said a word about what she called *the incident* to anyone in the department, and then when she'd been up for tenure Crawford had voted against her, citing the fact that she was, quote, unprofessional, unquote. BANG!

"Max," said Sloane, "the juice?"

"You want more juice, sweetie? Juice?" Max again put on the doting voice he always used to speak with Isla, the one that screamed *girl dad,* the one that Sloane had once been so sure meant she'd chosen the right partner in life—when she'd been so unassailably confident that the sexiest thing a man could be was tender with his child. "You know," he remarked, "we should really just give her water."

Something inside Sloane turned briefly molten.

"Max, I—" I tried that. I've *tried* that. Are you—? Are you suggesting that I'm—? Do you honestly think that I—? (Sometimes her mind went white with unproductive rage.) "Okay, give her water, then." See how that works out for you, fuckhead. Love of my life. Father of my child. Fucking fuckwit.

"Are you nervous about tomorrow?" Max had slipped a hand over Sloane's hip where she was angled on one leg, flamingo-like, beside the stove. He smelled of his usual bergamot, the detergent Sloane bought for them, not at all like a sweet baby head or its constant, inexplicable waft of maple syrup. Sometimes Sloane got alarmed by how much bigger he was than Isla.

Then Max slid by her, opened the fridge door, and bent to look inside.

"Nervous?" Sloane echoed belatedly.

"Where's the juice?"

She gestured sightlessly. "Right there, behind the thing."

"The thing?"

"Yeah, the thing. The fucking—the *thing,* Max, the thing." Since Sloane had gotten pregnant, she'd had trouble remembering certain words. It was like there was a sieve where her brain had once been. Her brain, which was worth hundreds of thousands of dollars. How much of that value fell out whenever she couldn't remember the word for the thing? The thing, the thing where— with the. That thing. (Had this single transaction put her twenty dollars in the red somehow?) Come on, Max, the thing!

Max announced profoundly, "Should I get out a new bottle? Looks like we're out."

"Max, we're not *out*, it's right—" Sloane hissed a breath she hoped he couldn't hear as she walked over and shifted aside the thing. (Water pitcher.) "There, it's right there."

"Oh!" Max sounded delighted with himself, like a child who'd done something hilarious, like someone on Twitter (whatever Twitter even was now) who'd misread a line, accidentally read the word six as sex, hahahahahahahahahahahahaahaha!!! "So, how are you feeling?"

"About what?" BANG! Isla had thrown the cup.

Now Isla was whining about the dropped cup. "About the new semester?"

Sloane imagined saying: "You mean about the job? The job that I have? That I've done for like eight years? The one we met doing? The job that we both do? That job?"

But she actually said: "I'm a little nervous about Isla."

"Oh, she'll be fine, daycare will be good for her."

"Well, sure, but you're not the one who'll be abandoning her." Sloane wiped some clammy sweat from her forehead and realized she wanted to stop breathing. She had maybe already stopped breathing just now, without noticing. The very normal thing that she was about to do, that all mothers did—that certainly all mothers without her socioeconomic privilege did—was actually the worst thing that had ever happened to her. She hadn't even wanted kids! Until she did. And now suddenly she was carrying around the atavistic weight of all the mothers before her whose children had been abandoned for eight hours a day, sacrificed on the altar of pointless labor.

Not pointless. She cared about her work. She took great pride in it, had always loved teaching, found sociology to be endlessly interesting in an esoteric way. But recontextualized by the tiny human being who depended on her for food, sleep, and comfort, it all just seemed kind of oppressive, or maybe that was what came of watching too much mommy content on VidStar.

(Which wasn't even to mention the trad wives! What a trainwreck. Sloane's sociologist brain couldn't look away.)

"That's true." Max kissed the back of her neck as Isla began to try to escape the high chair.

But wouldn't it be nice to return to work? Sloane was neither a housewife nor a "trad" one, and there was only so much time one could devote to poop consistency or creative ways to sneak iron into food. Wouldn't it be *invigorating* in some way to rejoin the realm of adults, who neither threw things nor had to be talked down, as with hostage negotiations? To have five minutes to stare at the water stain she could only assume would adorn the ceiling of her new adjunct office? Precious time to dissociate; time for devoted, unrelenting calculations about how to make thirty-five undergrads care more about the principles of sociology than how they'll next get laid. Impossible. Fucking Sisyphean. Of course, as with parenting, the trick was consistent methodology. You simply had to teach to the person who was most enthusiastic to be there, as Sloane had said last year—no, fuck, two years ago now—to a bright young female student who was interested in pursuing her doctorate. You can't think about all the yawns, the eyes glazing over—if you let that take you down, then you'll never get through the day, much less the semester. You have to *assume* you're reaching someone, but it's not your job to actually *see it happen*. It's not your job to know during any given lecture how many of those students will actually go on to become something great—it's only your job to give them the tools, the curiosity to do it. Sloane used to just say bullshit like that on command! It used to just pour out of her, it was honestly amazing.

"Max, can you—?" Isla was nearly out of her high chair now, valiantly approaching flight, and though Sloane prided herself on not being the sort of mother who fretted all the time about possible injury, everything her darling daughter was or ever would be was contained in that precious, partially formed skeleton head. "Baby girl, just wait two more minutes, dinner's coming—"

Isla commenced an eldritch howl.

"Juice!" cried Max jubilantly, presenting her with it. Isla promptly threw it on the ground. For the record, Max didn't do the cooking because Sloane had always cared more about food; she *liked* preparing food, she enjoyed cooking, she loved eating. (She used to do the fasting thing, where she only ate two meals a day, and she didn't want those two precious meals to be *Max's* idea of culinary delight—she wanted fucking pasta. She wanted pasta and fucking cheese!) Now, of course, she couldn't remember why she'd ever insisted on such a thing. At this point she imagined handing the spatula to Max and hearing wait, where's the pot? To which she would inevitably reply it's right there, behind the thing.

Eventually Sloane dished the spaghetti into bowls, into the carefully styled ceramics that had been her pride and joy for so many years. She said, "Max, the dog?" and Max charitably looked up from his phone and fed the dog. She said, "Frankie, sit," and Frankie did no such thing, so she said again, "Frankie, *I said sit,*" and she thought for a second about how she had loved the dog so much before, when Frankie had loved Max and only Max and Sloane had thought that was fine actually, the dog was a living thing, it didn't *have* to love her, but then she'd had Isla and fallen prey to the erotic motherlove and realized Frankie was a real drain on resources. She went inside to fill two water glasses from the thing and realized it was almost empty. Fine, Max could have the cold water, she didn't care anymore. She set down Isla's food, said, "Blow on it for her." She set down Max's food and then her own. She refilled the thing with water.

"I guess Daddy isn't eating," said Max playfully, in his doting voice, to Isla, which was how Sloane realized she had forgotten to put out the silverware. Her back hurt and she briefly folded over, trying to relieve the pressure. Max came up behind her and got a fork.

One fork.

Just one.

He returned to feed Isla, who knocked the spoon away from her mouth. "Isla, come on!" he yelped at her. *Come on.* Be cool, bro. Come on. As if that meant fucking anything to an eighteen-month-old.

"Isla." Sloane turned her voice sweet, dulcet, gentle. "Isla, try a bite? Mm, spaghetti, yum!"

Isla again batted the spoon away and looked sweetly, dulcetly, gently up at her. "All done," announced Isla proudly. Not a single bite eaten. It was the day before the first day of fall semester—the day before Isla would learn the meaning of desertion, the day before Sloane returned to work and became, again, a person. Seven days before she received a message in her inbox from Britt Landau asking a personal favor—a message claiming that Alex Carlisle had asked specifically for Sloane.

Dr. Sloane Hartley fell into her chair with a sense of dismal failure, the likes of which she had never experienced before, only to realize that she didn't have anything to eat with.

Max reached out a big hand, covering hers with his own, smiling the smile that had once driven her halfway to orgasm. They were different from other parents, from other marriages, theirs was a revolutionary union, if she needed something from him she only needed to ask!

"Try to take on some extracurriculars this year," Max suggested. "It might reassure Dean Burns."

Yes, Sloane thought encouragingly to herself, prove your worth to Burns. The problem is you're just not doing enough! Unfortunately, with all that free time and extra energy she'd had since giving birth, she simply couldn't summon the will to argue.

"Yeah," she said, "good idea," and stood up to get a fork.

2

Nina moved into the campus apartments a day early, with permission from the University, because fall recruitment started early.

Her sister, Jasleen, could not for the life of her understand why Nina had any interest in rushing a sorority. To be fair, Nina did have trouble explaining it. The best she could come up with was "it sounds fun," despite the fact that rush requirements were the opposite of fun, and were, in fact, punishing. Until rush was at an end and a bid from a house had been formally extended, there would be no drinking, no parties, no carousing of any sort, and Nina would have to come to class each day with her face and hair made up, operating under the watchful eye of every sorority girl on campus while pretending to be unaware this was the case. It was not unlike existing under the conditions of a debilitating crush, wherein one must appear effortless and casual despite slow, molten destruction at one's core, and the expectation of—indeed, hope for!—unrelenting surveillance. So possibly that was why Jas didn't believe her.

Of Nina's three apartment mates—one of which, Simone, was her randomly assigned roommate from last year, while the other two, Mei and Adelaide, had been suitemates in their eight-person cluster of rooms—only Adelaide was in a house, and she was extremely upbeat about the possibility of being Nina's sister. Adelaide's encouragement meant that Simone and Mei did not really ask questions, which was good, as Nina had a daily barrage of them from her sister, e.g., "Can't you just hang out with your friend without performing some kind of patronizing bonding ritual?"

Actually, Nina hoped not to be in the same house as Adelaide. Which was not to say that Adelaide wasn't beautiful and smart and generally deserving of great envy. Nina believed Adelaide had the prettiest face of all her friends, which was saying something, as Nina had always attracted pretty friends. But when it came to the known and publicly understood ranking of Adelaide's sorority compared to the other houses on the row, matters could frankly be improved upon. Adelaide herself could have done better had she not been a transplant from rural Idaho and therefore unaware of how to dress herself during her own recruitment. As dicey as it was to be a sophomore going through rush—by most panhellenic philosophies, you simply could not repair a sophomore's bad reputation, nor could you successfully mold her into the Ideal Woman of Two-to-Three Greek Letters—there was a profitable tradeoff with respect to the University's ecological learning curve. To Nina's mind, what she lacked in malleability she made up for in maturity and social expertise.

Approximately a quarter of the University's student body population was part of the Greek system, which statistically a person could take or leave as a matter of significance except for acknowledging the stratosphere *within* the system, wherein a person received an additional layer of value by association. An individual could be decently meritorious on their own, but a member of three-Greek-letters was already gifted a personality type and a corresponding likelihood of success. Acceptance by the gatekeepers of social capital meant that even on an ugly day, a bad hair day, a bloated day, you were automatically more beautiful than the vast majority of your peers. Even if you didn't look your most sexually delectable at any given moment, you were, in a more transcendent way, hot. Two sexy Greek letters had said so.

"You really think it matters what a bunch of white girls think of you?" said Jas. For having shared an upbringing and a womb, they had substantively very little in common. Jas was a comparative literature major with a minor in gender studies, whereas Nina daydreamed on occasion about girls too but she didn't announce it to the world. Also, they'd gone to the same predominantly white high school, which meant that if Nina didn't think about it very hard, she could easily forget she wasn't white. Her friends were white. Her boyfriends had mostly been white (she'd tried for Jonathan Zein, who was half Lebanese, but that had always been a pipe dream). The term "coconut" was often thrown around—brown on the outside, white on the inside. Thoughtless weaponry that was the height of disparagement to Jas, which to Nina could be easily laughed away.

The important thing was that Nina understood the trajectory of her chosen path. If she was going to go to a top twenty law school, which she had every intention of doing, followed by securing a spot at a big law firm in order to pay her various University debts as well as take care of her parents—in the only *actual* display of privilege Nina could think of, Jas had taken herself out of the running, filially speaking—she was going to need not only achievements, but connections.

The last year, her freshman year, had not gone as smoothly as expected. No need to ask why—bygones and such. Suffice it to say, this year was her second chance, her opportunity for necessary improvement. In order to win it all back ("it" being academic excellence, professional success, the ability to look at herself without a disemboweling sense of shame, so on and so forth), Nina was going to invent a new version of herself. It was baptism by initiation, transcendence to a better model, via glorious rebirth. And not just any reincarnation. To offset the previous year of her life, Nina needed to reach a better plane, a higher one.

She was going to need The House.

That was how she thought of them: in terms of the proper noun, perhaps even the royal. They were, of course, the same Greek jumble of meaninglessness as the others, but its members were in no way interchangeable with the community at large.

Each member of The House was not only noticeably beautiful, they were also peerlessly high-achieving, singular among the fray of their intended fields. Nina had, by then, experienced the presence of The House in a few of her classes—occasionally a small gaggle of them—and understood them to be exceptionally gifted as a group. The House's average GPA was a 3.86, which was unheard of. Their philanthropy had been lauded by multiple national media outlets. Among their recent alumnae were a sitting governor, an Oscar-nominated actress, a Pulitzer-winning playwright, an Olympic sprinter, multiple acclaimed academics, four celebrity lawyers, and a zoologist whose book on invertebrate sentience had been selected for a presidential honor.

The University at large was known for churning out the next generation of leaders, true, but The House was next level. Statistically, that degree of success was beyond made—those women were chosen. *Curated*. Being a member of The House was not only to be gifted *access* to the launching pad for eternal success, it was to be preselected for it. It was to be bestowed upon, dipped in the River Styx for an extra coating of invulnerability, because you were *already* worthy.

"Your desperation for external validation is honestly tragic," commented Jas over video call. Jas was watching Nina put on eyeliner, which she herself eschewed as a matter of principle. Despite this, if both of them had sat perfectly still it would have looked like Nina had taken a selfie. They wore twin expressions of fond disdain.

"I have to go," Nina replied. "I've got to suckle the teat of white greatness."

"That's not what I said because it's disgusting, but spiritually it's not untrue. You make me deeply ashamed of you." Jas sighed.

"Should I wear the purple dress or the red?" Nina asked. If she couldn't make the perfect first impression, forget it. The House was notoriously brutal. They slashed their numbers in half each day despite the University specifying daily percentages of call-backs. How could you argue with The House? It was almost like being a man.

"The red," said Jas. "And tell Arya I said hello."

"When I pass this greeting along to him," Nina posed, "should my eyes say, 'By the way, my sister is willing to compromise her feminism to suck your dick,' or would you prefer a coyer message?"

"That one will be sufficient," said Jas, before hanging up.

3

Sloane no longer understood how to dress herself and yet she came to work anyway. She vaguely recalled the sensation of caring what other people thought of her—about whether her waistline or the precision of her eyeliner had any bearing on her performance. She had never technically known herself without the gripping fear of being judged. Now, though, there was a window of less than five minutes with which to doubt herself. Mothering was favorable that way, redistributing gravity so that it no longer mattered whether her black button-down was too harsh for her skin tone or unseasonable for the time of year or too oversized for her frame. It did not have snot or milk stains that Sloane could see upon cursory inspection, which made it suitable. She would later learn this confidence was in fact unearned.

She and Max had agreed it made the most sense for her to drop off Isla, given that Max had the earlier lecture. This logistical element was considered more pressing than Sloane's desire to die. She had emotionally prepared herself for weeks in advance by imagining the worst-case scenarios: Isla screaming, Isla taking an enormous shit into Sloane's open blouse, Isla toddling off with delight to finally be free of her. All seemed equally plausible. Astoundingly, Sloane's painstaking efforts to torment herself in prologue did not help the situation on the day.

Sloane didn't know many other women in her same stage of motherhood; most of her peers were childless by choice and her high school and college friends (most of them gently estranged, a side effect of time and maturity) had much older children.

When Sloane scoured the internet for an applicable tribe, she'd been met with a variety of responses—the mothers who'd gone straight back to work were pleased she had finally given up the hopeless frivolity of day-to-day mothering and could no longer make them feel guilty over their own children forming substandard attachments; the mothers still at home queried whether this was really what was best for the child given that the early years were so tender; the mothers equally tormented by drop-offs suggested that at least Sloane was right there on campus and could easily drop by and visit, a privilege for which she ought to be grateful and, frankly, shut up. Sloane did not want to say, but visiting would torment me *and* her, don't you think? Because even Sloane understood it was a sign of Good Motherhood to casually surveil even if it felt counterproductive to Isla's engagement. Though, even the daycare itself had been apologetic about their play-based curriculum, meaning that formal instruction for Sloane's eighteen-month-old baby would be limited, and therefore much of the internet would purse their lips and say hmm.

Sloane had come in to meet the daycare teacher the week before, and Isla had seemed happy to play for the hour they'd spent among the other professorial offspring. Sloane had explained the situation with Max and the two-body problem and the whole thing where Sloane had been on a tenure track at her SLAC ("Small liberal arts college," Sloane clarified, slightly red-faced) but they'd decided that Max's offer was too good to turn down, even though here she would only be a spousal hire with uncertain benefits outside of her year-to-year contract and the first year they'd arrived there had been no courses for her to teach and the University daycare had been at capacity so she'd wound up staying home with Isla longer than she'd planned—leading to, well, kind of an attach-y attachment, case in point (Isla had started crying when Sloane tried to inch away while she played). But, of course, the whole benefits thing wasn't an issue, because Max was on a tenure track! And even though at Universities like these they often put several people on a track to one (1) tenured position, that was essentially irrelevant, because Max was brilliant and that was the whole reason Sloane had derailed her career for his. Not that she had *derailed* it, that was the wrong word, she'd just, you know, idled sideways into a suboptimal position given that she didn't care for this kind of high-stakes environment, and scholarship by Sloane's definition had different, more cerebral standards, something that was ultimately an ecclesiastical divergence, a slight disparity between beliefs. Although, as Max had argued—not argued, it wasn't an *argument,* he was just kind of contrarian by nature, a slight roll of the dice personality-wise that really, most people loved— Sloane had previously published a book that was exceedingly well-received, albeit modestly (*very* modestly) distributed, and even if research wasn't what she wanted to do, necessarily, the adjunct situation still kept her in her desired field of study, and she could always work her way into a tenure track position eventually. But even if she didn't, Max was basically a lock for tenure—provided that he didn't, like, accidentally piss off someone at a dinner party or something!—not that he would—it was pretty easy to forgive him basically anything—so the point was Sloane didn't have to worry about losing health insurance or whether they could afford their positively ludicrous mortgage, even though for some reason (?) she absolutely did.

Anyway, the teacher had been patient and sympathetic and reassuring, as if Sloane's was not a complicated story at all, and Isla's circumstances not so unusual. It was soothing, and Sloane vibrated at a slightly lower frequency, feeling marginally less likely to die. However, on the morning of the very first drop-off, a new teacher seemed frazzled to see her. She repeated Isla's name several times as if mentally referencing a section of a text she had once read in high school. Sloane asked where Miss Jamie was, and this new woman said Miss Jamie didn't work there in a way that suggested Miss Jamie had *never* worked there, and had in fact never existed, as with a ghost. Sloane realized she was dragging out the process of drop-off and this was unideal for Isla. She went to kiss her daughter's shock-white face and realized Isla was crying silently with fear, which was when Sloane understood that she was a monster. Then she went to her office because just because a person is a monster doesn't mean they don't have bills to pay.

Because Sloane would be a mere adjunct, only blessed with employment at the University thanks to Max's preeminence in the field and his arduous defense of her intellect, she was given one of the shared offices in the basement of the college of liberal arts, despite in fact belonging to the social sciences. This wasn't on its face a problem, given that when she and Max had been younger and Sloane had planned to stay at her previous SLAC where curriculum was more fluid and the necessity to publish more relaxed, she'd had the freedom to pursue scholarship any which way she chose, which could have easily involved literature or theology. But now that she was here, there was a sense of captivity to it all, something that felt almost Faustian but without the promise of artistic glory.

The shared office had a chalkboard-style nameplate, so Sloane wrote Dr. Hartley on the top and left the bottom blank for whoever her officemate would be. A single ribbon of string hung from the vent, unmoving. There were two small IKEA bookcases, two tiny wastebaskets, a stain on the rug beneath the worn office chair that belonged to the slightly cleaner desk. Sloane claimed it and set a framed copy of the previous year's Christmas card photo on her desk, trying to breathe through the pain in her chest at the thought of Isla, who would be fine. Probably. Isla would probably love the new teacher, Miss Lily, even more than she loved Sloane! Eventually Isla would grow up and have thoughts and opinions and believe that Sloane was stupid. Already Sloane was convinced that Isla was going to grow up with a flawed understanding of gender roles. "Oh, my mother did all the cooking," Isla would tell her friends. "It's just how things were at my house. She still called herself a feminist, though, it was honestly so sad," and then Isla and her Gen Alpha friends would pull Sloane's books (okay, *book*) off the shelves and cry with laughter.

Sloane wiped her eyes quickly and opened the document with the day's lecture. Then she went to class and delivered the lecture. It was mostly fine and she only brought up Isla twice (she was certainly not going to be the kind of woman who was A Mother™, noun, one who referenced nothing but her own motherhood; according to the internet, a Good Mother had many facets, including some modicum of a self). Sloane did repeatedly forget words and names and lose her place in her train of thought, which again had been happening since she'd gotten pregnant.

"Can I just say, I find it so refreshing to hear you talk," said a stunning freshman named Dalil Serrano whose hair was gleaming and whose perineum was intact and who would probably grow up to sit on the Supreme Court or something. "I have ADHD and I swear, something about the way you lecture tickles my brain."

Sloane did not have ADHD that she knew of. What Sloane *did* have was an arresting anxiety about her daughter and a body that had sacrificed its personal brain cells to the craft of Isla's perfection. But she was flattered in a way, because it was at least a compliment, and so she said thank you, and felt very online.

She returned to her office, noting the presence of a second person who had come and gone. She checked her watch—an hour until she could go get Isla. Luckily she had more work than she could possibly complete in an hour. She had more work than she could complete in three lifetimes, most of which existed only ephemerally, in theory. The work of becoming more inherently valuable, such that she might deserve job security or even, dare she say it, some presumption of competency that was not derived from her husband's accolades.

"Dr. Hartley?"

A voice startled Sloane because it sounded, at first, like it had come from somewhere inside her imagination. Like she'd dropped off into a pornographic fantasy. She shook herself awake, although she had definitely been awake and actively working, and because she no longer had the time or energy for an inner life.

"Yes?"

The man at the door introduced himself by a name that instantly disappeared into the ether, adding, "I'm sorry I'm late." A youngish man, maybe mid- or late-twenties—not an undergraduate student, that much was clear—stood there with . . . with shoulders. With shoulders and a jaw and a chin and that hair. It was almost impossible to take him in all at once without squinting. He sort of . . . gleamed.

"The office at the college didn't get in touch with me until about an hour ago—anyway." The man at the door cut himself off with a droll flap of one hand. "The point is, I'm glad I caught you."

He had a dimple. Just one dimple. This made everything substantially worse in some horrifying, Gothic way. "Oh, hi," said Sloane, and trailed off, which perhaps made her seem like she was stupid or geriatrically confused, neither of which would be entirely off base for a professor in this department.

"I'm your TA," added the youngish man charitably, who was most likely a doctoral student, Sloane concluded. "I'm in my third year in quantitative soc."

"Who's your advisor?" asked Sloane, faintly impressed she was still forming words.

"Burns."

"Oh, brutal."

"Yeah." Her new TA laughed and swept a hand through his

raven hair as he took the seat opposite hers at her desk. She had the vague sensation of wanting to witness him on horseback. "I don't sleep much."

Her phone buzzed on her desk. It was Max, asking if the daycare had sent any pictures of Isla. Max, who also possessed shoulders and a jaw and a generationally attractive respect for feminism.

Sloane recalled a conversation with her aunt from just after she'd gotten pregnant with Isla, about who would do the housework if Sloane planned to continue working full-time. "Oh, Max does the laundry and most of the cleaning," Sloane had said with a shrug, and later shared a conspiratorial laugh with Max about her aunt's look of dismay, reflecting the foolish gender roles of yore.

Thusly Sloane remembered her position of authority in the situation, and not a moment too soon. "Well, there's not much I'll need you to do for me," she offered in apology to the TA whose name she'd already forgotten. She had actually requested a TA for a different, more advanced course that she had not, ultimately, been assigned. This class on sociological methods was a stats class wearing a cardigan, or whatever bureaucrats wore to work. "I'll need some grading, maybe, and you can sit in on the course and the final projects, maybe deliver a lecture or two." Sloane was conscious, in her SLAC-y way, of the value of teaching; of the need to provide practical experience; of the desire to not reject a student who was probably in desperate need of a paycheck. She herself had gone to a SLAC that paid its grad students well, even admirably, rewarding their ability to wear many different hats, but this University felt the value of their degree was reaped later, by design, like how artists *necessarily* had to starve.

"I'll do whatever you need me to do," her TA said.

Sloane noticed again the presence of shoulders. His mouth.

Then her phone alarm went off. "Oh god," said Sloane, feeling as if someone in the room had started screaming. "How disruptive.

I'm so sorry." It was her alarm to pick up Isla, and she felt a thrill of relief, both at the reminder that she would soon hold her daughter in her arms again and the realization that even a man this handsome could not actually drive her to madness. "Could you email me your contact information, and I'll get you in the cloud drive with the syllabus?"

"Absolutely." Her TA stood up and slung one strap of a backpack over his shoulder, reaching out his free hand for hers. "Excited to work with you this semester."

His hand was warm and strong and his forearm was muscular and he smelled like fresh linen and a previous life. Sloane had the brief, overpowering sensation to pull the taut skin of his wrist to her lips—to brush them gently along the inner lining of his arm until she felt him shiver. It was humiliating to feel this way, but only a little.

At the same time that a hot flush reached Sloane's cheek, she realized she had yet to see the string tied to the vent move at all. Instead, it hung limply, forgotten, like the reflexes belonging to a form of existence she'd set down somewhere and lost.

4

"Mind you, my biggest piece of advice while going through recruitment is not to treat 'lower tier' houses as practice rounds. Use this time to forge *genuine* connections—that's the best way to get what you really want out of Greek life," said the first of Nina's recruitment counselors, who had clearly just outed herself as a member of an inferior house.

"I totally agree with Jen," said the second one, who was demonstrably prettier, although there were certainly pretty girls in every house (Nina was at least that charitable). The difference was in the details, most of which weren't immediately identifiable because the recruitment counselors were wearing the same shirt. They weren't all wearing it the same way, though—the first of Nina's RCs, Jen, was wearing her shirt adorably large, on top of trendy leggings that Nina also owned. The second, Mia, was wearing hers cropped, with jeans that fit almost impossibly, as if they were custom-tailored or wildly expensive. They were a barrel cut, magically oversized and yet impossibly snatched at the waist, in direct defiance of science.

"The important thing," Mia continued, "is that there's a house for everyone. Finding your tribe is *wayyyy* more important than choosing a house just for clout."

"You heard her, uggos," mock-whispered a freshman named Dalil Serrano to Nina. They'd become friends over the course of the previous four hours, wherein they'd visited every house on the row but one. "Not all of you can be in the hot houses," Dalil continued in a remarkable imitation of Mia's vocal fry, "so make your peace with it now."

Nina laughed. It wasn't exactly the height of wit, but there was nothing more intoxicating than talking shit after a day of being mercilessly judged. It swung the pendulum back, just a bit. "What do you tell them you're looking for?" Nina asked. "You know, when they ask why you *really* want to be in a sorority."

Dalil instantly transformed her face. "I'm just really craving a *community*," she said, her voice casually lowered in a way that exuded the perfect amount of intimacy—not too earnest, not too false. It was exactly the right amount of candor, like when a hot girl does a "get ready with me" video where she talks about her struggles with anxiety. "I love the philanthropy," Dalil continued, "but honestly? I want the sisterhood. That's what appeals to me most."

Nina was pleased that Dalil had chosen to bond with her, because it meant Dalil, a natural alpha, saw Nina as a peer. A promising start. Not that Nina felt any pressing anxiety—she told herself the stakes were almost laughably low, because if she didn't get the house she wanted, she would simply drop the process altogether and conjure up another transformation plan. It wasn't like there weren't countless other ways to fill her time. Right now, for example, her roommate Simone was at a party enjoying the hazards of her youth among the fray of future Wall Street financiers, and their suitemate Mei, a journalism major, was currently hooking up with the editor of the University paper, which was a helpful reminder that there were other ways to achieve an end. More than one way to skin a cat, as the saying went, and certainly to reinvent a future.

But then The House came into view, and a flutter of longing in Nina's belly felt like desire of the most urgent, erotic kind. The kind of craving that had once driven her to fumble with her clitoris until her fingers cramped.

It was clear she wasn't alone in her desperation. "See you on the other side," whispered Dalil, no longer mocking.

The lawn was perfectly manicured. The spectrum of pastel beach cruisers belonging to The House's chosen were tucked securely away from view. The whole place smelled like jasmine, like fucking roses. The house itself was Georgian, brick with regal front columns, like a sex dream authored by Jane Austen herself, on drugs.

The front door of the house opened and perfection spilled out in glossy waves, in Hollywood smiles. One by one The House materialized on the lawn, Nina's eyes tracking each member through a blur, a growing dazzle of white behind her eyes, like staring too long at the sun. She felt bewitched, intoxicated, more deeply taken the longer she looked. Like a sailor tied to the mast, Nina felt an element of torment, an animal longing she couldn't explain. A violence of feeling, a palpable hunger. Desperation to cast herself into the void and be deemed worthy, or perhaps not.

The lure of danger was half the desire; the other half unrealized, still wordless, unfulfilled.

Every outfit was on trend, easily worthy of a street-style feature, notably individualized (not cloyingly matched like the other houses had been, the lifeless equivalent of a dollhouse) but artfully cohesive. There was no theme, no specified color, no obvious palette, and yet from head to toe each girl was the well-crafted piece of an understood whole.

There was also, to Nina, an uncanny sense of the eternal. An undertow of syncopation, some soundless rhythm she struggled to put a finger on, being on the outside looking in. There was a visible unanimity, nothing robotic or Stepfordian, not even rehearsed—something closer to reflexive. The sleek orchestration of hunters in a pack. The feline prowl of an adroit pride.

There was a ripple of something, awareness, once The House had been assembled in full. A long period of silent looking, watchfulness that shifted the ground beneath Nina's feet to redefine the roles of predator and prey. Unmistakable tension, a crowded stillness, such that Nina could hear her blood crashing loudly in her ears. Arrhythmia to betray her vulnerability, an obvious and fatal flaw. Nina felt inexplicably certain that if a bird took flight at that moment, it would be caught one-handed; if she shifted a hair's breadth out of position, one of The House's members would effortlessly shoot her down. She could almost feel them taking breaths in unison, spurred on by a single, measured pulse. Aligned and carefully slowed, in tune with a steady beat that only they could feel. A thrum of constant frequency.

What would it be like, Nina wondered, to count among them? To live in the current of that stillness—that certainty of power.

What would it be like to sleep so well at night?

Three girls holding hands stepped down from the porch and into a stream of sun, glowing in perfect unison. Nina knew them. Everyone knew them. Leonie Monaghan, rush chair, biology major so arrestingly charismatic she had a VidStar following of over one hundred thousand due to her advocacy work, mostly in gifted designer swimwear. Alina Antwerp, VP Recruitment, public policy major, pre-law, dean's list. She'd wanted to be a senator since she was six years old and so far, it seemed a lock.

And then there was Fawn Carter, president. Half of the Greek system's golden couple (although rumor had it they'd broken up over the summer and Fawn had since hooked up with a literal prince). Blindingly beautiful, untouchably so. If Audrey Hepburn and Jackie Kennedy had some sort of sci-fi clone baby, she'd feel awkward standing next to Fawn. There was something otherworldly about her, an aura, or maybe an air of déjà vu, spiritually from a dream but actually from her stint as a prolific teen model. She could have walked the runway in Milan. She could have been an art-house muse, a baby Coppola. She could have run a boardroom or filled a stadium, she could have been anywhere else, worlds or lifetimes away, existing like a phantom, a face to grace the pages of a For You page, for you.

Instead, she was here. In front of Nina.

"Welcome," said Fawn. "We're so excited you're here."

Her eyes drifted to Nina, who felt the tug of their shared glance like a ray of fucking sun; like fate itself was in on the joke. Like the universe had willed it.

Fawn smiled.

She smiled *at Nina*.

"Jesus Christ, you sound like you have a crush on the entire house," Jas muttered later, when Nina called to report back on the first day of rush. (While Jas disapproved of the whole thing, she still felt the experience of going through recruitment secondhand was "of anthropological significance.")

But of course Nina didn't have a crush. It wasn't a *crush*.

She was in danger.

She was in love.

5

"Do you think there's a chance you could drop Isla off instead of me?" Sloane asked her husband, Max, after the fourth day of her new life. By that point, she understood that the air-conditioning in her office was broken, and that while multiple work orders had already been issued over its repair, it was unlikely to be fixed. Her officemate was an art history adjunct, a squirrelly, awkward man in his forties who was so plainly inadequate as a lecturer because he loved his work too much—so much so that his enthusiasm was unbearable. It was a common curse. As with dating, you couldn't lust too hard after your subject matter. Love it, yes. But coolly, with reserve.

"Hm?" said Max. "Hang on, just let me finish this email." He paused to think, then typed a response into his phone. "Okay, sorry, you have my attention." He reached out and gripped Sloane's shoulders playfully with both hands. "What was it?"

"I just . . ." How to put it into words. Sloane technically understood the nature of linear time, that a ten o'clock lecture took precedence over an eleven o'clock, but did it matter? Wasn't there some form of consideration within any relationship that meant easing life's burdens from the suffering partner's shoulders for a more evenly distributed collective load? "It's just so hard for me to watch her cry like that," Sloane attempted, and wilted from a general sense of shame. Her pediatrician had given her a similar look when she'd confessed to struggling with sleep training; it was the look of a mother who had simply gotten over it, as all Good Mothers do, or perhaps true Good Mothers never even considered sleep training. It remained unclear to Sloane despite much scrolling in pursuit of an answer.

"I know she's fine," Sloane argued with herself aloud. "I *know* that, I know she's safe, but still, it's just—I just—" She broke off, and beneath the sound of Frankie the dog licking the floor with an ardor once reserved in Sloane's brain for pornographic cunnilingus, resorted flaccidly to, "I don't like it."

Max gave her a look of sympathy, drawn deep from within their communal well. It was a gentleness Sloane was grateful for in the moment, because only Max could even come close to loving Isla the way she did. "But it's been getting better, hasn't it?"

The first day, Isla had visibly spent the entire morning crying. By the time Sloane had arrived to pick her up, her face was swollen with tears, and her voice—her tiny voice with which she produced little more than gibberish—was hoarse, like she'd spent the day chain-smoking. "She doesn't like to be comforted," said a slightly frazzled Miss Lily. "Obviously we try to hug and kiss her, but she prefers to soothe herself. It's a good thing!" she added, catching the dawn of apocalypse on Sloane's face.

A good thing, sure, but also tragic. After the first day, Isla had been mostly fine at pickup, but every morning, as it again came time for Sloane to leave, Isla clawed into Sloane's sweater with an animal desperation, her desire for Sloane eventually coalescing with pain and grief into a pterodactyl scream. The sound, if you could call it that, carried the weighty implication that Isla knew, she now bodily understood and could *never unknow*, abandonment. She would forever understand that Sloane's love had limits; that Sloane had chosen work over her; that love itself was fleeting and could fail.

It didn't help that the eighteen-month pediatric appointment had been an unmitigated disaster and the follow-up blood tests were looming, sinisterly. Despite purposefully selecting a female pediatrician after their first pediatrician, a man, had told Sloane within forty-eight hours of giving birth that firstborn monkeys often died of starvation due to their mothers' milk not coming in quickly enough (Sloane's underachieving tits had taken several days to set up production despite what she considered ample warning from the rest of the mother machine), Sloane still could not escape the dread of it—the numbers on the scale, the impossible tick box of achievements. It was almost worse, actually, that Isla's doctor was a woman, because at least if a man failed to credit Sloane's motherhood, she could remember that he was only a man. But now, Isla's development was actually a metric of Sloane's success or failure. Did Isla sleep a normal amount? Did she eat all her servings of leafy green vegetables? Was she suitably enriched with iron? No? Well, then Sloane should read to her more, she should engage her child with sign language and an endless stream of narration, she should try smoothies, these first three years were so important. To a Good Mother, nothing would matter more.

But in the face of Sloane's daily drop-off-related chest pains—Max sighed. He seemed to understand that there was no need to revisit logic. The problem was simply intestinal, some internal rupture, which did not require him to overturn his own carefully curated schedule.

Instead, he pulled Sloane into his arms and kissed her temple. "Isla's going to adjust, I promise, and it will be good for her. Social skills! Communication skills! She's already so much more playful at home. She's getting so much easier every day."

Easier? Watching Isla grow was remarkable, that went unquestioned, but it was also unsettling and occasionally depressing. She was more active, sure, climbing on every item of furniture and trying to engage with all the heavy textbooks on the bottom shelves, and as her vocabulary broadened she became increasingly capable of a personality that, already, Sloane treasured above every other human she'd ever met—but in achieving personhood, Isla was also more declarative, more mercurial, more expressive of a range of complex malcontents that exceeded simple matters of hunger or tiredness, and with that spark of consciousness came the probability of Isla noticing Sloane as something other than the beloved creator-god from whence she'd come. Sloane saw it in her daughter's eyes each time she left her behind; the more distance Sloane claimed, the more likely it would eventually become the way of things, irretrievable and lost.

Sloane supposed, in fairness, Isla was becoming easier *for Max*, who had never been able to calm her without the use of one or both of Sloane's boobs. But still, Sloane felt an acute loss of her baby; a loss she knew she wasn't supposed to resent because she hadn't had a child just to trap them in eternal infancy. She wanted Isla to become independent and strong-minded and curious, she just . . . wasn't ready for it to happen just yet.

She considered all this on Friday as she sat outside the daycare, crying silently into Isla's T-shirt. She scrolled VidStar from a fugue state of despair, not even stopping to properly digest her consumption until she found a new post from an account she particularly liked (by which she meant despised, but couldn't look away from) called @TheCountryWife. Objectively, Sloane understood that the nonsense about "traditional" gender roles conveniently forgot things like women being historically barred from having their own bank accounts; she knew that so much of what went viral on the platform was rooted in the corruption of evangelistic bigotry, white supremacy, and systemic power imbalances—a long, storied tradition of institutional misuse.

But still, it was so fucking *soothing*, watching someone wear linen dresses and putter around the garden, running the homestead and nursing baby pigs and curating holiday-themed mantels and declaring by virtue of God-given youth and beauty that women's work was something inherently profound. Sure, it was a lie, and the content was sponsored, but for the sweet love of fuck, The Country Wife's Sunday roasts looked genuinely life-changing. Her homemade bacon was seemingly to die for, and although in some very distant (albeit extremely real) way Sloane lacked the stomach for any kind of animal husbandry, in certain moments it seemed feasible that she herself could even . . . do it? Perhaps *she, too,* could abscond to a beautiful house in the country at a fraction of her current mortgage; she, too, could give up her highfalutin dreams, satisfy herself with the coziness of her home and the development of her child—who, of course, would only need her less and less as time went by, such that Sloane's mind would inevitably atrophy like her postpartum glutes, her capacity for intellect and ambition so shriveled from disuse she might not even stop to wonder when exactly she'd lost herself or who that person in the mirror even was.

Well, as always, the infinite scroll was doing wonders for her state of mind. Isla was wriggling disinterestedly in her arms, mewling for rocks on the ground or the freedom to charge headlong into traffic. Sloane's lecture wasn't until two that afternoon; still, she and Max and Miss Lily had agreed that consistency would be best with regard to easing Isla into her new schedule. Sloane had plenty of work to do in the meantime, but nothing pressing, which meant she wouldn't be properly distracted. Which was probably why she had the time to access the deep well of pain that seemed to have taken on an alarming level of sentience each time she paid it a visit, greeting it with little treats like intrusive thoughts and capitulation to the void.

"Are you okay?" came a voice.

Sloane jerked upright from where she'd been sitting on the cold stone bench outside the University daycare, clutching Isla to her chest like a shield and dropping her phone on the ground in the process. Isla, in turn, let out a shrieky barrage of nonsense, and Sloane's blurry eyes focused belatedly on a woman approximately her age.

The woman stood opposite Sloane wearing a red blazer over fashionable black trousers, with matching red lips and an air of perfection achievable only by some sort of cross between Helen of Troy and Anne Boleyn.

"Sorry to startle you." The woman looked genuinely sorry, in a way that was so lovely and kind that Sloane wanted to cry all over again. "First time at daycare?"

She gestured to Isla, and Sloane realized belatedly how silly it was to have to say aloud, "No, it's day five."

"Oh, it compounds," the woman assured her. She looked too fashionable to be a professor; unlikely to be a grad student. "Mine cried for the first four weeks."

"Four *weeks*?" echoed Sloane, as if she'd just been told her flight was canceled and wouldn't be rebooked until tomorrow.

"I'm not saying it'll definitely be that long," the woman said quickly, "but if it does take that long, it's still normal." She took a seat beside Sloane, fixing her attention with palpable sweetness on Isla, who now clung shyly to Sloane. "She looks about . . . eighteen months? Is that right?"

"She's eighteen months, yes." Sloane became aware of a fractional degree of ease in herself, a melting. She had the sense the woman was making idle conversation purely to calm her, and she was grateful for it. She was exceedingly grateful to talk about Isla specifically, because outside the cult of motherhood that was almost troublingly online, most people seemed to hope that Sloane would stop. *Sloane,* in fact, often hoped that she would stop. She could feel herself becoming less interesting, her capacity for thought shrinking down. This, the feeling that at all times she was Isla's mother in disguise, just Isla's mother in a trench coat trying desperately not to be caught except by someone who might understand, was a condition Sloane understood could not possibly last forever—like babyhood, the complete reorientation of her life would eventually change again. That was the point of venturing out among the adults and reclaiming her passions, the things that had once brought her such fulfillment and joy. Things that existed in a separate box from Isla, like the accolades that were about as taken with Isla as Isla could be moved to bat an eye for them.

And in a broader sense, Sloane was profoundly thankful to not be asked "what would make it better," for which there could be no reasonable answer. No one so far had been able or willing to increase the hours in the day. For the record, Sloane was technically willing to do her job at night, when Isla was sleeping, just to avoid the tearful drop-offs; to circumvent the sense that needing to do her own work and fulfill her own desire for personal, intellectual, and adult satisfaction was more pressing than Isla's desire to read *Trains, Trains, Trains!* for a fourth fucking time. Sloane was willing to eat spaghetti Bolognese every goddamn night if that's what it took. But nobody ever asked how much are you willing to suffer. They only asked what do you want.

"That's a great age." The woman, whose shirt was not stained and in fact looked to be magically unwrinkled silk, began playing peekaboo with Isla with the practiced ease of an exceedingly Good Mother.

"How old is yours? Are yours." Sloane wasn't sure whether to imply the existence of one or more children. She had once been asked while holding Isla on a particularly unkempt day if her older children were in school, which had felt somehow both innocuous and viscerally insulting.

"Just one, a boy. He's three now and all the baby fat's somehow melted off." The woman smiled wistfully at Isla. "Look at those cheeks."

"I miss her breath," Sloane said before she could stop herself, and she was about to explain it, that Isla's breath when she'd been only breastfeeding smelled so fucking heavenly that Sloane wanted to bury herself in her daughter's gummy mouth, when the woman suddenly lit up.

"Oh, I know! Everyone thought it was so weird, but I was obsessed. To be honest, I even thought Theo's farts smelled good. Like french fries in a hot car," the woman said dreamily.

Sloane laughed aloud, and the woman played one more peekaboo with Isla before picking Sloane's phone up off the ground, shifting slightly to hand it to her. "Sorry if this is a little strange, but— Would you want to go get a coffee?" the woman tentatively asked.

"Oh, thanks so much for asking, but I have some work to do before my lecture this afternoon," is what Sloane didn't say. She couldn't understand why she didn't say it. It *was* a little strange, and Sloane wasn't the kind of person to socialize with strangers— that was more Max's bag than hers. More importantly, she'd brought Isla to daycare that day because she had to work, and no other reason was a compelling one to be away from Isla.

Except that in the five minutes she'd been talking to this woman, Sloane suddenly felt like a person again, which she hadn't technically realized she still was.

And anyway, how long would a coffee take? Thirty minutes?

Thirty minutes was still long enough to betray Isla, but in that sense, Sloane was already a traitor. So, she said, "I guess I could use a coffee."

The woman smiled. "I'm Alex, by the way," she said.

I had coffee today with my friend Alex, Sloane imagined herself saying to Max. *My friend Alex said she even liked the smell of her baby's farts. I told you it wasn't weird!*

If Isla had cried that day at drop-off, maybe Sloane wouldn't have gone. Maybe she'd have changed her mind and stayed behind, replanting her nose in her daughter's T-shirt and deciding four weeks of tears was too much to ask of anyone's sanity. Perhaps in that alternate universe, the path before Sloane didn't alight so ethereally before her, doom's cavernous maw snapped safely shut with the splutter of a candle flame.

But Isla didn't cry. Instead, when Sloane set her down in the play area, Isla just toddled over to one of the squishy foam blocks and pulled herself up on it like a meerkat, giving Sloane a regal salute as if to say, good for you, girl. Good for you.

6

Nina immediately regretted having chosen a Friday lecture—it had been the only G.E. that knocked out two simultaneous requirements, a sort of operational hole-in-one, but at what cost? She felt groggy and exhausted, weighed down by the two previous days of recruitment, numbed by the three still to come.

The early days of gentle courtship were over—now, with recruitment numbers sliced in half each day like a scything of the undeserving, came the tracks to exclusivity (a tour of the house, introduction to each sisterhood's pet causes) and the moment of avowal (a preference ceremony tantamount to sacrament; the declaration of undying love that was, half the time, a bald-faced lie). Each morning was a cliff-edge of anxiety, waiting to be alerted whether this was the day Nina returned to the tedium of obsolescence. Whether The House had at last (inevitably) recognized the deficiency in her or somehow deemed her worthy of redemption and summoned her back. She fiddled with her phone all through her lecture, waiting apprehensively for the clock to strike noon, for the gods of linear time to take pity on her nerves. For Fawn Carter, supreme goddess of The House, to have made an almighty ruling.

Nina knew, objectively, that whether The House summoned her back wasn't Fawn's sole decision. Adelaide had already explained to Nina all the grimy intricacies of recruitment, the power differentials and secret codes. The way the so-called "door girl" wasn't just a pretty face but a discerning one; that she would leave Nina's bid card face-up if she liked her and turn it face-down if she didn't. That Nina would know she wasn't a frontrunner if she was seated far away from the front doors, relegated to the back of house like bad fish. If any of the girls hinted at something specific to Nina, like her major or her hobbies, it was because they already knew it. "We spend all summer going through every girl's social media and academic records," Adelaide explained, revealing all of this to Nina as if it were a slumber party revelation rather than a sacred rite of passage. "So, if you suspect they might have assigned someone to you for a reason, chances are they totally did."

Over the past two days—during which the recruitment pool remained largely indiscriminate, a mutual process of speed-dating before the real gore of selection began—Nina had spoken with the hottest non-white girl from every house on the row, many of whom spontaneously dropped details on their favorite K-pop band or Bollywood drama as if they had never seen Nina's Instagram stories or her Spotify account. They complimented Nina's nail beds and her hair. They made affectionate jokes about their immigrant parents. They told self-deprecating stories about henna stains on the white boys they'd kissed or the humiliation of bringing beans and rice to the fifth-grade cafeteria. They said things like "I'm an engineering major and screenwriting minor—my mom would *kill* me if I didn't get a degree in something practical" as if Nina could inherently understand. And Nina did understand. But all of this felt somehow unsettling, deeply unserious, as if they weren't flirting with her cleverly or sophisticatedly enough and would therefore never make it to a second date.

Not so at The House. On the first day, Nina's initial conversation partners were gleaming, golden blondes. Then a mahogany brunette and a redhead were inserted into the mix, alongside an olive-skinned beauty of indeterminate origin (her name, unhelpfully but accurately, was Summer). The second day, Nina met Tessa, who was half-Black, after two more blondes had welcomed her into the house. Perhaps it had been the long days getting to her, but Nina couldn't help asking, "Does it ever feel weird for you? Being one of the only people of color?"

Tessa laughed, then reached out at the precise moment that Fawn Carter was passing by, greeting the various potential recruits with a smile in her eyes but nothing more. "Fawn," Tessa said, and Nina's heart stopped. "C'mere for a sec."

Nina held her breath as Fawn turned playfully to Tessa, receiving a brief, telegraphed message before taking a seat beside her on the chaise. (Other girls, Nina noticed, had been relegated to ubiquitous rented furniture or uncomfortable surfaces like a nearby piano bench.)

"Hi," said Fawn, focusing her attention on Nina. Her eyes were a golden brown, a burst of amber. "You're Nina, right?"

"Yes." It didn't come out clearly but Nina knew it would be humiliating to clear her throat, to try again. "Hi."

"Nina was just asking me what it's like to be one of the only people of color," Tessa prompted knowingly to Fawn, who laughed.

"Wait," said Nina before she could stop herself. "Are you—?"

"I'm half, yeah," said Fawn, which was incredibly unclear to Nina. Half what? She didn't dare ask. "I'm what the kids call white-passing, which Tessa just *loves* to bring up."

"There's definitely been some problematic stuff in the past," Tessa said to Nina, finally answering the question, although Nina didn't initially understand what she meant.

"Hair rules," Fawn contributed in explanation. Tessa made a face.

"Hair rules?" echoed Nina.

"As in only certain styles. No natural hair, no dreads, no braids—" *Case in point,* Tessa's gesture seemed to say in reference to her own petite braids, which had been pulled back in a low, impossibly chic chignon.

"Let's just say we took a red pen to the rush bible," Fawn purred.

"*Several* red pens." Tessa snorted. "Years ago, though, before our time."

"We have really good advocates," Fawn said. "Peer advocacy, obviously, but also alumnae."

"Yeah, the alumnae club is great—"

"Alex is the best."

"—yeah, definitely, Alex is a game changer for sure."

"It's nice not to have to suffer the microaggressions on your own, you know? We really have someone in our corner. Last year Tessa had an issue with the English department—"

"The whole house had my back." Tessa's nod was firm, almost warlike. "And I don't know if you heard about the thing last year with Camille Strahan, her performance art at Take Back the Night—"

"Oh, Alex was *instrumental* in the disciplinary case the college launched against her. Against *her*, can you believe it? Not the guy who roofied her, but *her*, because somehow *Camille's* the one who made the University look bad."

Tessa's mouth was thin and grim. "The fucking *audacity*—"

"But look, exactly one white guy got any consequences from the University for sexual assault last year and it was him. So, you know—" Fawn's dispassionate shrug displaced her hair an inch, revealing the sharp edge of her clavicle. "Good riddance."

Tessa and Fawn had such a leisurely rapport, an affluence of fluency, that Nina only caught bits and pieces from their communal storytelling. What mattered more, the sense memory that Nina took away like a victory, was the warmth of camaraderie, inclusion by proxy. A contact high of sisterly feeling that could almost count for acceptance if she forgot for a moment that she didn't belong.

And she *could* forget, for which she couldn't be faulted. Nina was, after all, talking to the president of The House; two obviously valuable members were discussing their advisor with Nina by name, as if she, too, would meet her soon.

Alex is the best, Nina imagined herself saying one day, perhaps a year from now.

She also imagined herself telling Jas—See? These girls care about advocacy. They aren't mindless bimbos. They're not falling in line for the same misogynistic, whitewashed pipeline to weaponized femininity. Or whatever Jas's argument would have been.

"I will say, Nina," Fawn continued, as if Nina had been actively listening and not daydreaming about the conversations she would have with Tessa and Fawn in the kitchen, giggling over midnight burritos and a shared flask, "I'm sure you've heard that it's pretty unusual for us to take sophomores. We just like for everyone to be at the same stage, you know, life-wise. It's just a little more sisterly that way, for the pledge classes to literally go through *everything* together."

To Nina's discerning ear, there was a clear *but* that she was meant to leverage. "I totally understand," she said, stepping capably into the negotiation ring, ready to pre-lawyer. "I'd have rushed last year, but I don't think I was in the right frame of mind to really go into it with my heart open."

She'd seen someone say that on social media at some point. She realized only belatedly that it had been The House's public VidStar, in the caption for a beautiful, bikini-clad group collage before everyone's social media had gone on lockdown for fall recruitment. Was it too on-the-nose? Was she now the cringeworthy try-hard, the partner ultimately doomed to the power differentials of working harder, loving more, begging *stay*?

Frantically, Nina realized she should say something else, something better, something new and fresh and innovative—something funny, or witty, or for god's sake something she'd come up with on her own—

But Fawn and Tessa exchanged a glance then, consulting each other in silence. Nina tried to read the look between them but it was too quick. Too foreign.

"That's so true," Tessa agreed, and silently, Nina exhaled. "Timing is everything. Everybody's journey is different."

"It's really cool of you to know yourself that way," Fawn added. The light caught on her gold-plated lavalier, gleaming like a Byzantine painting. Divinity conveyed by the Greek letters of The House. "Honestly, most people who go through recruitment have no fucking clue what they're doing."

Nina had heard once from her roommate Adelaide that you weren't allowed to swear while wearing The House's letters. Nina wondered now if that was true, though either way, she liked Fawn more for doing it. "Right," she managed to say. "I just wasn't ready last year, but now I am. And I really think I could contribute a lot to the house." She meant to say it that way, the house generic, as if it were merely hypothetical that this could be the house she wound up in, but she knew Fawn and Tessa could hear what she really meant—The House. Nina's hunger for it was audible, maybe too audible. She tried hastily to pare down her thirst. "I think there's something to be said for a little more life experience. I mean, I'm definitely not going to be one of the girls throwing up on their first bus ride back from a party."

"She's got you there, Tess," Fawn teased, and Tessa laughed, unfazed.

"It's true, a little wisdom can do wonders for the bus insurance—"

"At least it wasn't the venue—"

"Can I have a little of my dignity, please?"

"Fine, fine, whatever's left of it—"

"The point is, Nina," said Tessa, turning back to Nina, who had again been basking in the glow of inclusion, "we're just really looking for girls who are committed to this. Who are ready to be involved—*really* involved, not just for events. For the sisterhood itself."

"It's for life, Nina." Fawn's voice then was deathly serious. Nina thought again of the heartbeat, the pulse, the tension that defined the hunt. The frequency she'd first sensed among The House's members, a vibration only the worthy could be trained to hear. "And I don't mean something trite, that these are the girls who will be your bridesmaids or whatever, even though they very likely will be. I mean that these are the women who will stand by you in your darkest moments. This house isn't just a four-year stopover. This house is your home—*our* home."

Fawn and Tessa seemed to lace fingers without even thinking, without consulting each other. As if the love that pulsed between them was too profound to be held with less than two hands.

"Every girl in this house will go on to become extraordinary," said Tessa. "We choose the best of the best for a reason. And look, you can be successful on your own. Of course you can. But what The House can offer you—"

Fawn cut her off with a look so swift that Nina almost missed it.

"It's a sisterhood," Tessa finished, a subtle, sunshiny sidestep from whatever she'd been about to say. "And that means you have to be willing to be a sister."

("Oh my god," Jas said later. "They actually *said* that? And you *bought* it?"

"I mean, who knows if I convinced them," said Nina, as if she didn't care, when in fact she'd stayed up all night replaying her answer, rewriting it, trying to determine if some other turn of phrase would have said it better; if, in her answer, she'd been cool enough, attractively aloof, while conveying with her eyes that she'd make it so good for them, baby, so good, if they'd only give her a chance.)

But now it was Friday, she was awaiting the results of her best efforts, and the clock had struck 11:58. Class would start in two minutes. The professor strode in, an unusually handsome man who looked possibly Latino, maybe even an Asian mix, though either way he had to be half, because his eyes were light, maybe green or hazel. He was tall and lean, elegant, with artist's fingers, brown-black curls that all but begged to be touched, a dimple below the scruff on his cheek that was the precise size and shape of her pointer finger. Nina sat up slightly straighter as he wrote his name on the board. 11:59. *PHIL 275, On the Nature of Being, Dr. Villanueva.* His lips looked soft.

"Welcome, welcome," said Professor Villanueva, and there was the dimple again. "You have thirty seconds to get your affairs in order and then, please, phones away. For the next fifty minutes, you have nothing to ponder except the meaning of existence and whether this is indeed oatmeal on my tie."

There was a low rumble of obligatory laughter.

"Please," said Professor Villanueva, with the bashfully sardonic motion of both hands. "Don't encourage me."

12:00. Nina hastily hit refresh on the window of her recruitment portal.

Congratulations! You are cordially invited back to—

"Time's up," said the professor, and possibly it was Nina's full-bodied rush of relief, but when she locked eyes with him just then, she couldn't remember ever having seen a more arresting shade of green. The sensation dropped hungrily into her vagina as Professor Villanueva leaned casually against the desk at the front of the auditorium, crossing his ankles right over left.

"Now, who can tell me," he invited, "is there such a thing as free will?"

7

It was the following week, on a Monday, when Sloane got the email from a woman named Britt Landau.

> *I'm sure you have a lot going on—I certainly know what those early days back at work are like!—but Alex was adamant that you'd be the perfect fit for our girls—*

Alex as in the woman Sloane had met last week. Alex, with whom Sloane had had a potentially ill-advised coffee, though she'd come out of it light as air, as if a burden had gently lifted.

"Do you hate me?" came from the doorframe of Sloane's office, and Sloane looked up, slightly bug-eyed from the glasses she didn't technically need at this distance. Still, her eyes had been hurting and she was on day two of a migraine, as she always seemed to be these days. Isla's naps had been disrupted all weekend, maybe teething, maybe the cruel pain of abandonment, maybe the sightless eldritch terror that was a sleep regression, it didn't matter the reason. The point was that Sloane was not, regardless of explanation, prepared.

"You can say it," Alex added with a sigh, falling into the chair opposite Sloane's desk. "I'm a monster. I've added yet another thing to your plate. I brought you a cappuccino with oat milk," she added, almost in the same breath, setting it down beside Sloane's ancient desktop. "It's decaf, don't worry."

Sloane had told Alex last week during their coffee date that she was still breastfeeding, which meant her caffeine intake was still limited, as was her ability to take pills for her headaches, or for anything really. She knew her milk supply was dropping but Isla wouldn't eat anything consistently enough for her to stop nursing completely, and anyway she loved it, sort of. There were definite moments when she loved it uncomplicatedly, the closeness and the hand-holding and the sweetness of time with nothing more pressing to do than nurture the baby she adored—but admittedly, the constancy of that love was fading; now it was pockmarked and brittle, the joy easily upended by the dread. The stronger Isla got, the less Sloane was able to keep her daughter from yanking her blouse open in public. She'd never thought twice about breastfeeding out in the open, but it took on a slightly more insidious, humiliating flavor when she couldn't say no.

At the time Sloane confessed it, Alex had then relayed a story about breastfeeding her then-almost-two-year-old while standing upright in the DMV line. "Honestly, I still miss the cuddles," Alex had said, and astoundingly, had not proceeded to add anything about when Sloane should stop, as all other adult humans seemed to do. "Seriously, people are bugging you about that? Dude, whatever," Alex had said with a flick of her golden hair. "Who is anyone to judge you for what you do to get through the day? We're all just trying our fucking best."

The words melted again like butter through Sloane's consciousness, drawing her gently back to the moment. To the version of Alex who stood now in her office unexpectedly, holding a coffee that Sloane hadn't asked for—that she hadn't needed to request.

"You think I should hate you?" Sloane echoed, reaching gratefully for the cup.

"Well, I assume you got the email from Britt. I was trying to beat her to it and ask you about it in person, but sometimes it's easier to just let Britt do Britt." Alex gave Sloane a wry smirk as if Sloane would know what that was like; she said it in the same tone with which she described the antics of her son, Theo, who was apparently some sort of jock prodigy, not that Alex (uncoordinated, more of an indoor cat, per Alex) knew what to make of that. "Anyway, look, it'd be a huge favor to me, and I really don't think it would be much work for you."

"You want me to be your sorority's faculty advisor?" Sloane asked, a little confused. She'd been in a sorority, at her mother's urging, a fact she'd thoughtlessly shared with Alex the previous week. Sloane's faculty advisor had been an eighty-year-old woman named Nancy who was semi-retired. She'd only ever come to the faculty brunch they threw to celebrate the girls on honor roll, which was paid for by the parents' club, so it was one of the few things Sloane participated in, again because her mother insisted.

Alex's house, however, was nothing like Sloane's had been. They'd walked by it on their way back from coffee, with Sloane pausing to take in the absurdity of The House's elegance. She'd begun to capitalize it in her mind, probably due to the way Alex spoke about it. The House required a great deal of maintenance. Similarly, The Girls. As in, The Girls were all so promising, so full of life. "Honestly, I wish I'd been like that when I was their age," Alex wistfully confessed. "I was more concerned with boys and parties. Plus I'm pretty sure we were all a little misogynistic then. I'm not saying I'm proud of it, but the subliminal messaging in TeenBop was 'Hate yourself, girl!' and I was nothing if not diligent about it."

Something about Alex's easy intimacy had spurred Sloane to say, "I think I was a pick-me girl."

"Oh god, were you *not like other girls?*" Alex's laughter then was contagious. Their coffee date stretched into ninety minutes before Alex had to run—she had only been on campus for a meeting she'd had with the administration that morning. She was actually a human rights lawyer who worked remotely for a firm in the city that Sloane had later googled. Alex had won a landmark case about a month before, one of several over the course of her career.

"Look," Alex said then, leaning across Sloane's desk with a slightly grim look on her face, "I know it sounds very rah-rah girlhood and all that, but we desperately need a new faculty advisor. Our last one got poached by Georgetown—that was inevitable, I'm sure I don't have to tell you how unreasonable the University can be—and we can't operate without one, per campus rules. And I really think you'll like everyone in the alumnae club—Britt included." Alex gave Sloane a conspiratorial wink. "It's just that she's the head of a PR firm and has twins, so, you know, time is money."

That was certainly true. With motherhood, the number one thing that had changed about Sloane's life was the value of her time. If she wasn't with Isla, then every minute had to have a purpose, because otherwise it was a minute that could have been spent with Isla but wasn't. Everything in Sloane's life had to be for sleep (so she wouldn't die) or for work, or for Max, or for Isla. This was so clearly none of the above.

"I don't know, Alex—I mean, I can appreciate that you're in a bind, but I'm only an adjunct—"

"You're still faculty! And I don't see you going anywhere anytime soon—"

"And with the time commitment, and me getting less time at home as it is—"

"Bring Isla," said Alex, without hesitation. "We've got a meeting this week to go over The Girls' new member education programming and to review academic standards with The House after bid night." Again, Sloane couldn't help hearing the proper nouns: The Girls. The House. "You can meet the rest of the volunteers. We're pretty much all working moms, so we get it—someone's always got an eye on all the kids, there's plenty of kid-friendly snacks. We do have the occasional boozy brunch, you know, for self-care," said Alex with a teasing smile. "But you don't have to commit to that. And they're useful to know, I promise. The smartest women I've ever met in my life. And Britt gave me this lipstick," Alex concluded with a playful shrug.

It was, Sloane admitted to herself reluctantly, the perfect red for Alex's skin tone, and seemed to be successfully transfer-free, which her own lipstick was not. Isla looked like she'd been attacked that morning, and all because Sloane had kissed her cheek unthinkingly—thinking only that she, an elite member of the educated class, might look fractionally more capable or less dead with some lipstick on.

"You could use an extracurricular," Max pointed out later, when Sloane brought it up as if it were a silly thing she wouldn't possibly do—be *faculty advisor* for a *sorority*. Tonally, it was all very *I mean, seriously, Max, who could possibly have the time and energy for that?* "It might look good to the University for you to be more active outside of just lecturing. They'd have a more compelling reason to install you on a tenure track, if that's still something you're set on doing."

Right, one of her frivolous expectations, job security and/or some vote of confidence in her proficiency at the thing she happened to know a lot about, not that she could get into that again. "But who knows how much time it'll take, Max. And what am I supposed to do with Isla? I mean, Alex mentioned brunch, and maybe sometimes meetings in the evenings—"

"I'll take Isla," Max said breezily, as if it were no big deal, as if he took Isla all the time, as if he'd been clamoring for more time with Isla and his pleas had simply gone unheard. "You're allowed to take some time for yourself, Sloane."

"But it's not *for* me, technically—"

"Sure it is. You need time to be around adults."

"By that logic, so do you." But Max played tennis at the University with a few of his department faculty twice a week after classes and did long bike rides with his recreational road cycling team at least three times a month. Sloane and Max went to dinner with

Max's friends on occasion, with Isla in tow, probably every few weeks. Both their social lives had definitely taken a hit since Isla's birth, but Sloane's was dead in the water in a way that Max's was not. And on purpose! Sloane had always been more concerned about Max's sanity than her own—her love for Isla was so consuming, so richly rewarding that Sloane never felt resentful of motherhood's undeniable pitfalls, nor did she necessarily long for stimulation outside of oxytocin and the pot-roasting VidStars she scrolled while Isla slept. But it didn't seem, from Sloane's perspective, that fatherhood was quite the same. Max's happiness was dependent on breaks from his child that Sloane had never personally felt she needed.

But the thought of brunch with Alex—with Alex's friends, who also missed the smell of their babies' farts and could tell Sloane what shape her jeans should be and whether her forehead necessitated bangs and how to successfully force-feed Isla iron so that, for once, Sloane could escape the inevitable, unbearable shaming by her pediatrician—*that* felt pleasurable in a way it never had before. It did not require Sloane to change shape or rearrange her priorities. She could be among others of her kind. She was a sociologist, for fuck's sake, this shit mattered, and that she was having to explain that to herself right now (to herself!) was suddenly hysterically absurd.

"Well, I guess I could try one meeting," Sloane said without waiting for Max to contribute, or maybe he already had and she hadn't been listening. She knew she'd harbored some resentment toward him since parenthood had taken its toll on his fundamental sexiness—he was still hot, obviously, it was just nominally less arousing when he failed to accomplish certain tasks or suffered from the executive dysfunction he protested not to have—but Sloane, too, had degraded a bit from the attentive wife and perfect hostess she'd once been, the Good Mother in waiting that was the Good Wife. Her ability to multitask, to listen to him while arranging her face in a way that suggested interest, was not at its most exceptional.

"Exactly," said Max, like any contemporary supportive spouse who did not conform to their mothers' gender roles and who did not cheapen her sense of individuality and who was, all in all, a really wonderful father. Sloane entertained the thought of offering him a blow job. In previous iterations of themselves, she had been the more sexually demanding of the two, a dynamic that had seen oceanic shifts since Sloane's sixth month of pregnancy. Other women got horny during the gestational period, but not Sloane. She got sciatica.

"What do you think about sex tonight?" Sloane suggested, in a tone not unlike the one an hour prior when she'd suggested pizza for dinner. (There was a 40 percent chance Isla would eat it and more importantly, it wasn't spaghetti, and *most* importantly, it wasn't spaghetti that Sloane had cooked.)

"Yes," said Max instantly, leaping to his feet to kiss her sweetly behind the ear. "Please."

"Assuming that Isla actually goes down and stays down."

"Yes. Listen," he said, turning over his shoulder to speak to Isla, who sat spreading sauce around in her high chair tray, "Daddy needs this. Go straight to bed, okay?"

"You know," Sloane gently teased, "if you really wanted to be comfortably sure I didn't get trapped in there with her, you could always be the one to put her down."

Max laughed at her clever, clever joke. It was only for humor, after all. Everyone knew Max used those ninety minutes to decompress alone with Frankie the dog, that slut, the two of them catching up on the latest prestige drama that everyone but Sloane had already seen.

But in the end, Isla did fall asleep within a reasonable time frame, and Sloane texted Max to meet her in their bedroom, and they were both naked within seconds. She began with a charitable blow job and Max went down on her in a perfunctory way as Sloane closed her eyes and told herself to come as quickly as possible, because Max was adamant about prioritizing her pleasure, primarily in the sense that if he didn't bring her to the throes of ecstasy he'd take it not as a personal failure from which to ambitiously learn, but a disappointing turn of events. She closed her eyes and tangled her fingers in his hair and enjoyed that her clitoris *was* more sensitive now, somehow, postpartum. She ran her hands over her husband's shoulders and dug into her personal file of erotic fiction, unveiling the slightly shameful visual of her TA's hands (his name was Arya, as she'd learned from his email address) and the imaginary sequence of being fucked on a nicer, cleaner version of her desk while the door remained flung open, risk of punishment be damned. She thought, absurdly, of Alex Carlisle's red lipstick while Max curled his fingers around the quaking elevated peaks of Sloane's thighs.

Of course, orgasm was ultimately an easy formula with an experienced partner of over five years. It didn't matter what Sloane thought about. Fatefully speaking it was always inevitable that she was going to come.

8

The final day of fall recruitment reunited Nina and Dalil, the only two of their initial rush group who had been extended invitations by The House. It was a dream of a Sunday morning—dewy beams of sun fell in weightless tendrils across the scenic stretch of campus, cocooning the creature that was the University off-duty, hungover and still abed. To Nina, clearer-eyed and more awake than it seemed she'd ever been before, it had all the ethereality of a wish. All the girls were dressed in white, and it felt like a baptism, or at least how Nina imagined a baptism would feel. There seemed to be both an agreement that this was silly—well, maybe not silly—possibly campy, which was like silly but with a sexier quirk of the lips—and also, in some way, profound.

On the final day, each of the potential new members was assigned a girl they'd spoken to before; someone who would conceivably vouch for them in the hours preceding bid night. It was a last shot, either to cement a bid or to lose, in effect, everything.

The girls processed from The House with their voices joined delicately in song, like living angels. Nina spotted two of the girls she'd spoken with, then three, then four. Each sister stepped forward to claim one of the potential new members. The girl Nina had laughed with the day before about an old sitcom stepped up—and chose Dalil. Nina held her breath, knowing someone was coming for her, but not knowing what it meant, or who it would be. She was one of ten girls left on the sidewalk, then one of seven, one of four . . . three . . . two . . .

She was last on the sidewalk when she thought she saw Fawn

Carter take a step from the center of the house's rose-lined path. Toward Nina? Her breath caught in her throat. Surely it wasn't allowed. Could that mean—?

Dreamily, she watched it happen in her mind. Fawn's lovely fingers; the gleam of a heady swallow along the notches of Fawn's throat. Rays of sun crowned both their heads from on high, a benediction and a blessing. Birdsong and benevolence. No need to playact when the thing between them was love—when the end of the story was fate.

Motion blossomed, petals of The House unfurling in outward peals of heavenly reach. But of course it wasn't Fawn progressing toward her from the roses. Be realistic!

The girl coming to collect her was Tessa. Reality coalesced again, and Nina exhaled sharply, relieved.

"I don't get it," Jas said later. "Why is it a good thing that it's Tessa?"

"Because Tessa is friends with Fawn." Nina didn't want to have this discussion with Jas, who obviously didn't care, but Simone was busy and Adelaide was still hoping Nina would choose her own house. Adelaide had, in fact, been the representative of her house to spend the morning with Nina. So, obviously there were worse things.

"But aren't they all friends with each other? Isn't that the point?"

Jas was being purposefully unhelpful. "They're still human, Jas. Some are closer friends than others."

"How do you know?"

It didn't seem productive for Nina to say *I can just tell*. She could tell, for example, that they liked her, but what would that mean if they didn't *pick* her? She could justify it by saying they didn't pick sophomores, but for the entirety of the week thus far she'd felt so glowingly the exception, like the heroine in a romance who couldn't turn anyone's head but his. If The House didn't choose her now, then the whole thing had been a lie—and could she really be that stupid? She didn't think so. She knew what it was like to hook up with someone who wasn't actually into her (thanks a lot, Jonathan Zein). That wasn't remotely what had happened at The House.

Or at least she hoped it wasn't.

Nina sighed, looking away from Jas's grainy presence on her screen, incapable now of focusing on her reading. The outcome of having to return to real life tomorrow—to anxiety about exam preparation and digestive regularity that had previously defined reality's constraints—whether she was welcomed into or cast out from Eden was fundamentally unimaginable, like living through the ravages of war. "I guess I—"

Just then her phone buzzed with a text. She glanced lazily at the banner that unfurled on the screen, expecting to hear from Simone about their dinner plans. Instead, it was an unknown number.

> **nina—this is tessa. the house is gridlocked. i'm so sorry to put you in this position. can you call me?**

"I gotta go," Nina said to Jas instantly.

"Wait, what does—"

She hung up on Jas and hit call on Tessa's unsaved number. "Hello?"

"Nina, this is so wildly against the rules, I'm sorry—"

"It's okay." Was it okay?

"You're on speaker. I'm here with Fawn, Alina, and Leonie. You remember them, right?"

"Yes, of course." Nina couldn't breathe. "What's up?"

"It's about Dalil."

Nina felt her lungs puncture, a tiny needle-thin prick of relief. "Dalil?"

"She was in your rush group, right?"

"Yeah, she was."

"Okay, great. We just . . . Fawn's not convinced."

"Don't tell her that, oh my god—Nina, it's me." And indeed it was Fawn, who had clearly grabbed the phone from Tessa. Nina became aware of the presence of something, tension, like gritted or chattering teeth. "Did you like Dalil? Like, did you get any weird vibes from her?"

"What? No, nothing like that. Wait, why?" Nina suddenly couldn't understand anything that was happening to her. Since the moment she'd seen Tessa's text, she had been compiling things in her head, lists of reasons why she would be a good choice, the perfect candidate. She'd go on to accomplish great things. She'd be a credit to The House. She would never throw up at a party, in public, *ever*. She would do more face masks if they were distracted by the occasional flare-up of hormonal acne on her chin. She'd switch her birth control. No she wouldn't! Ugh, fuck. That kind of desperation would rule her out completely. Something brain-rupturing had happened to her during rush. Something about the absence of reality had heightened the stakes, obscured them. If these three random girls didn't think she was hot enough then fine, so be it. She'd be a lawyer anyway. She'd be a fucking judge. Fuck them.

"We just . . . we found out something about Dalil that we're not sure about. It's not a big deal . . . it's stupid, it could be a total misunderstanding as far as we know, I just wanted to get your take. You know. As someone who was around her casually all week."

Nina's heart thudded in her chest. Panic was beginning to transfer rhythms to confusion. "Oh. I, um. I like Dalil a lot."

There was a triumphant sound in the background. A tinny voice said: "See?"

"I thought she was really cool," Nina said. "But I wouldn't say I know her."

"Did she seem . . . invested, to you? Sometimes these girls are just in it for the clout." That sounded like Alina Antwerp's voice, maybe.

"Oh god, really? I mean, I would never—" Nina cleared her throat. "*I'm* not, you know, like that, so I'm not sure if—"

"Oh *shit*." From somewhere on the other end, she heard Tessa burst out laughing. "Nina, babe! I'm so sorry! I just realized this must be *torture* for you. I'd forgotten you didn't know what we know."

"Oh my god, Tessa, did you not tell her? Nina." It was Fawn again. "Nina, you're in. You'll get your bid in a couple of hours. I thought Tessa would have *told you that* before breaking literally every fucking rule in the Panhellenic guidebook—"

"Oh." Nina felt so dizzy she could float.

"I honestly thought it was a given. Can you imagine if we'd illegally called you and then *didn't* extend a bid? Fucking Christ!" Tessa was still laughing. Nina pictured them all laughing about it together someday, a time that wasn't now but surely would be soon, like maybe tomorrow or next week or whenever she recovered from spiritually soiling herself.

"Please forgive my idiot friend Tessa," said Fawn. "She's your problem now."

"Anyway, can we please get back to the point? Alex will be back any second for our bid list and she'll kill us if she finds out we called you—"

"Alex of all people would want us to do this right. But yes, focus." That was an exchange between Alina and Leonie, Nina was pretty sure. She was fairly confident she knew Fawn's and Tessa's voices. "We have about ten seconds. Dalil, in or out?"

"In," said Nina instantly. She didn't know why. She didn't know who would take Dalil's place or what they'd found about Dalil. It didn't really matter. Nina was in and that was what mattered, so if something didn't work out with Dalil, then yes, Nina was the one who'd made that call, but even if they held that against her, so what?

She wondered whose idea it had been to ask her. Probably Fawn's. Probably Fawn had called in Tessa, who wasn't even one of the officers in charge of rush, and said *Wasn't she in Nina's group? Can you call Nina?* And so now time was of the essence and Nina wasn't going to hesitate. She liked Dalil. More importantly, Dalil didn't present a threat to her. Nothing did anymore.

"I like her," Nina said emphatically. "She's cool. She's funny. She's hot."

"She is definitely hot," Tessa agreed. "Well, Fawn? You're the last holdout."

"I mean, I trust Nina. I just think—"

There was a brief fumble and this time, the line went dead.

Nina pulled the phone away from her ear, catching her wide-eyed reflection on the black screen. Would she look different tomorrow? She exhaled with a laugh at her own expense. A picture of her with Jas, mirror images the day they both chose their respective University hoodies, flashed up at her to join the chorus.

Then a text materialized across Jas's face from Tessa's still-unsaved number. **sorry, alex came in and fawn dropped the phone!! lmao what a mess pls accept our bid see you later xxxxxxxx**

Nina carefully saved Tessa's name in her contacts, minus the last name, because she didn't know it yet. She wondered when Tessa would be able to take her social media public again, or if she even would. Nina vaguely recalled that every member of The House she'd ever searched for had a private account. Only The House itself had a public page.

She went to The House's VidStar account, searching through its followers for Tessa.

There. Tessa Alden.

Pleased, Nina went back to her contacts and changed Tessa Alden in her phone.

Unless that was creepy? What if Tessa looked at her phone later tonight?

Christ. Fuck.

Nina changed it back to just Tessa.

She got up and paced her room, realizing she still had two hours before everyone else could know. Before she would hold something in her hand as undeniable proof, incontrovertible evidence that she was one of them. True, she would still have to be initiated, but by the end of that semester, a year from the day things went astray—coincidence? no, again, it was fate—Nina could finally rewrite the story, reorienting herself on the path. In six weeks, she'd wear The House's letters like a badge of honor. Like a brand on her blessed, anointed chest.

Her mouth watered from the want of it, like chomping at the bit. Let me in. Let me in. Let me in.

"Bitch, did you seriously hang up on me?" were Jas's first words when Nina called her back.

"Bitch, you're not my only sister anymore," Nina said, as if it didn't matter. As if it never had.

9

The meeting wasn't in The House, because The Girls were preparing for bid night. Sloane recalled vaguely that bid night was a big deal; that she herself had wanted to throw up while waiting to find out what house had picked her. Not because she had wanted it herself, but because she knew that if she didn't wind up in her mother's house, it would mean she'd failed some kind of ultra-critical test. Everyone knew legacies got special treatment.

"That's actually not true for these girls," Alex said when Sloane confessed it. They were at Britt's house—the Britt that Alex said needed to "do Britt" in order to save time and energy for everyone else.

Sloane could see why. Britt had the most singularly toned biceps Sloane had ever seen and looked exactly like a Parisian influencer Sloane followed on VidStar who had four kids and a striking resemblance to young Jane Birkin. Britt had also served them a platter of fresh bread and artisan cheeses that Alex and Sloane were nibbling on while Britt picked a movie for all the kids—her twins, Alex's son, and Isla—to watch. (Isla was deep in concentration over one of the twins' toys, a puzzle from a subscription service that Britt swore by. "It's on the expensive side, I know, but they're all Montessori and so well made, honestly every other thing they own is a waste of money. I can give you the ones they've outgrown! I've been holding on to them for this exact reason. Anyway, I'll send you the link.") Britt's entire life was like a VidStar feed that Sloane would gaze at and ultimately fall well short of.

Telling herself the grass wasn't always greener didn't help—

Britt's boyishly handsome husband had popped in to offer Alex and Sloane refreshments and chat amicably with Alex about a book they'd both read, and then he'd given his wife a look so openly desirous it made Sloane's mouth go dry. Britt even had a similarly anarchistic dog to Sloane's, but there was no evidence of that, smell-wise, the way Sloane was sure there was at her own house.

"No legacies in The House?" echoed Sloane, biting into a spread of Camembert so rich it tasted like freshly churned butter.

"It's really uncommon," Alex said, and reconsidered. "Well, it's not uncommon to *try*. A lot of legacies come through, but they're so often of a different caliber. And honestly, The House underwent a pretty major shift about ten years ago, back when we were there. Most of the legacies we reject belong to alumnae of a very different generation."

"You were both members here?" asked Sloane, just as Britt took a seat across from them. (Britt's husband was now playing with Isla and Alex's son, Theo, making them laugh while the twins climbed on top of him.)

"Oh yeah. But Alex was two years ahead of me," said Britt, laughing as Alex tossed a piece of bread at her.

"You just had to remind me of my maturity, hm?"

"Nah, just your age." Britt kicked the foot of Alex's chair before turning back to Sloane. "You'll meet Priscilla, too. She's just running late. She was in Alex's pledge class."

"Oh, you'll love Skit." Presumably Alex was referring to Priscilla. "She doesn't have kids and doesn't want them, so we all live vicariously through her. Are you aware that she does whatever she wants, whenever she wants to?"

"Sounds fake," said Sloane, and Alex laughed.

"Priscilla is in publishing," Britt continued, with an air of not wanting to misuse their collective time. "She's executive editor for a boutique imprint that does mostly artsy shit. I make her send me advance copies of all the smutty stuff from one of the juicier imprints."

"I think that's great," said Sloane. "I like a little spice myself."

"I knew you'd be a perfect fit." Alex's smile broadened. Today her lips were a beautiful terra-cotta color, her hair falling in soft, honeyed waves that floated across her shoulder when she glanced at the kids playing in the living room. "Theo, take turns, baby!"

Sloane looked over at Isla, who was reaching for Britt's husband's face with a laugh. Sloane realized abruptly that she loved Britt's husband and would take a bullet for him, no questions asked. She also realized she didn't know Britt's husband's name until Britt suddenly called, "Finn, would you mind getting the rosé? Sloane looks thirsty."

"That she does," Finn blithely agreed, rising instantly to his feet. Isla reached for him, so he scooped her up one-handed, carrying her with him over to the fridge.

"I've never seen Isla take to someone so fast," Sloane commented to Britt in awe. "I mean, she loved Alex, but with men she's not usually so comfortable."

"Oh, Finn is great with children," Britt said, a slightly goofy look of adoration passing briefly over her no-nonsense features. "I didn't want any. He wanted ten. Naturally, the universe bent in his favor."

"Figures," said Alex, nudging Sloane. "Anyway, let's get the business portion over with, shall we? We just need to go over the bid list."

"What am I contributing?" asked Sloane, good-naturedly bewildered.

"Mostly a vibe," said Alex, handing her the list. "We offer fewer bids than International prefers us to extend, but The Girls are selective. We encourage it."

"International?"

"Two chapters in Canada," said Britt.

"Every house has a national or international form of governance," Alex explained. "Someone to rule over us and collect our dues."

"We have a somewhat strained relationship." Britt and Alex exchanged an eye roll. "International's job is to maximize profit by maximizing the number of members who pay dues. Not altogether productive for any goal that isn't financial."

"Sounds very bureaucratic," said Sloane, who was likewise on the hook for whatever her department decided whether she agreed with it or not, and yet couldn't get anyone to attend to her broken air-conditioning. She couldn't fault Britt or Alex for their obvious resentment.

Before either of the two women could say anything further, the front door opened, and with the bluster of a woman in a perfectly tailored black pantsuit arrived their wineglasses, courtesy of Finn (and Isla, who was putting her pudgy hand over Finn's mouth for loud, toddler-hilarious raspberries).

"Hi, hi, sorry I'm late." The woman who must have been Priscilla came over to kiss Alex's cheek, then Britt's, before falling into the vacant seat beside Sloane. "You must be the famous Dr. Hartley!"

"I wouldn't say famous," said Sloane.

"Well, live aspirationally, I always say. I noticed your last book did pretty well, considering the academic press. Obviously no bestseller, but still. Why haven't you written another?"

"Skit!" Alex gave Priscilla a disciplinary glance, which she ignored.

"No, she's right." Sloane laughed. "The dean of my department would probably like to ask me the same thing. And to that all I can say is something-something childbirth."

"Well, yeah, but I'm sure you've got something on the brain. Alex, honestly, I'm just making conversation—"

"Well, I do, kind of," Sloane admitted. "But I don't see the University going for it."

"Really?" Priscilla frowned at her. "Well, you never know. Are you on a tenure track?"

"She's hopeless," Alex said to Britt, who shrugged, taking a long pull from her wine before sitting up straighter to admonish one of her daughters.

"Eloise, be gentle with your sister, please!"

"Just an adjunct," Sloane answered Priscilla, who despite being in publishing seemed to know extensive amounts about academia. "I'd like a tenure track, but I think for now my husband's good graces are buying me time."

"Well, we'll see what we can do about that." Alex's hand settled warmly on Sloane's forearm then. "The University has a tendency to listen when I point out an asset."

"Meaning she's personally threatened every last motherfucker on that board," said Britt.

"It's why we love her," Priscilla confirmed, toasting Sloane with the fresh glass Finn had brought her.

Isla had tumbled slightly on the floor beside a set of beautifully hygge-painted blocks. Before Sloane could do anything, though, Alex's son Theo was at Isla's side, helping her to stand up. It was an incredibly sweet moment, almost surreally so. Sloane was temporarily rapt.

"If you're done interrogating Sloane about her personal life, we just need to go over the bid list," Alex said to Priscilla, who glanced at Sloane before reaching for the printed list.

"Have you looked at it already?"

"Oh, I mean—" Sloane shrugged. "Is it really my place to weigh in?"

"Oh good, they took the sophomore," said Britt, who glanced over the list before rising to her feet to refresh the cheese selection.

"I like her," she called from her walk to the fridge. "She's a good fit."

"She means Nina Kaur," explained Alex. "We don't normally take sophomores, but she has a lot of promise. Her freshman year was a bit mixed—" To this, she and Priscilla exchanged a look with mirrored shrugs. "—but her high school GPA was through the roof, and she's clearly ambitious. And dedicated. She's the kind of person who can really benefit from The House."

Sloane made a noncommittal noise in lieu of determining whether the girls' grades actually mattered (hadn't that always been a mere formality, academics in Greek life?) and scanned the bid list in front of her, realizing that was her main, and perhaps her only, job. "Dalil Serrano is in one of my lectures," Sloane realized aloud, with no small amount of surprise. She hadn't expected to recognize any names. In her experience, sorority girls were mostly comm majors. "I don't know anything about her yet, but I've spoken with her briefly."

"Mm, yes, Dalil." Alex exchanged another knowing glance with Priscilla. "We'll have to keep an eye on her."

"Why?" She'd seemed perfectly pleasant to Sloane.

Alex took a bite of cheese, so Priscilla took the first stab at answering. "She certainly won everybody over during rush, but she's . . ."

Priscilla looked at Alex, who shrugged as if to indicate it was silly, and yet. "She's what we in the business call a quitter," she said, one hand over her mouth.

"What?" Sloane couldn't help a laugh.

"Oh, you know," Priscilla said, waving a hand. "Did Girl Scouts for years but never completed her final project. Won a district essay competition but never wrote anything else. Champion debater for a year, then nothing. Played varsity soccer for two years and then stopped. She hasn't declared a major," Priscilla went on, ticking off Dalil's faults on her fingers, "has exceptional grades but transferred high schools twice, worked completely different jobs every summer of high school—"

"We just want to make sure she goes through with it," Alex concluded to Sloane. "We put a lot of time and effort into our new members and we expect a lot out of them, too. The House isn't for someone who can't be invested."

"A quitter," Sloane repeated quietly to herself, this time as if to turn it over and inspect it more closely. To make sure she didn't see herself reflected in any of its crevices, trapped somewhere unintentionally in its glare.

"Anyone else?" asked Alex, and Sloane looked again at the list.

"I don't think so—"

Britt was on her way back from the fridge when she paused, a strange look coming over her face. She doubled back and crouched down to coo warmly at Isla, her voice and expression transforming to something that even Sloane, a relative stranger, could tell was her Mommy Voice.

"Hi, sweetie," said Britt to Isla. "Did someone do a poo?"

"Poo!" exclaimed Theo.

"Oh, I'll get it," said Sloane, looking up with a sudden flush as if she'd been the one to poop her dress.

"Nah, I've got it. I haven't gotten to hold one this fresh in ages." Britt took a dramatic sniff of Isla's neck, making her giggle before scooping her up and sweeping Sloane's diaper bag from the floor in one smooth motion. "You keep working."

Working? This was working? This was the most relaxed Sloane had felt in almost two years. Maybe longer.

"What do you think?" asked Alex quietly, a tiny smile on her face. Priscilla had gone to get the cheese from the kitchen counter where Britt had left it. Britt's husband Finn was chasing his girls while playing catch with Alex's son Theo. Alex's bare feet were resting leisurely on Sloane's chair, her scarlet toenails tucked under

Sloane's thigh. Isla's diaper was changed, her butt had even been slicked with the French diaper cream Sloane always used but Max never did, and now Isla was lurching her drunken sailor sprint across the living room to the twins with her hand in Britt's, and Sloane wasn't being crushed under the weight of existential dread.

"So what do we do for The Girls, exactly?" asked Sloane, leaning back so Priscilla could set the cheese board on the table again.

Alex's smile broadened as she dug a knife into the Camembert. "I'm so glad you asked."

PART II

EDUCATION

POV: You can't understand why all your "career driven" friends are so miserable because you spend your days making healthy food for people you love . . .

—Transcript from a VidStar by @TheCountryWife

SIX

WEEKS

TO

INITIATION.

10

As if a spell had been lifted in the moments after Nina was extended a bid, The House seemed to unzip its pants and stretch out on the sofa, returning to a more authentic state of existence. Like petals unfurling in the sun, the uniform style of each bedroom began to change mere hours after bid night ended and festivities gave way to the light of day, taking on the fingerprints of its occupants. Now, the front window of the house boasted a glittery BLACK LIVES MATTER sign. The bedroom above it—belonging, Nina would later learn, to Alina Antwerp and Leonie Monaghan, who were best friends in real life in addition to being co-rush chairs—displayed a vintage presidential campaign banner for the most recent female nominee, which could be seen clearly from certain angles on the row depending on your position as you traversed the sidewalk. There was, as Nina had known to expect, an array of bikes now locked up against both sides of the house in a glittery spectrum of colors, freed from the polished veneer of recruitment. Perhaps most noticeable, though, was the way each girl had begun to shed her formal camouflage, settling back into some unknown personal aesthetic just as Nina finally got to shrug on the communal letters of The House.

Tessa, for example, had been wearing an oversized Kendrick Lamar T-shirt that read DAMN. in pastel letters across her chest while she'd been wandering the house, which she'd swapped for her bid night T-shirt just before accompanying Nina to class. The new members, which Nina had felt a thrill of self-satisfying pleasure to observe did include Dalil (thanks to Nina—or was that, as Nina often asked herself, the thought of a narcissist?), had been asked to come in early for a new member education meeting, where they were given their initiation bibles: binders including information they had to memorize and songs they had to learn before each sheet was burned and the details therein committed to memory and passed on orally, like the storytelling of yore. Dalil and Nina had exchanged a glance over the tops of their rush bibles, wordlessly expressing a sense of having been woken too early and assigned an unreadable amount of homework. Nina wanted to be a member of The House, yes, and therefore she understood that in some way it *should* feel difficult, as suffering was the only true way to weed out the unworthy. (She was, again, pre-law.) That being said, Nina was still taking eighteen credits for the semester and struggled to consider "sisterhood songs" a matter of supreme importance.

"Oh, I know, it's ridiculous," Tessa assured her as they walked. Nina didn't have a bike—her apartment was only just off-campus—but she understood that she would have to get one. She felt burdensome to Tessa, who was charitably walking her bike alongside Nina to keep pace. "As long as you're, like, fifty-*one* percent of the way there, muscle memory will eventually take over," Tessa assured her, with an air of jaunty conspiracy. "Everything's a ritual. You'll do it all a million times before you leave here, so as long as you can remember the things you're required to recite for initiation, the remaining lore will be mastered by virtue of time and bludgeoning repetition."

Tessa was a junior, one year Nina's senior, as was Fawn. Tessa had already explained that it was unusual to have a president that was a junior, as it meant Fawn had actually taken office when she was a sophomore, and typically speaking it took an extraordinary member to do that. Fawn had also not been selected by Slate, the election committee—meaning, she had not been appointed to run by the older girls whose business it was to decide who in The

House ought to take over. For most positions, Tessa explained, if nobody objected, then whichever girl was slated for a position won by default. Such was not often the case with the office of president, Tessa assured her. But Fawn had run anyway, and won what was essentially the popular vote.

"It's silly, honestly, since the president is mostly a figurehead," Tessa went on as Nina attempted to conceal a yawn. She had already learned during her first semester at college not to sign up for 8 A.M. lectures, as what had been doable, even luxurious in high school was no longer justifiably within reason. "A sorority president's job is basically to be the pinnacle of sisterhood. She doesn't have to be as pretty as the rush chairs or as organized as the VPs, but she can't have a single blemish on her reputation. She has to be a myth, basically. And sure, some of the girls disagree with Fawn's philosophy," Tessa qualified with an offhanded shrug, "but it's a house, not a cult, you know what I mean? There'll always be disagreement, but the difference between a hot girl and an It Girl is that ephemeral quality of making people either want you or want to be you, even against their will." She passed Nina an unreadable sidelong glance. "And I think we can agree that Fawn is very good at that."

Nina felt a slight tinge of embarrassment, as if Tessa had read her mind that morning while she'd been unable to keep herself from glancing around, waiting to see if Fawn might appear from the stairwell. Over the course of the new member meeting, a handful of The House's residents had slipped into the dining room groggily, returning to their rooms with an apple or cup of coffee in hand. A few others had come down the stairs fully dressed, cat-eyes sharp, to proceed directly out the door.

Tessa herself had come from the small in-house gym down the hall, sweaty from the treadmill, partway through Nina's meeting. Then, just as the girls were dismissed, she was waiting for Nina beside the door, her braids pulled back in a messy bun with tendrils casually hanging loose around her face. Nina had realized with a slight flush that Tessa had probably been assigned to her, given that someone had also called for Dalil from the dining room, inviting her to stay back. Presumably each of the other pledges had met a similar fate.

The intricacies of ritual seemed not to have left them despite the fact that rush was over. Nina had expected to feel that the period of time in which she would have to prove something about herself was at an end; that she would instantly blend and belong. But this, it seemed, would require a period of transition, and she couldn't decide if she should feel patronized by being assigned a guardian at all times or grateful that The House took care of its young, easing them in.

"You were Leonie's rush crush," Tessa remarked, jarring Nina out of her thoughts. Two very attractive frat guys nodded to Tessa, who gave a small, careless wave back. Nina felt their eyes linger subsequently on her, assessing. "Don't tell her I told you."

"Wait, rush crush?" echoed Nina.

"Yeah, you know, when you get obsessed with a girl you want to be your friend. You'll understand next year—it's unavoidable. You meet someone pretty and smart and cool and you just think wow, I want to share a bathroom with her for the next three years."

Tessa was clearly joking, and yet Nina had felt exactly that about the girls she'd met. She couldn't believe *Leonie* had felt that way about her—they'd barely spoken. And Leonie looked like a Barbie come to life. "Wow, that's crazy. I mean, I kinda get it already. I'm so excited."

That wasn't the right word. What Nina actually felt was a hot, molten desperation to skip over the next month and some change and be a proper member of The House—to know the rituals already; to already be familiar with where the coffee accoutrements were kept; to already know who had early classes and which days of the week Fawn and Tessa ate lunch on the quad; to tune in to the frequency of The House instead of jerking along in the wake of its current. She wanted to already possess the shorthand of sisterhood, the kind where she no longer had to wait to be invited, to wonder if she was included, if a stray comment was meant to encompass her among the *us*. She wanted to dissolve the barrier between herself and Tessa, the one where Tessa knew things about her and she didn't really know anything about Tessa, the one where she was new and Tessa was not, where as long as they remained on opposite sides of the invisible line they could never really be close. She wanted to stop questioning the right thing to say—to simply *know* it. She understood that theoretically speaking, every relationship began this way, that she had once not known Simone or Mei or Adelaide either, and had wondered whether they found it weird that she talked to her sister so much and had not started using tampons until partway through freshman year because her mother had not allowed it, despite the fact that Nina had not been a virgin since she'd slept with Jonathan Zein at his homecoming afterparty, and Jas had not been one since the year before that.

Did Fawn use tampons? Nina wondered. Did she wear period underwear instead, because tampons were bad for the environment, or did she worry about period underwear having carcinogens, as Nina did? Was Fawn's flow anything like Nina's, which was punishingly demented, diabolical like a plague of blood? Did Fawn use those discs that went up to your cervix, which Nina had seen at the student health center gynecologist's office and pondered the logistics of for so long she'd forgotten to get undressed and had to be reminded? Was Fawn on the kind of birth control that meant she only had a period every few months? Would Fawn want to sit on the couch watching crime procedurals for hours, a heat pack over her uterus while passing a pint of chocolate ice cream back and forth in solidarity, as

Nina and her roommate Simone often did? Nina couldn't picture Fawn having a period at all. She felt the phantom wave of a cramp just thinking about it.

"You don't have to worry about hazing," Tessa was saying, still playing the part of Nina's official House mentor. "I mean, International's rules are so strict that you're not even allowed to clear your own dishes at dinner. *We* have to serve *you*." She gave Nina an impish grin, letting her in on the joke. "But you do have to attend a bunch of meetings and memorize a bunch of stuff that some dead women wrote in the 1800s. And sorry about the shirt," she added, gesturing to the bid day shirt Nina was wearing, having been instructed the night before to wear it all day in class. It bore The House's letters and BID NIGHT in an old-school collegiate font. "It's tradition, but obviously the frat bros all use it as an excuse to be idiots and rank the new members like their male opinion even matters."

Nina knew about that. At the end of the day, there would be ample speculation on VidStar (and probably accompanying photo evidence) about which sorority had the hottest new members. It was always The House, though the occasional "hot take" might invoke someone else, just to be controversial. Adelaide had been very disgruntled about it last night, ranting for almost the entire time that she and Nina walked back from the row to their campus apartment. Nina understood that in Adelaide's case, intellectualizing the misogyny was a form of self-defense—that if everyone agreed it was chauvinistic and repulsive, then Adelaide didn't have to feel dejected about not being voted the best. A debate tactic, undermining the authenticity of the opponent, which in this case was almost laughably easy to do.

Nina, meanwhile, didn't care what a bunch of frat guys thought of her. She also understood that many of these disgusting frat guys would be competing against her for the same law schools and that, eventually, whether she liked it or not, their acceptance would determine her success in the workplace and in life. Two things could be true.

Tessa began to slow her pace, indicating to Nina that their paths would soon diverge. "I've got a lecture in the humanities building," she explained, before leaning in for a hug that smelled cosmopolitan and crisp. "When are you supposed to be back this week?"

"We've got another new member meeting Thursday night," said Nina.

"Oh okay, great. Text me if you need anything." Tessa's eyes were wandering slightly, like in her head she had already departed the conversation. "I'm so excited you're in The House!"

Again, it felt like the wrong word. It almost sounded like Tessa was saying she was relieved it was Nina and not someone worse, though it was possible Nina only felt that way because her period was imminent. She returned Tessa's hug and made a show of also needing to be somewhere, although she didn't, which was why they had already passed the building where her class would take place in half an hour.

She decided to get a coffee and call Jas, who would probably make fun of her shirt, though Nina felt it was tasteful and classic and so what if its purpose was to claim something specific about her—something that now belonged to The House by virtue of it choosing her? Basically the fact that she was fuckable, Jas would say. And Nina would say, What's wrong with that? If people were going to deem her fuckable or unfuckable regardless of whether she consented, wasn't it better to do it this way, without pretense? Forget dressing for men or for women. The fashion industry didn't care who you dressed for as long as you did so every season, changing color palettes and trends as a means of keeping classism alive. Short of making her own clothes, there was no way for Nina *not* to participate in the exploitation of desirability. So shouldn't she game the system and win?

You're so full of shit, Jas would say, in the same delighted voice she had used when Nina said she'd fucked Jonathan Zein despite Jas saying his forehead was too small for him to really be attractive.

Nina felt a surge of warmth, pleased now that she was awake so early, that she would have this time to decompress and be reminded that life did exist outside of The House. Of course, at the time this thought occurred to her, she realized that in parting from her company, Tessa had gone over to greet someone else. Tessa, who was currently locking up her bike in front of one of the humanities buildings, was chatting animatedly with a distinctly recognizable silhouette—specifically, the silhouette belonging to someone that Nina had to forcefully blink away, as if she'd conjured her up magically, from a dream. In a way that couldn't exist in any plausible reality, much less the one outside The House.

But she did exist. And in the breaths after Nina spotted her, Fawn Carter tilted her head back and laughed, and Nina felt a bone-crush of dread, wondering what Tessa had said about her, what Fawn thought was funny, all the things Tessa knew that Nina did not.

11

Sloane had never paid much attention to who in her classes was part of the Greek system, a non-issue at her previous college. She considered it a mere signifier of archetypes, not unlike the athletes and cheerleaders who dressed up for game days in high school. She supposed she could admit, grudgingly, that even now as a fully grown woman, she partitioned those sorts of associations into one of two categories: a try-hard mentality, if the student in question was unattractive, or a victim of pathological groupthink, if they were. She supposed she did have a sense for which Greek letters represented beauty, sophistication, money . . . Admitting this to herself felt embarrassing and juvenile, but it was true. She looked around during her lecture and spotted the letters belonging to The House, realizing that it was no wonder those girls eventually became women like Alex, like Priscilla and Britt. As Sloane had already observed, Dalil Serrano was breathtakingly beautiful, with wavy brown-black hair and breasts like the ones Sloane used to have before she'd sacrificed them on the altar of breastfeeding.

Which, Sloane recalled, she was meant to stop doing, per her pediatrician, who coincidentally did not have to deal with Isla's rage. Breast was best until apparently, mysteriously, it wasn't.

"Oh god, that's absurd," Britt had said when Sloane mentioned it offhandedly, after they determined that the twelve new members—well below the International standards that called for a pledge class of at least sixty given the size of the University at large—were all very good potential representatives of The House. "What's she complaining about?"

"Oh, she said I needed to night wean, because the sugar from breast milk was destroying Isla's teeth or something—"

"Oh, come on," growled Britt, whose twins looked up briefly at the declarative sound of their mother's ire, but then merely went back to their business of coloring, as if it happened all the time. "How often do you brush her teeth?"

"Well—" Sloane felt her face flush, not wanting to confess aloud that Isla was simply very noncompliant, and sometimes Sloane forgot to brush her teeth in the morning when she was in a hurry and didn't want Isla to wipe toothpaste on her shirt, and if she didn't do it then Max certainly wasn't going to do it because Sloane was the one who always did it, and because—despite the fact that Max was older and had therefore been brushing his teeth for even longer than Sloane had—when it came to Isla, Max simply didn't know how. "I mean, I'm *trying* to do it twice a day, but—"

"It's not a big deal," Britt concluded with a shrug, though Sloane detected a slight sense of disapproval. Britt, after all, had the time for it, and she had two sets of teeth requiring brushing, not to mention perfect abs and a slew of industry awards on display in her perfect house. "But if teeth are the concern, that's an easy fix."

"My trick is to use two toothbrushes," Alex offered. "One for Theo to 'brush' and one for me to sneak into his mouth at any given opportunity. I used to use two spoons to feed him, too."

"Oh god," said Sloane, who wanted to die at the mere thought of feeding Isla, a thing she did several times a day and yet couldn't imagine having to do again. "I can't get Isla to eat anything. She's not even a picky eater, really. She's just apathetic to food."

"Smoothies work really well," Britt said.

"Or ice pops," added Alex.

"Yeah, ice pops are great. And Trader Joe's has precooked beets, those have tons of protein, plus as a bonus they turn the smoothies pink."

"Sprinkles," said Alex, deathly serious. "Sprinkles are a game changer. I'll send you the link for the ones Theo loves."

"Oh, I forgot you're the one who got me started on sprinkles!" Britt laughed. "I avoided sugar for *so long,* and then you came around with the fucking sprinkles—"

"I mean, I randomly get the kid who loves broccoli," Alex said to Sloane with a little eye roll of *aren't kids such rascals.* "But all dairy products require sprinkles or it's not happening."

"I've got a great ragu that has liver in it," Britt said. "Lots of iron. The girls love it. I'll send you the recipe."

Alex nodded vigorously. "Theo loves it, too. You can make a huge batch and freeze it."

Quietly, Sloane considered saying that she didn't know how she would find the time. She was teaching a new-to-her course—the quantitative methods one—and wasn't confident in her syllabus yet. She wanted to have the time to be good at her job, to write something worth publishing by the end of the semester, and also to work out with the same frequency with which she had maintained her body previously, to cook extravagant meals her daughter would eat and her husband would celebrate her for, to read for pleasure, to feel sexual desire, to shower regularly. But in reality, doing any one of those things chipped away at any plausible time for the rest, and worse—any time Sloane did get a spare moment to herself, her exhausted brain misused it scrolling VidStar, hate-watching The Country Wife's homesteading montages like they were porn.

Sloane had looked longingly at Alex's nails, a trendy shade for autumn that Sloane had scrolled past while rocking a restless Isla to sleep the night before. Sloane had once been religious about her nail color, but since Isla was born there'd been no guarantee she'd be able to fix a chip in a timely manner, so she'd given it up. And yet Britt somehow had time to bake. Sloane had now eaten food prepared by Britt twice and offered nothing in exchange.

She felt a mix of longing and inadequacy, a desperation she hadn't felt since she was in her twenties, or maybe even earlier. It was a desire to do things correctly according to an invisible metric, to be good enough—not even better, but the same. To keep up, that was it.

Wasn't that supposed to have gone away? Sloane remembered turning thirty and realizing with relief that all of a sudden, she no longer depended on the opinions of others to define the outer constraints of her value. Did her professional success matter to her? Of course. But in a bigger way, she knew she was smart, understood she was deserving of respect, in a way she hadn't when she was younger. She had grown into self-acceptance, which was functionally the disposal of deep-seated inadequacy. She had always had something to prove, but no longer did that apply directly to her personhood.

Then she'd had Isla, and suddenly the bliss of maturity, of being a woman who understood how she made her way in the world, simply disintegrated overnight. Sloane remembered the exact moment she felt it leave her, replaced by a new version of an old doubt. She'd finally given birth in the late evening after two full days of labor, the hospital staff having changed shifts multiple times. After Sloane had held Isla, falling madly in love with the infant who'd curled kitten-like on her bare chest—after Sloane had been stitched up—after Sloane had taken the most terrifying, painful pee of her life—the nurses had set Isla, carefully swaddled and asleep, into the bassinet beside Sloane's hospital bed, turning off the lights. Max, on a cot on the opposite side of the room, fell instantly and heavily asleep. Sloane closed her eyes, aware for the first time that she'd been awake for almost forty-eight consecutive hours. Then Isla had begun to cry, and Sloane understood through an ineffable, cosmic jolt that this was her life now, and she didn't know what to do, and she might never again know what to do, and the best she could ever feel when it came to motherhood was that she had maybe gotten something sort of right in an acceptable, passing way, but never like she had really *achieved* something. She couldn't even win over the affections of her dog.

And she had once been full of achievement, literally all the time! She'd gotten As—so many As. She'd set *so many* curves. She gave blow jobs so good Max had once gone out while she was showering and bought her a box of donuts in gratitude. And the irony was that the whole time Sloane had been the best in her class or the prettiest or attracting the most envy from her peers, from her friends, and from other women, she had still felt on the inside like she should have gotten that one point she'd missed, and she needed to lose five pounds, and she had to learn to fix every little flaw she'd always previously lived with, because if she didn't then Max would inevitably leave her, because who could ever really see all her shit and still want to stay?

So it felt cruel, then, to eventually ease into the comfort with herself that no longer demanded her waist be the smallest or her hair be the shiniest or that she be the hottest professor in the department or the one with the best overall student rating, only to now have her mind consumed in different ways *to the exact same degree* with an overwhelming sense of constant failure. Not just in terms of what she did, but some more fundamental wrongness—something she couldn't articulate about who she actually was.

Sloane glanced, then—almost helplessly—at Dalil Serrano. Beautiful Dalil, who even in jeans looked like the *Vogue* profile of an up-and-coming movie star. God, Sloane thought with a sudden, visceral internal correction, Dalil wasn't just beautiful. The House didn't just have *beautiful* girls—it was so much more specific than that, like how the most gorgeous woman alive wasn't just *beautiful*. It was a bigotry-defying beauty, striking enough to dazzle the racism right out of anyone with eyes. And yet, breathtaking, perfect Dalil was glancing surreptitiously at her phone screen, probably checking to see whether some tall bland white dude had summoned the energy to venture *sup*.

In that moment, Sloane realized she'd rather die than be eighteen years old again. No matter how tired she was now, she wouldn't go back to some self-sabotaging youth, the version of her who felt like she might disappear without the attention of some fucking asshole, the stakes of the universe arranged not by any rational, objective measure but by how she felt about herself in her worst moments, by how others might feel about her. She'd take a bullet to the head rather than return to the fundamental question of who would she be, what would she accomplish, what was she good at, was she running out of time? The Sloane Hartley who stood in front of the class delivering a glorified statistics lecture already knew that life was long, that the world didn't stop at thirty, that maturity had only given her value rather than stripping it away, that her desirability to men had never offered her anything that actually mattered, even if it had felt like it at the time.

But *fuck,* Sloane thought, looking at Dalil Serrano with the same surreptitious pretense as Dalil's observation of her phone and the fuckhead frat bro no doubt haunting the poor girl's messages. If someone said Sloane Hartley, you have to be eighteen again, then she'd give anything to do it Dalil's way, with those letters printed on her perfect chest.

Just saying.

12

Nina didn't see Fawn on Thursday, and as the week crept into the weekend, she realized she was going to need to stop looking for Fawn. She felt a creeping tendril of embarrassment, like the first flush of a fever, realizing she had mistakenly thought of Fawn as a friend when really, Fawn had plenty of friends. And so, now, did Nina! She needed to stop lusting over some imaginary *SVU* marathon with an emotionally unavailable person she hardly knew. It was Jonathan Zein all over again.

The first weekend as a member of The House was a lively one, filled with innumerable fraternity house parties, all of which Nina was now able to attend, having fulfilled her puritanical recruitment abstention. She packed three super tampons into her clutch, took approximately eight thousand milligrams of Advil, and met up with Dalil and their fellow new members at The House before venturing out onto the row. Nina had promised to catch up with Simone and Adelaide at some unidentified point in time, at whichever party they happened to vibe with for the night, once she'd gotten her mandated hours of sisterhood out of the way. But then she'd lingered overlong at the particular frat house that was full of well-built crew-rowing nepo babies, both because they'd taken an unusual interest in her and because Nina had spotted Fawn out of the corner of her eye, one arm linked through Leonie's. A desperate part of Nina wanted to cry out, "Leonie! I was your rush crush, wasn't I? Can you tell me everything you admire about me in extreme, agonizing detail?" but of course she held it in, like a lady. She could feel The House settling like a cloak over her shoulders, a silky invisible material that heightened her magnetism and accentuated her natural social gifts.

Even her cramps seemed slightly easier, anxiety having briefly loosened its jaws. Suddenly Nina's hair seemed to fall perfectly, her jokes all seemed to land. Her pseudo-Parisian affectation of contrarian disinterest had sharpened so effectively that when a boy she would surely have gone home with the previous year invited her up to his room, Nina gave a coy laugh and flatly turned him down. It was as if the impulse to seek attention had dimmed, a prior necessity transformed into an erstwhile symptom of cringe-inducing youth, the high of casual hook-ups now rendered cheap and fleeting.

She could afford to be selective now. The gift of The House was the luxury of time and permission. Now, unlike before, Nina could wait. She could choose.

"Boring," said Jas. "Next you'll be telling me you're saving yourself for your husband, who will be named Tripp and have a family cabin in Sun Valley."

"Are you saying you wouldn't come along?"

"I mean, I'd go, but I wouldn't be happy about it."

"I'm not going to date a Tripp. But for the record, there are three of them and they're all friends with Tessa, so if you really wanted I could probably do it. A little Tripp, as a treat."

"Oh, see, you're making jokes, but I can tell you're drinking the Kool-Aid." Jas laughed. "By all means, though, keep going. I'm going to write about you for my term paper."

"Let me guess, it's about . . . Oh, I don't know, institutional power?"

"Second-wave feminism," Jas corrected, "but it's always best to draw an ominous conclusion, like how the systems you participate in that are meant to empower women are really only speaking to a certain class of privilege."

Nina scoffed. "Hello? Last I heard we share a DNA sequence, not to mention a tax bracket. If I'm privileged, you're privileged."

"Sure, but I'm not trying to *ingratiate* myself with that privilege. It's different."

"Is it?" As usual when it came to Jas there was no point getting into the weeds, but Nina couldn't help herself. "Look, the reality is that every douchebag at this school is using their privilege without a second thought. So why shouldn't I benefit?"

"Because you're not actually one of them, Nina!" Jas rolled her eyes. "This is all very 'I didn't think the leopards would eat *my* face' from the woman who voted for the Leopards Eating People's Faces Party."

"Touch some grass, J. I gotta go," said Nina, though she didn't have anywhere to be, she just couldn't continue discussing privilege or she'd get a headache and spontaneously start a podcast.

It was ironic, in Nina's mind, that there was no correct way to be a woman of color, just as there was no correct way to be a beautiful woman or a sexually active woman or just a woman, period. She didn't need Jas's help hating herself, or what was the cosmetics industry for? She sensed that family Thanksgiving would become unbearable as they aged, unless Jas did what every other left-leaning first gen queer person did and brought home a peaceable middle-class white woman. Which, ultimately, was no different from Nina joining The House—where so far, her two closest friends (three if you counted Fawn, which she wasn't, obviously) weren't even white!—so yeah, she had somewhere else to be.

Jas aside, Nina was coming to learn that The House wasn't quite as she'd expected. She understood, to some extent, that every one of her new sisters had a unique fingerprint, blah blah blah, but even taken as a collective, things were ultimately surprising.

Take their Monday night dinners, for example. Over the course of Nina's friendship with Adelaide—strike that. Over the course of Nina's friendship with other women, she had become accustomed to varying degrees of disordered eating. It was normal, in Nina's mind, for girls to allow themselves sweets and fries and various other culinary misbehaviors, but only with a sense of guilt, and a collective understanding that it was a sin-ridden act in some way, something they would all offer penance for in the gym, or perhaps in the bathroom, depending on how far gone the girl in question happened to be. True, there was a certain progressivism among Nina's close friends as opposed to her understanding of previous generations—there was no longer public acceptance of "body shaming," and people were just as quick to police fatphobia as they were to engage in any discourse on privilege—but it didn't change the fact that some girls really did appear to believe that nothing tasted as good as skinny felt, and even the ones who were healthier about it were still diligent about the optics of their bodies in ways that were hard-edged with shame.

So, Nina had expected dinner at The House to be a similar affair. She hadn't invented the stereotype of the sorority girl who asked about carbs and didn't eat gluten or dairy. She didn't even think she'd judge it if she came across it. The expectations for feminine eating were so patently common she doubted she would have even noticed if that had been the case. But it was the opposite—profoundly the opposite.

The first time Nina entered The House for Monday night dinner, she'd been struck by the eerie sense that she hadn't been invited—that she'd somehow broken in. The smart-tech front door opened for her fingerprint just as it previously had, but her awareness of The House's internal frequency was louder, a faint buzzing in her ears, in the space between her navel and her spine. It was like walking into a room where everyone had just been talking about you, but she could tell that wasn't the case—the energy wasn't directed at her, or directed anywhere, really. It was just a sense that something invisible was present, something tangible and pressing that Nina couldn't yet see.

The girls filed into the dining room in their pretty formal dresses without any particular sequence or hierarchy, but it was easy to tell who was a new member and who was not. The established, the old guard, the ones who *belonged* were all patently waiting for something, shoulders uniformly tensed beneath delicate straps of silk and linen as they walked.

Dozens of tables lined the dining room, with beautiful, intricate place settings for each girl. The silverware was heavy and antique, the glassware thick and iridescent, low-falling sun warming the view from the open windows, shadows of the candle-flames dancing blithely along the walls. As the space gradually filled, House members distributed themselves at random throughout the room—only the head table, where Fawn sat, was reserved—and Nina caught sight of a senior sniffing the air like a hunting dog. Two tables over, Summer Toft took desperate sips of her water like her throat was dry, her bottom lip nearly cracked open with wanting. Alina's and Leonie's knees jiggled in tandem; the girl across from Nina (someone Nina hadn't met yet) arranged and rearranged her jaw like she'd been steadily grinding her teeth.

There was an almost imperceptible thrum of apprehension, or desire. Like the moment you know a kiss isn't just a kiss anymore—it's going somewhere. The presence of anticipation passed through the dining room like a shiver, a sudden shift in the wind.

Plates were carried out from the kitchen by the hired catering staff, several heads snapping toward the pair of servers. Next to Nina, closer to the center aisle between the tables, there was an odd, almost cartoonish glint in Tessa's eye, a typewriter flick of unfaltering interest.

Amused by all this, Nina turned to find Dalil, who was two

tables behind her, but Dalil's gaze was fixed on a sophomore sitting across the table from her, whom Nina could see had begun to quietly pant.

Nina felt it again—the chattering teeth, the hum of inorganic stillness. The House's true members sat coiled and waiting, a collective bow strung taut. There it was again, that presence of something. Of waiting. Hunting.

Within moments, Nina thought she might have understood what it was.

Dinner at The House was, to put it plainly, a feast. Directly in front of Nina sat a platter with a colorful array of bright, festive vegetables, each roasted with golden crusts of Parmesan cheese. Beside her, thick, crusty slabs of bread were heartily dipped in velvety sauces, raised to still-chatting mouths, visibly dripping with richness like cream. A beautiful ceramic bowl was filled to the brim with fresh, hand-cut pasta. The main course was a short rib so tender it melted like butter in her mouth, and Nina felt her eyes close almost unconsciously, the word *savory* materializing unsolicited in her mind. For the first time she could remember since she'd gotten a period, she didn't think about her cramps at all.

"What if someone's vegetarian?" she asked Tessa beside her, who chuckled sardonically.

"No vegetarians in The House. We don't tolerate that sort of foolishness."

It was obviously a joke, and Nina laughed. "Seriously though, nobody's got any ethical hang-ups about meat? No religious oppositions?"

"The meat is all organic, butchered humanely, locally farmed, you name it," Tessa said. "We accommodate everyone as best we can, but these dinners are sacred. Once a week, we live deliciously."

"No allergies? No lactose intolerance?" Nina pressed, intrigued now. She wondered if her own occasional struggle with dairy would count against her on this particular occasion. Not officially, she told herself, either way.

"Nope," said Tessa.

"Is it like this at every house?" Nina couldn't imagine Adelaide eating this meal. Adelaide was vegan and struggled to keep weight off her thighs (according to her). Which wasn't to say Nina didn't have her own self-conscious moments, but she came from a household where food meant love, so she'd always simply lived with the existence of large celebratory meals where you ate until your stomach hurt. It was a philosophy she associated with immigrant roots, having a sort of inverse relationship to Americanness. Needless to say, Nina hadn't expected to find that sort of kinship anywhere in the Greek system, which was about as American as she felt you could get.

"No, this is pretty unique to us," Tessa confirmed, spooning more sauce onto Nina's plate. Nina hadn't even noticed she'd still been dipping her bread into it, physically unable to stop.

"Wait, there are *no* allergies?" she realized aloud, moving on to a completely separate pondering. "Nobody's got celiac?"

Tessa set the serving spoon down and licked her fingers. "Nope."

"No peanut allergies?" said Nina, slow to process whatever was mysteriously concerning to her about this, though Tessa's arched brow told her that Tessa had already lost interest. Nina glanced around the room, abruptly shocked to realize she'd heard no sneezing, no coughing, despite the viral cold that had been the subject of the health center's weekly email. "Is anyone on medication?"

"What is with these questions?" asked Tessa, though before she'd fully gotten it out, another House senior whose name Nina hadn't committed to memory yet commented vaguely, "I used to be on Adderall. And Lexapro."

"What happened?" Nina asked her, and she shrugged.

"Don't need it anymore."

Nina scanned the room again, still unsure what she was looking for. The girl who'd sniffed the air was now drawing circles on her empty plate with sauce, a strange, hollow look in her eye, like she wasn't quite satisfied.

Nina shook herself, turning back to Tessa. "What about glasses?" she asked, realizing that although several of the girls were barefaced or had clearly stumbled down the stairs with little effort at presentation, none seemed to wear prescription lenses of any kind. "Or what about . . . I don't know, asthma? Is everyone just completely perfect in every way? Or, like, does anyone else have—" She stopped.

"Have what?" Tessa asked, this time managing to resume her interest at the phrasing of *anyone else*.

Nina exhaled, regretting that she'd asked so many pointless questions, as she was now obligated to answer some of her own. Who cared whether anyone wore glasses or sometimes got the shits from dairy? Aside from her, who had ailments aplenty.

"Endometriosis," she said, with what she hoped was casual disinterest. "Maybe. Or just, like, periods that kick the shit out of you, basically." Since, depending on who you asked, Nina didn't have anything that was a real condition, or even one that had a real name.

"Oh." Tessa patted her shoulder, then slid Nina the butter knife and replaced her empty hand with another fresh slab of bread. "I'm sorry. That sucks."

Across the table, the senior snorted a laugh. "Doubt you'll have to worry about that anymore," she said, raising a piece of short rib to her mouth with her fingers.

The dining room was loud. "What?" said Nina, who wasn't confident she'd heard correctly.

Suddenly there was a tap on Nina's shoulder, distracting her just as she'd taken a large bite of rapaciously buttered bread.

"Hey! Just wanted to say hi." It was Fawn, of course. Nina

had seen her earlier, opening the evening's dinner with a recitation that Nina hadn't memorized yet. Not exactly a prayer before dinner, but not necessarily not, either. More like a pledge of allegiance. "How has your first week been? I've been meaning to check on you, I've just been so busy. You know how the start of the semester goes."

"Oh, yeah, totally, of course," said Nina meaninglessly, hurrying to finish her bite. She gestured to her mouth with a helpless, self-deprecating shrug; across the table, the senior who'd been chatting with them excused herself. "Sorry, I'm just—"

"No no, it's my fault! I'm the one harassing you while you're trying to eat. God, isn't it delicious tonight? I always miss Monday night dinner during the summer. Nothing else compares." Fawn sighed with contentment and Nina thought of silk sheets, clandestine poetry. The teeth-chatter of wanting, longing that pooled in her mouth.

"It's really amazing," Nina agreed, ecstatic to be talking to Fawn, wishing she could be sure her breath didn't smell like garlic, admiring the whirl of heady satisfaction that came from being so pleasantly full. "Do you guys always eat like this or is it just to impress the new pledges?"

"Honestly, this is mid," sniffed Tessa. "Like, no shade at all to Chef, but just wait until Thanksgiving. And solstice."

"Solstice?" echoed Nina. She felt a look pass between Fawn and Tessa from her periphery.

"You'll find out more about it after initiation," Fawn explained. "But it's the best dinner of the semester by far. We do one in December, one in May—"

"Supposed to be June, obviously, but we fudge it for the academic calendar," said Tessa with a grin.

"It's celebratory," Fawn confirmed. "A night of total sisterhood. Something to look forward to," she added, squeezing Nina's shoulder and straightening with obvious intention to leave. "But until then, don't forget to work on your rush bible. I saw you fumbling for words earlier," she playfully accused.

"What—I did not!" Nina ineffectively protested, and Fawn laughed, giving her an air kiss and wandering back to the table at the head of the room, where Nina realized Fawn would have had to stare eagle-eyed at Nina to catch her struggling with the dinner rites. Had she really been looking that closely? More likely it was a lucky guess. Nina shoved the thought aside and took another bite of bread, looking up to see the table being cleared for dessert.

"Okay, I take back what I said about being mid," said Tessa, who reached for the chocolate ganache cake with a look that bordered on orgasmic. "This is my absolute *favorite* dessert. Get your fill, because we only have it a few times each term."

"Oh my god, I'm so full, though—"

"Shut up and eat," said Tessa, piling a slice on Nina's plate as she laughed. "Self-care," Tessa added with a wink. "Good girls deserve a treat."

Nina felt woozy with pleasure, a little drunk, her cramps a steady, low-fi buzz, manageable and easy to forget. Punch-drunk and silly, she felt overwhelmingly fond of Tessa, and of Fawn, and of The House in general. It wasn't, as Jas had said, just paying money to eat food with her friends. Where else would she find this kind of community—this degree of letting her hair down? She'd die before eating this way in front of a boy, and she had the feeling most of the other girls would, too. This was just for them. Wasn't that feminist, and not just *in its way*, but generally speaking? Wasn't this the benefit of feminine spaces, to exist in celebration, authentically, with no restraint?

Nina thought suddenly of Dr. Villanueva's lecture from earlier in the week.

"There are, of course, countless ways to determine the proper form of existence," Dr. Villanueva had said, "and as a matter of charting a course, there is no singular methodology. The nature of philosophy is not to determine a life, but a way of living. A definition of what it means to live, and to what end."

His gaze lingered for a moment on Nina, who had been looking thoughtfully upward at the time. She'd always been one to crush easily, particularly on her teachers. Something about masculine authority was like competency porn, and Dr. Villanueva lacked for nothing in the physical realm. He remained of indeterminate ethnicity, though she'd tucked away a few more observations. His skin had a warm, olive tone, his hair falling casually in dark curls that he swept away from his deep, drowsy green eyes with apparent disregard for the outcome. When he caught Nina's eye it was like a temporary snare, a hook around her throat. Like he was looking at her from across an expanse of crisp white sheets.

He'd gone on to discuss the nature of ethics, of vice, of a life built on what Tessa called living deliciously. But was it strictly sinful to eat well among other women? It wasn't just the food, but the freedom. To eat among women unencumbered by shame was the actual delicious part, although the cake had admittedly been gluttonous.

For Nina, the decadence was in the company, in the collective, the shedding of the world and its narrow definition of reality for which the outer self was a constant and necessary performance. She had never before asked herself who she was when she removed the mask of backburning self-loathing, the one that called for self-deprecation and humility and constant, ritualistic assurance that it was not unpleasant or ugly, unfeminine or otherwise barbaric in its celebration of itself. Now, though, Nina understood that what lay beneath the theater of performative womanhood was a salivating desire for this—acceptance.

Rest.

She thought then that she understood what everyone had been waiting for, why the room had been so thick with tension. Everyone was hungry, simple as pie! But as the senior returned to her seat, distractedly avoiding Nina's eye, Nina realized the tension hadn't eased; the hunt, satiated, should have stretched out lazily in the sun, no longer so archly coiled.

But if anything, the frequency had intensified.

"So, anything interesting to report?" prompted Tessa, who was now licking ganache from her fingers with a ferocity that seemed unfulfilled; as if there was something else, something meatier she still needed, some cracked-open marrow she still craved.

Nina wanted to kiss the streak of chocolate on Tessa's chin; to snatch up her hand in gratitude for the freedom to be unladylike, to simply and wholly consume. It lit a match inside her, an epiphany of inspiration, or maybe just permission to ask for more.

"I kind of want to fuck my philosophy professor," she admitted, and Tessa laughed.

"To the fall semester," she cheered, toasting Nina with a glass of ice water so refreshing it felt like mountain spring water, a crystalline slither down her throat.

Nina clinked her glass jubilantly against Tessa's and looked up to find Fawn's distant eyes on hers, Fawn's glass lifting in quiet acknowledgment from afar.

13

Sloane, a creature of academia, was built on an operating system of deadlines and deliverables. Thus, living quietly in the back of her mind was the sinister ticking of a clock, the lofty presence of a mortgage. In order to achieve some semblance of long-term safety, she would need to advance from the position of mere short-term instructor, ideally by the end of the year. Which meant she ought to make herself valuable to her department, best accomplished by writing something publishable by the end of the semester, with chances of publication substantively heightened by getting the article submitted, pending revision, with a topic approved by Dean Wilson by midterms. She estimated about six weeks, then, to manage an impossible task. Then, in lieu of crying her eyes out, she simply told herself this would all happen, somehow, because alternatives did not exist.

"How was your weekend?" asked her TA, Arya, whose presence Sloane was gradually adjusting to. She liked him a great deal more than she expected, and interacted with him more often, too, given that he preferred to do his research work and grading at the frequently empty second desk in her office. Arya was older than the average TA, by Sloane's estimation—too old to be paid such paltry amounts to attend to her tedium, but that was academia for you—and the fact that Sloane knew that, or knew much of anything about Arya at all, was due to Arya being so forthcoming with the details of his life that she couldn't help but find herself fondly bemused by him—bewildered that he could share so freely, but also catching herself laughing nearly every time he opened his mouth.

It turned out that Arya had a family friend who was among the chosen few for The House—the sophomore, Nina Kaur. Sloane had mentioned her new faculty advisory position offhandedly to him after the contract had been left in her inbox, which Arya had seen. He'd chuckled and said he hadn't thought her the sorority type—and while Sloane privately agreed, warily she felt it was some subtle form of misogyny, as if he'd caught her reading a bodice ripper. But when she'd pushed back, Arya had explained that his cousin—not technically a cousin, just a thing they called each other despite Nina's twin, Jasleen, having given him a wolfish look since the tender age of twelve—was also among Sloane's charges, and that Sloane would surely make valuable contributions to the cult of femininity, which Arya presumed to involve blood oaths, ritual sacrifice, and probably Ozempic.

Arya's entire existence in her life was an invitation to be more forthcoming, but Sloane couldn't quite muster up the same energy. "Oh, it was fine," she answered vaguely with regard to the events of her weekend, and Arya, undeterred, proceeded to tell Sloane about a show he'd played with his band, showing her the latest damage to his phone screen as proudly as if he'd grown the placenta for it himself.

Sloane's weekend had actually been, as all weekends now seemed to be, both better and worse than usual. Aside from her pulsing interior deadlines (each passing day another gash of red in the ledger) and having to wrestle the dog to the vet for long-overdue vaccines (Sloane was instructed to brush Frankie's teeth more often, to which Sloane nodded enthusiastically as if she would definitely do this despite the fact that Isla was tugging at her blouse and then inevitably her hair and it was all so plainly a lie), Sloane had spent all of Saturday with Isla, which despite its ups and downs (Isla was, after all, becoming much more insistent on mysterious things, and often took over forty minutes to fall asleep for naps) retained a rosy glow of intimacy and pleasure for Sloane, who liked motherhood a great deal more than she had expected to. That felt a silly thing to say, given how miserable it often made her, but she had a newfound complexity, an ability to hold two things in her heart at one time. It was an indisputable fact that nobody made Sloane's life more magical than Isla—and nobody made her more miserable than Isla, either. Though occasionally it felt like Max was vying competitively for the spot.

In their previous life, when Max had been a rising department star and Sloane had been comfortably admired at her smaller college a short train ride away, Max had taken long bike rides through the woods on Saturday mornings, such that Sloane became accustomed to attending brunches alone, or accommodating these bike rides into wedding attendance or weekend travel as a means of support and also resignation, understanding that Max's outdoor proclivities made him who he was despite the fact that Saturday morning was a prime spot in Sloane's social calendar. (This kind of flexibility made Sloane an ideal partner; a very chill person, a deeply cool girl.) And it wasn't a terrible cost, not really. She loved a lazy morning with a book—even on weekdays, she liked to slowly adjust to waking by reading for thirty minutes in bed—but she also loved a trip to the farmer's market, a long walk, the purchase of fresh flowers to then arrange in her favorite vase that everyone oohed and ahhed over, guessing it was vintage. Saturday morning had once been a *lifestyle,* one to which Sloane had committed and coveted despite lacking any sort of discretionary slush fund at the time. To Sloane's thinking, just because her salary was barely enough to pay the rent didn't mean she couldn't revel in the riches of being young and healthy, and able to support the habit of placing petite wildflower bouquets in the Anthropologie vase she'd bought on sale.

Now, of course, things were different. Gone were Sloane's

leisurely mornings of reading. Gone, too, was the obsessive checking of her accounts, now that Max's salary as a tenure track professor paid the bills even without her paltry adjunct contribution. She could afford the off-season flowers, buy the organic berries, look at things that were new and therefore full price. And in an unexpected bonus, Max had given up his long Saturday rides.

When Isla was about four months old—back when Sloane still carried her everywhere in the baby wrap, strapped to Sloane's chest at all times with Sloane never, ever sitting because it was the only way Isla would sleep, despite the aforementioned crimes against Sloane's perineum that had taken the entirety of Isla's life up to that point to solve—Max's morning ride had been canceled, and he'd joined Sloane and baby Isla for what would have been a typical Saturday morning. It was beautifully temperate, not too hot, and the farmer's market was idyllic with fresh produce and tiny jars of cream and jam and overall not too crowded for Max, who liked attention but hated crowds. Isla had slept the whole time cozied up in Sloane's bosom, and Max and Sloane had held hands—as they had not found the time or luxury to do since Isla's birth—and they'd bought fresh pastries and split them as they walked, laughing about the days when they'd had no furniture, using stacks of textbooks as substitute nightstands instead. They revisited their high-minded, intellectual poverty years, this time as an aesthetic for early love, for the days when they could not keep their hands off each other, back when Sloane had gone to sleep naked every night because Max liked it and the ecosystem of her vagina was of no relevant concern and her breasts could be responsibly tasked with holding themselves up without assistance.

That one perfect Saturday had been enough to lure Max to Sloane's way of thinking, and at first it had felt like a wonderful new window of family life, until they had moved closer to the University for Max, and the local farmer's market there was too crowded in the fall and it was too cold to walk in the winter and by spring they'd forgotten that was a thing they used to do, and anyway Isla could no longer be put in the baby wrap, due not to size (she was a wee little thing) but incurable wiggling. These days, Max was still home on Saturday mornings, but now he used them to watch Formula One races or catch up on his periodicals or otherwise dominate the social spaces in the house—such that he was technically present, but not entirely *with* them.

Not in a way that Sloane could complain about, of course. Every Saturday, Max asked her if they had any plans. It was such an odd question, that. "Do we have any plans today?" he would say, despite a shared family calendar and a complete awareness that they did not have plans, and then at some point he would surprise her by saying *he* had plans. Usually it would go like this:

"Do we have any plans?"

"No, no plans."

"Okay, I thought so."

Then thirty minutes would pass, by which time Sloane would hold the question *do we have any plans* in her head like a test she'd failed. Why hadn't she made plans? Their daughter would only be this young once. It was still a lovely time of year. They hardly spent any time together now, both of them exhausted by the time Isla was down for the night. They should do something as a family, take the dog for some fresh air, get out of the house, stretch their legs!

"Max, what do you think about checking out [insert family activity here]?" The last time she'd done this, she had suggested a train ride nearby, one that went slowly in a circle. *Trains?* Max had asked quizzically, as if it was the dumbest idea anyone had ever had. *You want to ride a train? That goes in a circle?*

"Oh, sure, we could do that," Max would say in a voice that rang with a shoe yet to drop. "I'd planned [some personal activity that had gone unmentioned], but sure, if you want to." The last time this happened—the train occasion—Max had created secret plans to meet up with a colleague, and Sloane realized—she should have realized this sooner—that while she mentally earmarked the times when they all took up the same space with no particular programming as family time, Max instead saw them as free spaces on the board, where he could use them individually, as a person who existed outside of their unit.

"Oh, you can do that, it was just an idea," Sloane would say, and Max would protest that no, if she really wanted to they could do it, and she would say it's not like I *really want to* it was just an idea, and he'd say well I can cancel, and then later he would say did you still want to do that thing (the train ride)? And he'd say it in such a dubious voice that she'd suddenly feel she was fighting for her life over something she couldn't possibly defend. Why *did* she want to ride a train in a circle? Just because it would delight Isla, which it probably would? But there was all the faff to get there, and Isla needed a nap, and by the time Isla woke up it would already be late in the afternoon, and maybe next time she would just put this in their calendar so that when Max asked do we have any plans she could say yes, we have a plan to ride the train.

And Max would say, "A train?"

The point was that Max had ostensibly fallen out of love with Saturday mornings, but Sloane hadn't, and Saturday with Isla was a many-splendored thing. That particular Saturday morning, Sloane had given Max the go-ahead to do whatever it was he needed to do for his sanity—hers, as she told herself, was undisturbed—minus the throb of lost time, yet more sand in the hourglass of achievement—and anyway, she'd had the meet-up with Alex the previous evening and so didn't need any particular adult time, not counting hers and Max's Scheduled Evening of Marital Relations (a thing she had mentally earmarked, much like Family Time, when her sexual libido had first begun to noticeably lag, such that she never really felt like having sex—once it was started it was fine, she enjoyed it, but the desire to strip naked and exist in her body wasn't going to happen organically, so it was much easier logistically to prepare herself rather than let it go so long that Max looked at her, puppylike, while she had to fight the urge to make excuses). The days of their marriage revolving around frequent, spontaneous episodes of attraction (how handsy she got whenever she drank white wine, or the times they'd livened up their sex life with toys and silly games) were gone, and to Sloane's knowledge, both were accepting of the fact that the lull was temporary. Eventually desire would return, Isla would be less dependent on her, and Sloane would no longer be desperate to be left alone for five fucking seconds—unlike the current state of being, where a toddler was constantly tugging her clothes down for something, a less (more?) demoralizing version of a randy husband.

God, what Sloane wouldn't give sometimes for five minutes alone, except that she was also so desperate for Isla to stay precisely as she was that she sometimes stopped breathing from the pain. Sometimes, when Isla was sleeping in Sloane's arms, Sloane would have to physically fight the urge to nuzzle her, to kiss her pink cheeks, her rosebud mouth. It was a strange thing, motherhood. Sloane didn't want to freeze Isla in time, nor did she want to go backward, nor did she want to fast-forward. What she *wanted*, desperately, was to witness Isla in every form that Isla would ever take, all at once. She wanted to know Isla's future interests; she wanted to revisit the first gummy smiles Isla ever gave. Everyone else had warned Sloane that she'd eventually want children again, it was just biology, but Sloane had no interest in other children. Whenever she saw a fresh baby—*fresh*, her mind always said, like a vampire for milky breath—she never wanted another. She wanted five minutes of her *own* baby, a quick, crackpipe hit of the past.

Sloane understood that she would always feel that way; that

parenting was relentless and unsolvable. Impossible that she could ever truly do right by Isla. But by god, she was desperate to try.

So, that weekend, despite her theoretical deadline for survival, she'd taken Isla to the park, played on the playground, let Isla spend forty uninterrupted minutes on the swing. Isla had nuzzled her face, pretended to eat her nose, and as a rare treat, she'd fallen asleep quickly in Sloane's arms, and though Sloane almost always felt crossly desperate for Isla to drift off so Sloane could return to her ebook or sit down with some emails or god forbid, scroll The Country Wife and let her brain restart for a few minutes, this time she had sat quietly with the ache of love she felt for Isla, the one that made her wonder how Max could get through his day choosing anything that wasn't this.

But now, of course, they were well into the weekday drudgery where Sloane spent the first twenty minutes of every day hating herself for not being with her child. The irony being that she would rather die than be a stay-at-home mom (no offense). She'd always felt there was a two-part equation to happiness, a reason why romantic love wasn't enough for a happily ever after, because you had to feel another passion, too. You had to be productive in a way that was innate, ambitious to even the slightest degree, where if it wasn't professional success you were after, then it was some other self-driven desire for something, the ambiguous Thing for which to Live. The way some people tended gardens, and other people worked sixty hours a week so they could take a month off to travel every year. For Sloane, it was an intellectual desire, a need to play with some thought or ponderance, and she had chosen sociology for the way it felt like the most productive output she could personally contribute. Because if she could understand something fundamental about the way human beings innately deserved to live, then maybe it was possible to contribute some working understanding of how to ensure it. If making sense of the world meant unpacking forgotten labor movements or unearthing the origins of fascism or convincing hot girls to take public transportation, so be it. Sloane understood in some esoteric way how things were supposed to work.

Sloane's personal fixation had always been an eager blend of things. Unfortunately—the reason her deadline loomed, days and days peeled uselessly back without any particular promise of resolution—she had a tendency toward pulpy topics, like cults and psychology. Her first book had been about unruly women in history, which is why it had been well received by her predominantly female-identifying, overwhelmingly progressive liberal arts community.

Here, though, that sort of work was considered redundant, unnecessary, her expertise more history-minded than sociology, or so Burns had made clear when he'd questioned why she hadn't had more to contribute at a mandatory department seminar (Sloane had been watching the clock, calculating whether she could beat last call at Isla's daycare if she took the distance at a light jog).

"If you're still interested in achieving tenure here, we're really looking for you to focus on something a bit more . . . meaty," the dean had said, by which Sloane was almost 99 percent positive he meant men.

Sloane had mentioned that conversation, and the kamikaze mission that was giving herself six weeks to conjure a fully developed research topic from thin air, to Alex, who rolled her eyes about as hard as it was possible to do without facing medical injury. "I'm sure Skit would tell you to just write whatever makes the department happy," Alex said. "She'd say that once you could prove success by academic publishing's standards, eventually you could do whatever you wanted."

"I take it you disagree?" Sloane said with a lilting tone of amusement.

"Skit's industry is a dinosaur, so Skit thinks like a dinosaur. It's a coping mechanism. But you're an academic! It's your job to be innovative, to inspire. I mean, let's be honest, a barista provides a service more universally valued than yours or mine, but we get paid more to do our jobs." Alex had pointedly sipped her latte. "So shouldn't we be braver about how we do it?"

"What does being brave even mean, in my case?" Sloane sighed, because once you accepted that your work was mostly frivolous, there was no real way around it. "Correctly identifying that the world is a lot bigger than some guy who plays golf?"

"Don't get me started on golf," said Alex, commencing an obviously well-trodden rant. "I don't always agree with Malcolm Gladwell, but I'd love to be rid of golf. Every week my old partners did business on the green. I was lucky—I've got a fantastic drive thanks to my antisemitic stepdad—but what am I supposed to tell every bright-eyed girl in The House? That in addition to a 4.0 and a great ass, they needed a pitching wedge and a healthy tolerance for scotch? Fuck *off*," Alex finished conclusively, which was meant, obviously, as more of a playful comment, but which struck a chord in Sloane, who like all women had dealt with her own versions of Alex's hoops. "It's hard enough trying to protect these girls while they're still girls," Alex said with a tinge of sadness. "It's much harder to reconcile my concerns for their womanhood. What models do they even have, you know?"

"It's true," Sloane agreed. "They're told their paths are infinite, but really, they all boil down to these reductive little cults."

Cults again, she realized, as Alex picked up the thread like an improv player. *Yes, and.* "Yes, I totally know what you mean—the feminine archetypes. Madonna and whore."

"Do you think the distinction cleaves around whether you have kids or not?" Sloane wondered thoughtfully, playing again in her mental sandbox with the mommy blogs, the trad wives.

"Nah, only in fiction. In reality, there's still Madonna mother and whore mother." Alex sipped her coffee, drumming her fingers on the table, the inner workings of her thoughts in tune with Sloane's. "Even inside the Madonna cult, there's still a whore placement. Sex positivity—whore, obviously. That's uncomplicated, but there's other versions. Like: career advancement—whore. If they're ambitious, it's already too late. They're already on the whore pipeline."

"Are we whores?" asked Sloane, whimsically.

"Fuck yes, Sloane." Alex grinned.

"You know, when I did my unruly women book, most of the women I featured weren't mothers because I wasn't." Sloane felt contemplative. "I was afraid, when I had Isla, that I wouldn't have anything nuanced to say anymore. All the greatest female writers were childless by choice. It felt like choosing to be a mother meant giving up my own development—plus, pregnancy made me so stupid I can never remember the name of the thing in the fridge," Sloane sighed, "much less generate anything of profound sociological value."

"Okay, but value according to who?" Alex said, leaning forward in her seat. "According to some guy named Scott Burns?"

"God, well, that's a lost cause. I think he mostly sees me as distracted." And she was distracted—the worst part of his opinion of her was that it was true. Yes, she'd snuggled her daughter instead of thinking of the department. She would always snuggle her daughter, she'd drop everything to come to her daughter's aid, she'd clear her Saturday and choose Isla every goddamn time over the amorphous prestige of the University, and certainly over some optional department lecture. It was a truth that went beyond the rearrangement of Sloane's priorities to the reshifting of her entire self.

Sloane hadn't fully realized that she'd begun thinking about something since then, but she felt the motion of something forming. Something in her chest felt alive. Initially she'd thought it was the usual institutional rage, the one about Old White Men demanding that she cater to their tastes *or else,* but eventually she clocked that her mind was doing something it hadn't done since before Isla was born.

It was . . . churning.

14

"I hate those shirts. You know the ones. Fierce female. You go girl. Girls rule the world! God, it's so frustrating. It's . . . it's *infantilizing*, you know? Like, in what way do girls rule the world? Be specific. Because we can't even get our abusers to serve prison time. You know? So, like, what are you talking about, exactly? It's this absolutely bizarre collective delusion where we buy shirts and maybe one white female CEO gets rich but more likely it's a man. And we can't have equal representation in politics, we're too emotional for that. We get too excited about T-shirts. We get one good pop star but if she gets too rich then she was overhyped the whole time. Like, it's exhausting! Take off the shirt! Grow up!"

"I thought you were a feminist?" said Nina, for fun. There was nothing else to do with Jas except let her tire herself out. Sometimes it was more expedient to get her angrier faster, sometimes not. Either way, Nina was curling her hair, so she had nowhere else to be.

"I *am* a feminist, Nina, that's why the anger is *righteous*." Jas slammed a fist down on her desk, rattling the screen of her phone. "And you're over there participating in the rituals like a fucking sheep. You're not even listening to me."

"Mm-hmm," said Nina, partitioning another section of hair. "That sucks."

"I feel like I need to get off social media for a bit," said Jas.

"Yes," Nina agreed.

"It's stressing me out."

"Yes."

"Well, *the world* is stressing me out. I feel like we're not meant to know this much, you know? About sex trafficking and why things that seem good or at least different are actually problematic, and, like, sometimes I think about the fact that I'm safe and fed and healthy and somewhere out there a woman is probably being abused or attacked and the only solution anyone has to any of it is to donate the money I don't have to an organization where the CEO is almost *definitely* overpaid—or to, I don't know, vote. Like—!" Jas threw her hands inconclusively in the air. "Incremental change this, incremental change that! I get that any Democratic candidate is better than a Republican but, like, *how* much better, you know? How long do we have to settle for 'equally warmongering but not actively a bigot'? Why are those the only choices? It's exhausting. I'm exhausted." Jas slumped over at her desk, staring off into the middle distance while Nina wrapped a section of hair around the curling iron. "I really think the infinite scroll is ruining humanity."

"Maybe you should talk to someone," Nina said.

"I've been going to the counseling center," Jas confirmed with a sigh. "I sense I should probably take advantage of University medical services before I wind up working for a nonprofit that doesn't offer health insurance."

"You could . . . consider a different career path?" Nina posed as a revolutionary perspective.

"Well, you're fundamentally a sellout, so I can see I'm barking up the wrong tree." Even from the tiny phone screen, Jas looked morose.

"There's no need to take it out on me," said Nina. "That's not very feminist of you."

"Feminism is about allocating resources, Nina. You have the exact same resources as me. Maybe even more resources, since your nose is better."

"So you agree that beauty is a resource?" That was an interesting idea to Nina, more so than whether Jas approved of The House's homecoming T-shirts. (She didn't.)

"Why are you saying that in a meme voice?" said Jas.

"Well, you say you can't understand why I'd join a sorority, but being in the sorority is exactly what gives me more of the social capital you seem to think all women lack. Right?"

"No," countered Jas stubbornly. "So what if a bunch of girls think you're hot enough to party with them? That's not power."

"Isn't it? I get access," Nina pointed out. "To the exclusive networking events where I meet future executives—the exact future CEOs who will profit off *your* exploitation as a soon-to-be underpaid woman of color." She meant the exchange party she was getting ready for, which was a social event with a fraternity, where the entire fraternity collectively invited a whole sorority out on a date and they rented out an expensive venue and drank on the boys' tabs. Deeply gendered, with certain expectations implied. Without question, some of the girls would hook up with some of the boys, and that was basically the desired outcome. The exchange of money for sex.

Nina obviously didn't say that to herself in the same voice Jas did; being aware of something didn't mean it was a problem. It just was what it was. Beauty was a resource. So was desire. So was the supply of premium booze.

"What are you planning to wear?" said Jas desperately, with a hint of depression. As if she hated herself for being curious but couldn't help but ask, which was essentially proving Nina's point—that fuckability, too, was a resource, and therefore an allocated power.

The answer was a glittery silver bra, a pair of wide-legged jeans, and cheap platform heels that Nina was borrowing from another girl in The House, who'd donated them to a free-for-all supply of previously worn costumes. The exchange was seventies themed. Prior to the event, Nina had gone thrifting with a few other members of her pledge class, many of whom she was beginning to genuinely look forward to seeing. She understood in some hazy, objective way that while the twelve of them—"Oh, so like Jesus," had been Jas's snorted comment about that—had technically been won over by the established members of The House, what they had agreed to in practice was actually friendship with each other. As a pledge class, they did everything together—they saw each other multiple times a week, and it was understood that as a result, the experience of preparing for initiation and going through everything together first was a sort of binding ritual. It was why Tessa and Fawn would always choose each other over Nina, which Nina was not taking personally—*would* not take personally. Because that would be irrational.

So instead she focused on Dalil, her pledge sister whom she'd liked right from the beginning, and who was honestly very dry and funny in addition to being the same size as Nina, albeit with slightly shorter legs. "Why do you think we're not allowed to get ready at the house?" Dalil asked Nina when they met up to walk to the row, Dalil's hair in wild, suggestive bedroom waves with glitter so thick on her eyelids it seemed an effort just to blink. Nina had gone for more of a feathered thing, hair-wise, and a smoky eye that looked potentially too daytime. She was trying not to think about it.

"Probably the same reason we can't go into the chapter room," Nina said. A few places in The House were off-limits, belonging only to the initiated members. It felt fair to Nina to create a sense of exclusivity. (That, too, was a resource.)

"I like how everything toes the line of maybe normal, maybe sex cult," Dalil joked. Nina laughed.

"What, you think they have naked pillow fights before every event? Very male-gaze of you." Oops, she'd spent too long talking to Jas.

"I was thinking more like female pleasure-centric orgy. Much more sex positive," Dalil said, so maybe she was excessively online, too. Nina laughed again, the brief image of Tessa and Fawn applying each other's eyeliner to a bow-chicka-wow-wow porn soundtrack filling her mind until she realized that she and Dalil were catching stray glances from passersby, given that it wasn't yet dark out and they were both dressed like some pubescent teen's idea of a hooker.

"Does it ever feel weird to you?" said Dalil, who had probably clocked the same thing. "The dinner recitation, the whole concept of 'pledging,' the secret room in the house reserved for creepy rituals . . ."

"They might be sexy rituals," Nina reminded her. Dalil laughed. The whole thing felt airy, light, comfortable. Nina did not plan to ask if Dalil, too, felt a slightly sinister energy from time to time, a quiet insinuation of violence. The constant presence of an indeterminate hunt that lived in The House's walls like a host of silent ghosts.

It didn't seem productive, first of all. Secondly it made her sound like a dork.

With Dalil, Nina was reminded of the high of making a female friend, which wasn't unlike having a crush on a hot professor. She wanted to get an A in this conversation. She wanted to be pretty and mysterious to Dalil forever, despite falling harder for her platonically the more she psychologically undressed, revealing the comfort of her true self in layers. Nina was almost disappointed there would be boys at the exchange—it added a layer of performance that she was tiring of. Sex, a thing she liked and had sought to generally mediocre outcomes, now paled beside the pleasures of Monday night dinner with her friends.

"I guess it just feels a little silly sometimes—I don't know. Sometimes my mom asks me what the fuck I'm doing and my answer is, like, I'm playing dress-up, Ma! Leave me alone," joked Dalil.

"My sister doesn't get it either," Nina admitted. "But I don't know, what is there to get? It's fun. The little rituals are silly and weird but I don't mind. I like being part of it."

Dalil looked thoughtful. "Me too," she said eventually, in a slightly different tone of voice.

In the end, the party was about what Nina had expected. Tessa made out with a particularly hot guy, the two of them becoming aggressively acrobatic in one of the leather booths of a dark, cavernous event space. Alina Antwerp's boyfriend was in the frat, which perhaps explained The House's acceptance of the invitation despite receiving similar entreaties from all the other fraternities on the row.

"He looks like a knock-off Kennedy, doesn't he?" came a whisper in Nina's ear. Well, a shout, given the volume of the thudding bass, but it felt like a whisper. It felt like a fingernail had drawn a slender line along Nina's spine. "Alina's boyfriend. His name is fucking *Tripp*."

It was Fawn. Nina turned to take in the Twiggy-style eye makeup, the hair that had been fashioned into a faux bob. Fawn wore knee-high pink boots made of a crocodile material, visible beneath a slinky red dress with a thigh-high slit and a V-neckline that dipped to just above her navel. It was impossible that she could be wearing underwear. She looked both sexy and untouchable, which Nina suddenly realized was the height of feminine power—the inspiration of desire paired with a bar for worthiness that you could never, ever reach.

Nina giggled, looking again at Alina's boyfriend, who visibly rowed crew. "It's worse than a knock-off Kennedy, I fear," said Nina. "More like the guy you cast in the sequel to a Hallmark Christmas movie about the prince of knock-off Switzerland."

Fawn threw her head back with a laugh—an utter *gorge* of one. Heady, that was the word. Nina's vision nearly swam with pleasure at the sound, at the understanding of what it meant. A laugh that was better than sex because it was harder won. With Fawn's head thrown back like that, you could almost imagine her in bed.

Oops. Nina was drunk.

"That is *so* specific," Fawn said in Nina's ear. "God. Who wants to fuck that guy?"

"What's your type?" asked Nina, lifting her glass to her lips. The venue didn't serve anyone underage, but she and Jas had gotten fake IDs for each other for Christmas in a rare episode of honest-to-god twinning.

"Mm, I like a man's man," said Fawn. "A really *thick* thigh, you know what I mean? Like a cartoon Christmas ham." Fawn giggled. She sounded a little drunk, too. "I like to feel tiny by comparison."

"You *are* tiny," Nina said. Her own voice came out breathy.

"Yeah, well, teeny-tiny. Pocket-sized. I like to be with a guy that makes me spontaneously think the word *girthy*."

Nina erupted in a fit of bubbly laughter. "You mean like Superman?"

Fawn leaned closer, giving Nina a quizzical look as she sucked her cocktail straw, suggesting she hadn't heard. Nina took a step toward her, half-shouting in Fawn's ear, "So your type is Superman?"

"In guys, yeah." To that, Nina's heart bang-banged ham-handedly in her chest. "In girls I like the opposite. I'm a narcissist. I like someone really femme, painfully petite, practically no boobs at all." Fawn giggled again, the straw caught between her teeth. "Well, okay, sometimes I love boobs. The point is it's really more Narcissus than Sappho in terms of vibes. I like an hourglass, you know—hips and a small waist. Something to grab onto."

It was too dark to tell if Fawn's eyes had drifted down to Nina's goose-fleshed midriff.

"So yeah, I guess in conclusion, Superman and Lois, too," remarked Fawn, idly, her fingers still clutching the straw. Before

Nina could begin to process a response, she was jostled into Fawn by someone from behind.

"Oh Nina, I'm so sorry—Taylor, you fucking idiot!" blasted Summer Toft at some laughing frat bro before she rolled her eyes and turned back to Nina. "I'm so sorry. He's a child. Are you having fun?" She seemed to register Fawn's presence belatedly, her expression transforming. Still friendly, just . . . less inviting. "Fawn," Summer acknowledged, her smile approximately five degrees cooler than it had been.

"Summer," Fawn replied, her eyes already drifting away. Then she waved at someone, some meaty dude who came over and plucked Fawn up in both arms, twirling her until she shrieked. Both staggered slightly, then they touched each other's faces.

Mating ritual, Nina thought.

"God," remarked Summer near Nina's ear, a little huff of indignation. Unclear who was the recipient. "So," Summer said, turning to Nina, "how is everything? Semester going well? Everyone being nice?"

Before Nina could answer (*good, yes, of course!*) the initial frat bro, the jostler, was back, one arm suddenly slung around Summer's bare waist from behind. "Taylor, for *fuck's sake*," said Summer, throwing him off and shaking her head before knocking her elbow affectionately against Nina's. "I better go, sorry, Nina. I think Geoff's on risk tonight—he's gonna need to call a cab stat." Summer was already mentally several feet away from where she stood. "Listen, have fun, okay?"

"You too," said Nina. She blew Summer a kiss, something she'd never done in her life, which Summer readily returned. Then Nina turned back to the bar for another drink, exhaling with a brief sense of melancholy. Probably from one drink too many, though history suggested she'd still likely have a few more after that.

"Hey," said a guy who stood near her at the bar.

"No thanks," said Nina.

"Ooh, feisty," said the guy.

"Hard pass," said Nina.

"Hey," said Dalil, stumbling a little as she blazed a path to Nina. She grabbed onto Nina's shoulders, trying to steady herself. "Important sisterly question. Is this guy I'm with a pledge?"

Nina glanced over Dalil's shoulder, surveying the guy in question. He was average height, sandy hair, seemed golden retriever-y and young. "I think so."

"Is he at least hot?" said Dalil, frowning.

"I mean, he's fine," said Nina. Who did think a lot of the guys present were hot. They just weren't her kind of hot. They all seemed like they'd been captain of their high school water polo team. They were mostly boyish hot. She liked her boys to be men. Professorial. With an air of experience. With eyes that could undress you while they whispered sweet nothings about philosophy to your clit. Or, you know, something else.

Dalil looked over her shoulder, then back at Nina, having seemingly drawn a conclusion. "I have to pee!" Dalil announced to the boy before taking off, dragging Nina behind her by the wrist.

When they got to the single-stall restroom, they collapsed inside in a fit of giggles. Dalil tumbled so hard into Nina's arms that Nina could almost taste the sweat on her skin. Nina licked her shoulder, just for fun, and Dalil let out a squeal of delighted protest.

"No, really, I have to pee," said Dalil, shimmying out of her jumpsuit and squatting expertly over the toilet. Dalil grinned, her stick-on gel bra pads defying gravity while the uneven stream hit porcelain. Nina held her hand to her stomach and laughed and laughed.

15

Weeks to deadline: four and some change. Progress made: substantively none.

Then, on the Wednesday of Isla's first daycare plague, which Sloane had been meaninglessly assured by Miss Lily was "a light one" despite her having to flee the lecture hall, Sloane managed—with some logistical sorcery and much groveling—to secure one of Max's colleague's wives to watch Isla nap on the monitor while Sloane formally introduced herself to the alumnae club at The House.

The Women, as she thought of them, who were once The Girls. At which point the hollow urgency of her deadline abruptly shifted, becoming something else.

Alex introduced Sloane last, as the final item on the agenda, which left Sloane an excessive amount of time (certainly too much time for a woman with a sick baby at home, said the Good Mother mommy blogger who lived in Sloane's brain) to observe The Women. She could see how they had once been the archetypes on campus—there was a uniform quality, as if the correct amount of polish had been apportioned evenly but executed in different ways. Most were white, but even the ones who weren't had a similar look of having recently had their highlights refreshed or gotten a chemical peel. All seemed youthful in the same way, where Sloane didn't know whether to identify something as cosmetic or genetic, but it seemed unlikely that this many women could go so long without crow's feet or gray hair. (She herself had woken up one day to discover she was visibly getting older. She was also no longer carded at restaurants or at the grocery store, which could be due to the fact that she was usually holding a baby, or maybe everyone could already tell the light had gone out in her eyes.)

"This is Dr. Sloane Hartley," Alex said, startling Sloane back to cognizance. "She's a sociology professor at the University, soon to be tenured. We're hoping she'll be with us for a good long time." She smiled warmly at Sloane, who couldn't tell where the tenure thing had come from. Optimism? Solidarity? Not wanting to admit they couldn't do better than an adjunct lecturer who hadn't had her eyebrows done in two years? Sloane had one of those plastic facial razors and was pretty sure it wasn't cutting it, but she didn't have time for vanity anymore. Only shame. "Sloane, would you like to say anything? Share a little about yourself?"

"Oh, um." Sloane rose to her feet, waving awkwardly to The Women, who uniformly smiled back. "Hi, I'm Sloane. I previously taught at a small college up north. I was in a sorority myself, albeit a different one." She paused, wondering what else was relevant, and as usual came up with only one thing. "I have a daughter."

The room seemed to warm in a few pockets of space. "How old?" asked one of The Women, whose eyes shined a little with the prospect of bonding.

"Eighteen months. Almost nineteen," said Sloane, feeling again the crush of guilt that Isla was somewhere else sleeping, or maybe not. Maybe she was awake, and Sloane wasn't there.

"Oh," one of them sighed. "Still squishy."

A few other women laughed, and Sloane managed a wan smile. "Yeah, she's a squish, that's for sure."

"What's her name?" A different Woman.

"Isla," said Sloane.

"Oh, so sweet. That's perfect," said another Woman who seemed to genuinely mean it, that a name could be sweet, and be not only suitable but perfect as well, based purely on its phonetics.

"I wanted an Isla," said another Woman. "But my husband

was hell-bent on naming her after his mother, so as a compromise I had a boy."

Sloane startled herself with a laugh, realizing only when Alex looked expectantly at her that she was still standing. "Right, well, I'm really looking forward to working with you, and doing... whatever a faculty advisor does," she impressively concluded.

"Inspiring them, I hope," said Alex with an eye roll that Sloane didn't entirely understand. "Given what some of The Girls seem to be into these days, they desperately need a fresh dose of professional aspiration in their midst."

Sloane wanted to ask what that meant, but she could see that the other Women were looking eager to end the meeting, so she decided to leave it to later, when everyone was filtering out.

"What did you mean about inspiring them?" Sloane asked curiously, and the same look crossed Alex's face, the one that was a mix of dejection and irritation.

"It's just... sometimes The Girls and I don't see eye to eye," she said. "I think I feel very different to them, generationally. They have very different idols."

Sloane frowned. "What do you mean?"

"The official House account is following this girl, an alum from a few years back," Alex said with the air of a recent argument. "Caroline Pang was her maiden name... Britt," Alex called, "what's Caroline's name now? Or her username?"

"The Country Wife," said Britt without looking up. Britt had been getting something in her calendar with another alum—even having been around her only a few times, Sloane understood that Britt was always getting something in her calendar.

"The Country Wife? That's a huge account," said Sloane, with no mention of her own obsessive following.

"Right, well, I think I'm willfully forgetting," Alex said with a grimace. "It's just..." She hesitated for a second. "It's important, Sloane, that you understand the way we choose our Girls.

They're . . . ambitious, they're hungry. We encourage that. We *want* them to be politically active, to participate in counterculture, to have divisive beliefs. We want them to think for themselves—to feel that the world is theirs to conquer. What we do *not* want is for them to believe life would be easier if they no longer had choices," said Alex, zipping her bag shut with such force that Sloane decided it would be better not to question it.

"The point is," Alex said, sensing perhaps that she had lost the thread, "we want The Girls to find role models in the women who've come before them. The women like you, who are accomplished and prominent in their fields in addition to being thoughtful, caring mothers. Women who can do it all," Alex concluded.

Women like Us, Sloane heard, glancing again around the room and realizing that this was it, the final evolution. The Girls would eventually become Good Women—meaning, in this instance, women who could Do It All.

The thought stayed with her the rest of the week, lurking politely in the background of dog walks and diaper changes without disruption. Then, the following Friday, after Isla's fever had broken and Sloane's pre-apportioned twenty minutes of self-loathing were up, Sloane clicked on the weekly minutes Britt had sent over from The House's alumnae committee and sat back in her chair, scrutinizing the list of names for something she hadn't yet put words to.

Arbitrarily, she highlighted one (Aimee Rivera-Hughes, which felt suitably unique) and searched her name, pulling up a LinkedIn page and a VidStar account. Sloane glanced at the professional portrait and chose to visit the VidStar profile instead—which had an immediately recognizable visual theme. Soft blues, creamy pastels, low contrast and high brightness. Sloane wasn't a designer of any sort, but she could tell the overall effect had been curated—that visually speaking, there was a story here.

Aimee posted pictures and videos of her young family that

were a mix of posed and candid. Aimee's kids had the same toys as Britt's twins, thoughtfully arranged in a Montessori-style playroom. Aimee wore the same type of cable-knit cardigan that Priscilla had worn to a dinner at Britt's house, the one she called her "work sweater" for when the office air-conditioning—determined by her overlords at the Big Five publishing house to which Priscilla's imprint belonged—got too cold. Aimee's ballet flats, which appeared in several of the photos, were so covetable that Sloane wanted desperately to know what they were—she could tell at a glance that Aimee could chase after her kids in them, that she ran errands in them, that she looked impressively pulled together at all times despite the fact that her outfits were simple, elevated basics in a minimalist capsule wardrobe. Aimee's husband even looked a little bit like Max. Then VidStar timed Sloane out, prompting her to log in to the app, so she pulled out her phone.

"Arya," Sloane called to her TA, who was dutifully at work on his laptop, without looking up from her phone screen. This time she looked up another name, Deirdre Voss. Deirdre, that was the one who'd made Sloane laugh. Her son had the same kids' play couch as Britt's twins. Deirdre had the same shiny hair as Aimee, as Alex. There was that same unique and yet interchangeable, aspirational quality, the sense that Deirdre *just knew* what was cool, what was expensive while still being achievable. She had a Nancy Meyers kitchen, a sun-soaked playroom for her child, a wardrobe that was practical and beautiful at the same time. She had the thing Sloane didn't know how to explain—the one that was so easily shorthanded as Taste. It made Sloane want to ask her what books she read, what music she listened to. Sloane felt confident it would be an eclectic mix, and that Deirdre would have the perfect recipe for some hearty, provincial food that her iron-enriched offspring consistently ate.

"What's up?" replied Arya, turning away from the grades he was inputting on his laptop. (Also pulled up on his laptop screen was a playlist called Grading Vibes, which had previously made

Sloane wonder aloud how many different vibes he had. He'd given her a sly look that sent her attention briefly to his mouth. He was, he informed her, a man of many vibes.)

"What do you think about mommy bloggers?" asked Sloane.

"Love 'em," said Arya instantly. "Why, thinking of starting one?"

"No, I—" Sloane stared hard into the distance, trying to accommodate a sudden onslaught of unarticulated thought. "I feel like there's . . . something to it." She was mentally arranging the many, many accounts she'd scrolled on VidStar as she breastfed Isla in the early days, fighting to stay awake at 3 A.M. "Have you heard of crunchy moms?"

"Crunchy? Like they're edible?"

Sloane flapped a hand, swiping left on his knowingly dumb joke. "There's crunchy, or maybe I'm thinking of scrunchy." She couldn't remember which—it had never mattered to her before. "Whichever one means, like, not a total hippie but not totally anal. Someone who uses gentle parenting techniques but also, I don't know, fosters independence—"

"I know gentle parenting was kind of a hot social movement a few years ago." Right, Sloane recalled—Arya's dissertation on post-9/11 cultural responses to patriotism relied on observing generational trends.

Arya twisted around in his seat to look at her then, a thoughtful expression crossing his face. "My mom thinks it's stupid and making us all soft. And I mean, it's definitely problematic, though not for the reasons my mom thinks, but still. Not surprising that gentle parenting coincides with trad wife stuff, considering that it basically requires the mother to stay home with the children."

"Trad wife." Sloane could practically hear herself delivering it in a presentation: *Women who believe in, and practice—as in religion—traditional sex roles.* "Like this one?" On Sloane's screen, as if she'd been summoned by magic, a young woman no older than twenty-five was once again baking a loaf of bread to pair with her home-cured prosciutto, beside which sat a bloodred apothecary jar of freshly decanted wine.

It was, of course, The Country Wife.

Caroline Collins plaited her long hair, dressed in a linen shift that made her waist unavoidably envious, referred to her husband as Dear Husband, and—now that Sloane knew that her maiden name was Pang and that she'd graduated from this University rather than, say, growing up in a fairy commune—seemed, in context, an entirely different person from the one Sloane had watched so many times before.

"Yeah," said Arya, who'd come around his desk to look at Sloane's screen. "I wish I knew less about this, truthfully," he said with a grimace, "but my cousin Jas talks nonstop about this shit. She thinks it's setting feminism back at least a century and that homeschooling is—" He paused to get the wording right. "Something about 'unsubscribing from community' and also, inevitably, fascism."

Sloane looked up to regard his expression of resigned ambivalence. "What?" said Arya, meeting Sloane's glance with a candor that made her cheeks heat. "She's not wrong. She just also doesn't have an off switch."

"Does your family sit down regularly for these kinds of sociological accords?"

Arya shrugged. "She and my mom rile each other up. It's a love language."

"I bet." Having looked away from him by then, for survival reasons, Sloane's mind was back on its track to something she still hadn't named. "So is it inherently problematic, do you think?" she asked, scrolling through The Country Wife's recent content as if she hadn't already seen it all. Sloane wondered, for the first time, not how long it took to collect vampiric apothecary jars, but to gain the editing skills to create this sort of viral content—to make a living full-time on something you had to pretend wasn't a job. Money, definitely, lots of it, and there was no way this girl had children, but how much longer could she hypothetically Madonna without them before she became a Whore?

"I mean, it's a pendulum swing," Arya pointed out. "Ten years ago, everything was *you go, girlboss*. Then the wellness bubble faltered. Maybe the girlbosses got tired of having to have it all, you know? Maybe they decided to have one thing with the volume turned all the way up."

Sloane thought back to what Alex said about ambition. About hunger. About the loss of aspiration, the desire for tradition that was quietly synonymous with oppression.

Just how dangerous *was* it to drool over the aesthetic of a wife?

Because it was true, even Sloane couldn't honestly resist it. Whether she consumed this content ironically or with intent to hate-watch, she was still a view. She contributed to the virality, and therefore who was she to say it wasn't valid?

Sloane tried to imagine her daughter growing up with social media, wearing these linen *Handmaid's Tale* dresses and buying into this shit, whatever it was. If Sloane explained to Isla that this shit was stupid but then she still engaged with it herself, what would Isla believe? And what was the line between the cult of The Women and, per Arya's inevitability, fascism? Did moderation exist, or did the pendulum always swing, like Arya had said?

Something in Sloane's brain was speed running, drawing up disparate considerations—trad wife? Good Woman™? Madonna and Whore?—and determining a thread, one she couldn't see yet but that she trusted did exist. She thought of beautiful Dalil Serrano in her lecture hall with her precious Greek letters, the brand of The House emblazoned across her perfect tits. Was progress the freedom to have babies, to embrace domesticity, to abscond sexily to the woods? Was it resources; was it capital? Was progress *necessarily* presidential office? Was Sloane an accomplished woman who might achieve tenure (pending the next four weeks) or was she just a woman who half-heartedly shaved her eyebrows and worried about sun exposure? And if she was both, who was the model for *her* womanhood? In what ways was Sloane merely a woman and not A Woman, and how hard would it be to become, like Alex Carlisle, some tangible epitome of womanhood itself?

What was the difference between Alex Carlisle and The Country Wife? Was it, as visuals suggested, a throwaway matter of a handful of years? Was it sociopolitical assignations? Was it how they had each been raised? Was it nature? Was it nurture? Was it society?

Was it The House?

Was The House some kind of laboratory for high-achieving womanhood, and if so, was Caroline Collins a failure or a success?

"I've got something," Sloane said aloud to Arya, who gave her a cheeky, knowing grin.

"Is it good?" he asked, scouring her face. "It looks good."

"I don't know what it is yet. Maybe." Sloane's fingers drummed of their own accord, agitation via inspiration. "Maybe it's something."

From a long-dormant tomb, the vestiges of Sloane's passion were suddenly thunderstruck. Whatever this was, it felt undeniably important. It felt *interesting*. And honestly, it felt—

Fuck, it felt possible! Achievable by semester's end, even, because it wouldn't divide her resources any more than she'd already spliced them up. And that alone was good enough to feel miraculous. Like water to wine, a future from nothing. Sanctified and glorious. #Blessed.

16

On one of the Thursday new member meetings, the weeks to initiation draining faster the closer they got, Nina and her pledge sisters were allowed to drink alcohol in the house. "Allowed" being a loose term, as nobody else could know about it, but in this singular instance, the use of wine as a conversational lubricant was encouraged among the rest of the girls. It was an expensive bottle, too—one of Nina's pledge sisters, Ryoko, who had grown up on a vineyard that her parents owned and operated, said it was a vintage. All Nina knew was that it went down smooth and warm, giving her an uncurling sensation akin to stretching out her legs.

"Look, we get it, shedding trauma is a big deal," said Nicole, one of their pledge class's two new member educators, as she addressed them in the large, formal living room that most of The House's occupants didn't use. (Dalil liked to mock Nicole's title, which was also very formal. The concept that they were participating in an *education,* rather than a set of hoops performed with slight variations by every house along the row, was among the things Dalil deemed "silly," though just because something was objectively ridiculous didn't mean it didn't get done). "Part of what makes The House so special is that here, with your sisters, you're allowed to be vulnerable. Obviously, though, we respect your boundaries," Nicole added, exchanging a glance with Mallory, her counterpart.

"Right. Don't feel like you're being forced. Undress to your comfort level," Mallory emphasized. "The point isn't to *make* you do anything. Just to give you the space to feel like you can share parts of your life that you haven't been able to with anyone before."

"This feels kind of cult-y," Dalil whispered to Nina in a voice warmed by alcohol, and Nicole, who was close enough to hear, gave an easy laugh.

"I mean, everything about this is cult-y, let's be real," Nicole said to a replying chorus of chuckles. "Right, Mal?"

"Monumentally, yes," Mallory agreed. "But don't worry, you won't be asked to commit any ritual murders. Yet." More laughter.

"If all you want to do is drink good wine and shoot the shit, go for it," Nicole said when the laughter subsided. "This is your time. You might also want to consider the lyrics to your pledge class's dirty song. It's pretty atrocious so far."

They had been trying to rewrite an old pop song so that it was filthier. The problem was that the song they had chosen was already about sex, and none of them were very good at lyric writing. ("This is what comes of defunding the arts," bemoaned Maud, the lone English major of the group, who, despite frequent interjected disapproval, still could not think of anything but slant rhymes.)

"In any case, we're going to do something very unusual and shut up now," Mallory announced, and turned to the door, gesturing for Nicole to follow. "You guys have two hours to yourselves. When your time's up, Nic and I'll come get you. And if you all prefer to pass out here, don't worry, you can stay the night."

"You're still pledges, so even though we're bending the rules for tonight, upstairs is still off-limits and so is the kitchen," Nicole warned, as if their eyes had collectively lit up. "If you get the munchies, that's what all these snacks are for."

Indeed, the coffee table was laden with a variety of sweets and savories—exported dark-chocolate almond-butter cups, chocolate-covered cherries, champagne-flavored gummy bears, an array of salty and nutty cheeses paired with tiny sourdough toasts, a rubied spectrum of fine charcuterie, an oozing wedge of honeycomb, tiny quiches laced with onions so caramelized they shone. And, of course, three more bottles of vintage wine, two a pale gold and the last a rich, glittering garnet. Nina felt dazed just beholding the wealth of it.

"Well," said Maud when Nicole and Mallory were gone, the French doors to the living room shutting cleanly behind them. "Should we make a game of it? Never Have I Ever? Truth or Dare?"

"Let's expedite the bonding," said Dalil. "Let's go around in a circle and each say the worst thing we've ever done."

It was in these controversial moments that Nina was fondest of Dalil, who had a technique for mastering every scenario. She settled in beside Dalil on the floor, realizing as she did so that all twelve of them had had the same instincts; that this sort of intimacy was best suited for the ground. Closer to hell, Nina playfully figured, pulling a pillow down from the nearest couch as the other girls gathered a collection of sinfully soft sherpa throw blankets from the various other sofas and hunkered down in a sort of modified slumber party fort.

"Who wants to go first?" called Dalil, pouring more wine into Nina's emptying cup.

"I once cheated on a math test," said Francisca, whom they mostly called Fran.

"Basic," called Maud through an improvised foghorn.

"Terrible," Dalil agreed. "Do better. Next?"

Nina ran through her mental sins. She had masturbated many times and had also frequently gotten drunk, occasionally high. She'd snuck Jonathan Zein into her bedroom once when her parents weren't home. She wasn't always a very good friend and could occasionally be known to leave people on read, basically at constant risk of doing so with everyone who wasn't Jas. She knew Jas had a desperate, pseudo-incestual crush on their not-cousin

Arya, which Nina didn't technically share, but it felt weird just to know about it. She didn't always do all the reading for class and sometimes she scrolled her phone instead of paying attention in lecture. Was any of that really the juiciest thing she could choose to say aloud?

"I want to fuck my philosophy professor," she decided when the circle came around to her.

"Boooooo," said Dalil. "I always want to fuck my teachers."

"It's true," Maud agreed. "It's an ongoing fetish."

"Fine. I think I'm probably bi," said Nina, who had the sense that all her blood had rushed to her cheeks.

"So? I said *worst* thing, not just 'a' thing. Who in this day and age isn't bi?" scoffed Dalil.

"Um, me?" said Maud. "I'm a lesbian."

"Good for you, Maud, no need to show off—"

"I'm pretty sure most of us are straight," said Ryoko tentatively.

"Why? Do better," said Dalil into her glass.

"I guess I kind of want to fuck Fawn," Nina admitted, as if the thought had only recently crossed her mind. She was prepared to regret it instantly, to walk it back, but nobody seemed even remotely fazed to hear it. Maybe because the truth was that wanting to fuck Fawn was too innocently unspecific. What Nina actually wanted to do was sit in The House's big leather armchair with her legs hiked up on either side while Fawn looked up at Nina with those big Twiggy eyes, dragging her bubblegum tongue along Nina's clit and telling her how fucking femme her waist was. (Nina had a similar set of fantasies for Professor Villanueva—but in those, it was a leather office chair.)

"Dude," said Maud, reaching to spread honey and Brie over a cracker. "Fawn loves you. She basically *only* talks to you, have you noticed that?"

"I get the feeling she pissed off half the House somehow," remarked Quinn, whose cheeks and forehead were a wine-flushed crimson. Though, because she had said it with very little conviction, nobody responded or acknowledged that it had been said.

Nina, for example, was far more fixated on what Maud said next, which was, "The point is Fawn probably wants to fuck you, too."

"Yeah, I'd buy that theory," Dalil agreed, which Nina tried not to dwell on or feel smug over, choosing instead another swallow of fancy wine. "I wouldn't be surprised if Tessa does, too."

"I'd fuck you, Nina," Maud offered charitably through a mouthful of crackers.

"Me too," said Fran. "If I had to pick a girl, I mean."

"Oh sure, *had to*—"

Dalil forged ahead, undeterred. "I heard The House *never* takes sophomores, and yet here you are, so—"

"Wait, I've been wondering about that. Why did you wait to rush?" asked soft-spoken Melanie, who was French-Canadian, which was the only thing Nina knew about her. Well, that, and that apparently Melanie had once been caught tripping "absolute balls" at school, as Nina had discovered over the course of the past hour.

The wine warmed its way into Nina's stomach. "Oh, um. I just wasn't sure I wanted to," Nina said. "Immigrant parents, you know."

"I hear that," said Maud, who was half Thai.

Dalil nodded vigorously midsip, spilling her wine down the front of her shirt. "None of you sluts look," she warned as she dabbed at her cleavage, then paused. "I take that back," she corrected on second thought, pushing out her chest. "Please look, I need the validation."

"That doesn't sound like the whole story," said Fran, who was apparently still waiting for Nina's answer. (Ryoko glanced at Dalil's boobs and Nina made a mental note to bring it up to Dalil later.)

"Oh. Well. I mean, honestly, my sister asked me the same thing. I'm glad I didn't rush last year," Nina added, "because I don't think I would be here if I had. I'm kind of a late bloomer." She paused. "And last year was . . . tough."

"Not answering the question," Dalil said loudly, having given up on the spilled wine. There was a bloodstain of liquid on her T-shirt, a rosebud splash left unattended on her skin.

"Well, I mean—" Nina pondered how to put it into words; how to gently brush up against the truth without crashing headlong into it. It wasn't like she was confessing to flirting with her priest, as Fran had done, or to serialized petty theft, per Dalil's extended brush with shoplifting. "I guess I just . . . I mean, this place is such a boy's club," she exhaled, referring to the University. Not wanting to get into the stupid little nothings, obviously. The accountability to which none of her male peers were ever held. The things that had happened to her last year that wouldn't have happened if she'd been smarter, or had more value, or been part of an established, self-protecting group.

"I just . . . I realized how hard it was going to be, just being here," Nina admitted quietly, "and I wanted, I don't know—to be part of something bigger. Something that already had a reputation that was scarier than mine. I wanted the right kind of attention—I wanted to be noticed, I wanted to be valued. And I wanted it to happen on my terms."

Nina felt her cheeks flame, realizing this was now, officially, the worst thing she had ever confessed. The nakedest secret she had in her arsenal, which not even Jas could understand, because to Jas this was victimhood or worse, it was clout-chasing, it was peddling desperately for some fundamental falsehood. Greek letters around her neck to help her mythologize the better future that she singularly deserved.

"I wanted to be beautiful," Nina croaked, unable to stop herself, the truth wrenching out of her like an uncontrollable sick.

"No, I wanted to be untouchable. I wanted to be *hot*. I wanted to be *smart*. I wanted to be *tough*." Now the truth was a marching rhythm, a slapping pulse. "I wanted to count for more, I wanted to be *unbreakable,* and I just wanted more—"

"Power," Dalil cut in, breathless. Her voice was almost a whisper.

Nina felt it again, the teeth-chatter of want. The House hummed in her veins, the exact frequency of longing. A hunt for something. Maybe blood.

"Yeah," said Nina. It left her like a sigh. "Yes. That's exactly it."

PART III

INITIATION

How it feels to sip fresh coffee in your beautiful home, planting nourishing food in your very own garden while your man works hard to provide for you and grow his business . . .

**—Transcript from a VidStar by
@TheCountryWife**

TWO

WEEKS

TO

INITIATION.

17

Weeks to deadline: two. Progress: don't ask.

Despite the high of inspiration—or, rather, because of it—Sloane had had a bad day. The follow-up tests her pediatrician requested *in re* Isla's low iron had gone about as poorly as expected. Isla remained, how else to put this, sickeningly malnourished. This was Sloane's fault. Also, per the pediatrician's disappointed scolding, Sloane was reminded that Isla had not yet gone for her first dental appointment. This was also Sloane's fault, because it was very obvious now to everyone involved that she simply didn't care about her precious daughter's teeth. What exactly did she think motherhood was, just hugging your child when they were scared? Just loving them so fiercely you had chronic chest pains and a perennial state of survivable dehydration?

"I'm glad she's in daycare now," the pediatrician said, implying heavily that any given stranger would be much better for Isla than Sloane, a decorated academic who nonetheless could not nurture her only child to save either of their lives. "That'll be good for her to get some real social stimulation," the doctor added, which ostensibly meant that Sloane had done something wrong by virtue of . . . being an adult? Unclear. The point was that Sloane was a bad mother, or at least an inadequate one. Was she even reading to Isla? Had she considered simply being better at this, or flaying herself more deeply, beyond the subcutaneous level of skin and sweat and into the marrow of her sanity and time?

Then, after that month's department meeting, Sloane's subsequent chat with Dean Burns—for which she had been publicly asked to *stay behind,* like a child being sent to the principal's office, despite her civilized request for a scheduled tête-á-tête—had also not gone well. In fairness, he had heard the word VidStar and shut down immediately, so that was on Sloane for her ill-fated attempts to inject the situation with logic and facts.

"Dean Burns," Sloane attempted, "with all due respect," she had none, "this department has two thousand followers on Instagram," pitiable. "This Christian girl trad wife has over four million across multiple platforms. Are you really telling me your current faculty is having more of an impact on society than she is?" In retrospect, a bad move.

Burns flapped a hand, looking idly over Sloane's shoulder for the proverbial gal with the great gams who could run off and fetch him a coffee. "She's an ad, nothing more than the latest form of monetizing lifestyle publications. A glorified sales tactic."

"But in this neocapitalist day and age," Sloane had unwisely postured, "what is sociology if not an attempt to understand why something sells? The Country Wife has concrete, quantitative value whether or not you find her to be intellectually serious."

To Sloane's thinking, The Country Wife was *objectively* serious, not to mention academically so. A tool of viral misinformation on one hand, given the quagmirical popularity of conservative feminine clout, and also a case study in feminized labor. The Country Wife was proof of several things: one, that a Good Woman instinctively knew how to provide. The Good Woman was an effortless cook; she could throw a meal together with nothing, because her talents were innate. The Country Wife's argument, which existed by virtue of not only her existence but her popularity, was that modern women (Sloane and her fellow whores) could no longer cultivate the divine feminine because they had been forced to seek some Western capitalist sense of meaning—to take demeaning jobs and suffer, only to prove they were worth a fraction of a man. Meanwhile, men who performed women's tasks were paid well for it—professional kitchens were run by men who primarily learned their craft from a woman. When a woman knitted, she was a spinster; when a man did it, he was a designer. When a woman made something, it was arts and crafts; when a man did it, it was engineering. Anything innate was simultaneously valueless. Burns's response to the movement The Country Wife belonged to could be taken as proof that feminine labor was worth less, sociologically speaking, because it was the product of some mythologized instinct rather than a learned trade or a craft.

Sloane had heard, though, as soon as she said it aloud, that due to her flood of inspiration, she had begun to sound passionate, which meant that what Burns was hearing was a woman who had become emotional, which was obviously a sign that it was Sloane who was not being serious, which meant Burns had a fiduciary responsibility as the owner of a penis to condescend to her, so as to fulfill his masculine duty of securing the ongoing prestige of a lifeless dinosaur (i.e., the University at large).

Truthfully, Sloane did love social media. She thought, academically, that one *could* view it as something that was rewiring our collective brain, actively rewriting society. Or one could think of it as exceptionally powerful hypnosis. Either way, it was proof that everyone was inherently interested in sociology, even if sociology as an institution was not interested in them.

Case in point.

"The question we must ask ourselves, Sloane, is will this be a question of relevance in five years? Ten?" pondered Burns in a tone of utter superiority. "Will it even be relevant beyond the end of the week?"

Sloane wanted to ask just how long Burns and his cohort planned to remain relevant themselves, but on second thought reconsidered that it might be a touchy subject. She began instead to say, "This is a very charged time, politically speaking, with regard to the rights of marginalized groups, which do"—per silly matters of demographics and facts—"include women. Reproductive rights, for example"—a hot-button issue presently driving all levels of politics—"are a question of agency. But whether or not the state can meddle with a person's uterus is only a symptom of a larger problem—of the basic fact that agency is conditional if the person in question identifies as or is visibly a woman." Oh no. She'd gotten worked up again. Scale it back. Retreat! "The point is," Sloane attempted again, "even if something is merely a trend, does that make it less significant? We're in a critical time of radically right-leaning politics, which is of interest to at least half of this population." Whereas most of the work this department does is aimed at twelve or so people who do your same job, Sloane didn't add.

Burns gave her a kindly smile. Poor thing. Poor Sloane. She tried so hard to matter and yet here she was, someone's mother, and barely even a good one at that. Where, after all, was her child? Did she even know?

"I'm sure there's something there," Burns said, as if, if Sloane merely thought a bit harder, she could find a man at the center of this thought experiment, and that man could speak to Burns, and together they could find a way. "By the way, how is Max?"

"Max has downloaded a Scrabble app," Sloane didn't say, because Burns wouldn't understand the point, because Burns couldn't understand a point if it walked up and flicked his balls.

Alex, meanwhile, had not required explanation.

"Oh, no," Alex had said with a shake of her head. She'd called Sloane and invited her and Isla over, something Alex occasionally did now that they'd become friends. Alex's house was clean (a weekly housekeeper) and Montessori-ed (it was important to her to have everything be a "yes" space for Theo) and she always had a beautifully stocked kitchen (Theo actually loved grocery shopping—it was a way they bonded, both sharing a love of fine yogurts and fresh berries and other such treats). Theo was a remarkably social child who seemed to enjoy Isla's primordial efforts at play, which Alex attributed to him having been in daycare since he was four months old. Not a situation Alex delighted in, she confessed—oh, the nightmare that was pumping in the bathroom at work for almost two years until she'd riled up enough support for a proper nursing facility!—but Alex was a single mother, by design. Theo was the result of a sperm donor and Alex's desire to focus on her child without simultaneously addressing a husband's dirty socks or his disinterest in family time.

"So, wait," Alex said upon learning of The Scrabble Betrayal, "does that mean he's on his phone even more now?"

Let us be clear: Sloane did not want to complain about Max. She wanted (needed) (desperately *needed*) Alex to believe that Sloane was an intelligent woman who, in a time of profound feminine progress, had chosen a radical feminist for a partner from a place of deep love and sexual attraction, not economic necessity or any pressing sociological need to marry like she was some kind of basic pumpkin spice bitch.

That being said, Alex had immediately spotted the issue—the further erosion of Sloane's husband's time and mental acuity was weighing heavily on her, such that she didn't think she could prevent herself from bringing it up, which she most certainly did not want to accidentally do in public or worse, in front of Britt, whose husband openly delighted in the routine tasks of domesticity that Max seemed to intellectually discard. But Sloane also didn't particularly want to go into detail about the research Burns had dismissed, because it did feel a bit invasive, or perhaps judgmental—Sloane didn't want Alex to think she saw her as an experiment, a subject to write about like Jane Goodall's apes. So, of the available discussion topics, it would obviously have to be Max.

"It's just . . . sometimes I look over and want to slap the phone out of his hand," Sloane admitted, resigning herself to the guilty pleasure of shit-talking the love of her life. "But it's not as if I don't get the impulse. I mean, truly. What I wouldn't give to sit there and scroll my phone for thirty minutes uninterrupted. Honestly, just the idea of sitting down for thirty minutes without thinking about whether I should be googling baby sign language or preparing iron-rich foods—"

"Fuck the pediatrician, first of all," Alex said. "You should switch, although given how infrequently you have to see the doctor I don't see the point of wrestling over the phone with your HMO. So basically fuck her, end of story."

It was a relief to know that Alex had already done the math of convenience, which was the main thing Sloane's mind was still capable of doing when it wasn't spiraling about how she'd become the kind of person she'd once considered ridiculous before Isla had come along to drive a stake through her image of herself. Before Sloane had understood, in a visceral way, that a man could be authentically progressive and fundamentally useless at the same time.

God, it was fucking *marvelous* to feel as if someone else understood the value of Sloane's time. Typically, after thirty minutes or more of uncharitable feelings toward Max, Sloane made a productive effort to remember things she liked about him. He was funny and he was very sexy and while he might be less capable of executive function than she was, he was smart and doting and, someday, when the grime of early motherhood wore off, Sloane would recall the spontaneous bursts of love she'd always felt for him; the waves of gratitude when she looked at him and remembered he was hers.

Presently, though, she could only see him with his phone in hand, ignoring Frankie the dog who was in turn ignoring Sloane, looking at something that wasn't their precious miracle, the child they had made with every functioning brain cell and iota of energy that Sloane no longer possessed.

So then later, when Alex called Sloane about having a meeting to discuss The House's initiation standards—after Isla's bedtime, which Sloane had accepted, because although Isla needed to be rocked to sleep each night and was liable to wake within hours, maybe even moments, wasn't it acceptable for Sloane to ask one thing of Max, who had *specifically said* she needed to engage in some University extracurriculars?—Sloane had been playing the "I love Max just as he is, I don't need him to change, I will simply change myself and it will be fine!" game for several consecutive days, and had accepted the glass of wine she was offered at the door, and then the two refills after that one.

"The thing is," Sloane said, by then feeling the whorl of catharsis mixing jauntily with rosé, "isn't it unfair, that we're supposed to be independent and successful *and* do everything our mothers did?"

Alex's eyes were shining when she looked at Sloane. It was like a glimmer of something had come alive in her. Like love, or lust.

"But there's a difference between our mothers and us," Alex said as she refilled Sloane's wine. "We don't have to be martyrs. We don't have to just sit there and take it, Sloane. Why should we sacrifice ourselves and make no demands of others?"

Alex was close to Sloane then, the gentle hint of her perfume a sudden, salacious warmth.

"Honoring ourselves is how we take our power back," Alex said, and perhaps in retrospect it wasn't directly in Sloane's ear, but maybe it was.

Then Alex withdrew, the glass of wine in Sloane's hand like a cool mist of sanity. Sloane shivered a little from the temperature drop.

"That's true," she said. "I guess the difference is that everything I agree to is conditional. I make my own money." Sort of. Max made more as a tenured professor, but Sloane was educated, she had been published, she was capable of demanding more of herself, and most importantly, she wasn't trapped. If Max left her because she took issue with him playing Scrabble instead of participating in the raising of their child—which Max wouldn't do, because he wasn't a monster, just a normal, unconscientious and occasionally selfish but not actively bigoted man—then Sloane, unlike her mother, *would* be fine, because whether she admitted it to herself or not, she'd erected The Deadline specifically to ensure that she'd be fine. Maybe not right away, but Sloane had social capital now, thanks to Alex, and Sloane could make her own network outside of the University if necessary, because now she knew women like Alex who could help.

Which *also* meant that Sloane could probably find someone else to publish her research, should it come to that. If it wasn't important to the Almighty Department of Sociology, then couldn't she get more creative, more innovative—what about a book deal, a newsletter, a platform, something? Not that she was preparing for a worst-case scenario, per se, but wasn't Alex right that what Sloane had was agency, the very agency she'd tried to legitimize to Burns—the very agency that the fucking Country Wife had so infantilely given up?

Yes! She would talk to Priscilla about it, Sloane decided. After all, she hadn't gone into sociology just to impress an old man whose opinions she didn't even respect. She wasn't having a meeting about a bunch of teenagers being initiated to their social club just to kiss the crest of the University, like indoctrination to a cult. And also, she should stop worrying about whether Isla was crying for her at home, where Isla's father also lived.

Sometimes it was about *Sloane,* goddamnit!

She lifted her wine to her lips with a sigh, something that was equal parts resignation and relief. "At very least I deserve a little treat," she said. After all, she worked hard for the money. So hard for it, honey! The silliness of intoxication was getting to her, but Sloane felt certain that somewhere in there she'd had a point.

"Self-care," confirmed Alex with a wink, popping a chocolate-covered cherry in her mouth.

18

Nina was surprised to discover that after four weeks of Monday night dinners, she had somehow unintentionally learned the words to the dinner blessing. She had also learned the words to what she couldn't stop calling their "profession of faith" after Dalil had called it that, jokingly. The bit about believing in her sorority, in the sanctity of sisterhood; the things Nina *did* believe in, sort of, but mostly knew she had to say in order to cross the finish line that was initiation, the reinvention of herself. (Dalil said that as a lapsed Catholic she felt she was uniquely skilled for this sort of thing, the numb recitations and excessive ceremony invoking body and blood.)

Since their evening of intoxicated confession, Nina had gotten so accustomed to the presence of her pledge sisters that she no longer felt so blistered by the mercurial nature of Fawn's attention, and was thus a little taken aback on the next occasion they spoke.

Nina had stopped by the house to pick up the day's little sis gifts—a week of charitable gift-giving from a mysterious Big Sis (almost certainly Tessa) wherein each of the pledges was showered with cozy socks and rich chocolate truffles and bath bombs that made her skin smell like dessert, the exact opposite of everything the media had led Nina to believe about the treatment of pledges—when she heard voices coming from somewhere in the corridor beside the kitchen. One was older, an adult. The other was noticeably angrier.

"Isn't the point of all of this that we get a right to choose?"

demanded the second voice. "How are you any different from everything else holding us back?"

"You're telling me you think what Caroline's doing is rational?"

"No, I'm saying it's Caroline's choice to do whatever stupid thing she thinks is worth doing. I mean, would you be this mad if it was sex work? If she was selling her content on OnlyFans, would you call her a slut?"

"Fawn, please. This isn't slut-shaming." Now the adult voice sounded irritated. "What Caroline is doing is diving down an insane alt-right pipeline that has actual repercussions for the rest of the women in this very house. You think the fucking Country Wife is inspiring a generation of women who'll fight for their reproductive rights? And she's from Dallas! If *anyone* should know how draconian abortion bans can get—"

"You're our *chapter advisor*, Alex, not our career counselor. It doesn't matter what you think of our decisions. You don't get to choose our futures, or how are you any different from the very same male politicians you claim to hate? When we graduate, you essentially vanish into obsolescence."

"I'm not telling Caroline what she can and can't do. I'm asking *you*, Fawn, as president of this house, to take accountability for the alumnae programming you bring into it."

"I'm not saying I want Caroline to come and give a lecture, but if she's just asking to drop by at dinner and introduce her book—"

"Get Exec to vote on it." The adult voice was clipped now in addition to annoyed. "Let's see what Alina has to say about this 'trad wife' shit."

Nina sensed a shift in the conversation, like a gauntlet had just been thrown.

"Alina may not like Caroline, but she still understands the fucking concept of, like, freedom of speech—"

"Let me know how the vote goes. And make sure your pledges

are ready for initiation, okay? *That's* your job. *They* are your job. You owe nothing to Caroline. Do you understand?" There was a pause, and then the adult voice added, "If I were you, Fawn, I'd choose my battles carefully. Come December, it'll be your throne that topples, not mine."

There was an unclear mumble in response, then footsteps. Nina ducked into the dining room and out of sight, heart quickening as she heard the front door open and fall shut with the telltale signs of the adult presence leaving. Then, just as Nina prepared to venture back into the hall, she felt the nearness of someone else in her periphery.

"Hey," said Fawn, her mouth tight with irritation. "Want to get a drink?"

Nina swiveled to look at her, surprised. "What, now?" It was three in the afternoon.

"Yeah." Fawn seemed fidgety. "Before anyone else sees and tries to come with. Come on."

She turned swiftly and headed for the back of the house. Nina, laden down with a giant poster of an incomplete family tree, set her things down in an unclaimed corner of the dining room and followed hastily, unintentionally holding her breath when she realized they were passing the kitchen into the carport behind the house.

Fawn unlocked her car, an ice-blue coupe, with her phone. Nina slipped into the passenger side without a word. "I know you overheard us," said Fawn as she shifted into reverse, pulling out into the back alley behind the house. "That was Alex, the chapter advisor."

"Oh. Yeah, I gathered." Nina had met Alex briefly, back when Alex had introduced herself to The House at a dinner early on in their new member period. They'd had a roast chicken that night with crispy skin, meat that slid off the bone, alongside tiny, delicate Yorkshire puddings into which Nina had ladled a gravy so smooth and delicious she wanted to drink it straight. By comparison, Alex hadn't left much of an impression.

"The thing is," Fawn sighed, parking the car at the big-box grocery store nearest to campus, "I fucking hate Caroline. But she's my GrandBig—my Big Sis's Big," she explained unnecessarily to Nina, who could put two and two together, "and, like, all those followers . . . that's not nothing, you know?"

It was true Nina had no idea what it took to achieve success as an influencer. She had a sense, as someone who'd come of age on the internet, that what was viral about Caroline probably had something to do with her face or boobs, which didn't seem to be Fawn's point. Fawn didn't have any social media herself, which made sense to Nina—it went unsaid that a large part of Fawn's general mystique was the fact that her face and thoughts and life were not available for consumption. Instead she was . . . not to be insufferable, but an *experience.* An asset, too valuable to simply give away, unbranded and more importantly, unbrandable—above the fray of algorithmic grift.

But Nina had enough self-preservation to know these were the thoughts of an idiot, and anyway, Fawn was still talking, so she kept it to herself.

"I just don't like the idea that *Alex* gets to decide what's appropriate for any of us," Fawn continued. "Like, I don't personally think Alex has it all, you know? She's just another lawyer with a kid. So what? She's not some revolutionary act of feminism. She's literally the institution. She's not *changing* anything—she's just playing the same losing game. Like, we lost abortion rights under her watch, you know? Not her *personally,* but you get the point." Fawn slumped down in the driver's seat, not getting out of the car.

Then she turned to Nina. "Anyway, I've been meaning to check on you. Feeling ready for initiation?"

Nina wanted to contribute something to Fawn's argument,

though even with Jas constantly in her ear, she couldn't think of what. She didn't know any of the details; had nothing reasonable to offer in response. So she cleared her throat and said, "Yeah, I think so."

"Good. Great." Fawn smacked a hand onto the steering wheel in ongoing frustration, a clear sign the tangent hadn't taken root. "Ugh. I'm sorry." She exhaled swiftly. "I'm in a shit mood. Midterms. This shit with Alex. Getting ready for initiation." She shook her head. "I don't want to burden you with it, it's just—"

"It's not a burden." That much felt natural to say, and quickly. Nina twisted in her seat to face Fawn, who scrunched up her nose in disagreement. "Seriously, it's not."

"I'm your president," Fawn said bitterly. "I'm supposed to be, like, better than this."

"You're perfect," said Nina, who corrected quickly, "Like, perfect for the job. And I think it's cool that you can be real with me," she added.

"Well, I do love mess," Fawn said with a grimace.

"No, seriously, it's—I mean, you're great." Nina felt her cheeks flush. "And you obviously care so much, and that's . . . yeah." Way to stick the landing, she thought resentfully. "If you want to talk about it, I'm here." She looked at Fawn then, trying to express it in a meaningful way, something that was sincere and rare and not just some kind of sad, sycophantic pledge crush.

Rush crush, she thought. Girl crush.

"Ha, well, let's just get through initiation first before I unburden myself all over you." Fawn gave her a meaningful look in return, albeit not one Nina knew how to translate. "By the way, how's it going with your hot professor?"

Nina's cheeks went hotter still. Recently, Nina had begun sitting closer to the front of Dr. Villanueva's lecture hall. He seemed to continuously catch her eye, asking all his theoretical questions of her personally, like a discussion the two of them were having in private. The rest of the class, all philosophy or English majors, were on their phones. Nina, meanwhile, was riveted. She'd stopped by Dr. Villanueva's office hours just the other day to ask some questions about the reading—she was surprised to discover that Dr. Villanueva's philosophical pairings were ample food for thought.

Every day of her new life felt stimulating, enriching. Roast chicken and intellectualism. Fawn's long fingers casually brushed the gearshift, drawing Nina's eye.

"How'd you know about the professor?"

"Your Big told me." Fawn winked. "So how hot is he? Show me a pic."

"Oh, it's not . . . I mean, the picture won't really do it justice." Nina had shown Jas his department headshot the week before, to which Jas had said *ew*, which was a bit harsh. Though, to Jas, there were no men on earth compared to Arya. Still, Nina preemptively explained, "It's more about, like, his mannerisms. The way he talks." His lecture on existentialism and ennui had made Nina's toes curl with sapiosexual longing. She didn't know how to express that in terms Fawn could properly understand. "But, I mean, here."

Fawn leaned closer to see him on Nina's phone screen. "Ooh, no, I totally see it. He's hot." She said it vigorously. Too vigorously? Like she wanted Nina to know she really loved dick. Or maybe Nina was overthinking. "Love that. I don't have anyone interesting on my radar these days," sighed Fawn, fashionably listless.

Nina realized she physically couldn't bear to discuss the possibility of Fawn dating or even lusting after someone, despite that being a fundamental cornerstone of girl talk. Problematic. "Well, still time." Nina gestured to the grocery store they still hadn't entered. "So, what was the plan here, again?"

"Ah. Well." Now Fawn's cheeks were peach with casual embarrassment, the faintest hint of shame that paired so expertly with a vivacious episode of recklessness. "I guess the plan was to get a handle of cheap vodka and douse it in even cheaper fruit punch while sitting in the carport of my sorority house with the pledge I abducted in a moment of weakness. Did I miss anything?"

"I mean, it's definitely *a* plan," said Nina charitably, and Fawn laughed.

"Forget it, let's get a tube of cookie dough instead." She threw open the driver's side door and gestured for Nina to come along. "Though you're still welcome to do illicit things with me in the carport, if you want."

Nina ignored the flutter of innuendo from a place of self-preservation. "Like tax evasion?" she offered instead, getting out of the car.

Fawn tossed her head back with a laugh, reaching for Nina's arm and leaning companionably into her, drawing multiple sets of eyes to the pretty pair they made, shiny-haired and young, full of possibility and talking only a handful of decibels too loud. A forgivable offense when you looked like this, attending this University—wearing these letters, as Fawn currently was, like a glimmer of protection, an amulet around her neck.

"You know, I never saw you as a sorority girl," Dr. Villanueva commented to Nina the following day, leaning against the podium at the front of the auditorium while Nina packed up her things from lecture. She had thrown on her Bid Night shirt in a rush, having accidentally slept in that morning.

For whatever reason—the implication, perhaps, that Tessa and Fawn and Dalil were anti-intellectual in some way—or the hint of misogyny buried deep within the concept that a woman couldn't be beautiful and worth taking seriously at the same time—Nina felt her crush waver, no longer so distracting she couldn't look him in the eye for fear that he might somehow read her mind.

"I take it you don't think much of sororities? Groundbreaking."

Nina's voice was more dull than cold, but ultimately there was a dearth of flirtation that felt appropriate under the circumstances.

"I didn't say that. My wife was in a sorority." Dr. Villanueva's wedding ring glinted purposefully, utilitarian on his finger, like punishment for stepping jarringly out of the game.

"You say that like 'I have a Black friend' or 'I'm a feminist because I have a daughter,'" challenged Nina.

Dr. Villanueva laughed, breaking their momentary tension. "I do have a daughter and a Black friend, so you might be onto me."

Nina could feel the other students' eyes on them, realizing she had somehow begun to be comfortable with it. The power that came with being interesting. Magnetic. She grit her teeth around it, that same feeling, the urgency to hunt. Dr. Villanueva seemed to sense it from her in the same moment, leaning away, distracting himself with the process of packing his laptop back into the leather messenger bag that bore his initials. The kind of thing that had probably been given to him by a colleague, or his wife.

It was something about his behavior, his obvious desire to clutter up his tracks with misdirection that made Nina realize he actually wanted to fuck her. Not a tease with no chance of follow-through, but foreplay with a destination. If this was just flirtation, if it was a game he played with every young woman in his classroom, then he wouldn't have bothered to end or conceal it. At the moment, he wasn't looking at Nina—was in fact looking pointedly away, like The House's letters were temporarily blinding him, or maybe it was her youth.

She felt a different thrill then; a sudden, sharp stab of agency. This wasn't some infantile crush on a teacher that was safe because it could never, would never happen. This was real. This was a man, a man who knew how to fuck, who wanted to fuck her. It was repellant and also sexy, in that by virtue of her awareness of his desire, *he* suddenly became the object.

Power, Nina thought. Power.

Her heart thudded while she dressed for the Big Sis reveal, imagining what she might tell Fawn. *Oh, him? Turns out he's a creep.*

Never trust a man, Fawn might say. Or maybe Nina was totally off base and she'd offer some variation on *Get it, girl!* When it came to The House, it was difficult to predict where sex ended and power began.

"Respectability politics can suck my dick," Tessa had once told Nina over Monday night dinner, nearly bludgeoning her with a Portuguese egg tart that tasted like the afterglow of orgasm. "What's the point of being a 'good girl,' hm?" This Tessa had put in air quotes. "Like, there's a real threshold for effort, you know. Code-switching gets me *this* far"—Tessa made a small motion with her thumb and forefinger—"and anything beyond that is won by whatever means necessary or it's not given at all."

("I like her," Jas had said when Nina relayed this conversation to her. "I still think this whole pledge thing is dumb, but I do love supporting women's wrongs.")

"I'm certainly not earning anyone's respect by straightening my hair or 'maintaining boundaries' with my TA," Tessa ranted. "At best, all I'm ever doing is dodging vitriol. Because in the end, I'm still having to prove my worth to someone who requires proof, aka an *impossible task*. Because if they were going to respect me or even see me as a person, they would have done it. You can't earn your way to personhood or some shit. You know?"

"So what'd you say when your TA asked you out?" said Nina, because that was what had started the whole thing—the discussion about whether going out with the dude who inputted your grades was a slutty move or a savvy one.

Tessa shrugged. "I said I'd think about it, and I will. Now pass the gravy, pledge."

Nina was glad that Tessa was her Big—glad that Tessa wanted her and not one of the baby freshmen who might be more docilely in her thrall. Which wasn't to say Nina *wasn't* in Tessa's thrall to some degree, because Tessa was brash and charismatic and unapologetic, things that Nina could only be when she focused her energy very hard, like trying to blow things up with her mind. She was glad when her scavenger hunt led her to Tessa, because she earnestly felt the relationship was lasting—that one day, when Nina was sad or lonely or desperately in need of some advice, she would pick up her phone and call her Big Sis Tessa, the next Great American Novelist, and it would be like calling her actual sister Jas, except that Tessa wasn't obsessed with their cousin and had no working knowledge of what Nina had looked like in the sixth grade. The Nina that Tessa knew was someone Tessa couldn't weaponize against her—was even someone Nina felt she could grow into being in a more permanent way, like finally finding her signature perfume.

"But I thought you wanted that other girl. *Fawn.*" Jas couldn't say Fawn's name without pairing it with a weird, melodic singsong, ostensibly meant to pitch her voice into the babygirl register, where someone of Fawn's nomenclature belonged.

"Fawn's the president, Jas. She can't take a Little, it would be unfair."

"Oh, so she's like the entire house's Big Sis?"

"I can hear you mocking me, Jasleen. And yeah, sure, basically."

"But she has her special friends, right? She gets to *participate in the rituals,* does she not?"

"Stop."

"You're making it sound like she's some kind of living saint. A vessel of sisterhood. Mother Sister, Most High."

Fawn's title was actually Lady Superior, not that Nina would be caught dead admitting that to Jas. "The point is, I like Tessa. She's cool. She's fun. And she's probably going to be famous one day."

"Is she one of the important ones?"

"On Exec, you mean?"

"Yeah, is she on the Holy Council?"

"It's called Exec, and no, she's not." Tessa "didn't care for group projects," in her words.

"Wouldn't it be better to have a Big Sis with some political capital? What's Fawn's major, anyway? Is she pre-law too?"

The former remark was typical Jas meaninglessness; the latter felt like the start of a tangent, or possibly a trap. "She's a business major."

Jas let out a mocking snort, so definitely a trap. "What kind of business?"

"How should I know?" Fawn's general approach to academics implied some pressure from her parents, presumably not the white one. (The other, Nina had eventually gathered with the compulsive desperation of an alcoholic noir detective, was Filipino—a critical commonality! Asian parents! Something-something not a monolith, but still.) Fawn wasn't unambitious—she spoke generally of getting her MBA at some point in the future, pending whatever greatness she felt like attending to in the meantime—but overall, Nina got the feeling Fawn had chosen something broadly applicable for a reason, and not one she felt compelled to share. "And for the record, I don't think anyone on Exec is taking a Little this year."

That part might have been a lie, or maybe not. Either way, Nina wasn't going to let Jas make her feel like she was failing at sorority politics. As far as Nina was concerned, The House was fundamentally egalitarian. To her, The House was like the Greek agora, a free-flowing place of ideas, where the theoretical idea of womanhood could become dynamic and real. Nina felt she could almost touch it, the woman she would one day be, which was different from the version she might have been before she'd let the letters kiss her skin. She could see the many routes and pathways, the language she would need to speak but didn't yet, couldn't. The glimmer of possibilities that would eventually be bestowed by The House, by virtue of being one of its inhabitants—but it was also not strictly The House that conferred their womanhood upon them, because it was *they* who were The House.

Of course, waxing poetic to Jas about The House's egalitarianism would not have been productively received. It also undermined Nina's whole thing about Fawn not taking a Little, which was something Nina needed to believe for purposes of personal survival.

In fact, when it did eventually come time for the Big Sis reveal, Nina was ashamed to say that despite this, there had been a perilous second while making her way down the papier-mâché yellow brick road to her mysterious Big Sis where her heart had soared—a brief nanosecond of time during which she spotted Fawn first before she saw Tessa, and thought perhaps it was indeed Fawn who was waiting for her, like the sparkling manifestation of the dream.

Then, once Tessa came into view and the situation played out exactly as anticipated, and, indeed, entirely as she had pre-reasoned with Jas, Nina had thought *but actually,* wasn't it sweet that Fawn was so close to Tessa that her choosing to be *with* Tessa during this momentous ritual ("Stop referring to them as rituals or I'm going to start doing it too," Nina had growled to Jas that morning for the hundredth time, and for good reason!) meant that Nina was kind of *both* their Littles, like a polyamorous circle of sisterly fondness and trust?

And then, as Nina leapt excitedly into Tessa's open arms like throwing herself directly back into girlhood, she caught Fawn's eyes traveling over her shoulder—over Nina entirely—away from Nina—toward . . . something else? Yes, to someone else who was a person that wasn't Nina. To a figure entering the room at Nina's back—to the person who was more important than Nina. Prettier, probably. Funnier. A closer friend. A forever kind of person.

Nina clung tightly to Tessa. *Rush crush. Self-care. Respectability politics can suck my dick. Participation in the rituals.* She tapped sisterhood like a tree and waited for that new-old golden feeling, the sweetness of utter relief.

"I would have taken you," Fawn explained in Nina's ear at the end of the night, when the slumber party energy had taken them from silly games to the retro dance party of their pre-teenage dreams. "But Tessa really wanted you, and the others already think you're my favorite. Plus, we're already so close, you know? And Dalil doesn't show it, but she's kind of struggling to find her place here."

Fawn and Nina both glanced over to where Dalil was swaying to the music with her eyes closed, dappled by the shoddily installed mirror ball overhead. They watched her in silence for a long moment, and then eventually, Fawn said, "She needed someone who would really make her feel like she belonged."

Nina understood, then, the sweetest thing that is possible for anyone to understand. She didn't need to be told that she belonged because she already belonged—had always belonged, as if from another life. Intrinsic sisterhood. A natural conclusion.

"Besides," Fawn added, raising a glass of lemonade to her lips as she lowered her voice, "can't exactly do illicit things in the carport with my Little Sis, can I?"

Nina choked on her swallow, messily spluttering liquid back into her cup.

"Like tax evasion," Fawn said, straight-faced.

But Nina, still choking, couldn't laugh.

19

Days to deadline: three. Prospects: abysmal. Possibility of deadline abandonment: high. Sloane couldn't think of anything new or interesting. All she had was her previous idea, the one deemed unacceptable. Beyond that was the presence of a loud ringing noise, like the ongoing scream of a kettle, from which no cognition could be drawn.

Problems, or perhaps at this stage merely facts: Isla, the sweetest, most darling child alive, was also a violent sociopath. While the headbutting had begun around the advent of Isla's first birthday, the increase in muscle tone since then had taken things to a savage new degree. Constancy of plagues aside—one such virus forcing Sloane to beg Arya to look after Isla for the length of a lecture, which he had cheerily done, which made everything somehow both better and worse—Isla had also begun shoving Sloane away when they arrived for daycare, not out of excitement to see her teachers, but rather a spiteful way to impress upon Sloane the force of her many disappointments. It expressed some version of "Fuck off, Mother. Just take your pathetic apologies and go."

"I feel like she's starting to love me less," Sloane confided in Max while scouring the internet for some way to escape actively brushing Frankie the dog's teeth. Admittedly, though, her timing had not been ideal, as Max was composing an email or perhaps researching word game strategies—Sloane was presently unsure and didn't have the time or energy to ask. Possibly this was her fault? She had lost interest in his interests. She remembered, vaguely, having ample space and tenderness and romantic curiosity for the contents of Max's mind, for the ways it twisted and turned to derive such fascinating conclusions. The way his intellect was so fluid and capable; his vibrant sense of humor that took her so charmingly by surprise. He seemed stressed these days; but then again, so did she.

"You're not the one abandoning her every day, so you get a pass," Sloane helplessly continued, hitting buy on some dog treats she hoped did not contain lead. "And now Isla has an entire life separate from me with Miss Lily at the daycare. I'm losing her, I can feel it—and I also feel like, I don't know, it'll only go downhill from here, you know? I've let her babyhood slip away from me without even noticing."

Sloane let out a deep sigh, realizing she hadn't the faintest idea what to make for dinner. For the last two nights Isla hadn't touched her food, opting only to suck some ketchup from her fingers. The doubts in Sloane's competency continued unabated, as with the slow trudge toward mortality. Memento mori, amen. "And I gave it all up for what, some teenagers who only sometimes do the reading? Who are mostly all scrolling their social media while I ramble on about frequency distribution?"

"At the very worst, Isla's gone from you having ninety-nine percent of her love to ninety-five," said Max, who managed to transfer his attention briefly from his screen to Sloane, although his eyes were the last to make it. "She still loves you the most."

"Yeah, but that'll end." Sloane slumped down in her chair, though as usual, she had the distinct feeling she shouldn't be sitting, that there was something else she ought to be doing, because eight thousand tasks remained unattended to or half-finished somewhere in the ether of her life. "She'll hate me the moment she turns thirteen, it's just part of the cycle. Which is fine, obviously. That's her right as a woman and a citizen of the world." Sloane had once been told that her ability to rationalize aloud was impressively diabolical, a symptom of being too online. To which she had pointed out that her job was to exist as part of *society*, she was literally a *sociologist*, burying her head in the sand was unacceptable, silence was violence, the end! "This is all I get, and I feel like I'm wasting it."

Sloane remembered all the things left undone that she had previously not cared about. Once she had been so grateful to Max for being the one to do the laundry, to clean the bathroom, to tend to the kitchen stove and the care and keeping of the butcher block, freeing up Sloane's mind for other, less trivial tasks. She used to be able to think about things! Now she was distracted by the presence of grime, the NOW NOW NOW of Isla's needs. Isla deserved a clean home, she deserved a mother who looked up from her phone, who knew exactly what Isla liked and didn't like because every moment of Isla's life came from inside the sanctity of the mother-daughter bond.

At the same time, Sloane wanted to think more deeply about femininity as a social construct and the ways in which it was an unsolvable curse, specifically *in re* The Country Wife. Which, again, was a topic that had been soundly rejected, and so she was back where she started, with an incurable research obsession that was worth the same to her department as having no research at all.

"Do you want to have sex?" Sloane asked in a fit of desperation.

"Oh, sure." Max stood without removing his eyes from the screen. Eventually he looked at her, his mouth in a cheeky little grin, and Sloane felt a flood of fondness that was mixed with . . . observation. Max looked tired; he looked suddenly much older, like she'd blinked at some point five years ago and arrived at this moment, and couldn't remember now if the age in his face was new.

Reliably, though, Sloane's brain was quick to acknowledge that with things as they were in Gaza and the Congo and the Sudan, she could not reasonably afford to think of growing old as anything but a blessing, even if it meant she lost some elasticity here and there and so did Max.

"Honestly, the real fuckery about getting older is this absurd resistance to *looking* old," Alex said when she joined Sloane for coffee later that week. "Which is ridiculous. Because as I tell The Girls all the time, getting older increases your value as a woman. It's a gift." She sipped her coffee with a shrug. "Needless to say, they don't believe me."

"In fairness to them," commented Sloane with that same diabolical rationalization, "there is a very palpable tipping point where becoming undesirable as a sexual object diminishes the mythology of your acceptance by men. But since that acceptance was a myth to begin with, the loss is imaginary, and yet absolutely crushing at the same time."

Alex nodded, a tangent clearly forming behind her eyes. "One of The Girls—Fawn, who's a real pain in my ass," she added, rolling her eyes in a way that was laden with wry affection for The House's current president, "once pointed out that if I thought it was true that getting older was a gift, then wasn't it hypocritical to cover up my gray hair? And I had to tell that little asshole that I wasn't a hypocrite because I don't dye my hair."

Sloane cut a glance sideways to Alex's perfect highlights, and knowingly, Alex grinned.

"Yet," she said with a pointed sip of her coffee. "I'm not a hypocrite *yet*. It's not my fault she didn't think to ask if I have gray hair. I still pull them out like a normal person."

"There's a fine line, though, no pun intended," said Sloane, who had indeed been about to launch into a discussion of crow's feet. "I always think about how much of what we do is for us and how much of it is for, you know, the feminine mythos. I used to think getting Brazilians was disgustingly infantilizing until I realized they actually improved sex. And if it bothers me so much to look older, is Botox then the more empowered choice?"

"God, I should lock you and Fawn in a room together." Alex

rolled her eyes. "I believe Fawn's stance on this is that feminine conventions of beauty are just another form of exploitation. Then again, who knows if that's actually her opinion. Fawn is addicted to playing devil's advocate—she loves to argue, but she can't take a meaningful stance on anything to save her life."

"Really?" This was vaguely interesting to Sloane.

"Really." Alex's nod was long-suffering and firm. "She'll go to bat for a stranger if it suits her but stab her best friend in the back. There was a whole thing last year, one of the girls got in trouble with the University for a political post that went viral and Fawn tried to—" Alex waved a hand. "Long story. The point is, it's impossible to tell what Fawn actually cares about or believes."

"Do you often disagree with her?" asked Sloane, intrigued enough to have temporarily forgotten the host of other quandaries in her head, like how her daughter would probably one day hate her. She felt grateful to Alex for that reprieve, even if she didn't quite know what to make of Alex's position on the matter.

"The fact is that we can argue about all of this until we're fucking comatose and it won't matter," Alex said. "The problem is systemic, institutional. The problem is the patriarchy, and the answer to literally every question is that of course we're being exploited. Of *course* we are. But does that *necessarily* mean we are also powerless? The only way to win is to be in the room. Whatever it takes to sit at the table is the empowered choice," Alex concluded.

"So then what is choosing not to even acknowledge the table?" Sloane asked, thinking of The Country Wife, who sat primarily at her husband's table and presumably didn't ask herself these things.

"It's naive, unforgivably so. The table exists whether you acknowledge it or not—it *impacts* you, and others, regardless. So honestly, it's a betrayal," said Alex. "Plain and simple."

"I see," said Sloane, with potentially too much excitement. Because it *was* exciting! That kind of black-and-white stance was invigorating. It gave her something: a hypothesis. A question.

Essentially, what was power? Was it the woman who used her desirability and the conventions set for her by the institutional penises-that-be to exist in the room, or was it the woman who said "Fuck this room, I don't even want it"? Was the Good Woman the one who molded herself on the accepted path? But, of course, then every woman who couldn't achieve acceptability was . . . what, rejected from the holy church of Whatever It Takes? Alex could promise to leave the ladder down behind her all she wanted, but how many Alexes were actually required in order to dominate the room? If modeling "appropriate" conventions was the necessary bar for all women to clear, what behavior did Alex expect from the queer woman, the BIPOC woman, the disabled woman, the trans woman . . . ? Which was not even to speak of the *unattractive* woman, god forbid!

"What's going on in there?" asked Alex, playfully squinting at Sloane's face. "You look deep in thought."

"I am, a little," Sloane admitted, and took a sip of her coffee before gambling with, "What do you think about me using this experience to write something?"

"Which experience?" Alex asked. "Our inevitable demise or the descent into geriatrics?"

"Oh, I meant The House," Sloane said, as Alex froze with her cup partway to her mouth. "I'm not going to exploit the girls, I promise," she said quickly. "I'm more . . . curious about the uncanny volume of high-achieving women The House produces."

"Uncanny? Next you'll be calling us witches." Alex's brow was pointedly arched, her eyes elsewhere.

"Unusual, then. Remarkable. Not occult." Sloane forced a laugh. "And anyway, I meant more like its philosophies and values, and why that culture works or doesn't work."

"I see," said Alex, her brows now stitched neatly together.

"Not *doesn't* work, just—I don't know, I'm fleshing it out," Sloane amended quickly, realizing this was not the time to bring up The Country Wife or Alex's disappointment in her ostensible failure. "Basically," Sloane summarized, "I want to look into the values of feminine institutions, and structures of power in feminine spaces. You know, what *is* female power?" she riffed, realizing that Alex had begun to nod slowly, then with increasing fervor, despite this not at all being the thing Sloane wanted to research. Well, not that it *wasn't*, but there was definitely something more micro at work, something best paraphrased as "What the fuck is up with this sorority cult?" Which Sloane was at least smart enough to know wasn't going to be taken well by Alex. "So, you know, in addition to The House, there'd be some discussion about wellness influencers, or momfluencers, for example. The way women themselves give shape and definition to traditionally patriarchally understood power and agency."

"That's incredible," said Alex, who was still chewing something, unclear what. "But that's still way too pop-psychology for the University, though, isn't it? Given what you said about the dean."

"I was thinking about maybe chatting with Priscilla about it," said Sloane, hoping Alex wouldn't find that too inappropriately buddy-buddy, given that Alex was their common ground. "Maybe there's some nonfiction imprint she knows about that would find it interesting? Something non-academic?" Distantly, Sloane felt her deadline disintegrating blithely into space. Progress: ??

(No really, was it progress??)

"Oh, good idea. I can ask her for you." Alex seemed to be gradually coming around, shifting her ideological weight from foot to foot. "I'd have to ask you to be cognizant of The Girls and their privacy, though. No real names, nothing like that. Might be better if you focus on alumnae rather than current members."

"Oh yeah, completely doable," said Sloane. She would have to be in touch with more than just The Country Wife, anyway, to find out where things really diverged.

"I can help connect you, if you want," Alex said. "A lot of our best and brightest have gatekeepers, but I can make sure you get through. All of our alums have great connections, too—the breadth of interviews here could be really interesting."

Oh, this would definitely be a book, Sloane realized. The list of high-profile women who might be willing to be interviewed . . . it *was* pop-sociology, but why should that have to be a bad thing? If Burns still couldn't be convinced, then to hell with the tenure track. She could really build something with this. "That would be amazing, thank you *so* much—"

"Absolutely. You're an honorary sister now." Alex beamed at her, and Sloane felt an irritation, a tiny patch of friction, at the knowledge that she was misleading what currently seemed to be her only real friend.

She mulled it over later, in her office, watching Arya's head bounce soundlessly along to the Enya he listened to while plugging in grades. She pondered, staring into space, too distracted to attend to her correspondences (mainly students requesting extra credit). Then she suddenly stood and tapped Arya's shoulder to get his attention.

He jumped. "Whoa, hi," he exhaled, grinning up at her as he removed his headphones. "Got a little too in the zone there. What's up?"

This close his eyes were a velvety brown, Parisian ganache. His lower lip was bitten red from concentration. The impetus had been innocent, purely academic, but the choreography of how this all played out was somehow suspect. From where Sloane stood and Arya leaned in his office chair, his mouth was very close to the apex of her thighs.

"The, um. The influencer I told you about," Sloane said. "The Country Wife."

"Oh yeah, the homesteading trad wife." Arya nodded.

"I want to write about her," Sloane said, and trailed off, because she wasn't sure how to use words for *I want to write about her but my friend might be mad.* Was she a professional or wasn't she? She couldn't reasonably leave out such a notable outlier. And wasn't that part of the undressing of feminine power? Was it power for Caroline Collins to have a significant, financially viable platform of acolytes even if the values her brand espoused were harmful—or even, as Alex had put it, a betrayal to her kind? Was there *ever* real power in the subversion of power? Was it simply committing to the bit when it came to exploitation, or was it in some way exactly the same as Alex's approach—parlaying desirability into money, influence, and the increasingly relevant social capital of ultra-niche microfame? Was Alex's success by traditionally masculine markers less significant than Caroline's success by traditionally feminine ones? Was gendering power even a thing that could be done, or was it already a failure because it was inherently buying into a system ruled by heteronormative cisgender men?

"Cool, cool," said Arya, as if he were now vibing to the low-fi bass of Sloane's private thoughts. "I think it's interesting, but more importantly, *you* think it's interesting. So, you know. What would you say to anyone who told you they were inspired?"

"I'd say chase it," Sloane admitted aloud. "I'd say to follow it down the rabbit hole, because only in madness lies genius. But then again—" She laughed. "I'm full of shit."

"No, you're not." She'd been lost in thought, albeit not so lost that she didn't feel it like a fever flush when Arya leaned closer. "It's true, and you know it. So who better to take advice from than you?" he pointed out, the curl of his wry smile landing somewhere in her stomach.

Sex with Max that night was unusually good, apropos of nothing. "Twice in one week," Max panted, "I must have been a very, very good boy," but Sloane's thoughts were once again elsewhere, so she had replied with little more than a distracted laugh. Though she was all too cognizant later when her screen lit up with an email confirming her meeting with Priscilla. Too buzzed to sleep, she slid out of bed to sit at her computer, typing up what would become the proposal for her book while Frankie the dog seized casually with halting snores.

I have to figure it out for my daughter. I have to become the right kind of woman so that she will have a model and a path. That urgency, it keeps me up at night. I thought I had stakes before but I had no idea. It's a new form of seeking perfection—knowing with abject certainty that I will fail.

(Deadline: already slipping through her fingers. Circumstances: exigent. Progress: irreversible. A long, long way.)

20

The night of initiation was a quiet one, a Sunday, the sky foggy and heavy, late now into October. The pledges had all been instructed to wear no makeup, no jewelry, to enter the house in a state of virginal simplicity with which to be reborn. For Nina, whose reinvention timeline was right on track, this went beyond mere aesthetic, rising from symbolic to borderline literal. Unfortunately there was about a 97 percent chance she would bleed through her tampon, maybe even vomit. How easily in uterine time four weeks had come and gone, the whims of her period an everlasting inconvenience.

"It feels cult-y," said Jas, commenting idly while Nina searched around for a suitable white dress. "Don't you think it feels cult-y? Like you're being indoctrinated into a priestess sect or something. The Jedi."

Of all Jas's commentary, Nina felt these were among the comments she could fairly and rationally discard. "Yes," she said, ignoring the stab of pain radiating to her back, "I am joining a cult. Are you happy now?"

"I guess, kind of," said Jas with an unusual listless energy. "Maybe I should find a cult to join. You seem more at peace than the average person."

Nina suspected that was actually true. Cramps aside, she had never before felt this absence of anxiety. Midterms were going fine—her personal rebirth was already underway, with sparkling results in academia specifically. She was also far less concerned with the mating rituals that had so dominated the previous year, of which Jas had been previously disdainful (before Jas had taken up the sorority-related disdain). Increasingly, though, Nina felt Jas had become accustomed to the idea of The House, perhaps even in a way that mirrored envy. The more mocking Jas became of its little absurdities here and there, the more Nina detected a shadow to her sister's tone, a longing for similar mundanities that might make daily life a little easier, a little more protected. Which was, indeed, how Nina felt.

She bid farewell to Jas in a bit of a rush, having agreed to meet Dalil on campus before walking over to The House together. In the days since discovering that Fawn was her Big Sis, Dalil seemed substantially lighter, to the point where Nina was finally able to pinpoint the aspects of her that Fawn must have been wary of at the start. Only in retrospect could Nina grasp that Dalil's attitude about the various hoops of recruitment had previously represented something tactile, a cynicism she had worn like a mantle.

"It's mainly an issue of retention rates," Tessa had explained to Nina at the end of Big night, when she'd caught Nina watching Fawn and Dalil taking pictures together with a variety of props. Dalil wore an uproarious false mustache that Fawn had smoothed down with her fingers. "Since we take so few pledges," Tessa explained, "it looks bad if any of them fail to initiate. The last thing we need is International breathing down our necks, or Alex."

"Is there something weird about Alex?" Nina asked, thinking of the argument she'd overheard Alex having with Fawn.

"Mm, I'm really not the person to ask about that. Fawn would have a much longer speech prepared, probably because she's the one who's always having to deal with Alex." Tessa shrugged. "In my opinion, Alex isn't weird, she's just . . . basic. She's controlling, you know? She's a micromanager, but not in an abnormal or problematic way. More like the prom queen who keeps going back for homecoming because she peaked a long time ago."

"But she's a lawyer," Nina said, leaving out that her own aspirations were essentially to become exactly like Alex. "It's not like she's worse off now than she was when she was our age."

"Well, who knows about her private life. In any case, she's way more invested than I plan to be," said Tessa. "Isn't the point to reap what we can and move on? If you stay, it just gets sad."

This assessment crossed Nina's mind again when she and Dalil arrived at the house to discover it was fully unlit, and at first glance, completely empty.

Except for Alex. She stood alone in the corridor from the foyer to the kitchen, looking up from her phone as the pledges began to slowly file in, with Nina and Dalil being among the first to arrive.

The entryway to the house had the original dark wood floors, which gleamed with polish beneath the tastefully selected entryway rug. The walls, which were generally covered in fashionable House of Hackney wallpaper, were newly lined with framed composites of portraits that Nina hadn't seen before. Even from a distance she could see they were filled with the faces of alumnae, like an ancestral record or collection of family heirlooms that had ostensibly been carefully stored during the brief period that usurpers—pledges—roamed the house floors.

Unlike the pledges in their stark communion gowns, Alex wore a red wrap sweater, her lips painted a blazing scarlet to match. Her hair was pulled away from her face, and there was . . . something, Nina thought. Some tension to her expression, the queen bee fretting over the hive. *Basic,* Tessa had said, but Nina saw something even older than that, almost fairytale-like in its familiarity. An archetype, which Nina supposed was "basic" in the narrative sense. Someone whose power would inevitably be lost, worrying about whether her power was being lost.

That, and a familiar teeth-chatter of longing.

Nina realized as she set her bag down on the floor that Alex was watching her specifically, observing her from a distance with a divot of thought between her brows. Before Nina could say anything, though, Alex tore her gaze away to return her attention to her phone, then turned to exit the house through the rear door, by the carport. Evidently she didn't plan to address them.

Then the rest of the pledges arrived, vermilion vestiges of sun burning low through the foyer windows.

"What are we supposed to be doing?" whispered Maud, loudly, to Fran, who shrugged. Without consulting each other, the pledges seemed to have agreed the waiting period should be silent.

Then, just as the sun began to fade into darkness and Nina struggled to discern the expressions on the faces of her cohort, a faint flicker of candlelight appeared from the foyer's rear corridor. Nina nudged Dalil, who instantly stood a little straighter. They felt the hum, the presence of the sisterhood, its precise and unignorable frequency, before any of The House's members came into sight.

Then, stepping into view from the darkness, their new member educators Nicole and Mallory appeared, each holding a lit votive candle.

"Welcome, sisters," they said in unison, their voices low and solemn, something that would have ordinarily made Dalil's eyes cut to Nina's with exasperation at the campiness. Instead, Dalil stood unusually still at Nina's side, a look of contemplation on her face, like a new bride.

Nina realized that in addition to baptism, this also seemed a lot like a wedding. The House was both religion and spouse, institution and lover. She wanted to point it out to Dalil, but realized she didn't feel mockery about it. Slowly, gradually over time, she'd developed not just an opposition to derogation, but a genuinely protective feeling, not unlike how she might have felt about her religion or her partner. Of course everything to do with The House could be odd and silly and imperfect. Did that necessarily make the love less pure?

"Tonight, we will commune with our sisters past, and beseech them for acceptance. May the sisters who came before us welcome you into the auspices of The House."

Nina felt a shiver of something down her spine. Renewed, collective teeth-chatter. Air-conditioning, or ghosts.

"As you know," Nicole recited, "The House was established centuries ago to celebrate sisterhood, and the improvement of both heart and mind. Our founders believed that we are stronger together, and that binding together as a sisterhood would create new opportunities for women—opportunities to learn and grow.

"The House was built on the ideals our founders believed to be imperative for the growth of women. Truth, honor, and loyalty are the foundation of our sisterhood. These ideals are as important today as they were to our founders over one hundred and fifty years ago.

"Tonight, you are but one step from becoming a member of The House. We as a sisterhood have found in you the qualities we cherish in one another. Sincerity, honor, friendship, and love are the hallmarks of our sisterhood, as are the hunger of our hearts and the protection of those we call our own."

Mallory passed around a box, gesturing for each of the pledges to take their own white votive candle. Nicole began to walk around the circle they'd formed in the foyer, one hand cupped around the open flame she held in her hands.

"On this special night," said Mallory, "we invite you to share in our bond. But first, we must ask you to complete your vows before crossing the threshold of our sisterhood."

Nina was last in the circle. Nicole held her eye for a brief moment, kissing her own candle flame to Nina's wick before rejoining Mallory, all the pledges' candles having been lit. The house was so unnaturally quiet they could hear the creak of every floorboard beneath Nicole's careful footfall, not a sound coming from the row outside, nor the occupants upstairs. Briefly, Nina wondered how they'd done it. What she would have done for this kind of silence under other circumstances—even the library was quiet but profoundly unsacred, easily pierced by the undignified crunch of someone's midnight Lay's.

Just as Nina's thoughts began to wander, Mallory spoke again. "Before you enter the hearth of our sisterhood, we must ask you to complete these vows. Do you accept our foundational beliefs of loyalty, honor, and friendship?"

This part they'd been schooled in answering. "I do," Nina said quietly. Beside her, she heard Dalil murmur the same.

"Do you reject the temptations of envy and deceit?"

"I do," came the low-thrumming chorus. The hum was there again, louder, or perhaps nearer. Nina felt the space between her shoulder blades constrict, her body centralizing, condensed, as in the moments before the shotgun start.

"Will you put first the high ideals of friendship, generosity, and trust?"

"I will." She could hear every sound in The House, perhaps even miles beyond it. The snap of a twig, a branch on the ground. Any threat to her sisters.

"Do you share in our goals of betterment and growth, that together we may become women of higher scholarship, achievement, and self-worth?"

"I do." She could feel Quinn's breathing. She could taste Maud's lip balm.

"Will you choose the beating hearts of your sisters and place this love above all others?"

"I will." Dalil exhaled softly. The hairs rose on Nina's arms.

"Do you swear to guard the secrets of our sisterhood with integrity, until death?"

The invocation of death in the moment felt appropriate. The solemnity felt earned.

"I do." The hum fell away.

The thing was: Nina wanted to believe it. She wanted more than anything to come to these promises without irony—with no hypocrisy, no fear. Truthfully, she *missed* the earnestness of girlhood, aware that in her ordinary University life, with its mimicry of adulthood, she constantly straddled a line of something unknown with one foot in and one foot out. But what had she been as a girl if not capable of magic, both vengeful and pure? What womanhood would she possibly want where those things were gone from her, all because she had willingly unclenched her fingers, let them go so as not to be humiliated, caught in the act of wanting without moderation or restraint? Better to be gauche than to be ordinary, to have pulled herself back from this kind of devotion at the cost of herself. To receive nothing more from social convention than a tired adulthood filled with playing someone else's games.

Already Nina felt nostalgia for this moment, for this person, for this version of herself. She understood that after tonight, she would likely never be able to speak like this, so openly. Swearing a blood oath to be friends forever. She could never again reasonably ask that of anyone. After tonight it would always be too painful, too naive.

So she was glad, more than glad, that Dalil seemed just as rapt as she was. In that moment, Nina wanted every promise that passed her lips to be true—that these women would forever be hers, that nothing would ever change, that she would protect them with her life or let her be struck down where she stood for her failure. She wanted desperately to invoke the ghosts, to join the thrumming chorus, however sinister it was. To opt in to the promise of this haunting. It was the closest she had ever felt to actually *mattering*—like if she could strengthen herself with the mortar of this sisterhood, then no one would ever be able to hurt her. She could never again fall apart.

"May the memory of tonight stay with you always," Nicole said softly, while Nina prayed to her girl-gods and ghosts. She bargained with the universe in silence. Let there be safety in this house, she prayed, for she already knew there would be none outside of it.

21

Midterms arrived and Isla had another stuffy nose. Maybe she was worryingly sick, maybe she wasn't. Max seemed disinterested in tissues, in holding Isla down to use the electronic snot-sucker everyone hated, to petition the gods and wrestle the titans all to try to help their baby breathe. Isla sounded increasingly like a French bulldog (or their actual dog, Frankie) when she slept, and Sloane contemplated buying a new humidifier, although she paused when she realized it would then become her job to clean it, and how exactly did she plan to do that when she was already so busy abandoning her child, for reasons unclear?

"Oh god, we all feel that way," Britt said over dinner, having invited Sloane once again into her home upon learning (from Alex) that Sloane intended to conduct interviews with the alumnae of The House. (Sloane, for her part, tried very hard not to *audibly* capitalize The Women, though indeed she was equally as interested in The Women as she was in The Girls.) Britt's husband, Finn, was loyally and usefully elsewhere in the house playing with the twins, though Britt had prepared a beautiful rack of lamb for Sloane that she claimed was, quote, much less difficult than people thought. (She then sent Sloane the link.)

"There's just no getting it right as a mother, is there?" Britt remarked. "The whole thing is just . . . watching yourself get torn into usable slivers and constantly trying to decide which balls are acceptable to drop."

This was a very hilarious assertion to Sloane, as Britt did not appear to be dropping anything, not even crumbs. While Sloane did understand that Britt was a person and therefore likely flawed, Sloane couldn't imagine what in Britt's life would represent a failure or a disappointment. "How did it start for you?" Sloane asked, becoming more and more curious about this. "What exactly was it about The House that made you so . . ."

She trailed off unintentionally, searching around for a word that meant "inordinately poised" or "immaculately put-together" with a slight hint of "acceptably Stepfordian," but Britt laughed before she could.

"Some of it is innate," Britt admitted with a shrug. "I'm not an anxious person. And I *am* an ambitious one, so admittedly there are moments when I make choices that other mothers might not. But it was The House that gave me the ability to do that." Coincidentally, when Britt spoke of The House there was a warm glow on her molten highlights; on the styling that looked like a professional blowout, which Britt said was "just a really good ceramic curling iron, I'll send you the link."

"The thing is," Britt continued, "coming of age in an all-female space was extremely rewarding. And I don't think you could argue it had anything to do with academia—I'm not advocating for all-girls high schools, believe me. It was an extracurricular space, a second home, a second chance at the kind of personal growth I'd needed as a teenager. I learned how to be a woman in The House."

Priscilla, who met Sloane at her office for coffee, said similar things. Priscilla had arrived with a batch of chocolate zucchini bread that was so decadent and rich that Sloane had to fight the impulse to moan aloud. "You have to understand, I'm not naturally good at making connections with people," Priscilla said, after dutifully sending Sloane the link for the zucchini bread. "I think the word for it these days is 'on the spectrum,' but the whole point of a spectrum is that everyone is on it somewhere, so yes, adapting is something we can do to varying degrees of success. And if I hadn't had The House, I don't think I would have felt comfortable enough—*safe* enough—to express my dreams, my ambitions, my desires. Nor would I have really learned how to make the kind of professional connections I needed later in life, especially in this industry."

It was a constant refrain, Sloane was learning. This theme of safety—The House as the ultimate safe place, in a way that felt like the witch's house in a fairy tale, something of near-magical significance. Sisterhood, Sloane learned, was a proper noun, as in: The House was a hearth for Sisterhood, where The Women grew into themselves.

She continued her interviews with a sort of mechanical probe, unsure what she was hoping to unearth, inert or perhaps merely circular in her narrative. What was the specific magic of Sisterhood that seemed so influential, such that it cast off the expectations of society, and, also, had set each woman on an almost inconceivable and certainly unreproducible domino-fall of social capital and luck? Each woman Sloane spoke to seemed to have benefitted from the "Who Run the World?" philosophy of womanhood—something very close to the girlboss, "*She*-E-O" mentality that eschewed traditional female constraints—and yet each woman was also hypercompetent at performing domestic femininity.

"It *is* uncanny, honestly," Sloane commented mindlessly to Max, eating from the container of autumn stew that Deirdre Voss had urged her to take home with her. ("You have a sick baby at home," Deirdre had said, "and I made a fucking vat of the stuff. It'll save you a night of cooking," she added, as if Sloane had any idea what made beef this tender or squash this bright. Sloane was a good cook, but it was like The Women had all taken some advanced symposium on adulthood that she had slept through that day.)

"I can't even form a pattern, really. I mean, what do they all have? The prestige of their University degrees, sure, and maybe there's something to this idea of all-female spaces being focused on personal growth, but how exactly does that lead to a Supreme Court clerkship or the fucking Pulitzer? Are they sacrificing virgins in the basement? Is it something in the water?"

"Where exactly is this research going?" Max asked, pausing beside Sloane at the kitchen table where she was again scrolling VidStar, ostensibly for the book. So far, there had been nothing especially illuminating. She supposed she could seek out other all-female spaces and see if she could discover the secret sauce via elementary compare-and-contrast, but where was she supposed to go? Did convents still exist? Should she pop by a gymnastics training center?

"I'm not sure yet," Sloane admitted, leaning back with a sigh. One of the other women Alex had recommended she speak with had made a bulgogi some days ago that made Sloane want to weep for craving it. The recipe was apparently pulled from *Bon Appétit*—she'd sent Sloane the link—and yet Sloane simply could not achieve the same rust-colored, caramelized result. Was it patience? Did Sloane lack patience? Did she lack *practice*? But then the others aside from Priscilla were all mothers whose time was equally as limited. How had they sprouted more time, and did it have something to do with unlocking a level of the game somehow?

Did Sloane need a cheat code?

"Well, just remember, this isn't the best use of your time if Burns isn't interested in it," Max pointed out, which was somehow more frustrating than Max leaving the microwave door open despite the fact that he was right. Maybe it was *because* he was right. Couldn't he be right about something else, such as what was best for engaging their daughter developmentally? Or performing the laundry with something beyond a perfunctory, indiscriminate cold-water cycle?

Alex needed Sloane to review the midterm grades for The Girls—a requirement from International, or so Sloane was informed—so, the following night, Sloane took Isla over to Alex's house, relieved to smell Bolognese already simmering on the stove. (Sloane hadn't even bothered cooking, which was starting to weigh on her socially, but not so much that she'd bring some half-assed version of her spaghetti down on Alex's door.)

"Lyla!" said Theo, which was his toddler-speak for Isla. In response, Isla smiled and waved with one pudgy hand from Sloane's arms.

"God, she's so precious," Alex said dreamily, which was another thing Sloane appreciated. Sloane didn't technically believe a more darling baby than Isla existed, so for all The Women to acknowledge this made her warm to them automatically, in a way that made her feel she was perhaps too close to what were supposed to be her subjects.

"What a magnificent squish she is," Alex declared with a quick tickle to Isla's side.

"Oh, you're a godsend," Sloane said the moment she clocked the parenting strongholds: curly pasta that Isla could eat with her hands, cheese ready for Isla to sprinkle. Sloane wanted to cry with relief—alarmingly, she realized that wasn't even hyperbole. Her eyes actually pricked from the kindness, the honest-to-god benevolence. "I swear, Isla's given up eating just to spite me."

"Oh, they get that way sometimes," Alex said. "It'll pass. And anyway, she's alive. She's safe. She's healthy. You're doing great."

"Low bar to clear," Sloane muttered, lowering Isla to the floor so she could wander over to where Theo was stacking his favorite set of beautiful, hygge-colored cups (Alex had sent her the link).

"It's not, though," Alex reassured her. "Come. Sit. Relax." She patted the cushioned chair.

"You've done so much," Sloane moaned, and Alex laughed. "I have to feed my son too, you know. It's really nothing. You're the one doing me a favor," she added, gesturing to the printed sheet of grades.

"God, as if! You got me all those interviews. And Priscilla said she wants me to submit a book proposal officially. She said she knows an agent who'd love the project—not that I know for sure what the project even is," Sloane said, glancing cursorily over the grades. They were good? What else did an academic advisor even do?

"So you've decided to go the non-academic route with Skit, then?" Alex asked, turning to stir the sauce on the stove.

"Well, I'll send Burns the same proposal, I guess. But maybe having some outside interest will make him . . . more amenable to it, I don't know." Sloane realized that even she had some doubt in what she was saying. Delusion was powerful stuff.

"He's an obstacle," Alex said, leveling a wooden spoon at Sloane as she appeared to come to the same conclusion. "Not an ally. After a certain point you have to allow yourself to stop jumping through hoops. If he won't recognize you as a person worthy of respect, nothing you do can change that. And that's not your fault, it's his."

The words struck Sloane unexpectedly, like the crack of a whip. "Wow." She exhaled swiftly. "I guess I hadn't thought about it that way."

"It's the same thing I tell The Girls," Alex said with a shrug. "You have limited reserves of energy. Don't keep throwing yourself at something that won't move. Find another way in. There's always another way."

"Do you think that's actually true, though?" Sloane said, and watched an odd wave of something pass over Alex's expression. "Not everyone will find a way in. I mean, in terms of, like, marginalized identities, or social capital, or *actual* capital—"

"The world is unfair," Alex said coolly, setting the wooden spoon down on the ceramic plate beside the stove. "But that's the purpose of sisterhood, to raise each other up. To help each other up the ladder. *They* are each other's allies. They are faithful to each other, and that's how we create the means to succeed. *We do it*," said Alex, with an almost biting acerbity. "We don't wait for someone to give us credit, because if we did we'd all toil in obscurity until we died."

Sloane glanced over her shoulder, checking on Isla and Theo. The two children were playing side by side, Theo stacking cups while Isla appeared to be organizing them.

"You know, I did notice," Sloane remarked over her shoulder to Alex, "that many of the alumnae have similar backgrounds. Difficult adolescences, maybe even some trauma. They all credit The House with giving them some kind of second chance."

She turned back to Alex in time to see her shrug. "That's what college is, isn't it?" Alex replied simply. "It's a bridge between adolescence and adulthood. A place to explore things intellectually, to decide who you want to be."

"But within The House specifically—"

"Sloane," said Alex with a laugh, "are you investigating us or something?"

"I think I'm jealous, honestly." It was only after Sloane said it that she realized it was true. "I just . . . I wish I felt that secure, I guess. But that's not much of a research topic, is it? I mean, what's the conclusion to the book? What's the ending?"

"That when women help women, we all win," said Alex, easily.

"Sure, but how can we apply that to the average reader when you just admitted that this kind of success only exists for people with access to The House's connections?"

"Are you writing a self-help book?" asked Alex wryly, before beginning to plate the spaghetti. "Just . . . let it marinate for a bit, let it stew. I'm sure it'll come to you."

"What about you?" Sloane suddenly asked, struck that she hadn't thought to ask sooner.

"What about me?" Alex replied without looking up.

"Did you . . . what was your life like, before The House?"

"Oh, Sloane." Alex shook her head with a mirthful sigh. "I'm just another girl who got let down by men, that's all. I really think that's what everything comes down to."

The following day Sloane sat in her office, residual self-loathing from Isla's daily drop-off fading to an unproductive replay of the dinner. The rest of the meal had been focused on the children—Theo had been especially proud to show off to Sloane and Isla his new technique for jumping from his play-couch to the sofa—with a few minutes of looking over grades. The Girls now had a 3.89 cumulative GPA, which struck Sloane as wildly above the campus average but that Alex waved away, saying they chose smart women in the first place, and the emphasis they placed on scholarship accounted for the rest.

"What about The Country Wife?" asked Arya from his chair.

Sloane hadn't realized she'd been mulling her notes aloud. "What?"

"You interviewed everyone who fit the pattern," Arya said. "So what about the outlier?"

"Oh." Sloane tried to play this off like an oversight rather than what it actually was—procrastination. Intellectually she understood that she could not move forward without talking to Caroline Collins; in a deeper, more amorphous way, she also understood she would be betraying Alex the moment she did.

"God, do you think she'll want to talk to me?" Sloane play-acted hesitation, trying to make her protestations true, as if they could be presented as evidence to the court of her good intentions sometime later. "I mean, what am I even going to tell her? I'm writing a book about her sorority? And I doubt I could ask Alex for her contact information—"

"She's an influencer," Arya said with a shrug. "She definitely checks her DMs. And I think you should tell her the truth. She's probably interested in telling her story—that's what her whole account is."

"A story?"

"Of course. What's a brand other than another way to tell a story?" Arya was grinning at Sloane like a dog who'd set a tennis ball at her feet.

Sloane hemmed and hawed uselessly, a function of being ethically stuck. "I already know Burns isn't interested in this, though."

"You keep going back and forth on whether Burns's opinion matters," Arya observed. "Either you care or you don't."

"It's not really Burns." It was something, though, Sloane realized. She wanted Burns's approval, followed by Burns's apology, to prove her instincts sound. And of course she felt that way! Max had wanted the University, to put down roots, to let their daughter grow up in this mecca of elite intellectualism, to afford Isla every resource in the world, even though—as Sloane knew—many of those resources would still regard her as someone whose interests weren't serious, meaningful, or profound.

"Look." Before she fully noticed it, Arya was on his feet, bending over the edge of her desk to lean on his elbows, his face floating before hers. "Your idea is solid. It's interesting, objectively so. If some old white dude doesn't like it, so what? Plenty of other people will." He paused, his mouth quirking up at the corners in a way that drew Sloane's eye. "But you gotta be okay with danger, Doc. You can't just talk to the people that the Sorority Queen wants you to talk to. She's treating you like the media, putting her best face forward, which is fine, that's her job. But your job?" He leaned closer. "Yours is to find the ugly. You want the skeletons. You want the sins."

Sloane couldn't help a shiver. The presence of Arya's mouth so close to hers helped nothing. She thought of Alex's red lipstick, the cool knife-edge of her voice when Sloane seemed occasionally to get too close, to break the rules. A part of Sloane unfurled like a petal, stretching out, reaching. Dancing close to something wild, something hot.

"The sins?" Sloane echoed.

"The sins." Arya's eyes glinted. "That's where the real story lives."

22

The pledges were taken to the second floor, blindfolded (a *thin* blindfold—Nina could still safely see the glow of her votive candle), and led to separate rooms in pairs. Every heartbeat seemed accelerated; each perfect forehead was suddenly host to a sheen of clammy sweat.

The hum was back and ever nearer. Time alone moved too slowly; everything else was too fast. More than once Nina had seen their new member educator Nicole slightly twitch; small spasms of something.

Dalil reached out for Nina with the hand that wasn't holding the candle, gripping Nina's fingers with something that was part nerves, part childlike excitement.

"I hope we see a ghost," Dalil whispered to Nina, her voice warm in Nina's ear.

"I hope we see ten ghosts," Nina whispered back, and Dalil giggled.

"Quiet," said Nicole's voice. Nina felt dizzy, or possibly dazed. The wave of a cramp metastasized and she rode it, ignored it. Nicole was leading Dalil, who in turn led Nina. "Watch your step."

Nina tripped a little over the threshold despite having been warned. This was probably Tessa's room, then, which had an uneven board in the entrance that Tessa frequently complained about. Nina knew this was all very silly, that nothing scary could possibly happen to her, that all of this was for performance, for drama. Still, she enjoyed the mystery, the unknown that was her crossing from one version of herself to the next.

"State your name, sisters," came Nicole's voice again as she maneuvered Nina to one spot in the room, Dalil to another. She seemed to be speaking to someone other than Dalil and Nina.

"Fawn Carter," answered a low breath of Fawn's voice across the room.

"Tessa Alden." That came from somewhere just behind Nina, a handful of inches away.

"Will you speak for these new members?" asked Nicole.

"With the blessings of our founders, I speak for Nina Kaur," said Tessa.

"With the blessings of our founders, I speak for Dalil Serrano," Fawn replied.

"Do you know these women to be of righteous honor and upstanding caliber? Are they fit to join our ranks?"

"They are," said Tessa and Fawn.

"Sisters, we call upon you now," said Nicole's voice. "Be with us. Guide us."

Nina felt another unexpected shiver as Tessa undid her blindfold. The room was dark and still, the moon glowing brightly just outside the frame. The only light came from the votive candles still clutched in each of the girls' hands.

Across from Nina was Dalil, Fawn's free hand on her shoulder. Nina caught Fawn's eye, and Fawn raised a finger to her lips. Like Nina and Dalil, Fawn wore no makeup, no jewelry. Her dress was white muslin, angelic. She seemed younger than Nina had ever seen her, impossible and distantly familiar, like someone Nina had known from a previous life. Tessa's hand mirrored Fawn's, set on Nina's shoulder.

Later, Nina would learn that the rest of her pledge class had been distributed in larger groups, three or four pairs to a room. She was glad to have been in a smaller setting, for a more intimate avowal. The implication that anyone else even existed outside their foursome would have seemed silly, almost absurd. The humming frequency wrapped tighter, lassoing in around the room. To Nina it seemed they were the center of the universe; that nothing of consequence would happen outside this space, this fellowship, these breaths.

"Sisters," whispered Fawn. "Speak."

And abruptly, Nina's candle went out.

23

Deadline: imminent. Answers: here.

When Caroline Collins opened the door to her recently renovated farmhouse, Sloane caught a rush of freshly baked bread, the savory tang of meat roasting in the oven, and a top note of freshly picked flowers—a conflagration of experience that was at once folksy and alive.

The homestead was a good thirty or so miles outside the University, a journey that departed the highway for a two-lane interstate until finally the asphalt dwindled down to an unpaved road. From the drive in, as the sun gradually bled into the endless stretch of horizon, Sloane had spotted familiar hallmarks of The Country Wife's fantasy theater—the barn with the small drift of pigs and the dairy cow named Dolly, after Dolly Parton (one of the pigs was named Jolene). Sloane had parked self-consciously in the finished drive outside the farmhouse, a little jarred by her own admiration for the stonework beneath her feet. Before she could knock, the house's video doorbell had flashed with acknowledgment of her presence, and the door opened as if by magic.

Caroline wore one of those milkmaid-style linen dresses, her skin dewy and effortless, her natural black hair fading artfully to gold. "Come in," she said, breezing aside in the doorway for Sloane to enter. "I hope the traffic wasn't too bad."

It hadn't been great, but that seemed an unpleasant place to start a conversation. Nor would it be appropriate for Sloane to mention the argument she'd just had with Max, who was irritated at having to stay home with a cranky, newly pink-eyed Isla (as if Sloane had planned on pink eye, of all the fucking things!), and wanted to know why exactly Sloane was throwing away the job he'd pulled so many strings to secure for her, which she insisted she wasn't doing, or would have insisted on, except she hadn't heard him put it in those terms before.

"Are you saying that I owe you?" Sloane asked him, and it must have shown on her face, the proverbial blow and her consequential reeling. The unexpected confirmation that her progressive marriage, her domestic safe place that she had built with her own two hands—the love that she had chosen without question or doubt!—had been contained within an invisible expectation this whole time. "Is that what you're saying?"

"Of course not." Max raised one hand to his forehead as Isla began to cry, as if this were something Sloane was doing to him; as if it did not destroy Sloane in every conceivable way not to reach for her daughter and give up all pretense of existing beyond Isla's immediate needs. "I'm just tired, Sloane. I've got term papers to grade, lectures to finish. You haven't exactly been present lately." Oh, nice, as if she hadn't hated herself enough.

"I'm here exactly as often as you're here. More so." Sloane couldn't believe what Max was telling her, that what she had anecdotally observed to be true was actual, concrete fact to him: that her job was less serious than his; that her job only existed because of him; that her absence was a burden while his was earned. That she, as the mother, owed more to Isla than he did, or worse—that Sloane, as the less valuable person in the partnership, could not equitably rely on the importance of her own work. "I'm doing what you said, Max. I'm trying to show Burns that I'm valuable enough for tenure." She heard Alex in her head then: *You can't show a man that you have value. Either he believes it or he doesn't.* "Max, I know you're under a lot of pressure, but have you considered that maybe so am I?"

Oh, but Sloane's tolerance for hardship was so much higher, had always been higher. Her ability to withstand stress, to bend but never break, had always exceeded his. People were imperfect; of course they had their flaws. Sloane could be overly sensitive, she could be unpredictable and a little too rigid, she had a temper she often lost. But Sloane could also handle exhaustion better than Max could; she could roll with every disruption, whatever conflict might arise. She took on the heavier burdens because she could; because her love was naturally generous; because she understood that stress cost her less than it did him. Max, he just didn't bounce like her, he simply couldn't do it. A personality detail. Surely not structural. Surely not something he could improve.

Which was bullshit, wasn't it? Because when Sloane had a flaw, she adjusted. When Max identified a weakness in her, she fixed it. When something wasn't working, she simply fucking *changed*.

But none of that did anything to make her feel less guilty about leaving her daughter, nor did it soothe the brittle annoyance she currently felt about Max.

So Sloane turned to Caroline Collins, who referred to her own husband as Dear, and said, "I'm just grateful you were willing to chat with me."

"Oh Dr. Hartley, believe me, it's my pleasure." Caroline turned, motioning for Sloane to follow into her open-plan kitchen, a familiar sight by now. The other alumnae of The House—The Women—had similar tastes, and the bottle of wine set out on the island with two glasses beside it was no longer an unfamiliar sight for Sloane. There was a now-predictable spread of three cheeses, the crusty bread that Sloane had smelled from the entryway, and a small dusting of purple pansies and orange dahlias, ostensibly for decoration. There was also a selection of grapes so shiny they almost looked candied, or fake.

"Help yourself," Caroline said, bending to check something in the oven. "Dinner's nearly finished, just needs about ten minutes to rest." She poured herself some wine, then offered the bottle to

Sloane. "I know you're driving, but you've got to try this one. The vineyard I'm partnering with sent some over last week and it is *genuinely* to die for."

In real life, Caroline's voice was just as soothing as her VidStar content suggested. Sloane accepted a small amount in her glass, wondering aloud, "Do you get these kinds of interview requests often?"

"I do hear from potential advertisers a fair amount," Caroline said. "Not usually any sociologists, though, much less any that are associated with The House."

Sloane wondered if she detected a tone of irony in there somewhere, although she could have been imagining it. "I'll be honest, I don't know The Girls very well," she attempted. "I've only been an advisor for a short period of time, and truthfully, I'm still in awe. Everyone who's walked those halls has turned out incredibly impressive—I feel a bit humbled, honestly, being just a lowly adjunct," Sloane said with a fashionably self-deprecating laugh.

Caroline said nothing, so Sloane continued, "Like I said, I'm so grateful you were willing to talk to me. I mean, you've had such a wildly successful couple of years," she added, hoping to soften Caroline's placid homemaker mask, "so I'm sure you must get all kinds of interest."

Caroline stopped pouring, looking down for a moment before her eyes rose shrewdly to Sloane's.

"Alex doesn't know you're here," she said. "Does she?"

Sloane's heart seized. "What?"

"Oh, come on," Caroline said lightly, with the disdain of a woman twice her age. "Alex doesn't consider me successful. Neither do you."

She gave Sloane a look, which Sloane attempted to refute.

"Alex was very encouraging, actually, of the project. Because the book isn't *about* The House, really," Sloane added hastily, scraping a knife over what was almost certainly hand-churned honey butter, if only to busy her hands. "It's more about feminine power generally, and what makes a 'good' woman, and the ways that success in feminine terms can be—"

"And I am, what, powerful?" Caroline seemed amused by this. Sloane very wisely said nothing.

"I bought this," said Caroline, gesturing vaguely to her farmhouse. "I made over a million dollars in sponsored content alone last year. I manage our finances and investments. My husband's aunt left him ten thousand dollars a few years ago and I turned it into this."

Caroline's heels clipped on the kitchen floor as she walked over and bent down, knees together, to check on the steaks broiling in the oven.

"I do think you're very successful," Sloane said. "I'm not surprised you're the savvy one in your relationship, especially given what I know about The House." She paused, reevaluating whether candor might take her further than flattery. "I guess I just wonder, then, about the . . . values."

"You mean the cross between anti-vaxxer Barbie and *Little House on the Prairie*?" asked Caroline, checking the temperature of her meat before rising to fetch her oven mitts, which were pristine, natural fibers with the modern-looking monogram of CC.

"I wouldn't say that," Sloane hedged, and Caroline laughed.

"Alex would. More accurately, she already has. I believe she once called my audience 'a slew of fascist bimbos.'" Caroline set the meat on a wooden carving board to rest, reaching for her glass of wine. "Of course, it's not exactly *bimboism*, is it? So there's that for Alex's spirit of accuracy."

"I don't want to suggest I've come here as Alex's missionary or something," said Sloane, frowning a little. Maybe she should have leaned harder into the idea that Alex didn't approve of her presence. "I find all of this interesting, I really do—"

"All of what?" Caroline asked, arching one polished brow.

"Well, I suppose—" Sloane hesitated. "Is it real?" she asked. "Is this you building a brand, or is it sincere?"

"Can't I be sincere in my brand?" Caroline seemed to carefully dance away from delivering an outright challenge. Still, Sloane saw a flicker of extreme calculation behind Caroline's eyes. She understood almost innately that this was a woman well-trained by Alex.

"Well." Sloane took a sip of her wine to buy some time. "Speaking as a sociologist, I think I can safely guess that your demographic is—"

"Young, impressionable women," Caroline confirmed. "Give or take some horny incels and neofascists." Caroline's lips curled up, inviting Sloane to take up arms. "Say the word 'traitor' out loud and maybe we can take the gloves off."

"Well, that's the question, isn't it? Is Alex right about you—are you dangerous?" Sloane said, settling more comfortably on the kitchen stool. "Are you exploiting other women and profiting off their adoration while knowingly contributing to a system that holds them back? The traditional patriarchal system that your content appears to uphold can only be damaging to them," Sloane remarked. "Conservative women are, arguably, aligning with men for power that will only be used against them, whether they grasp that or not. Do you feel any sense of accountability, or even awareness?"

Sloane paused to watch Caroline watch her. There was something very prowling about her, something meticulously on the hunt.

"Do you think, for example," Sloane attempted, spinning out the thought experiment, "that you will have to have a child in the next few years purely for the sake of the brand?"

"That's an interesting question." Caroline's eyes flashed. "You're a mother, aren't you?"

"Yes," said Sloane. "I have a daughter."

"And you wouldn't want her watching my content."

"No," Sloane said honestly. "I would not."

Caroline leaned against the counter, appearing thoughtful. Unhurried.

"What do you think a good woman is?" Caroline asked. She seemed genuinely pensive, and Sloane considered it.

"I suppose it's kind of impossible to remove the constraints of the patriarchy from that question," Sloane hedged.

"Oh, come on." Caroline smirked at her. "Take off your sociology hat for a moment. What would *you* be, if you were a good woman? What would you know how to do then that you don't know now?"

"God. Almost anything." The answer seemed snatched from somewhere in Sloane's lungs. "I wish I had a better temper and no dysmorphia. I wish I had thicker skin, or that I could put down my goddamn phone. But isn't that more a question of what do I wish I were?" Sloane mused aloud. "Not what a good woman is generally."

"Yes and no, though, right? Because the answer to a good woman should be a good person," said Caroline shrewdly. "If we were really *free*—if this were a winnable game—then your womanhood would have nothing to do with it."

"Is that possible? Removing my womanhood from the equation?" Sloane was intrigued, both by the idea this was all a game and by the question of whether she could exist outside her social identity. But then again, Caroline Collins had gone to a prestigious University, where she had been selected and shepherded by the most high-achieving women Sloane had ever met.

"The Country Wife posits not." Caroline seemed playful, or possibly more toying, as if with her food, when it came to dissociating her identity. "Of course, The Country Wife is a moment, not an institution. That's the nature of content and consumption, don't you think?"

"So then this is a job," Sloane observed aloud.

"Digital content creation has always been a job," countered Caroline. "And lifestyle content is a uniquely feminine space. It follows that if there is money to be made, someone will make it. If not me, then someone worse."

Sloane sipped her wine. "Worse in that they're more sincere?"

"Possibly." A timer went off, an old-fashioned egg timer that looked quaintly vintage. Caroline began slicing into a large, irregularly shaped steak, which sagged juicily, visibly tender.

"Maybe I'm just very good at it," Caroline said, carving up the meat. "The domestic roles. The homesteading. Maybe there's no harm in monetizing the fact that I'm pretty and I like animals and I can cook. Maybe," she said, looking up for a moment, "the truly unfeminist thing would be to devote my life to my husband *without* an audience, so that *only he* benefited from the things that I know. From the woman that I am, which is considered good specifically because I'm a nurturer. A natural caregiver."

"So that's a good woman?" prodded Sloane. "A good wife? A good mother?"

Caroline rolled her eyes, turning to Sloane to distribute thin-sliced pieces of steak across filigreed Italianate porcelain. "Wife and mother are roles. Womanhood is intrinsic. Not," she said, stabbing a warning blade into the air at Sloane, "in the biological sense. I'm not a fucking Republican."

"But you're enabling Republican values," argued Sloane. "Aren't you? Could you even say you're not one publicly without alienating the vast majority of your audience?" Caroline was carefully arranging the steaks on the plate, adding a sprig of fresh rosemary for garnish. "You're the first step down a dystopian rabbit hole, algorithmically speaking," Sloane continued. "You're the entry point to alt-right content, and to the belief that what you do is what women were meant to do, *for* men."

"Let me tell you something. The women who believe this? They're going to believe anything they're told," said Caroline without looking up. "I mean, come on. You think any Black women are buying into this shit? You think many disability advocates are into doing everything the long way around?"

"So you're both complicit and unaccountable, then," Sloane challenged. "And you don't see the hypocrisy in that?"

Caroline's eyes had a hungry glint, like someone looking at a pig for slaughter. Pity, that's what it was. "You don't win this game with virtue, Dr. Hartley. Convincing people that you're smart or that you're right doesn't change anything. All there is in this world is money. Either you make it and use it or someone else will."

"That's what you took from Alex?" Sloane found herself genuinely disappointed, almost hurt, even though Alex had only been Caroline's sorority advisor, not her personal sensei. Still, somehow, irrationally, it was as if Caroline had left a papercut on Sloane's heart.

She almost wished Caroline had turned out completely brainwashed, earnestly praising her husband and kissing the flag while spewing vitriol about vaccinations. It would have been easier, more detached from reality, but more honest. This—this was unbearable, because Sloane had no argument. Because Sloane could only say what she had always been told, which was to try anyway. Try harder. And though it was true, it had never particularly moved her to anything but exhaustion and anxiety and fear.

Caroline slid the plated steak toward Sloane, a silver meat fork in the shape of a decorative trident placed ever so carefully beside it.

"I don't hate Alex," Caroline said, appearing to concede to some internal monologue. "I'm grateful to Alex. She taught me something invaluable. She gave me an enormous gift, and I will always treasure it. She and I just disagree about the broader mission. The greater goal."

Sloane picked up the trident, spearing a slice of steak to transfer to her plate. It spilled over with shining juices, though it had taken more effort to pierce than she'd expected. It had to be a particularly muscular cut, which seemed like a rookie mistake for someone who made a living on domesticity.

"I wish I were better at this," Sloane said, realizing that weeks of research with women her age had probably made her expect too much from a twenty-five-year-old hobbyist. "I wish I could cook—like, *really* cook, and know how to do everything correctly, not just prepare meals from instructions. You're right, I do feel like I should be better at all this stuff. The caretaking, the homemaking. Your taste is beautiful, and it's so obviously innate." Sloane shook her head, sluicing a crust of bread through the juices of the steak. "I can see why you have such a following."

"You think this is innate?" Caroline looked amused, partitioning a bit of steak for herself. "When I joined The House I couldn't even boil an egg. I'm still not very good at my mom's recipes. Most of her stuff says to ask the gods, who never answer for me." She paused, half smiling to herself. "Probably because I'm a traitor."

"So do you think that's it?" asked Sloane, taking a sip of wine. "Does leaning into the hearth, the womanhood of it all—does that somehow give us more than it takes from us?"

Caroline, who had been drinking her wine, snorted. "What?"

"I just—" Sloane felt her cheeks flush. "I'm just, you know, speculating. That having a women-dominated space must allow for something unique. That something about sisterhood must have a genuine impact on personal growth that contributes to the success of everyone who comes out of it. Maybe that's the reason for the mommy blogging, the trad wife thing, these micro-collectives of women that are really just . . . just *safe spaces,* and maybe that's enough t—"

"Jesus Christ. Stop." Caroline set down her glass, looking at Sloane with something like amusement. "You have no idea, do you?"

"Well, I was in a house, but not *The* House," said Sloane, before Caroline held up a hand.

"Look, Dr. Hartley, let's be clear about something. I'm a hypocrite," she said flatly. "I know it and I've made my peace with it, because I think there's something easier than Alex's version of killing yourself just to lose a race against the ministry of dudes who couldn't care less if you're dead or alive. I don't care if some fucking white woman in Omaha votes for a sex offender just because I gave her a recipe to make bread. I've given up on what I can't control, and if I don't wear the costume and say the lines, Karen and her friends decide I'm out here spreading China flu. But you? You should ask better questions." Caroline leaned closer, a manic spark in her eye. "Stop asking if I'm some brainwashed cunt and start considering why I'd want anyone to *think* I was."

Caroline gently speared a thin slice of steak, raising it to her lips. She closed her eyes, breathing it in. "The marinade," she said, "really ties the meal together."

She took a bite and chewed, gesturing to Sloane's plate.

"Bon appétit," Caroline offered, inviting Sloane to follow suit with a distant toast of her wineglass.

Obligingly, Sloane dressed her fork with a velvety ribbon of meat, folding it over on itself until it was perfectly bite-sized. It smelled rich, hot with chili oil, something almost earthy. She raised it to her lips and realizing Caroline was watching her—waiting with something like anticipation for Sloane's verdict on the marinade.

The meat was, as Sloane had anticipated from her initial glance, dense and a little gamey. Savory and mild in flavor beneath the chili glaze, but hardly the kind of disintegrating perfection she'd experience from any of the other Women—the kind of cut that melted sensually away, almost like a kiss.

"How is it?" asked Caroline, her voice slightly husky with fascination.

There was a new energy present in her posture now, something tightly coiled. Sloane tried and failed to think what it could be.

"You said you learned to cook at The House?" Sloane asked, or tried to ask. The meat was unyielding and tough to swallow; she held a hand guardedly over her mouth, struggling for dignity as she chewed. "When I was in a sorority—sorry," she said, referencing her mouth and its ongoing endeavors. "Mouth's full—it's just that when I was in a sorority, we lived off Red Vines and stale Cheetos. I always thought romanticized, high-minded starvation was a sort of rite of passage for the college years."

Caroline shrugged, running her finger through the pink-tinted juices on her plate before bringing it back up to her mouth, sucking lightly. "We all developed a very . . . distinctive palate over the course of our time there, I suppose."

Sloane said nothing, and Caroline laughed. She drained her glass of wine and poured herself another, holding it aloft for another toast.

"To good women," she said. "May we be them, may we raise them, and may they all enjoy their little treats."

Sloane tried to echo the toast but couldn't. She felt like she'd been chewing for an absolute age. "Cheers," she managed to choke out, forcing a swallow, and clinked her glass against Caroline's before finally washing the bite down with a gulp. "What kind of meat is this?"

"I know it's a bit tough to swallow at first, but of all the organs, heart has a very mild flavor that I quite enjoy," said Caroline. "You get used to it. Eventually you even develop a taste for it. Plus, god, all those nutrients." She took an overlong sip. "It's worth it just for the health benefits, you know?"

"Heart?" The swallow of wine stuck like a tennis ball in Sloane's throat. "Beef heart?"

"Do you like it?" The Country Wife's eyes twinkled with something. Low burning derangement? Sloane's heart canted, then thundered; her stomach churned. "I'll send you the link."

Then Caroline smiled vacantly, as if reliving a happy memory in the recesses of her mind. "You know what you haven't asked me, Dr. Hartley? If The Country Wife is more than a lie. I mean, it's absurd, right? It's just funny to me that you haven't even wondered whether it's *so* dishonest that maybe it's a cover for something . . . bigger," she mused, her eyes flicking down to the steak on Sloane's plate. "Or something worse."

"What am I eating?" Sloane suddenly asked. Her tongue was rubbery, almost ashy with sediment from the steak, and she gagged, doubling over on her stool. "What did you give me?"

Caroline leaned toward Sloane, bracing herself over the kitchen island. Her eyes, Sloane realized, were almost black.

"If you think *I'm* bad," whispered Caroline, "just wait 'til you find out what they're doing in that house."

24

Nina couldn't prove there were ghosts in the room with them. She couldn't prove there weren't. Everything felt electrically charged, sensually tensed. Behind her eyes she kept seeing flashes of something, rippling flanks. The glimmer of an ax falling. An osseous glint of bared teeth. Girl glitter, Nina thought, and shivered, lightheaded, through another wave of cramps.

"And now," said Fawn, "to end the ritual, you'll each take a drink from the loving cup."

She turned first to Nina and Tessa, passing them the three-handled, wrought-iron goblet with her fingers still on one of the handles.

"It has to be drunk with three hands," Fawn said softly, her eyes finding Nina's in the dark. Suddenly the pain in Nina's core felt deeper, more of an ache. "Hold it while Tess and I drink, okay?"

Nina nodded, unable to speak even if she'd been asked to. She accepted the third handle and watched, teeth clenched, as Fawn raised the cup to her lips. Her long sip brought Nina swaying closer, the fulcrum of their triad shifting to the zenith of Fawn's mouth. Then Fawn ran her tongue over her lips, her eyes straying to Nina's as Tessa took her turn.

Nina was next. Behind her, Dalil stood waiting. Nina reached her free hand back for Dalil, who squeezed once, then let go. Nina's pulse was in her throat. She thought again of teeth, the caress of a blade gliding smoothly over skin. The invulnerability of safety. The wave of a cramp nearly brought her to her knees.

"We're here with you, Nina," Tessa said.

Fawn's voice was hardly a whisper, her empty hand finding the base of Nina's spine to rest on the axis of pressure. "Just bring it to your lips and drink."

The words climbed gently up the notches of Nina's spine. Nina held the cup with her left hand, Tessa on her right, Fawn tilting the goblet toward her as Nina raised it to her mouth. In the dimness of the unlit room she couldn't see its color; could only smell the tang of something deep and unfamiliar.

Even in the dark, she could see the faint stains on Fawn's white teeth, the viscous wine that slicked her gums. Girl glitter.

It touched Nina's lips and was biting, sharp, like copper. Nina choked with surprise, and Fawn's free hand settled on hers.

"Be careful," Tessa warned. "Don't waste a drop."

Fawn's lips were so close to hers. So close.

Still, the smell from the cup was overwhelming, acrid. Nina struggled not to gag. "But—"

Tessa's hand was on her waist, her grip reassuringly tight. "We'll explain later," she whispered. "You'll see. As soon as we explain it, you'll understand."

The smell of iron seemed to pulse behind Nina's sinuses, throbbing like a migraine. She felt dizzy and uncertain, like if either girl loosened their grips, she might sway.

Fawn's voice when she spoke again was low and intimate. The way a lover said *good morning*. The way a mother said *trust me*.

"Nina. Drink."

Nina closed her eyes, she inhaled deeply, and she drank. She choked again, coughing, and felt Tessa release her, moving a step to shift the cup to Dalil.

Fawn hung back, reaching out for Nina. She stroked the side of Nina's mouth gently with the outer edge of her thumb, dragging the nail lightly across Nina's lips until they parted for a soundless sigh. Painless.

Then Fawn wiped the last of the blood away, and Nina's vision swam.

PART IV

INVITATION

Is it just me or has no one else noticed that the "feminist" lifestyle is destroying their happiness?? I don't want to girlboss for 40+ hours a week, I want to be outside!

—Transcript from a VidStar by @TheCountryWife

NINE

WEEKS

TO

DINNER.

25

"What kind of meat is this?" Sloane felt herself reaching behind her for her purse, unsure what exactly the move would be from here. Did she really believe Caroline was dangerous? Yes, actually, she did, though it seemed sillier and sillier, feeling threatened by this girl in a white linen dress. White! Did she actually cook in *white linen*? Was that somehow the most insane part?

Never mind, Sloane thought as Caroline reached down with the opulent pitchfork, selecting a particularly moist-looking slice of meat. She nudged it, letting the liquid ooze out, candy-colored, as Sloane took another step in retreat. Caroline herself was definitely the most insane part.

"Just tell me," Sloane felt herself plead, and Caroline laughed, raising the pitchfork to her lips.

"Do you really think I get clear skin from a water bottle?" Caroline asked. "That my hair's this fucking shiny because of some shampoo that anyone can buy on Amazon?"

"What the fuck did you give me?" Sloane felt sure she was going to vomit. She gagged again, this time on the sense that whatever still lived in her throat might vengefully resurrect.

"It's a common historical ritual, you know," said Caroline, swirling the wine in her glass as Sloane retched dangerously into her palm. "The ancient Egyptians believed blood was an elixir. The Germans believed drinking blood from a wise person meant ingesting their wisdom—not to mention the myriad health benefits of the organs themselves. And surely you've heard of women who eat their own placenta? Lots of mammals do it," Caroline said sweetly. "It's because the body naturally offers you exactly what you need."

"Stop," Sloane said into her hand, retching perilously again as the door behind them opened and slammed shut. "Oh god—"

"Caroline." The sudden materialization of another voice in the room was so shocking to Sloane she managed to swallow her forthcoming vomit. "For fuck's sake."

"Oh, Alex!" Caroline exclaimed, with a gleeful, put-on voice of girlish innocence. "I suppose you decided to join us after all. Wine?" she offered pleasantly.

Sloane looked up to find Alex standing beside the door of Caroline's farmhouse with her arms tightly crossed, a look of annoyance etched explicitly across her face.

"Get in the car," Alex said to Sloane, her eyes still fixed on Caroline. "Now."

"What? *Fuck* no." Sloane shuddered, the brine of her own stomach acid now curdling on her tongue.

"Get in the car," Alex repeated, her eyes sliding sharply to Sloane, "*now*. We're leaving."

Sloane gagged again, desperate for water, unsure whether anything here could be trusted. "No way," she rasped. "My car is here, and if you think I'm going anywhere with you—"

"It's *beef heart*," Alex snapped, her impatience a sudden, horrific surge of perspective—the disappointment of a mother rather than the unhinged rantings of a maybe-cannibal.

For a moment, Sloane was able to recall a thread of sensations she'd always hated, like realizing it was April Fool's Day, or the third night with no contact after having trusted that a boy would call you back.

From behind the kitchen island, Caroline let out a bray of a laugh at Sloane's expense.

"She's just fucking with you, dumbass," said Alex flatly. "Get in the car, okay? I'll get your car for you tomorrow. You're in shock, you shouldn't be driving."

It was true, Sloane was in no position to drive. The new-old reminder, the one that had been there ever since Isla's birth, rang out again in Sloane's head: the fact that she could not die, she simply couldn't. She had to come home to Isla or who would raise her daughter, who would comfort her, who would protect her from harm, who would teach Isla how to be? Who would tell Isla who *Sloane* had been, and how could Isla ever know how hard and desperately Sloane had tried to do right by her if Sloane threw her life away now?

Alex was here, a new character in Sloane's waking nightmare, for better or worse, and thank god she was. Sloane wanted to crumble with relief. She felt like a child, but for a moment, there was something beautiful in that. What she wanted most desperately then was for Alex to take her away, to stroke her hair, to tell her the monsters under her bed weren't real. Her hands were shaking, she felt impotently nauseated, cold chills still running up and down her spine.

How could she be a mother when she was still just an idiot baby? How could she get up every morning and not sob to death over being so fucking dumb?

Sloane picked up her purse and did what she was told. She walked silently to the door, Caroline's laughter unignorable behind her. "Bon appétit, *Dr.* Hartley," Caroline called again at Sloane's back, and Sloane shuddered.

Alex's hand gripped her shoulder, hard, once she came within reach. "I'll explain everything in the car," Alex said in a low voice.

Sloane said nothing, only climbing obediently into the passenger's side of Alex's electric SUV.

Alex got into the driver's side, starting the car and cranking the heat. Sloane still felt like she might throw up if she opened her mouth. Alex's car smelled familiar, clean, and alive. In the backseat was Theo's car seat, his toys.

Alex was real, Sloane realized. Alex was a normal person, and Caroline was not. The nightmare was slowly fading.

"It's my fault," Alex muttered to herself, reversing out of Caroline's driveway. "I knew you were a little too curious about Caroline, but I just—" She sighed. "I thought if you just spoke to some of the others . . . I don't know. I guess I thought you'd lose interest." She paused, then shook her head with a scoff. "Nah. I just trusted you. That's on me."

Sloane said nothing.

"Caroline's a problem," Alex acknowledged after another moment, leaning onto her left elbow as she guided the steering wheel with her right hand. They'd pulled into the remote country road Sloane had taken earlier while it was still light out, which seemed eerier now than it had on the drive in. "I'm handling it."

"You're *handling* it?" Sloane felt herself speak without realizing she'd meant to, her voice almost slurred when it finally came out. "I really thought she was giving me, you know. *Human* heart."

She knew how ridiculous she sounded; how little she could explain the sense that had nonetheless lodged deeply in her soul that something about Caroline's behavior was dangerously off, and that Sloane's sense of wrongness about Caroline had come from the same place as her unshakeable curiosity about The House. But then, that was exactly what Caroline had wanted her to believe, wasn't it?

Maybe what had driven Sloane to investigate The House had nothing to do with sociology—or everything to do with it. Maybe it was born from the usual instinct women had to hate each other, to sniff out the *other,* the weakness, the root cause of envy that invariably became the thing that didn't belong. Maybe Sloane, too, was a vessel for the patriarchal flaw that meant a group of inordinately successful women simply *had* to be doing something unnatural. Maybe it was a resentment so natural and socially programmed that Sloane hadn't needed more than a prank to be convinced she'd been right to judge.

Still, she couldn't shake it. The feeling like she'd finally found the sticky gear in the overall workings of the fallacy—the thing that logically hadn't fit between The Girls who entered The House and The Women who came out.

Its skeletons. Its sins.

"I know it's stupid," Sloane sighed, "but for a second, I really believed her. She didn't seem crazy. She seemed—"

"She was fucking with you," Alex said again, confidently.

"But can you prove that? Because I've never eaten anything like that." Sloane shuddered. "And you didn't see her face when she was talking about the ancient fucking Egyptians."

Alex didn't answer. Sloane felt her cheeks heat with something, some desire for an appropriate counterweight. For Alex to be angry, either at Sloane or at Caroline, to react in some extreme way because it was what the moment was owed. "I mean, what a prank, right? It seems so . . . so . . . I don't know, it just doesn't make sense!" Sloane blurted out, interrupting herself. "Why would she do that to me? What problem did she have with me?"

"It's not you." Sloane caught the motion of Alex's jaw tensing in the low glimmer of a rare passing streetlight. "It's me, Sloane. It's a tantrum, that's all. She told me you were coming. I would've been there sooner, but my usual babysitter was booked and I had to drop Theo off at Britt's—anyway." Alex's mouth tightened. "The point is, it's not you, it's me." She paused, drumming her fingers on the wheel. "And anyway, I was going to tell you."

"Tell me what, exactly?" Sloane said with a tired, sardonic grumble. "That Caroline's crazy, or that all this time you've been commiserating with me and playing with my baby and encouraging my research, you've actually been running a sorority house full of cannibals?"

It sounded so ridiculous out loud. Too ridiculous.

And yet what had Caroline said? That it wasn't water that kept her skin clear? What a weird—honestly, what a fucking diabolical thing to say. It was unhinged, it was deranged, it was actively fucking stupid.

The one thing it *hadn't* sounded like was a lie.

Alex rolled her eyes, which Sloane took as temporarily bolstering, even if all evidence should have suggested it really, profoundly wasn't.

"I honestly thought it was human," Sloane admitted, more to herself now than to Alex. "I'm still not convinced it wasn't. I really don't think she was kidding. And even after you told me it was beef," Sloane realized, replaying it in her head, trying to decide whether it was more absurd that she couldn't let it go or that she might actually believe it, "Caroline laughed, but she didn't confirm or deny it. She didn't deny anything. And she didn't, like, reveal the twist, you know? She was never like 'HA, gotcha!' so—"

"Jesus, Sloane." Alex sighed, gripping the wheel tightly now with both hands. "It was beef, okay? Maybe ox, but probably beef."

"Probably?" Sloane cried, or wanted to cry.

"I wasn't there, Sloane, and she does have a fucking farm—"

"But can you *actually* be sure it wasn't something else?"

"I'm sure, okay? One hundred percent sure."

"Okay, but can anyone ever *really* be that sure—"

"Look, it's not like human hearts grow on trees, Sloane. She wouldn't waste a real one on you just to fuck with me," snapped Alex exhaustedly, like Sloane was the cause of all her misfortunes—like Sloane had personally planted obstacles in Alex's path for inner peace. "Okay? This isn't about you and I've had a hell of a week. So calm your goddamn tits."

"Waste a real—" Sloane gaped at Alex. "So it's true, then. Everything she said?"

Alex's mouth stiffened. "Sloane—"

"You're actually cannibals? Oh my god. You really are cannibals. That's *actually* the secret." Sloane wanted to throw up again. Her brain short-circuited, misfired. She couldn't understand her thoughts in sequence. She saw, mostly, a bright, white flash of rage. "You're . . . you're *all* cannibals? Jesus *fucking* Christ, I've eaten all of your cooking—I fed it to *my daughter*—"

"Oh my *god*." Alex looked wearily heavenward. "Sloane. My Bolognese is beef and pork. Okay? Relax. Not all of the human body is worth preparing into food, and even if casually preparing human flesh to be consumed without your consent *was* something we did for everyone, we couldn't eat it all the time, it causes neurological disease."

"Oh my god." Sloane's heart was thundering in her chest. "Oh my *god*."

"For the record, if I *did* give your daughter human liver in her spaghetti, she'd no longer be iron deficient," Alex said with the same tone of weariness, "and she'd probably start sleeping through the night. But far be it from me to solve all your problems for you."

"That's the secret? That's the literal secret? CANNIBALISM?" Sloane felt hysterical.

"One dinner a semester, we perform a ritual as a house," said Alex, as if she were coaxing a small child or negotiating with a terrorist. "We don't eat *everything*, Sloane, it's not some kind of disturbing gorge. It's a ritual. Everything is followed *to the letter*. We do it very seldomly. We do not get caught. We do not endanger our members. We partake in communion as a sisterhood. And the result is that everyone has more energy, clearer ambitions . . . not to mention the physical effects. It's rejuvenating and cleansing."

"What the *fuck* are you saying right now?" Sloane demanded.

"What Caroline told you is true," Alex said with a shrug. "Clear skin, shiny hair. That's the least of it. Check the House lineage from the last decade and you'll find no cancer, no disabilities, no serious illness of any kind. Not even the flu. Everyone who partakes in communion is healthy, beautiful, and successful. It really is purely medicinal in nature, and the benefits are—"

"I'm going to tell," Sloane rasped. She couldn't believe what she was hearing. "I'm—you can't seriously think I'll just *let you*—"

"Okay," said Alex. "Who are you going to tell?"

"The police!" Sloane snapped. "The University!"

"Okay," Alex said amiably. "What are you going to tell them?"

"That you're a *fucking cannibal*, Alex—"

"Well, seeing as they'll find the kitchen completely unstocked with human flesh," said Alex, "I don't really understand what you think is going to happen."

"I'm writing a *book* about it, for fuck's sake—"

"Well, if you make those kinds of claims, then a book that no one will publish because it's unequivocally absurd."

"I don't care!" Sloane shrieked. "You can't just—*you can't*—"

"Sloane." Alex turned her head to look at her. "Come on. Be real with me. You knew there was something weird going on. Right? And now you know what it is."

"*Weird* is hardly the fucking word, Alex!"

"You know, there are a lot of things people find abominable," Alex calmly said. "Homosexuality. Transgender identity. I'm pretty sure if it were up to the current Supreme Court we'd lose interracial marriage any day now."

"That's—" Sloane couldn't speak in a normal register. "That's *not the same thing*—"

"Why not? Taboo is taboo," Alex said with a shrug. "You don't understand it, so it's wrong. That's the general conclusion you're drawing here. Right?"

"What's to *understand*?" Sloane wanted to tear her hair out. Nothing about Alex's face or voice or demeanor made any sense.

"You really think I'll buy into cannibalism as some kind of . . . of *wellness regimen?*"

"Why not? People get stung by bees on purpose. They swallow charcoal and coat their faces in snail mucus. Plenty of people support the consumption of raw meat. It's very European."

"Jesus, Alex, *stop*—"

Alex began enumerating on her fingers. "Bull testicles, raw ox heart—"

"—I'm going to throw up all over your fucking car—"

"—not to mention all the weird shit people say to shove in your vagina on VidStar. Have you heard of perineum sunning?"

"None of those things involve eating humans!" Sloane wanted to primal scream with frustration. "You can't *eat humans,* Alex, it's a very simple rule!"

"Sloane." Alex turned to look at her again. "What do you want to be in life? Conventional or extraordinary?"

"You're not seriously telling me *I'm too conventional* right now—"

"I'm not telling you anything, Sloane. I'm not threatening you, I'm not convincing you, I'm not doing a single fucking thing. I'm asking you a simple question." Alex glanced again at Sloane's face before turning back to the road. "Just sit with it for a second, Sloane. Nobody's making you do anything. No one's asking you to be complicit. You can tell whoever you want. You can publish your book about it for all I care. I just want you to be honest for a second—not even with me, just with yourself. If I told you that you could be beautiful, innovative, able-bodied, successful, powerful, rich—if I said you could have everything you've ever wanted and nobody would ever know or even guess what you had to do to get it—would you really choose convention, even then?"

That's completely fucking bullshit and you know it, Sloane

thought but didn't say, at first because it felt so obvious, so undeniably real.

But as they drove silently over the two-lane road, the darkness a blur beside the windows, Sloane gradually understood that the believable window for authentic disagreement had closed, and the last-ditch window of necessary sanity was even more rapidly diminishing. Because did she think cannibalism was fucking disgusting? Absogoddamnfuckinglutely yes. But she also understood that she didn't *have* to say anything. Of course Alex could tell her all of this, openly and without fear, because nobody would ever believe Sloane even if she did point fingers, and worse than that—it wasn't as if Sloane couldn't understand Alex's point.

Because what *wouldn't* Sloane do if it meant a loving marriage, a happy child, a rewarding career? Forget the other two things, even. What wouldn't she do to guarantee a healthy life for Isla, a life for herself where she could see her daughter grow up strong and well, where she had the resources to personally ensure that nobody ever caused her daughter harm, where her daughter would never have to know abandonment or pain or fear? It was impossible, of course, irrational, but what else was motherhood? What was womanhood if not a lifelong desperation for things that were not and could never be guaranteed?

As usual, Sloane collapsed into thoughts of Isla. A missing of her, eternal, that disappeared only momentarily for things like irritation, when Isla wouldn't sleep or wouldn't eat. Nothing felt natural to Sloane anymore but Isla, such that sometimes, with Max, Sloane would even feel a sort of hunger for Isla's smallness, the smell of her skin. Sloane's desire had transformed itself, now an unrecognizable mutant.

So many things had disappeared from Sloane when she became a mother. Her younger self, her ability to make mistakes. Her capacity for judging the desperation of others. There was suddenly no limit to the person she could be—to what she genuinely believed you could become.

It was true there was a loss of something; in the unsurgical cleaving of her life, some fragments had simply fallen away. Caretaking was draining work, her time ruled by not just the presence of but the worry and the longing for The Child. There was so much capacity for resentment, for all the grains of life in the hourglass lost to the wee hours, the distant specter of the capable adult she used to be, hovering out of reach like a ghost while she swayed half-asleep but still upright. The things she used to love, the loathing for herself she used to feel, were suddenly immaterial. The person staring back in the glass had already shape-shifted irretrievably, the old her was gone. If it wasn't baby weight, it was the pain of being torn in two or the atrophy from months of being forced out of her natural shape, first the belly and then the carrying of the child, the soothing, the protecting, the strength she would reach for and use whether she possessed it in actuality or not.

But all those things were nothing. The physical shape-shifting only camouflaged a love that was more like insanity, contortions of the body to cage the madness inside. A love that defied reason and felt closer to pain. It would never be reciprocated—impossible, who had ever loved their parent as they loved their child? Who could ever reasonably ask for that kind of love in return? This, it was a rush of maternal carnage, love like nothing she'd been capable of before because it fell so close to violence. It was a love that didn't whisper about the atrocities it would gladly commit.

So Sloane said nothing, and the silence didn't necessarily feel like complicity or assent. It did feel like nausea. It felt uncomfortable—unlivable.

But then again, Sloane was a mother. She had lived through nine months of the unlivable before.

"I need a drink," said Sloane.

"In the thermos in the door," said Alex with a gesture from her chin, because she'd thought of everything. Because of course she did. Because—cannibalism included!—she'd done more for Sloane's sanity in two months than anyone else had done in Sloane's entire life.

No wonder Caroline couldn't hate her. Sloane laughed through a mouthful of straight whiskey, not even knowing where to start.

26

Nina opened her eyes to the bright obscenity of midmorning, a metallic, coppery taste filling her mouth. So this was rebirth.

She lay very still for as long as felt reasonable, retracing the evening's events in her mind. The funny, unfocused look in Dalil's eyes. The feel of Tessa's pressure on her shoulder. It was day two of her period, typically a slaughterhouse, and yet the odd absence of cramps—how could she put it into words, the sudden relief, the glorious nothingness? That erstwhile dinner prophecy, spun now from silver in her mind: *Doubt you'll have that problem anymore.* Fawn's lips beside her ear, the blood in Fawn's gums, the stains on her teeth. The way the row had looked from the roof in the dark of the wee hours, the sound of laughter from the chapter room—a plain, unremarkable room that Nina would have guessed from the outside was just a closet—echoing at their backs. Her own breath and Tessa's making ghosts in the chilly autumn air. Tessa taking a long drag of midnight, neither of them suggesting they go back inside, where it was warm.

At around three in the morning, Nina and the rest of her pledge sisters were left alone in the chapter room to process everything they'd seen. To adjust to the new frequency of reality, the hum that had fallen away, unheard, unnoticeable—inseverable—because they had been welcomed inside it. Because, as Nina had so consumptively craved, they now belonged. But had they really never questioned what belonging might entail? Nina waited for Maud to lead the group in rebellion, for Dalil to storm out, for Fran or Ryoko or Ella to rant and protest that this was unnatural, disgusting—but then nothing, not a word. It seemed everyone had had a conversation that night; one that had rewritten them, or at least temporarily silenced them. One by one, the girls had fallen asleep, strewn across each other like puppies, until Nina had slid out from under Ryoko and caught Dalil's eye, the two of them tiptoeing out of the chapter room and through the bone-quiet house to the front door.

When Dalil finally spoke, her voice was hoarse with disuse, as if the other, less informed side of initiation had been years, even centuries in the past.

"We should be repulsed," Dalil said. "Right? We should . . . tell."

Nina said nothing. They slid out the front door, both glancing around to see if anyone would stop them.

The grass was dewy and wet, the air laden with something. Change.

"What did Tessa say to you?" asked Dalil. "When you two were outside."

It's still on my tongue. Nina's absent-minded, intoxicated musing.

Tessa's reply, her breath warm on Nina's cheek. *Doesn't it feel good?* she said. *Knowing that for once, you don't have to be the one to bleed.*

Nina pressed a fist into her abdomen again, massaging the pain that wasn't there. She had taken her tampon out hours ago to find the answer she'd suspected. That the bleeding had already stopped, as if The House had cauterized the wounds.

But Tessa told her it was more than that. As if Nina's painlessness alone was nothing. *For the old guard, Alex's pledge class and the other alums, it's so different. They push this wellness bullshit, Orientalism like you wouldn't believe. But for us, ever since Fawn and I rushed—or maybe even since Caroline, I don't know—it's not about some fucking whitewashed beauty standard, it's not pay gaps or presidential office or barking like a big dog so some dude named Harold will finally give you the time of day. That's what Alex doesn't* get. *It's not just about what we get from the dinner. It's what we can take from the hunt.*

Tessa had looked at Nina closely then. *Every fucking day, the world takes a bite out of us. So now, we bite back.*

Nina and Dalil both paused before reaching the sidewalk. Nina turned first, looking at The House. Then at Dalil.

"I don't want to go to my apartment," Nina admitted. Her voice wasn't a whisper, exactly. It felt different, though. Like how everything is different once you tell a lover how you feel.

"Yeah," said Dalil, as if Nina had answered the question.

Without further conversation, they made their way back inside the house. Dalil headed straight for the chapter room while Nina paused, making the excuse of needing water, to tiptoe through the darkness of the dining room.

Nina stopped to cradle newness like a superpower, a sixth sense. She remembered being outside of it, naming it insidious, thinking it uncanny, and it was. But was it ugly?

From elsewhere in the house, Nina could feel Tessa breathing deeply, sleeping soundly. She could sense Maud stirring, turning quietly, resettling. Fran snored, a steady buzz.

Eventually Nina poured herself a glass, her hand steady, and leaned back onto the counter, waiting for something. Punishment? She was an eldritch thing now herself, a mistress of the hunt. Would there be a price now for her malfeasance? A sign, a bolt of lightning, in answer to her sins?

Instead, she caught the presence of someone in the threshold of the dining room.

"I was horrified, too," said Fawn softly. "Until I wasn't."

Fawn was wearing a matching pointelle set, a thin tank top with a pair of cropped white pants, her hair down and loose where it skimmed her waistline. It looked undone and unkempt but thick and long and glossy, even in the dark. Nina felt the urge to wrap some of it around her knuckles, pulling savagely taut.

She'd thought the hunger would fade, that blood would sate it. Too many vampire novels. Instead the tension remained throughout The House, their appetites only whetted. Upstairs, someone was panting through dreams of carnage, legs twitching like a dog's.

Nina took a long drink of water, then set the glass down empty.

"I'm not horrified," she finally said. "That's the problem. That's the part I'm not sure about."

She felt Fawn come closer, treading softly over creaking beams.

The rest felt like a dream until Nina awoke to the gentle sound of slumber carrying on restfully beside her, beams of sunlight streaking over their bare waists.

She kept her eyes closed, replaying the night like choreography, like narration.

Fawn had taken her hand and pulled her wordlessly up the stairs. "You should be with your pledge sisters, I know," Fawn said, a half-hearted apology, a set of words in random order with a meaning she so obviously didn't believe. So Nina didn't answer. Instead, Nina pulled Fawn back to pause beside the composites of their sisterhood, holding her still to run a finger lightly over the thin pointelle fabric. Easing it down until her thumb brushed over the bead of Fawn's bare nipple.

"Stop me if this isn't what you want," Nina breathed.

"Don't you understand? We chose The House. Now we *only* do what we want," said Fawn, and caught Nina's lips with hers.

Fawn's mouth on hers was hot, her motions still slow and pliant. Too slow. Too pliant. Nina pressed against her harder, then hard. Fawn laughed, pulling Nina's hand again. "Be quiet," she warned, tiptoeing up the stairs to the highest room; to what Nina had learned that evening was The House's only single. Fawn slipped inside the president's suite and tugged Nina after her, shutting the door as Nina fell heavily onto the bed.

The sheets were cold to the touch, unmade but unslept in. Fawn paused to lean back against the door, grinning at Nina like a fox. Like the groom in a bodice ripper. Nina, however, wanted nothing coquettish, nothing so coy. She wanted to grind on Fawn's leg like a fucking dog. Her dignity was an unbearable weight, nothing cool about her longing. She pulled her white dress over her head and let it fall to the floor, shivering a little where she sat at the edge of Fawn's bed in nothing but her bra and underwear. Nina hadn't dressed for sex, but for baptism. She waited for the benediction to fall.

Fawn crept forward from the door, taking hold of Nina's shoulders and climbing onto her lap, making a low soothing sound as she drew a finger over the dip of Nina's clavicle. "Don't rush this," whispered Fawn.

But all Nina wanted to do was rush. She tugged Fawn's tank top lower, burying her face between Fawn's breasts and inhaling deeply, like taking a line of cocaine. Fawn gave a shuddering groan, tightening her fingers in Nina's ponytail. Nina slipped her tongue out, tasting the skin of Fawn's decolletage. How sweet the words seemed for sex when it was two women. Decolletage. Neck. Throat. Lips.

To her embarrassment, Nina moaned into Fawn's mouth, an unhinged, unexpected sound that tore from her throat. Fawn laughed and tugged Nina's hair, deepening the kiss. Fawn's lips were soft—cosmetic soft, perfection you couldn't achieve, maybe it's Maybelline. Her tongue danced, sweet and uncommitted. Nina still tasted blood in her mouth, but now it was rich and inviting, closer to flame.

She made another humiliating noise when Fawn reached down, taking Nina's hand and placing it between her legs. Nina lifted a hesitant thumb and stroked, electrified when Fawn inhaled audibly, sharply, at her touch. Nina shifted until she was flattening Fawn down against the mattress, drawing her deeper into the sheets. She pressed her mouth to Fawn's crotch, lingering hungrily over the fabric, saturating it with the broad flat of her tongue. Fawn jutted her hips up, mewling expectantly for more. Nina let one hand fall, slipping her fingers beneath her own underwear.

Her eyes met Fawn's between the pillars of Fawn's thighs. Nina licked, hard and rough, and touched the slickness of herself at the precise moment that Fawn's thighs shook with sudden vigor, like coming alive. Nina licked again, harder. Harder. She slid her fingers to her own clitoris and widened her legs, bracing them against the bed.

Something told Nina she no longer had to wait for pleasure. Something in her life had profoundly, unalterably changed. Fawn watched Nina with interest, with expectation. Nina fucked herself with two greedy fingers until she came with alarming quickness, a seething grit of relief between her teeth.

Fawn propped herself up on her elbows then, waiting to be rewarded for her patience. Nina pulled Fawn's pants down, then smacked Fawn's hip with one hand. Fawn smiled a knowing, Cheshire smile, closing her eyes and lying back down. Then, inexpertly, with the ardor of an amateur, Nina sucked and sucked until Fawn came like a gunshot.

They fell asleep close to five in the morning. Blood and orgasm on Nina's tongue.

She rose carefully now from Fawn's bed and looked in the mirror, inspecting herself. The abdominal pain was gone as if it never existed, barely a phantom ache to memorialize a lifetime's curse. No wonder no one wore glasses, used an inhaler, took Adderall to study. Nina felt clear-eyed, mindful, in tune with something— groundedness, she thought. She felt grounded, no longer adrift. Her hair seemed . . . shinier. It seemed longer, thicker, like she'd gotten it blown out for hours instead of just dry humping for a cool forty-five.

Whose blood was it? she'd whispered to Fawn before they drifted off.

Something we had in the reserves, said Fawn. *I think he was a state senate candidate.*

Nina looked at her cheeks in the mirror. They seemed... dewy. Her skin seemed radiant, like something was glowing from underneath.

In her montage of the night, Fawn flipped over on the mattress to face Nina, her palm steady around Nina's cheek.

What you're tasting is revenge. Tessa's voice was laced with Fawn's sweetness, or maybe the other way around. *It's reprisal. It's violence. It's the guns they won't ban no matter how many abusive assholes kill their wives. It's the choices they strip from us and the formula they lock up so the babies they forced on us will starve. It's every time you were called a bitch for saying no and a slut for saying yes.*

Peaceful protest only works if the enemy has a conscience. The two-headed monster of Tessa/Fawn blew out a breath like a smoke ring, coolness personified. *If they have none, why should we?*

Nina had shivered gladly then, wondering if anyone knew, if anyone could ever know. Whether anyone could really judge her if they actually understood.

And Fawn had stroked her thumb over the bone of Nina's cheek, a play of sympathy spilling over her delicate features. *Hey. Let's keep this between us for now. Okay?*

Nina would have kept anything Fawn gave her. Hair, a vial of blood, all her secrets.

Okay.

In Fawn's mirror, Nina could see her lips were bitten red. Her eyes seemed clearer, brighter. A deeper, more otherworldly brown.

She almost gasped. She seemed so . . . beautiful. Not that she couldn't have called herself pretty before, if pressed, but now it was different. Her tawny skin looked less sallow around her eyes, the dark circles vanished in accommodation of the new inner light. Despite not having slept more than a couple of hours, she didn't look tired. There was more depth to the color of her hair, highlights and lowlights, every motion as she turned her head from side to side a new spectrum of radiance from ebony to gold.

Her first day as a member of The House. So this was rebirth, and yet the clock went on ticking. Unbeknownst to Nina, her timeline had always been off.

"You know," came Fawn's voice from the bed behind her, "you should really move in here."

"To your bed?" Nina joked, turning to look at her. In the morning light, Fawn was still perfection, a groggy smile on her petal-pink lips.

"The House, but you knew that." The smile faltered, becoming a flicker of something else. Desire, Nina realized.

"Get back in here before everyone else wakes up," whispered Fawn.

Nina knew she would mentally record this, skip class in favor of playing it back. She saw a long shower in her future, all the excuses she would make to her roommate Simone. She'd suck more expertly this time, with something like control, or at very least restraint. Or she'd just masturbate violently in parallel to Fawn—who could really say, given her new appetite?

Everything would be different now.

"How's the cult?" Jas asked when Nina finally called her back, smelling primly of body wash and lotion.

"You'd like them," Nina said. "They're your people." On her phone was a missed call from Dalil, followed by a text: **where'd u go last night?**

"Why," Jas sighed, "because they knit pussy hats?"

"No, because they slaughter men and eat them," Nina said.

"Ha ha," muttered Jas, slumping down in her desk chair with her usual gloom of systemic frustration. "Well, then good for them, I guess."

27

Deadline: ??? Progress: Loads. Or several steps backward. Unclear.

As Alex had promised, Sloane's car was parked in the driveway the next morning. Sloane had been fully prepared to offer Max a story about why she'd left her car behind, but she hadn't even had to lie. Instead, she woke up to Isla (who'd roused sobbing around midnight and gotten in bed with them for the night as usual) kissing her face (sweet, if inconvenient) and then they came down to the kitchen to find Max drinking coffee, the dishes from the breakfast he'd prepared for himself—just him—waiting patiently for someone's attention in the sink, beside the unloaded dishwasher.

"Why'd you park in the driveway instead of the garage?" Max offered in greeting. Sloane shifted Isla to her other hip, searching around in the cabinets for something suitable to eat.

"I didn't want to wake you. Is there any more oatmeal?"

"Oh, sorry, no." Max kissed her forehead, an apology for last night's argument. "How was dinner with your friend?"

Isla began pointing urgently to something mysterious. "It was a meeting, Max, for the book I'm writing. Not dinner with my friend."

"Right, how was it?"

"Can you get her juice, please? It was fine."

"Where's her cup?"

Sloane paused to try and remember. "I don't know, somewhere. And the meeting was fine. She's a cannibal."

"What?" Max laughed.

"The Country Wife. She's a cannibal. So is that whole sorority."

"Okay," said Max, getting distracted by something on his phone. "Sounds like a productive meeting."

Isla wriggled to get down, then darted into the living room to either cuddle or harass the dog, depending on who you asked. "Make sure Frankie doesn't snap at her, Max, please. Did you find her cup?"

"What cup?"

"What do you mean *what* cup?"

And so on. Such was the morning, and so Sloane did not think about cannibalism again for at least another hour, after Isla had been dressed (Max's morning activity, though Sloane had to pick it out first or he'd try to dress Isla in something that didn't fit and had, in fact, been shoved into the back of the closet because Sloane didn't have time to organize things, not even for the person she cared most about on this earth, and Max was busy playing Scrabble on his phone) and dropped off at daycare. Once in her office, Sloane spotted a note from Alex on her desk, and lifted her phone to her ear with a weighty sense of having lost the plot completely.

"When you say Caroline's a problem," Sloane began without preamble the moment Alex picked up, hoping Alex wouldn't call her out for her failure to condemn cannibalism one more time. (Alex didn't, because she was a very good friend, if also *an insane fucking cannibal.*) "She said The Country Wife is a cover. Does that mean . . . ?"

Despite everything that Sloane had willingly said aloud that day, she still couldn't bring herself to say things like "murder," although she couldn't imagine how else one procured human organs. Still, Alex had said there was a ritual. What kind? Was it like when ethical vampires on TV shows used blood banks? Was it worse? Did Sloane even want to know?

"Caroline is . . . taking things too far," Alex said, an ominous place to end a sentence. "I didn't teach her that. I don't approve—" She stopped. "I strongly condemn Caroline's philosophies and actions. You could turn her in if you wanted," Alex added, "but I don't have any proof of wrongdoing and I doubt you'd find any if you tried. Caroline is very smart, and very careful."

Even to Sloane, that sounded like a weak attempt at reverse psychology. Not to mention a little bit *too* doting, like a mother describing the bare accomplishments of her degenerate son.

"You think she's killing people?" Sloane asked. When Alex didn't immediately answer, she added, "And you haven't tried to turn her in yourself?"

For once, Sloane's tone of incredulity was rewarded with a sigh from Alex that felt genuinely disturbed rather than purely tired.

"She's one of mine," Alex concluded simply. "I want to fix her. I want to stop her. I want to help her. But what will prison do for her? I don't even believe in the carceral system as a means to cure social ills. And she has a code of morality, I know that."

"So she kills . . . ?"

"Bad men. Violent sexual offenders are mainly her targets, I believe, unless she's changed her internal manifesto. Either way, it's some vigilante shit." Alex hesitated, then said, "The other girls, the ones currently in The House . . . some of them do know about Caroline, but they think it's . . . earned, I guess. That violence has been their only option for a long time. I'm working on it," Alex said quickly, "but it's exactly why you're necessary. You're smart, you're academic, you can appeal to them from a place of—I don't fucking know—logic, I guess. You can remind them of what the mission is and what it isn't."

Sloane found this both exasperating and intriguing. "What *is* the mission?" she asked, intending to sound sarcastic but finding herself genuinely curious. "Like, seriously, what on earth is your validation for any of this?"

"The point is to win," said Alex. "To grow. Achieve. Lift each other up."

"But—"

"Sloane, come on. It's fucking hell being a woman," said Alex. "Do I really have to explain that to you, of all people? Your husband's on a tenure track and his record as an academic is barely even with yours. You're a better writer and you're smarter."

"We're in different fields."

"Who cares? It'd be even worse if you were in the same field and you know it. Who had to quit their job to take care of the baby?"

"Come on." Sloane didn't want to be forced to defend that decision again, least of all to Alex. "You're supposed to get this, you're supposed to understand that I *wanted* to—"

"I do get it," Alex said. "But why didn't *he* want to? Why didn't he *fight* you for the right to stay home with his child? Because it's less important work, Sloane." Sloane's head rang out like she'd been slapped. "What you contribute to the life and health of his child is less important to Max than what he provides, intellectually, to the world at large."

"Alex, who are you right now, Betty Friedan?"

"I'm not saying this is new or revolutionary, Sloane. In fact, I'm saying it's so baked-in that there's no point fighting about it."

"What Max and I decided privately has no bearing on what you're suggesting is completely normal behavior," Sloane muttered just as her office door opened. Arya slipped inside, lifting a hand in greeting. He was bobbing his head to whatever beat was emanating from his headphones as he took his usual seat at her absent colleague's desk, pulling his laptop out of his bag.

"Sloane, while I'd love to beat this dead horse with you again, you're obviously in no place for a meaningful conversation and I have about eight thousand meetings today for five million things that don't matter," said Alex. "Can we table this for now? You can call the cops on me if you want, just please, as a fellow mother, spare me having to hold your hand through an ethical crisis when I only slept three hours last night."

"You know I don't trust cops," muttered Sloane. Arya turned around in his chair to grin at her.

"We'll talk later, okay? I just have to get through the hellscape that is my average Thursday." Then Alex hung up, and Sloane slumped lower in her chair.

"Fuck," said Sloane, to no one.

"That bad?" said Arya.

"The Country Wife is a cannibal," she said.

"Juicy," said Arya. "Though I assume that would be difficult to prove."

"Is cannibalism actually an ancient Egyptian practice?"

"Nah, that's just what medieval Europeans said to get away with it."

"Of course. Classic medieval Europe." Sloane, to her great despair, was sulking.

"It's not just medieval fetishism," Arya continued. "It still exists in some parts of the world. A lot of those places also acknowledge and legally define sorcery. It's one of those conversations that's hard to have, anthropologically speaking, because culture is relative. There's no universal standard to measure what is culturally wrong or right—once you go down that path, it's a slippery slope. Homosexuality is often penalized, but love is love. But then, is love also love when it's your close blood relative? How do we draw those lines?"

"You can't compare queer relationships with *incest*," Sloane moaned, and Arya laughed.

"Why not? You can theoretically define 'acceptable' love as nothing more than consensual love. Once you start making arguments based on biology, things go awry."

"Stop," said Sloane. "I know you're rationalizing all this to prove a point, but it's making me physically ill."

"There's even some research to suggest Genetic Sexual Attraction is a real, biological phenomenon—"

"First of all, conflating taboos feels like a really unproductive headspace," said Sloane. "Secondly, ew."

"I'm trying to help." Arya's face was sweetly puppylike. "And I seem to have distracted you, which is good work by me, I think."

"I wonder if I should ask Max what he thinks about all this." Sloane exhaled deeply. "He's a philosopher. He'll talk himself in circles and I can just watch."

Arya's expression flickered ever so slightly, or perhaps Sloane imagined it. "You could. I do love a little logical contortion."

"God." Sloane checked her watch and closed her eyes. "The last thing I want to do right now is a lecture about categorical variables."

"What would you rather do?" asked Arya.

"I don't know. Kiss my daughter. Sleep for a hundred years." Sloane pressed two cold fingers into the throb of her sinuses, glancing up at the unmoving string tied to the vent of their malfunctioning air-conditioning. "At least it's cold enough now that I can suffer at a different temperature in here."

"Go get Isla, then." Arya rose to his feet and walked over to Sloane's desk, gently removing her laptop from her hands. "Is this today's lecture?" he asked, glancing at her screen.

"I can't just *go get her,* Arya, I've got thirty barely conscious undergraduates to enthrall—"

"I'll do it," he said, bending down over her laptop to email her open slides to himself. "Go get Isla, spend the day with her. I'm sure you could both use the time."

Sloane cracked one eye, frowning at him. "Is this you trying to get some extra lecturing hours in at my expense?"

Arya laughed, full and throaty, and turned his bright smile directly on her, like someone suddenly turning on the sun. "Maybe I want you to owe me a favor," he said. "Or maybe I think there's a good chance you'll have a full mental breakdown in that lecture hall. Who can say?"

"You don't believe me, do you?" Sloane asked, and realized she'd inflected wrong. She'd meant to dryly suggest that Arya couldn't believe her because doing so would be categorically impossible, but instead it came out as if she were tentatively curious, like she'd asked is this okay, or can I touch you here.

"It just seems to me like you've got a lot going on in there," Arya said, tapping Sloane's forehead gently with one finger. "And I know it's been tough on you, not having as much time with Isla as you'd like. So take the morning off, I'll cover for you."

Sloane's heart was already racing across campus, though she made a show of holding back. "This is why Burns won't give me tenure, isn't it? Because I put my daughter before *the craft*," she sighed.

"Burns won't give you tenure because he's a fucking goblin," said Arya. "And what kind of person would you be if you didn't choose your daughter over everything?"

"A man," said Sloane.

"Not to 'not all men,' Dr. Hartley, but I must protest, not all men." Arya played dramatically at injury and hit her with another of those obscene smiles. Sloane felt the sunrise of it down to her geriatric bikini, a heat that drifted up from her vagina through her soul.

"How old are you?" asked Sloane abruptly.

"Old enough," said Arya without missing a beat. "Why?"

Well, fuck! That time she rose to her feet, recognizing an opportune exit and deciding there was no point being a martyr, fighting for the idea of respect at the cost of her very real heart. Not today, anyway. Maybe tomorrow.

"Don't make me fire you," she called over her shoulder, gathering her things and quickening her pace as she went, the rush of blood in her ear singing *Isla, Isla, Isla* until she flung open the daycare door and could breathe.

28

"How has it been since you told your roommates you were moving out?" Jas asked from Nina's phone screen where it rested on the bathroom sink.

"Conditions have . . . worsened," Nina acknowledged, closing one eye to examine whether her cat-eye could, in fact, kill a man. Not quite. Unless blunt force trauma was an option.

"That's too bad," Jas sighed. "I like Simone."

"Simone is actually not the problem." Nina had always been the ideal audience for Simone's benevolent indifference, which was a quality that was appealing if you enjoyed the ups and downs of striving for hard-won approval and less so if you liked knowing you were unconditionally loved and cherished. As a roommate, Simone had been clean and beautifully uninterested in Nina's daily activities. There was no telling whether the same would be true for the foursome soon to be shared with Nina by Dalil, Maud, and Ryoko. Would they be so respectful of her migraines, her occasional need for quiet?

Not that Nina had migraines anymore. Even her bowels worked like clockwork. The inefficiencies of a normal human body had simply faded away, like she'd outgrown them. Her only problem now was her interior awareness of how many weeks remained until finals. The collective thrall that was the ongoing hunt.

"Simone's going abroad next semester, which means Adelaide and Mei are going to be assigned two new roommates."

"Ah." Jas, an empath, required no further explanation. "But at least they have each other, right?"

"Well, Mei has her boyfriend. And Adelaide isn't very fond of change."

"Deal with it, white girl," said Jas succinctly.

"It's not like I blame her," said Nina, with Nina's pre-law tendency to argue both sides in a way that was so consistently performative she no longer knew how to skip it as a step. Fawn had already laughingly pointed it out as what she called a charming inefficiency; even post-initiation, it seemed some elements of humanity yet remained. Quelle tragédie. "I *am* kind of leaving them in a lurch."

"Not really. It's campus housing, so they'll just be assigned new roommates, right? It's not like they have to rush to find a subletter."

"True, but still." There was a knock at the door and Nina set down her eyeliner with a sigh. "That's Arya. I assume you want to stay on and say hi?"

"Fuck yes, asshole. I still can't believe you're actually going out with him."

Nina picked up the phone, carrying her sister's image to the apartment's front door. "I told you, I just needed a date for invite."

"Why are you pronouncing it like that? *In*-vite?"

"It's just what it's called. And like I said, I needed a date." Nina swung the door open, waving in a slightly awkward manner as Arya finished typing a message into his phone. "Hey," she said, thrusting her phone into his hand. "Talk to Jas while I find a tutorial on eyeliner."

"Oh, let me do it," said Arya, happily accepting the phone. "I do a little calligraphy on the side and my Etsy reviews are unparalleled. Hey, Jas."

"Oh, hi, Arya!" Nina nearly let out a burst of laughter at the sound of Jas's breathless imitation of surprise. "What are you doing with my whore of a sister?"

"Not defiling her, if that's what you're asking. Here," he offered to Nina, "give me the pen."

"It's not a *pen,* Arya, and I'm not letting you near my eye."

"It's essentially a pen, Nina, and I have to fix you, you're a mess."

"I didn't know you did calligraphy!" exclaimed Jas, her voice several octaves too high.

"Oh, only because I'm a starving academic," replied Arya gamely. He beckoned again to Nina with one hand, offering her Jas with the other. "Here, take your sister while I make you presentable."

"You're going to stab me in the eye," said Nina. "Again!"

"You're going to have to get over that," Arya informed her seriously. "I was, like, fifteen. And you stole my lightsaber. Didn't anyone ever tell you that crime doesn't pay?"

Nina handed over the eyeliner with a groan, realizing as she swapped for the phone that she hadn't properly looked at Arya's outfit.

"You look good," Nina realized aloud, and Arya did a little spin. "Did you just have that lying around?"

The theme of the invite was Malibu Barbie, which Nina had mostly underperformed. She was wearing a dress she'd bought cheaply online in a Tropicana spectrum of pinks and turquoise, paired with some sequin knee-high boots she'd borrowed from Tessa. Arya, meanwhile, had managed to procure a pair of tiny coral shorts that ended well above his knees, which he'd paired with a frayed denim vest he'd left open. It almost appeared as though he'd contoured his abs with self-tanner, though it was also possible they simply looked like that.

"First of all, I used to be young," said Arya, maneuvering Nina into the dining room chair and gesturing for her to close one eye. "I have a vault of secrets. Secondly," he said through a peering look of concentration, "I did have to borrow the vest."

"Explain the shorts?"

"No," said Arya. "Now stop moving. I never have this problem with place cards."

"You're going to stab me in the eye, aren't you?"

"Hello, I wanna see Arya's outfit," said Jas, who'd been left forgotten in Nina's hand. "Bitch, show me!"

Nina shifted to try and capture Arya's entire appearance while Arya scolded her again, sounding unerotically like their auntie.

"I can't see shit, Nina. You're really letting me down here," Jas bemoaned.

"Done," Arya announced triumphantly, leaning back to survey his handiwork. "Now *that's* the cat's meow."

"Don't," sighed Nina.

"Now can I see?" demanded Jas.

"Whoa, damn," said Mei, appearing in the corridor on her way from her bedroom to the bathroom. She hadn't put in her contacts and was terribly nearsighted, so the Coke-bottle lenses made her eyes appear especially magnified as she gaped at Arya from afar. "Are you some kind of underwear model?"

"Close! I am an underpaid TA," said Arya, as Nina picked up her phone for Jas to see him.

"Arya, stop," said Jas, after what Nina observed to be a hard moment's pause. "You can't go out like that. Your mother will kill you. *Our* mother will kill you. Everyone can see your—"

"Bye, Jas!" said Arya cheerfully, reaching forward to hang up Nina's phone. "Now can we go, please? This is the sort of outfit that looks much better in company."

"It looks pretty good from here," said Mei, who had been joined by Simone, who was appreciatively clicking her retainer.

"Nina," said Arya. "I am doing you this very cool favor. I am being a very cool guy. Can we leave?"

It took only a few more tries to get Nina out the door, once she had forced Arya to take pictures with both her roommates (much funnier to send to her mother than a picture of Arya with her, because it did not involve anyone asking if Nina "really considered that a dress") and arranged to meet up with Dalil at the corner of campus closest to the row. Dalil, who was usually reliable, had been delayed due to the less admirable time-management qualities of her latest situationship. (The two could not date "for real," said Dalil, because she could not in good conscience take seriously a person named Yarden.)

Outside it was rudely crisp, borderline frigid. Nina hopped from foot to foot, desperately taking sips from a flask she passed to Arya as she texted Dalil with increasing urgency (????????) and looked up again at his outfit, trying not to laugh. "I really can't believe you did this for me," she said, accepting the flask back from Arya after he'd taken a long, covert sip. "It's so . . . I mean, it's impressive, really, this level of commitment."

"I am very fond of you," said Arya, whose teeth were chattering as Nina raised the flask shakily to her lips, "though my benevolence does diminish by the second."

Nina passed the flask back to him and hugged herself tightly, texting Dalil again purely for want of something to fixate on besides the cold. "Have you been to one of these before?" she asked Arya. "You know, sorority things?"

"Here and there," Arya confirmed. The rate at which the vodka blanket was being passed from hand to hand was influenced by a mix of glacial temperature drop and awkwardness—they hadn't spent this much time alone together without Jas or their parents since they were kids. "I don't own these shorts for my health."

"Certainly not your reproductive health, no." Nina grinned, and Arya played theatrically at offense.

"I'll have you know I'm wearing just as much short as you are skirt."

"Well, as Jas would say, something-something gender roles—"

"You look good," Arya said abruptly, as an apparent tangent, in something that struck Nina as an unusual tone of voice. He was inspecting her closely, searching her face with something that made Nina sharply aware of her bare legs, her upstanding nipples. "I mean . . . you look healthy, and happy, and . . . something."

She groped his hand for the vodka, fingers stiff with cold. "You are a man of many very good words," Nina offered drily, into the flask.

"I don't know, you just seem different. You . . . glow." Arya made a brief gesture in the general direction of her face. "I don't mean it in a gross way."

"I'm telling Jas you said my rack was huge."

"Please," said Arya, pained, "do not do that. Come on, I thought we had a kinship."

"Really?" Nina said, unable to disguise her genuine surprise. "What have we ever had in common?"

"We," Arya said, snatching the flask back from her, "are keen observers. We reflect more than we say." He took a long pull from the flask and shuddered. "God, and I thought I'd matured. Oh well, when in Rome."

"If we're both apparently mirrors, what are we reflecting in each other right now?" Could Arya see it? Nina wondered. All these things that she had done.

"Extreme cold," said Arya, so no. "And if I had to guess, a taste for distant authority figures."

Nina didn't hear him, having been tackled out of the blue.

"NINA," screeched Dalil, barreling into Nina's side from somewhere on her left. "I'M FUCKING FREEZING. And what's eight hundred goblin emojis supposed to mean?" she demanded, showing Nina their messages on her screen.

"I don't know, Dalil, let's just get the hell out of here—"

There was a brief flurry of introduction as Yarden appeared, wearing a very similar outfit to Arya's but without the impressive muscular tone that apparently came with achieving physical maturation. His blond hair flopped over in something that was deeply, J.Crew-ily catalog. Nina slipped the flask from Arya's proffered fist into Dalil's hand, both of them tripping over themselves with giggles as they made their way to the house to board the waiting buses.

"Everyone on the buses, let's go!" shouted Alina, who was flanked on one side by her impassive-looking date—the boyfriend, Tripp, that Fawn had previously called a knockoff Kennedy—and on the other, recognizable with a hard lurch from Nina's chest, Fawn.

Fawn had opted for evening-gown Barbie, wearing a tight satin dress that stretched across her hips. She looked too refined, almost upsettingly so, compared to everyone—Nina included—who seemed now, unmistakably, to be a partially drunken clown. Fawn stood out from the crowd, peerless, alone. How had she chosen Nina; how could she while away her time with *Nina* when there were so many others more worthy—prettier, kinder, smarter, better tasting, probably? Why was Fawn always alone when surely there were throngs of admirers, mobs of desirers, countless throbbing bodies pulsing amorously with want? Nina had the sudden, distressing urge to shove Arya in front of her like a shield until she could regain some poise, sober up, change all her clothes.

Too late. Fawn spotted her, a brief, wolfish look coming over her face as her mouth twisted up in a smile.

"Little Sis!" Fawn said, holding out her arms for what Nina realized belatedly was Dalil, not her. She held herself back half an inch, and then it was her turn, like a peasant in line for the queen, to bask in the gracious light of Fawn's attention. "Wow," Fawn breathed in Nina's ear. "Your date is fucking *hot*. Should I be jealous?"

"No" was all Nina could manage. She wanted to laugh, honestly. Arya was basically a sibling, or furniture. Arya could start a disco flash mob or flawlessly perform a sonnet or drop dead on the sidewalk and Nina would still be looking at Fawn. "Where's your date?"

"Oh, I never bring one to these," Fawn said with a dismissive flap of her hand. "Have to stay sober for liability stuff anyway, so—oh my god, Maud, I *love* that bodysuit!"

Nina felt herself being pulled by the tide onto the bus, shivering again as her moment in the sun passed away. She glanced over her shoulder, catching Fawn's wink, and let herself be directed to the fray, Fawn still the fulcrum of everything. But the chorus of bawdy songs had already caught like wildfire, and Nina found herself in the thrall of the night before she even knew it had begun.

29

"We should go out," Max had said to Sloane earlier that evening, in an unusual display of interest. Performative? Maybe just inspired. "It's been a while, don't you think?"

As she often had over the course of the previous fortnight, Sloane suppressed the urge to discuss cannibalism. She also fought the reflexive grimace that came with the thought of hyping herself up for sex. It would, she realized with a sprig of optimism, be much easier with the lubrication of wine and dinner conversation. Max had always sparkled in social situations, even among just the two of them. It was Max's brain that Sloane had been most drawn to, despite the benefit of his aesthetic. He could—often did—dazzle her conversationally, by virtue of a singularly brilliant or humorful thought.

There was, of course, the hesitation at the thought of leaving Isla, even for an hour or two. Max's colleague whose wife had been helpful in the past was unavailable, and it wasn't as if Sloane was going to call a random number off the Starbucks job posting board.

Grudgingly, Sloane realized there was always one person she could reliably call.

"Of course, no problem at all," said Alex on the phone, a knowing hint of something in her voice. "Are you at all concerned that I'll try to feed her human flesh?"

"Thanks, Alex," Sloane said loudly, giving Max a thumbs-up. "I really appreciate it."

"It's my pleasure. Theo and I'll be over at six with the freshly slaughtered corpse." Click.

"It's nice that you finally have someone you trust," Max observed, materializing from behind Sloane to wrap his arms around her in the kitchen. He'd been particularly touchy lately, a sudden, sharp increase that had driven Sloane to ask him about the Scrabble app.

"You're not using that thing to cheat on me, right? I've heard about people DMing their paramours using the chat features in games like that," she'd said, astonished that she'd said it aloud. Surely it wasn't a *serious* concern, right, if she could ask him that, flat out? If she actually thought it was a possibility, she'd just check on his phone while he showered. Was this growth? Maturity? Lunacy?

"Of course not," Max said, rolling his eyes, and that was that. "Seriously? A guy can't like wordplay without getting his dick sucked?"

"Who knows what you men are capable of," teased Sloane, in a tone of voice she hoped did not suggest that she knew of any women who might take such generalizations to a malicious or culinary extreme.

The more time had passed since Alex's confession, the less Sloane really believed it. It was true, apparently, that humans could adapt to almost any condition, including the one where you walked around knowing some fundamental wrong was occurring in the world and yet you still worried about the tedium of what to make for breakfast. Though, that was true of all things, Sloane realized increasingly, her brain digesting the truth of Alex's atrocities as if it were a brick of shredded wheat. (Slowly, but digesting nonetheless.) It was true that Sloane walked around in the world knowing that at any given time there were at least three ongoing genocides; that at least one city in the United States could not give its residents lead-free water; that in all likelihood, her life's work was trivial at best. That the daily disappointments of her husband were far more likely to crush her than any distant loss of human life. The brain simply couldn't cope with the scope of plausible trauma. Instead it wondered what to wear, or how to make small talk with a woman who had been eating people on and off for the last decade of her life.

Of course, Alex and Theo arrived while Sloane was still choosing an outfit—nothing seemed to fit her as it had before; this was not an existential state, and yet—and so she walked into the kitchen with Isla on her hip to discover that Max was already chatting animatedly with Alex, who wore a look of mild rapture.

Sloane walked over to Theo, who was picking up a die-cast car from Isla's new Montessori shelf, purchased via a link that had been sent to Sloane by Britt. "Hi, sweetie," Sloane said quietly, and Theo looked up at her with big, innocent eyes, waving a shy hello before scrunching up his nose in greeting to Isla.

Sloane looked up, noticing that Max was now gesturing broadly with his hands. She caught Alex's eye, and there was a moment—a little slip of pretense—where Sloane became aware that Alex was performing attentiveness. Sloane realized from that single blitz of contact that Alex was incredibly bored and unimpressed, and then Sloane became aware, in perhaps the lowest moment of her life thus far, that she had married the kind of man who didn't understand when a woman wasn't interested in what he was saying.

"Max. Ready to go?" Sloane's voice was forcefully chipper. For god's sake. Why did it matter whether Alex found her husband interesting? Personality divergences were natural, even expected. This wasn't one of those situations where the husband was an uncharismatic blob—some generic, unremarkable Dad Bod wearing clothes she'd bought for him (although he was). Max was incredibly handsome, almost unreasonably smart. Yes, Sloane had considered in the past that his charisma sometimes bordered on controversial, but never in any *real* way. People loved Max. He was a very interesting person on a tenure track at a prestigious University and for fuck's sake, Sloane couldn't wait to have dinner with him!!! The end!!!

"Ah, there she is!" Max said, shepherding Alex into the living room. "I was just telling Alex how nice it is that you've got such a good friend."

"I, of course, assured him that good was highly relative," said Alex, whose face changed at the sight of Isla. "Hi there, Miss Isla!"

There was something so warming, so fondly *assuring* about people who loved your baby. Sloane had told Max just that morning that sometimes, when Isla said hi to random passersby on the street who didn't look up or wave back, she felt capable of murder. "It's just this wash of something, this total hatred," she mirthfully explained as she scrubbed a spot of mold from the straw of Isla's sippy cup. "Like, my brain goes white for a second. Why wouldn't you wave back to this precious little baby?"

"One of these days you'll really have to check your violent impulses," said Max.

"I'm just *joking*," Sloane insisted, although she wasn't, really. It wasn't as if she was *actually* going to snap and kill a stranger on the street, but that feeling—that inexplicable, primal desire to tear something down with her teeth—she realized only belatedly that she'd said it to the wrong person.

Because of course Alex would understand.

"She's started saying hi to random people," Sloane said now as Alex got on her knees to play, apparently unbothered about the pleats in her casual trousers. (Did they iron themselves? Was that a benefit of consuming human organs? Where was the line, exactly? That was a real question, Sloane registered. Suddenly she wished she were staying behind.)

"Oh god, that's so cute. Theo did that as well, always waving to people. Sometimes when people don't wave back I feel this need to shove them into traffic," Alex said without looking up, because in that moment, Isla was offering Alex a cup from her singing tea set, and therefore Isla was more important to look at than Sloane.

Gratified, hot tears pricked inexplicably behind Sloane's eyes.

"Should we go?" asked Max, checking his watch. "Should leave a little time for parking."

"Right. Yes, thank you." Sloane rose to her feet, lingering for a moment. "Call me if you need *anything*," she said. "Seriously. Nothing is too small."

Alex did look up at her then, a small glimmer of sympathy like a balm to Sloane's senses. "I will, I promise."

"Okay." Sloane backed away. Did she really trust a cannibal? Did that even mean anything to her anymore? Was it like when you said a word too many times and it stopped making sense? "There's dinner for her in the fridge."

"Perfect. I brought some zucchini bread, too, just in case."

"Oh, that's great, thank you."

"Sloane," said Max. "Ready?"

"Bye, Isla," said Sloane softly. Isla looked up then, a beautiful, open look of childlike adoration on her face.

"Bye bye, Mama," said Isla. The first time she'd ever said it like that, in sequence, like a big girl. Sloane wanted to stay and stay and stay, to make her repeat it one hundred times, to eat her cheeks and cry all over her hair until Isla smelled like Sloane forever.

Sloane got in the car and slumped down in the passenger seat, suffering the same rush of self-loathing she felt every day at drop-off.

"God, I'm absolutely starving, I hope the traffic downtown's not too bad. I'd have picked somewhere less busy, but Chris over in Classics said we had to give it a go." Max tinkered with the vents, looking quizzically over at her. "What's up?"

"Oh, nothing," Sloane sighed. "The usual thought spiral."

"Oh yeah?"

"Yeah. It's like a permanent recording in my head. What if Isla feels abandoned?" Sloane mused, mimicking her own depressing thoughts. "What if she wants me at bedtime and I'm not there? What if this is how she learns to stop asking for me, because sometimes I won't come when she calls?" Sloane looked out of the window as Max pulled into reverse. "What if she starts to love Alex more than me?"

"Then I guess Alex is moving in," Max joked, which wasn't what Alex would have said.

Alex would have said: *You are her mother, and she will never love anyone like she loves you.*

Then Alex would have said: *Now go have a nice meal with your stupid husband before I boil him in a soup.*

Faintly, Sloane smiled.

"What?" asked Max, amused.

"Nothing," she said. Fucking Christ.

She'd gotten used to it, just like that.

30

Arya was an incredibly bad dancer. He was, however (relatedly?), very generous with his fist pumps. He also seemed to know the words to every song, no matter what genre, which was very amusing. Nina couldn't help matching his energy, enjoying herself more than she'd expected at what was essentially a more naked version of prom.

"Your date looks like Aladdin!" Ryoko screamed in Nina's ear.

"What?" Nina shouted back. The song changed to something from Arya's youth, which was funny and terrible in terms of the reaction it provoked in Arya.

"My sooooong!" he roared. Three other frat guys roared back, hypermasculine call and response.

"Oh my god," said Nina faintly.

"He's really hot, like Aladdin!" Ryoko yelled.

"Arya, they can't all be your song," Nina shouted at him. He ignored her, attempting something that might have been the Dougie, and her phone buzzed. "Hey, Arya? I'm going to the bathroom."

"What?" said Arya.

"I have to pee!"

"Okay! This is my song," Arya shouted at her, gesturing to the speakers.

"I'm peeing," Nina informed him, and began to push her way through the sea of sweaty Kens, emerging onto the edge of the dance floor and making her way toward the front entrance.

The venue was a restaurant that had closed down for the event, something that had seemed an absurd thing for a restaurant to do until Tessa explained how much The House prepaid for alcohol. Nina said she'd been trying not to think about stuff like that—she'd spent the first month after bid night bracing silently for the bill, like every spare breath of enjoyment in The House was being added to her tab—and Tessa had said, quote, dude, you're in The House, you never have to worry about money again!

Nina had felt dazed at the time, fully dazzled.

Really?

Really really. Everything's paid for. Alumnae funds.

Seriously, everything?

Seriously, everything. SISTERHOOD, BABY!

"There you are, *finally*—"

Someone grabbed Nina's hand and pulled her into the corridor leading to the bathrooms. Nina hiccuped a laugh, letting herself be pressed flush against the wall.

"Missed me?" she whispered to Fawn, letting her palms trace the silk of Fawn's dress.

"Absolutely. I'm bored as fuck. You look hot." Fawn's lips brushed Nina's neck as she laughed. "But you smell like sweat and vodka."

"Mmm," Nina said in an exaggerated moan. She felt electric as Fawn's hand slipped under her skirt.

"Not leaving much to the imagination, are you?" said Fawn.

"Good. Who has the time."

Nina giggled, a little breathy moan slipping out. Vodka did something to her volume control. And her balance.

"Fawn?" came a voice, and Fawn stepped coolly away from Nina, turning to look at Summer Toft, who Nina now understood was Fawn's executive vice president.

"Everything okay, Sum?" The nickname felt weaponized, somehow. Nina shifted like she'd poked herself on it.

"Oh yeah, just Katy's date throwing up in the bathroom. I sent them off in a cab—Katy's fine, she's taking him home."

"Great," said Fawn. "Thanks."

"Just doing my job." Summer smiled at Nina. From a blurry place of observation, Nina felt there was a strangeness, some blockade between Summer and Fawn, such that one or both were pretending the other was invisible or simply did not exist. "Having fun, Nina? Your date is really hot," Summer informed her with a wink. "Even Alina's boyfriend thinks so. I think he might have turned half the guys in that room."

"Oh, Arya's a family friend," Nina started to say, but Fawn gripped her hand covertly.

"We'll be back in a sec," Fawn said to Summer, who shifted her attention away from Nina and back to Fawn with something that might have been a grimace, although the corridor was only dimly lit. "I'm taking Nina outside to get some air. She's feeling faint."

"Oh shit, I'm sorry, Nina," said Summer, looking genuine in her concern. Probably because they were sisters, and sisters cared! "Do you want me to get you some water?"

Fawn interjected, "I've got her, Summer, thanks. I'll be back in a couple minutes."

"Okay, take your time." This, too, was directed at Nina, who suddenly couldn't remember what it looked like to feel faint, and wondered if she were committing appropriately to the improvisation. Summer's voice was already growing distant, Nina tripping casually toward the door in Fawn's thrall. "It's not like it's the first time we've lost a cleaning deposit—"

Fawn tugged Nina out the side door, the cold night air like a knife to Nina's lungs. The venue was one in a row of high street restaurants, beside which was another hot downtown spot with a long line of respectable-looking middle-aged adults. Fawn guided Nina out of sight, into the narrow entry path between buildings.

"Holy fuck, it's cold out here," Nina gasped, and then Fawn's mouth was on hers, warm and delicious. She capitulated with a sigh, or maybe something louder, before licking the inside of

Fawn's mouth. Like catching drips of maple syrup, honey falling on her tongue.

Fawn laughed. "You're horny as fuck. Down, girl." She gestured over her shoulder, taking a step away. "We're in public."

"I'm drunk," said Nina. "You're hot. Do the math. What'd we come outside for anyway, if not this?"

"Not my best plan, all things considered." Fawn kissed Nina hard, then stepped away, back toward the restaurant's side door and in view of the street. "Are you gonna be hooking up with your date tonight?"

"Depends," Nina said coyly, reaching out in an attempt to find Fawn's nipple through the whalebone of her shapewear and then giving up once she realized it was an impossible task in her current state. "What are you doing later?"

"Not me, dummy, your *actual* date. What's his name? Arya?"

"Oh," Nina said, her hand slipping to find Fawn's. "No way. I told you, Arya's just—"

She stopped, unintentionally locking eyes with one of the people in line for the restaurant next door. He was looking curiously over at her as a woman stood impassively beside him, typing something into her phone.

"Professor Villanueva?" Nina registered aloud without thinking.

"Nina!" exclaimed Professor Villanueva, his voice excessively upbeat. "I thought that was you."

"Oh, yeah," said Nina, realizing now how ridiculous she must look. Her hand was still floating midair, untaken for obvious reasons. "It's an invite. It's Malibu Barbie themed."

"Oh, a classic," said Professor Villanueva meaninglessly. Something felt off, Nina realized. She knew she was drunk and dressed like a sex object, but there was something much more off than that. The woman had looked up from her phone, frowning slightly at her. Then a different look passed over her face, which Nina didn't know what to do with.

"This is my friend Fawn," Nina said to fill the silence. "This is my philosophy professor," she added to Fawn, hoping she'd catch her drift.

"Oh, right, I forgot you were taking that class this semester," said Fawn. "Nice to see you, Professor!"

Odd phrasing, Nina thought. Or was it? Fawn had so many voices, Nina realized, as if from a dream. She could sound like so many people, with so many timbres and meanings and aims.

"This is my wife, Dr. Hartley," Professor Villanueva told Nina, maneuvering slightly out of the way. The woman beside him had a curious look on her face, like she was solving a math equation, though she managed to lift a hand in greeting.

Something lit inside of Nina like a sudden, distant triumph. She knew, like glimpsing another life through a keyhole, that this was what she had narrowly avoided by saying yes to The House. A boring life, waiting in line for a restaurant, having nothing to say to a man who probably fucks his students, who'll think about Nina's tits tonight when he comes in missionary while the baby sleeps.

"Dr. Hartley!" said Fawn in an animated voice. "You're our academic advisor, right?"

"Yes, oh, hi," said Dr. Hartley politely, like an email ending with the phrase *all best*. She wrapped her coat tighter around her—it was red, so beautifully tailored, effortless like she'd just pulled it on over her outfit, no forethought required. "God, aren't you girls cold?"

The side entrance opened, revealing a stumbling Arya in the frame.

"There you are!" he announced when he spotted Nina. "I was checking on you in the bathroom but then one of the other Barbies said—"

He stopped, straightening, when his eyes drifted over Nina's shoulder to Professor Villanueva and Dr. Hartley.

"Oh, Sloane," Arya said as if he couldn't help himself.

"Arya," Dr. Hartley replied in a low, amused voice. She looked suddenly more awake than she had in the moments previous.

"This is . . . I don't normally—" Arya coughed. "I don't usually refer to women as Barbies. I just—Well, I told you about my cousin Nina, right?"

"I do recall that you have one, yes." Dr. Hartley sounded like she was trying not to laugh. Nina thought she was really pretty, actually, especially now that she'd become interested in the conversation. She seemed like someone who probably knew what a good wine was and how to wash delicate fabrics and why that coat fit her so perfectly, like a glove.

"Well, that's us, I think," announced Professor Villanueva, gesturing to the name the host had just called, and that was when Nina clocked it. The strangeness. Professor Villanueva hadn't even glanced at Fawn, and was conspicuously not looking at her now. "Nice to see you! Enjoy your evening!"

"Looking forward to our hedonism discussion on Monday!" Nina called back unthinkingly.

Dr. Hartley gave something of a strangled laugh before following Professor Villanueva inside.

"That's the professor, isn't it?" Fawn said to Nina, who had forgotten they'd been joined by Arya.

"What professor?" he asked.

"The one Nina has the hots for." Fawn had a strange smile on her face, like it was forced. Was she jealous? Something in Nina roared with heat.

"Not really," said Nina. "I mean, he's hot. But I think he might actually do it, which makes it less fun."

"True, the fantasy is the fun part," Fawn agreed. Her gaze drifted sideways, interest lost.

"Oh, I don't know," said Arya quietly, half to himself. "Sometimes the fun is the fun part."

He looked like he'd sobered up in the past five minutes, or had tried to and failed. He no longer seemed joyful or free.

Then he turned to Nina, who, by contrast, was lightheaded with something she couldn't yet articulate. "You okay? One of your friends told me you were feeling sick."

"No, I'm—I mean, I'm fine now," Nina assured him, fumbling the lie. "I do still have to pee, though. Fawn?" she asked, turning to her. "Want to come?"

She didn't know what she'd accomplish sneaking into the bathroom, but she had a feeling that whatever it was, it wouldn't take long. Seeing Professor Villanueva in the wild could have been awkward and embarrassing—it certainly wasn't not—but what it really did was make Nina feel even more craven about her real life. About the little treats she deserved.

"Sorry, you know how girls are," Fawn offered to Arya, alive again, interested again, following Nina to the bathroom with a giggle once the three of them had gone back inside.

The stalls were roomy and ideal. Nina and Fawn slipped into one and kissed soundlessly, Fawn's fingers shoving Nina's flimsy thong aside to dive inside her. "This can't take long," she said in Nina's ear. "Someone will notice I've been gone."

"I won't take long," Nina assured her. "God, Fawn—"

"Don't say my name," Fawn whispered. Then: "Not until I make you come."

Nina nearly came on the spot. "I think you're onto something with the sneaking around."

Behind closed eyes she saw Dr. Hartley's red coat, like a lipstick stain on a starched collar. Fresh blood from a shallow cut. She wondered if elsewhere in the venue someone would feel it, the way the flutter of her orgasm around Fawn's fingers could spell out *I love you* in Morse code.

"I think I'm onto more than that." Fawn grinned wickedly, quickening her pace as she slipped her fingers in and out of Nina, pausing to rhythmically circle her clit. "This'll be so much easier when you move into the house," she murmured.

The thought of it made Nina sick with pleasure. "One more week."

"Mm." Fawn's tongue slipped out between her lips. "What do you think about your professor?"

"What?" Nina felt fucking indecent, riding the knuckles of Enchanted Evening Barbie like she'd never had a pure thought in her life. It felt ecstatic, freeing. She couldn't imagine the version of herself who'd wanted to fuck Professor Villanueva, even just for fun. It had seemed exciting once as a fantasy, but now it was pathetic, some grown-ass man who'd probably shove his dick down her throat while his wife checked on the casserole and changed diapers alone. Fucking disgusting. "I'm over him."

"I don't mean that." Fawn's eyes looked a little glazed over, watching Nina's breath quicken as she worked her fingers in and slowly out, one hand covering Nina's mouth to stifle her animal groans of urgency. "As a candidate."

"Candidate for what?" The words were muffled into Fawn's hand. Nina was so close it was physically painful. The angle was ever so slightly off; she wanted to part her legs wider, to be fucked somewhere she could leisurely spread out. She wanted nothing more than to scream for Fawn's mouth. The words *suck me, please, I beg you* crossed the forefront of her mind, which somehow made everything even more explosive.

Outside the door, the pulse of bodies was a minor revelry, a fleeting high. Not a hunt. The House in heat. Fawn pressed her hand flat against Nina, letting her grind herself hard into Fawn's palm until Nina finally, blessedly, came with a strangled moan.

"For dinner," whispered Fawn in Nina's ear, biting down hard on her lip.

31

"It's hard to believe we were ever that young," said Sloane in the car. Nina Kaur. She remembered Nina, the sophomore; had recognized her the moment she saw her from the pictures Alex had shown her of all the candidates. She'd had a certain look in her eye tonight, a sort of wild recklessness. Maybe just intoxication, or maybe the look of someone who'd fuck a professor because he seemed like more of a man than the average college boy.

Poor thing, she had no idea. Wash a man's underwear and all of a sudden the mystery was gone. "They looked like children, you know? Like little girls." Beautiful ones, almost unbelievably so, like their very existence defied any preexisting constraints on the limits of physical perfection, but still.

"I wouldn't go that far," said Max, shifting in the driver's seat. He'd seemed distracted through most of dinner, and still was. "What about that guy, your TA? He seemed way too old to be dressed like that."

"Well, he is," said Sloane. "He's a grown-ass man wearing a silly costume."

"And that's not weird to you?"

"Not really," said Sloane, with a shrug. "He was just there with his cousin. You're supposed to find a date for invite and she probably needed one. It's sweet."

"I guess," said Max.

Sloane couldn't wait to get home.

Theo was asleep with his head in Alex's lap when they arrived, so Sloane and Alex whispered their goodbyes and then Sloane pulled Max into the bedroom, greedily tugging down his trousers and getting to her knees.

She could feel herself throbbing with something, desperation. Max groaned when she slid a hand between her own legs, unable to wait. As soon as they both were adequately lubricated she shoved him back on the bed, digging out her vibrator and holding it to her clit as she rode him, holding in her mind's eye the desperate, fleeting thoughts of desk-fucking and bare Malibu abs.

By Sunday, Isla had come down with another runny nose and was beginning to be more verbally expressive. She was starting to say "please" and "thank you" unprompted. She remained uninterested in food or sleep. Her hair was almost long enough to be considered girly. She was growing and changing, minus the disinterest in food or sleep. "Babe, look," whispered Sloane urgently, hoping Max would see that Isla was singing to herself.

"What?" said Max, because maybe it was only visible to Sloane. Or maybe only Sloane had ever cared.

On Monday she had a check-in meeting with Dean Burns. "We're concerned you're not showing a commitment to this department," he said. "You rarely come to department events. Your colleagues routinely observe you leaving early."

"I have a child," said Sloane. "A *baby*. She's not even two years old."

"Of course, Sloane, we understand that, but Max spends time with the other members of his department and has already published in a journal this semester, and your only pitch so far has been—"

Right, of course. Given everything (cannibalism), Sloane had lost track of the deadline in recent weeks, her timeline irrevocably and necessarily shifting, such that "her future with the department"—a thing that evidently wouldn't exist if Burns had his way—could fucking wait.

"Aren't you concerned that Max spends more time with his

department than with his daughter?" said Sloane. "Who even reads academic journals, Dr. Burns? Do you really think that contribution is worth becoming an absence in your own child's life?"

"Sloane, please understand, when we're choosing tenured faculty members, we do have to consider whether they will put the University first. It's an honor, not a given, to be selected for the University's permanent faculty—"

"Do you really want me to tell you that you're more important than my daughter?" asked Sloane, incredulous. "Because you're not, Dean Burns. I think if you considered this for even a moment you'd realize that what you're asking is unfair."

"Many members of our faculty are parents, Sloane. You're not the first woman to have a child."

"No," Sloane agreed, not mentioning that she was also not the first woman to be passed over within the department as retaliation for having one. "Dean Burns, I *am* doing research, even if you don't care for it, but of course my time is limited right now. My child is young and my daily responsibility to her is substantial. As she grows older and more independent, then yes, I will be able to make the choice to spend longer hours away from home and contribute more enthusiastically to faculty research and programming. Until then—"

"Until then, I suppose it makes sense to table this discussion for now." Burns symbolically flipped her file closed. "And it's possible we may need to cut your lecturing hours next semester, to make room for more invested faculty."

Though she'd felt so gorgeously, coolly in control at the beginning of their conversation, Sloane's heart briefly stopped at that. "But then I'd only be a part-time adjunct." She inhaled, slowly, and exhaled. "I'd lose benefits. I'd lose childcare."

"Well, fortunately you have Max," said Dean Burns, as if this was something Sloane should have considered—as if she ought to have known this would be the only plausible end.

Sloane walked slowly back to her office with the thought that it really didn't matter, did it? What she said, what she did, the impossibilities she magically performed. Every day was laden with the guilt of being away from her child, of being an inadequate employee, of failing to be maximally exploited and thus losing the parts of the paycheck she needed to keep the abandoned child alive. Would anything be different if she were prettier or dressed better? If she had a nanny and stayed behind to hear from her colleagues about what hot new sociology trends were sweeping the nation and whether Janet had fucked Robert in the bursar's office, would anything really be better? Would life really be easier, or would it just be something else?

What did Sloane even want out of life, really? She realized Alex had asked her that question; that Caroline had essentially said the same thing. What even *was* a Good Woman? Sloane wanted uproariously to laugh. A good woman was just a good loser, because there was no fucking way to win. You fall in love, you marry someone devoted and interesting, and bam, you still somehow turn into your mother, and *his* mother, and every mother since the dawn of time. Was heterosexual marriage the problem? But then there was still the matter of being denied tenure, of being told the details of your life are uninteresting to serious men. Were men the problem? But then you made a new friend, a new circle of friends, and it turned out they had the same problems as you except their hair was nicer because they were goddamn cannibals. So maybe the problem was that *Sloane* was a woman, born with a losing hand. Where the motherfuck did it end?

She walked through her office door and stopped when she spotted Arya there, sitting at the usual desk, typing something diligently into the grading system. She saw him again in his tiny orange shorts, the pattern of his abs like a blazing beacon of youth and sex. That little quirk in his mouth, the way he undressed her when he looked at her, unwrapping her like the treat for which he had been so decadently patient, so impeccably behaved.

Arya looked up when he saw her, a warp of pleasant surprise melting to blithe confusion in the moment their eyes finally met.

"What?" he asked her.

Sloane shut the office door behind her and locked it. She let her bag fall from her shoulder onto the floor. The clock ticked down the twenty minutes left until her next lecture, which was plenty of time to cross an invisible line.

"Oh," said Arya.

So Sloane wasn't a good woman.

But did it really even matter anymore?

PART V

DINNER

*A simple life is a good life. Stay home.
Eat meat. Be happy.*

—Transcript from a VidStar by
@TheCountryWife

?

DAYS

UNTIL

?

BRIEF,

UNMISTAKABLE

SOUND

OF

CHATTERING

TEETH.

32

Nina found Professor Villanueva's lecture on hedonism to be something of a letdown. Prior to bumping into him in the outside world, she had believed him to be an enigmatic intellectual who did not belong to a class of people capable of gas or furtive masturbation. Now she understood him to be a human being, which was disappointing on many levels. She realized that he, like her, was fallible and very likely making things up as he went. Philosophy was not an exact science. He could interpret things as he wished, possibly incorrectly. And yet, somehow, it was his job to interpret her opinions in a way that would be forever reflected on her transcripts. It might very well determine the difference between a top twenty law school and virtual impoverishment.

Nina shook herself. No, it did not mean that.

"I constantly feel I'm in danger of doomscrolling over a very real cliff," Jas said while Nina was lounging in her new four-person bedroom—a large, spacious room at the back of the house called the Icebox, due to its hyper-enthusiastic air-conditioning. There were two sets of bunk beds lining one wall, then four dressers placed against the leftover wall space, with a walk-in closet that all four of them shared. It was aesthetically juvenile, like being a child at sleepaway camp, but simultaneously it was freeing. The four inhabitants mostly occupied the center of the room, on the floor, where they casually threw around topics such as what to wear to the evening's social events (the closet was really socialist in nature) and who they'd kill if given the chance.

"You know that you control the phone, right," Nina reminded her sister exhaustedly. "You can turn it off anytime you want."

"I just feel very un-grounded," Jas said, before asking tangentially, "You didn't fuck Arya, did you?"

"No. Seriously? Of course not. And you're not *grounded*, Jas, you never have been."

"Right, right, I should be more like you. Good Nina, calm Nina, such an easy baby—"

"Don't bring Mom into this. I mean it as a good thing. You're not grounded because you think about everyone constantly all the time. You somehow manage to hold in your head all of your friends in addition to every atrocity you come across on social media. I'm not sure it's even possible to be considered sane under those conditions."

"Just because I hold them in my head doesn't mean anything is coming back *out* of me," said Jas. "It's very unproductive to care this much and do nothing about it."

Nina threw up her hands. "But what can you even do?"

"That's it exactly, isn't it? I can't do anything because I can petition my representatives who are all paid by billionaires and they don't care and I can rant at everyone around me who also doesn't care and I can donate money to organizations who try to convince the people who don't care *to* care but then really just skim off the top. And at night, do you know what I think about?"

"How much your head hurts?"

"How I'd probably just shut up about all of it if I could marry Arya." Jas sighed heavily. "It's very disappointing to discover I'm just an ordinary person who wants stupid things. When I'm done thinking about Arya, I usually think about how unfair it is that I was born with plenty of food and clean water and access to electricity and all the time in the world to lust over a man who thinks I'm his cousin."

"Hi, Jas," called Dalil, who had just come in from her morning statistics lecture.

"Hi, Dalil," Jas had replied morosely. "Anyway, I'll stop bothering you, Nina, I know you have an actual life to get around to."

"Jasleen," said Nina. "I really think you need to delete Twitter."

"It's not even called that anymore, Nina. And believe it or not, that's *also* something I worry about. I mean, a lot of journalists found jobs that way. How am I supposed to be part of a disappearing industry? I was too busy seeking intellectual purity to go around blowing rich dudes who could give me jobs, like you."

"No offense taken," said Nina.

"Will you hire me, Nina? When I'm unemployable and homeless?"

"You won't be homeless, Jas. You have me, and I'm very high achieving."

"See?" moaned Jas. "My life is so easy and yet everything hurts."

"Have you considered just . . . going out and having a little treat?" said Nina. "I don't think your existential suffering is doing anything specific for the Sudan."

Which brought her back to the philosophy lecture, and the distinct sense as she watched Professor Villanueva that he'd lost a significant bit of shine. It seemed unfair, really, the certainty with which he made declarative statements, the exercises he posed as if humanity were hypothetical—something they simply *were,* ineffably, rather than something they did or chose. Was it because he methodically set aside the parts of the world that were untenable? Maybe that was the problem, that a certain percentage of the truth was meant to remain unexamined. Maybe Jas had opened herself up to too much information and now she was short-circuiting. Maybe when you looked an entire problem in the face you had to give up a bit of your ability to function. There was a peak, Nina thought, or a quota. At some point there was a ceiling on the darkness with which you could empathize, beyond which you had to compromise for the power of omniscience. The more you could see, the less you could care.

Nina hated to continue learning from a man who'd already revealed himself to be nothing more than a man, but wasn't he teaching her something critical now? That the only way to do any good at all was to focus on only a very, very small sliver of what could be controlled, and not wonder why some people were given power and agency and authority over others. Because those people would claim something about bootstraps anyway, which might not even be false in an overarching, universal, objective way. Was there really a metric for who deserved to be fed and who deserved to be eaten? What qualified Nina to be part of the hunt?

"You really think you're the only young female student he's willing to exploit?" Fawn had said to Nina the other day, lying together on the floor of the Icebox after Fawn had wandered by under the pretense of seeing how the new residents were settling in. Or maybe that's what Fawn had *actually* been there to do, except Nina was alone, so they got each other off in the socialist closet with one hand over the other's mouth. "Trust me," Fawn said from the postcoital haze, "you wouldn't be his first or his last."

"It just seems like there must be someone more deserving of slaughter," Nina commented. "Like a white man, at least."

Fawn flicked this away as she would a fly. "Ritualistically speaking, you don't want some shitty, shriveled organ," she said. "There's some parity here in terms of the quality of exchange."

"So it's a wellness thing now?"

Fawn gave Nina a hard look. "Who are you, Tessa?"

"No, I just mean—" Nina didn't understand the question. "I just meant, like, are you serious about this?" Nina attempted again. "Like, when you say 'the ritual,' are you talking about magic, or . . . ?"

In her head she became aware of something pressing in on her thoughts from the inside. She already understood the world consisted of untenable choices. In many ways she had been primed for this by Jas, and by Jas's understanding of the world as an unwinnable place that cannibalized itself inherently. The women who voted for men who stripped the rights of women. The rich who sacrificed the poor to perpetuate the myth that the rich alone could earn their wealth. Jas had recently ranted to Nina that prior to the Reagan administration, the wealthy had paid substantial taxes, such that it could not be argued that the suggestion of a wealth tax now was in any way unprecedented. Those same taxes had previously funded many of the social programs that no longer existed, many of which had ironically been cut by Democrats.

Not ironically. Hypocritically. Hypocrisy, that was the word, and it was also the world. Nina understood that she could live with all of these truths existing at once, the knowledge of what was right and what was necessary, and what was technically unnecessary but would still be done because it led to something that *had* to mean something, because otherwise what were any of us doing toiling away under capitalism, striving emptily for the intangibles of purpose and meaning while half the world clawed for the basic right to be alive, and starve?

The thing was, really, that when you broke it down like that, down into the little crumbs, really staring into the face of the problem and looking at it from all angles, it wasn't possible or ethical to be happy, and yet it was also completely unethical to be miserable, given the circumstances of her life. Okay, so Nina would be discriminated against for various reasons, she could be powerful or she could be beautiful but she could not really be both, she would always be exploited and yet to succeed she must always exploit someone else, and it was true that her success would always come at the cost of someone else's but, also, that was true for everyone, and therefore choosing *not* to be successful was a waste of resources that also meant Jas would almost certainly turn up homeless, and giving up or simply choosing not to accept the power Nina was offered was also, in some way, untenable.

Things could . . . change? Occasionally Nina almost believed this. But then she saw some impressively moronic opinion on the internet that assured her stupidity was not generational, that apathy wouldn't die out. One simply could not "Okay, Boomer" the entire world's injustices. Someone was always eating. Someone else was always being eaten. Was it magic? Was it balance? Was it a simple exchange of energies, neither lost nor destroyed?

The point was: Nina believed in it. The ritual. She could no longer remember a version of herself that did not. She was, after all, the reincarnated version of herself who understood the sisterhood that sat plated before her every Monday evening, piled high with love and care and compassion and unconditional support. It was more than just painlessness, more than wellness. It was utopia, it was womanhood the collective, it was the mercy and benediction of The House. The House was the Mother, they the Daughters, indivisible from the Holy Spirit. This was communion on high.

"We should ask what Caroline thinks. She's crazy," Fawn acknowledged aloud to the expression on Nina's face, "but she has a lot more experience with getting the most out of the ritual."

"I thought it was Alex who took care of the ritual?"

Nina thought of the woman called Dr. Hartley, the academic advisor who looked a lot like Alex. They had the same aesthetic build, like two white women exiting yoga together and going to the organic grocery store to talk about how their husbands never emptied the dishwasher. Nina felt an awareness of something then, a low-burning hatred, not like the hatred she had for The Patriarchy, which was the mortal enemy of The House, but something more like frustration or the feeling when you're having sex you didn't really want to have.

Alex represented something, an old guard, maybe, the kind of woman who might want Nina to succeed but wouldn't bat an eye if Jas were starving. Nina couldn't put a finger on why she knew this, exactly, but she just knew it, like some essential calculation in her soul. Dr. Hartley, she wasn't quite that, but her husband was Dr. Villanueva, and didn't that have to mean something? Wasn't there something wrong there somewhere, something off, with a woman who had chosen a man who was probably a predator, or was it just that she had chosen a man? But then Nina wasn't against men, romantically or sexually. She just didn't understand why Dr. Hartley had not had the same feeling Nina had, that to Professor Villanueva she was interchangeable, one of many—or maybe what Nina disliked was her certainty that Dr. Hartley *had* had that feeling but she had wanted to feel chosen anyway, because there was something inherent in being that choice that felt a little bit like winning, even from inside the game that nobody could win.

Nina didn't *respect* it, was the thing. She knew it was hypocritical, her joining The House because its acceptance would give her power, or her willingness to defy a fundamental tenet of human ethics because it would taste (ha) like victory in some way. But if it was all hypocrisy anyway, then who the fuck cared? Better this version of fake power than some guy who didn't unload the dishwasher, right? Or one who behaved and acted and voted from a place of solidarity, to make sure that power never transferred hands.

"First of all, Alex is completely full of shit," said Fawn. "Apparently the first ritual only happened because she accidentally killed some guy who'd roofied her. It was her pledge sisters who came up with the idea—no body, no crime." Fawn laughed faintly. "That's why she won't leave the ritual alone. She can't."

Nothing about that tracked for Nina. "I mean, isn't it only getting worse, though, the longer she keeps herself involved? Criminally speaking?" Nina recalled that Alex was a lawyer. She recalled even more hazily that she herself wanted to be a lawyer. It was another choice that tasted like safety. There was a savoriness there, a kind of maple-smoked essence, like a really complex barbecue rub. It existed from a place of hypocrisy. Nina wanted to make money. She wanted to do good. She couldn't do both, because in order to accomplish anything meaningful, goodness needed power behind it, but power without exploitation didn't exist. Or maybe this was just the hypocrisy thing again.

Fawn rolled her eyes. "Alex just needs control. If she's not in control then she's out of control. Then it's wrong."

"*Is* it wrong?" asked Nina.

Fawn said nothing for a second. For a moment, Nina wished she were having this conversation with Tessa. Sometimes, when she spoke to Fawn, she had the feeling she was staring directly into a shiny surface. Granite countertop. Vintage mirror. Glassy lake. Something that could change depending on where the wind might blow.

Then Fawn pushed herself up to one elbow from the Icebox floor. "Come here," she said, and slipped her tongue between Nina's lips, brushing the roof of her mouth. "Is that wrong?"

Without hesitation: "No."

Fawn's hand slipped under Nina's shirt, under her bra, taking a greedy palmful of Nina's breast. "Is this wrong?"

"No."

"Are you sure?"

"Not in any way that means anything."

Fawn laughed and pinched Nina's nipple.

"After a certain point you just don't give a fuck, you know?" she said. "I don't do 'wrong' or 'right' anymore."

"Did something happen to you?" Nina asked. She didn't know why she asked it then. She just had a feeling. She felt it in the Icebox, in the chapter room. That was it, she realized. The hum. The frequency. The way each of her new sisters carried something around with them. Someone who hadn't accepted the word no. Someone else who had never even asked permission. She couldn't tell if that was true of every roomful of women or if it was specific to The House—if The House's collective heart could only beat against a dissonance, a fundamental wrongness, a desperation to believe in a goodness that everyone else had denied them up to that point. A worthiness that only their personal gods could judge. They each had a starting point—then a definitive endpoint—of the girlhood they'd all endlessly fought to win back.

Nina's was last year. He had a name, but she hadn't asked it. She'd been the one wearing that dress, she'd been the one drinking to excess, she'd said yes to everything—except for the thing that she hadn't.

And for that, she knew there would never be justice. There would only be dinner.

"Yes," said Fawn, and kissed Nina again; quickly, hungrily. The real Fawn was always hungry, Nina realized.

So anyway, hedonism. Professor Villanueva didn't seem to understand it, but he taught Nina something about it all the same.

33

The problem was that Sloane had lost track of the deadline. The problem was that she'd been lured by a homicidal cult. The problem was that the skin of Arya's bare torso was pebbled over lightly, a whisper of indecency. Sloane pressed her hand flat along the ridges of his stomach like she might still push him away. "Can't keep doing this," she managed to say.

"Remind me why not?"

"Because it's wrong. Because it can't go anywhere. Because I love my husband. Because this is twenty minutes I could be spending with my daughter. Take your pick."

"Mm, could save you an extra five." His hand was deep in her jeans, cupping her groin where she leaned, straddling him with acrobatics she hardly knew she'd possessed, against her colleague's unused desk. "If you only want one this time."

"This is ridiculous," gasped Sloane, and it was. Two of Arya's fingers had worked their way inside her, curling up to hit a meticulously targeted spot. She felt her balance give way and leaned harder onto Arya, pondering briefly how disgusting it would be to move all this to the floor. She knew for a fact the custodial staff paid no attention to this part of the offices, probably because Burns's board cronies didn't pay them enough.

This deep underground, the eyes of all the buildings could be turned conveniently away. The real problem was that Sloane suffered the constant pain of her injustices, the slights against her that she knew to be outrageous, indefensible. The way every simulation still drove her right here. But if she'd had a cock. Would any of this be what it was?

Speaking of cocks. Arya's leapt where it was pressed to the inside of her thigh. They could fuck right now; technically speaking, Sloane had the time. She wondered what Isla was doing. It was music day at the daycare. Every Friday they brought in a young guy with a guitar who sang "Old MacDonald" to her precious baby daughter, whose eyes shined bright with love for any chance to say moo. Her daughter, who also didn't have a cock, and would get so horrifically fucked one day, in a way that Sloane could predict but not prevent.

Sloane ran a hand up the back of Arya's neck, grabbed a handful of dark strands, and pulled. If Isla was lucky, she would know love before sex. But statistically speaking the odds were against her.

Sloane wouldn't have worn pants if not for telling herself this wouldn't happen. She told herself a lot of things these days. Cannibalism, for example, continued to be ethically wrong but it was somehow better if it only happened once or twice a year; if some kind of reasonable steps were taken to mitigate harm. Arya got on his knees and pulled Sloane's new trousers down. Britt had sent her the link for these pants. They made her ass look shapely and full and young again; they yanked her back into her most desirably grabbable form. From his knees, Arya shifted her around and bit the curve of her ass to prove it. Lovely Arya, who could have any woman still in her physical prime, before she became aware of her back. Before she had to routinely account for the place where her perineum had been imperfectly restitched. A woman who still believed that desire had reasonable limits, or maybe the opposite, a woman who did not yet know the desperation she could feel; that she could find a man sexy and want his babies without fully understanding the kind of person he'd one day become under middle-aged circumstances. Sloane closed her eyes as Arya pushed aside her underwear, widening her legs so he could fit his mouth carnivorously between her thighs.

The first time she'd initiated this little lapse in judgment, they'd simply fucked, hard and penetrative, no frills. The second time, Arya had begun to exhibit some finesse, ostensibly to prove something. Like showing her his résumé. He seemed to understand that there were limits to the work product he'd be given the opportunity to share—his position, such as it was, had time constraints.

Sloane felt powerful in that deeply frustrating way, because there was no real power here. She was at least old enough now to understand that, which was what made her, in her mind, less attractive than Arya's other theoretical options. The imaginary younger woman who still felt like making a man come was the same thing as having power over him. But could it get you tenure? Okay, well, maybe. Sloane could try to fuck Burns and see where that got her. But as soon as she stepped a foot wrong—as soon as it became clear that her interests and his were no longer aligned—it would stop being power and be what it was, which was sex. Which this also was. And there was no power here, nothing being exchanged, because Sloane was having her lecturing hours cut to part time, and Max suddenly wanted to take a sabbatical, because he had work he needed to do on his book, for which he apparently did not have the time right now despite having so very much of it compared to Sloane.

"You can't be serious," Sloane had said when Max informed her of his intentions that morning, a few hours before she unwisely failed to suck Dean Burns's dick during the department lecture he'd heavily implied was mandatory. "If you take a sabbatical then we lose Isla's daycare. I'm not considered full time anymore."

"I told you not to piss off Burns," Max muttered. Max, it appeared, was frustrated with *her*. "You know the University requires tenure track faculty to publish. And there was never any guarantee they could keep you on as an adjunct full time."

"I'm aware of that, Max." She, after all, had been working all semester on something extremely viable to publish, which she would have the time to do if Isla could stay in daycare, but not if she couldn't. "But if you take a sabbatical now—"

"You complain *every day* about the time you're missing with Isla," Max snapped at her in visible frustration. "Now you can spend more time with her. Or is that something to complain about, too?"

"Okay, so are you going to watch her while I teach?"

Max waved a hand irritably. "Yes, fine, as long as it doesn't interfere with my writing schedule, or we can just get a babysitter for a couple of hours—" Never mind how much that would cost.

"How much of this book do you need to write?" Sloane could feel herself becoming more shrill, which was never a good sign. "I haven't even heard you mention a book all semester."

"I talk about it all the time, not that you're ever listening to me anymore—" The second half was a mutter under his breath, another jabbed accusation.

"I don't understand why you need an entire semester to do it—I mean, can't it just wait until the summer? Wait a minute." It struck Sloane belatedly. "I have my courses for next semester—you should have yours. Why are you just now trying to take a sabbatical?"

Max sighed again, pushing to his feet. "Sloane—"

"Are they pushing you into it?" A dull thud sounded somewhere in Sloane's inner ear, like the fall of the other shoe, the one she had known for so long was coming. "What did you do?"

"I didn't do *anything*, Sloane, I just need t—"

"It's that girl, isn't it? That undergrad? Nina Kaur." Sloane swallowed hard, the truth materializing in her head, like finally recognizing the silhouette of a shadow on the wall. "What'd you do, fuck her? Did she report you or did you get caught?"

Max looked briefly torn between walking out and clenching a fist. "Sloane, *Jesus,* I am not fucking my student—"

"Then why do they want you out, Max?"

She had him, she knew she had him. There was a darkness over his face, an obvious inability to meet her eye. Maybe she didn't have the details exactly right, but she had *something*—she was right about some of it, if not all of it. Sabbatical! Please. Not a chance that was his choice. Who would laud Max then? Who would laugh at his jokes? How would he avoid being at home with his wife and daughter if he committed himself to staying home? And say that Sloane *did* leave Isla at home with him, knowing he wouldn't engage her as Miss Lily did, as Sloane did, as Alex did. How was she to know he'd even *be* there—that she could trust him even a little, or at all?

The resentment Sloane had been fighting spilled over, revealing the truth of itself. The fact that Sloane trusted a bunch of fucking cannibals to take better care of Isla than her child's own father. She felt the tireless, jaw-tensing sensation of not allowing herself to reveal her disappointment, her fucking mortification over being the kind of woman who'd fallen right into the everywoman trap. It didn't matter how smart she was! How fuckable! How beautifully she was aging! How much she hydrated or paid for eye cream! There was no power in beauty because it still couldn't grant her a faithful husband! It couldn't give her lasting value in the workplace! It didn't offer her a goddamn thing!

"No," said Isla then, sweetly, in response to the oatmeal she wasn't eating. Sloane wanted to throw up and jump off a cliff.

"I'll get her one of those Clif Bars," Max muttered.

"Those aren't real food. Fucking Christ," said Sloane, to herself, to Isla, to everyone and everything. "She still doesn't drink milk, she's still not getting enough iron—"

"What do you want to do about it?"

"I don't know, Max! *Who are you fucking?*" shrieked Sloane, and Max had said something about not being able to reason with her and then he left to go to work, which was a thing he did every day, for hours and hours, with Sloane now forced to acknowledge that she didn't know how he filled that time—whether it was haunted by thoughts of his daughter, as hers was, and whether he would ever live up to the person his daughter deserved, or if he was just getting blown by some pretty teenager who didn't yet have crow's feet or a fucking sense of solidarity to her kind.

No, no. Sloane forced herself to calm down, to think rationally. This wasn't the pretty teenager's fault. Sloane thought then about Nina Kaur, about her beautiful face and her lovely breasts and her dry, drunken remark that had so undressed Max—so prodigiously unnerved him.

It had to have been Nina Kaur. Sloane hadn't seen Max that shrunken up before, like someone had shined a harsh, unflattering light on his face. Interrogation lighting. He'd looked old to Sloane then, newly a little paunchy, a curve she hadn't noticed before spilling over the top of his jeans. Not like Arya, who'd looked ridiculous at the time, and yet also like he'd been carved from stone.

So yes, Sloane had gone to her office the following Monday intending to write and then she'd fucked the twentysomething who worked for her, so there was that for her dignity. Because yes, Sloane could feel that cannibalism was fundamentally wrong, but so was adultery, and was there any real way to compare? (Yes, but Sloane was close now, so close her thoughts were blurring, her hand wrapped painfully tight in Arya's hair.) Okay, so her husband had cheated on her—was cheating on her?—and now she would probably lose her office and she would have to stay home with Isla, because the amount she brought in as a part-time lecturer was essentially equal to the cost of non-University childcare, and that math simply didn't make sense. And yes, it was true, Sloane wanted desperately to stay home with Isla, but didn't it matter that *she* had a book? One that might actually sell, unlike whatever self-indulgent monstrosity Max would write about the unbearable [blank]-ness of being! She could leave him, she recalled. That was technically an option. She could go it alone like Alex, who might be a cannibal but who was also a really good mom. Couldn't a person be two things without one counteracting the other? Maybe a man could.

Sloane came so hard that she choked, a little saliva spilling helplessly from her lips. She wiped it away quickly, feeling something about herself that was mainly disgust. She hated that she could still feel that way so easily—that nothing ever changed, not really.

"You okay?" Arya looked up at her, his lips slick, mouth red. "Sloane."

Some young girl was out there right now accomplishing things, becoming an interesting person with innovative thoughts, exercising regularly and taking care of her skin, spending money on clothes that made her waist look small and her legs seem long so that she could be noticed by a guy like Arya, who would make her feel like she wasn't alone anymore, like she mattered, like there was so much love in her heart that she could share it with somebody else, and she'd love him so much, so profoundly, that she'd long so intrinsically for a person she hadn't yet met and then she'd feel that person's heart beating inside her, and then theoretical-Arya would become someone different, a person who didn't particularly want to change—or maybe some other version of the exact same fate, the one where you're a woman and it's your job to make everything easier for everyone around you, even though nobody will ever think of you.

You're a woman, and it's your job to fade into the background. It's your job to make sure your children love their father and never know what a fucking idiot he is, or how little he is capable of accomplishing without you. You're a woman, and it's your job to have it all but never complain about how heavy it is to carry. You're a woman, so you must strive to achieve, even if those achievements will drive the envy that means you will always be disparaged and never be embraced. You're a woman, and you were put here to suffer and feel pain, or so people will say, and so they will act, and so you will never be properly treated and your borne-in aches will never be taken for the fatal blows that they are. You are a woman, and so the transgressions against you will always be justified in some way by what you wore or what you said or who you are, and everything bad that happens to you will always somehow be deserved. Unless you die a martyr, for your children, which is the only sure way to be a Good Woman. Because then, when you are dust and unexamined, important only for the act of ending, you will finally have the honor of being a saint.

"No," said Sloane, "I'm not all right," but she knew there was only one person who could fix it. It wasn't Arya, who was a good man, or maybe he wasn't a good man, who even knew anymore, but good things didn't grow from poisoned earth. If this could have ever been real, Sloane had fucked that up the moment she took him at the expense of her own goodness.

And she still wanted it, the goodness. That was the fuckery! She still wanted to be a Good Woman, a thing that didn't exist, some utter fucking mythology—except that even in this world, the one that she already understood was on fire, there was still the glowing light of Isla. The only untainted piece of Sloane's heart.

So later, she dialed the number, and the other line answered: "Hello?"

"Hey," said Sloane, taking a deep, sustaining breath. "Sorry to bother you. Are you free right now?"

"I've got a few minutes," said Caroline Collins. "What can I do for you, Dr. Hartley?"

34

Post-initiation, with all The House's secrets bared, life took on a certain elasticity, a looseness that came from an absence of conflict. Dalil—for whom ADHD was regarded, even venerated, as a foundational personality trait—was sailing through her classes with ease; Nina, likewise, found her schoolwork invigorating, her mind well-rested and her intellect freshly ripe. She read with a voracity she hadn't felt in years, absorbing new information intravenously. The rich marination of her thoughts derived new, caramel bursts of inspired conclusions, like the first bite into tender, slow-cooked ribs.

By contrast, Monday night dinners took on a heightened revolutionary energy. Nina had sensed some element of this before, but now it was clear that the dinners were meant to stave off some deeper, wilder appetite. The decadence of the food no longer seemed the point, or even the main event; the dinners were, instead, increasingly like opulent rounds of amuse-bouche to whet the palate. The usual tension, like chattering teeth, radiated in waves among all the sisters, emanating from the older ones who already knew what to expect.

That particular semester had always carried with it a forward momentum, one that Nina had mistakenly associated with her own reinvention, where initiation was the finish line. But no. It had nothing to do with her, except that she now belonged to the feeling rather than observing it from outside.

The week after she'd moved into The House, as the nights grew darker and colder and the leaves fell swirling from the trees, dinner was a hearty beef bourguignon that was a rich, viscous garnet, dripping pearls of ruby red over thick, tender cuts of meat from an ensorcelling vat of vintage Burgundy wine. The chapter meeting, to which Nina and her pledge class were now not only invited but expected, took place afterward, each of the girls licking stew from her lips with distraction, an air of ongoing hunger, despite the pear and cardamom tart that had followed, crumbling with butter and slick with crystalline sugar like the daydream of a Dickensian orphan or the glossy prelude to sex.

The chapter meetings were overseen by Fawn—Lady Superior, within The House's nomenclature—and Nina adjusted to seeing herself during these hours as Sister Kaur, Dalil as Sister Serrano, another element of cultlike behavior that instead felt leavening, as if drawing them up to an equal, shared height.

The hunt had no hierarchy. Only a leader. Nina watched Fawn as she always had, but differently now, more protectively than searchingly. Fawn scratched an itch and Nina noticed. Fawn's gaze went temporarily distracted and Nina wondered who, where, what.

There were no phones allowed in the chapter room. Disrespectful. Chapter was about togetherness, about sisterhood, about honoring the body, the collective whole. The House voted on which exchange invitations to accept. The House was informed of the changes in study hours (The House had its own library, with predictable, institutional rules) and advised how best to take notes. There was occasional extracurricular programming, sexual health workshops, disaster preparedness, even notably a mini-course on self-defense. Beauty programming was also present, but it focused obsessively on inner wellness. They weren't educated on the use of exfoliants or the latest beauty fads because it was broadly accepted, Nina observed, that such things were mere tedium. Real sisters understood that beauty came from within.

(Not the soul, obviously. The digestive system. From the energy you consumed, which became the tools your body used to perform its necessary, natural tasks.)

Weeks passed in a flurry of midterms, liaisons, and meat. Then Monday night dinner was steak tartare, served beneath lustrous, runny eggs that were an almost umber, alongside salty mouthfuls of acid capers. Nina and Tessa took turns tearing off pieces of the accompanying bread, a rustic French loaf, with sips of the liquified chocolate that was the evening's beverage, bittersweet lechery topped with a spellbinding cream.

"I haven't seen much of you lately," Tessa confided in a whisper during the chapter meeting, when both she and Nina were full to groaning, such that even Nina couldn't think of sex. She wanted only to slumber deeply, uninterrupted, for several years, or until her next meal.

"Oh," Nina said, feeling her cheeks heat at the reason for her distraction that she already knew she couldn't give. "I know, sorry, I just—"

"Sisters," Fawn called out to the room in greeting as she rose ceremoniously to her feet, and so Tessa motioned quickly to Nina a thing that meant *later*, they had business to attend to now.

"As you know," Fawn continued, "chapter elections for next year's executive board will be taking place soon. Slate will be meeting this evening, with candidates being announced tomorrow morning. We will also," she said, with a slight gleam in her eye, "be discussing the matter of our annual solstice dinner, which will take place next month on the evening of elections, per House tradition."

There was a ripple of motion throughout the chapter room. Nina looked over at Dalil, whose gaze had sharpened, somehow. Nina thought idly of stakes, and then steaks.

"For those of you who are new to the matter of dinner, you are each asked to present a candidate on the evening of the feast," said Fawn, whose sly smile quirked then. "Dinner is, as you know, best prepared fresh."

"Wait, what?" Nina whispered to Tessa, managing to sit up slightly despite the compression of her waistband. "We have to bring a guest?"

"They all get slipped something right away," Tessa assured her, "don't worry. Assuming they're not chosen, they have basically no memory of the evening." She made another quieting motion of her hands—they'd discuss the details later, as if Nina could so easily be made to wait. *Assuming they're not chosen.*

"The matter of deliberation should be as expedient as possible. Let's not have a repeat of last year, ladies," said Fawn, with a knowing look in her eye. "Please come prepared."

"What?" said Nina again, only for her chair to be kicked by Alina, who was sitting behind her.

Tessa leaned closer to Nina, her voice barely audible as she explained. "Everyone has about two minutes to explain who they brought as a candidate and why, and then we vote. Last year we ran a little behind and had to do a couple of rounds of voting—The House was gridlocked between four candidates, and the whole thing took so long that someone's guest woke up."

"God." Nina's hand flew to her mouth. "Then what happened?"

"Oh, it was fine," said Tessa with a shrug. "Alex took care of it."

"Wait, but—"

"As you know," Fawn continued, "the ultimate honor of preparing dinner goes to our seniors, whose participation in the ritual means they're allotted the best portions as a reward. It's only fair," Fawn added, "since they're the ones who are about to enter the real world. Or grad school," she joked, "for those who can't cut it quite yet."

"Booooooo," called Sienna, a senior.

"I'm joking, Sister Lee, we know you're going to be a very

talented surgeon. We're less sure about Sister Antwerp's aspirations. Doesn't the world have enough PhDs?"

Behind Nina, Alina lazily flipped Fawn off and the room collectively laughed.

"All jokes aside," Fawn said once the laughter had subsided, "I invite you to think very carefully when you make your selection." Fawn's eyes got a hardened look to them. "Consider what is being asked of you as you make your choices this year. We must protect the sisterhood as well as nourish it. We do not only eat. We also decide."

There was a ripple throughout the room of something; an unusual current of discord. Someone had nudged Summer's shoulder as if to gesture at something unsaid. A few girls shifted in their seats, exchanging glances. Something had clearly energized or disgruntled the crowd, though Nina couldn't tell what.

She looked at Tessa, who shook her head. "Later," Tessa mouthed, this time without an aside.

"With that, chapter is adjourned," said Fawn, recovering some of her usual brightness. "Slate, you've got a long night ahead of you, so we'll take some volunteers to send up an assortment of pastries and other snacks—"

There was a bustle of movement, Tessa taking an iron hold of Nina's hand to drag her out of the room and out to the roof, where they had last spoken privately during initiation.

"Okay, where do you want me to start?"

"Fawn," said Nina instantly, which was so clearly not the answer Tessa wanted to hear. Nina, too, didn't know why she'd said it. She supposed she'd meant something along the lines of *why was Fawn being so weird and serious for a second there,* or maybe just *let's talk about Fawn, isn't she so pretty?* like any idiot with a crush, but Tessa—probably for the best—had other interpretations.

"The truth is, she's probably going to lose," Tessa confirmed, a shocking answer to something Nina hadn't even intended to suggest. Tessa, meanwhile, glanced over her shoulder as if she feared someone might hear. The two of them were alone on the roof, but even Nina understood The House was always listening. "I'm not sure if she plans to run again, actually," Tessa continued in a low voice, "and it really might be better if she turns down Slate, but if she doesn't, it won't be easy. She'll have at least one challenger for sure."

"What?" Nina was rattled to hear it—the possibility that Fawn was in any way unpopular. "Are you serious? But she's so perfect for the job. And everyone loves her."

Tessa gave Nina a surprisingly hard look. "No, Nina. *You* love her. But the others think she's . . . I don't know, fickle. That her agenda doesn't fit with theirs."

By the look on Tessa's face, Nina could see she wasn't talking about someone obvious, like Summer, who even Nina knew wasn't overly close to Fawn. If anything, Tessa seemed to be suggesting that the person Fawn's agenda didn't fit with was Tessa's own.

"But—" Nina couldn't think of how to voice her protest. "But I thought—didn't you say . . . ?" Nothing more dignified came to mind aside from *but Daddy I love him!*

"Look, compared to the rest of The House, I've got some . . . particularly charged views about the purpose of the dinner." Tessa raised her hands in a portrait of sardonic innocence. "And there's probably a reason Fawn chose to invoke them, even though I wasn't so sure she still agreed with me these days."

"But—"

"Maybe she does," Tessa qualified with a shrug. "Or maybe she has something else in mind, and honestly, that's her prerogative." There was an unreadable tone to Tessa's voice. Or rather, to a less informed ear, it might sound like Tessa harbored some resentment toward Fawn.

"But . . . you're friends," said Nina.

"Yep," said Tessa. Her voice was edged with something, possibly sarcasm. Maybe disappointment. Maybe Nina had imagined it.

"But sisterhood," Nina insisted with juvenile fervor, and then Tessa laughed.

"All sisters disagree," she reminded Nina. "For most of The House, the important thing is the future. *Their* futures, specifically."

"But isn't the future important to everyone?" They'd all chosen the University before they ever chose The House. So wasn't it obvious they all had aspirations?

"That's not what I mean. It's . . . you know, dogma. The ritual as, like, supplement. A juice cleanse. Some magical alternative to retinol or something."

Nina made a face. "But it isn't, because—?"

"You know my feelings on it." Tessa shrugged. "The violence of the ritual isn't just some unfortunate side effect. This isn't a 'thoughts and prayers' situation. It's a choice, which means it can be a meaningful one. It should be; it has to be."

"But that's how Fawn sees it, too," Nina insisted, although in retrospect, she realized that Tessa's explanation for the ritual on the night of initiation had blurred with her memories of being with Fawn. Maybe Fawn hadn't explained what she really felt about the ritual—maybe Nina had drawn conclusions from disparate pieces, unrelated parts.

"It's more than that, honestly," Tessa said with a shake of her head. "It's not like Fawn's completely uncontroversial. She's still pretty close to Caroline—"

"Oh," said Nina. Not that Fawn had any flaws in Nina's mind, but with a gun to her head—if Nina had to pick one little nit when it came to Fawn's judgment—The Country Wife was the obvious one. Nina had scrolled through Caroline's VidStar feed and marveled for a second at the raw physicality of her own reaction. A low-boiling knot of rage had formed in Nina's stomach, one that she couldn't quite name or identify, so she had simply closed the app and told herself that Fawn was just a proponent of free speech, and anyway, real feminism meant not judging women who lived unconventional lifestyles—right? The feminist choice was the one that every woman was empowered to make. (Charitably assuming that Caroline was actually unconventional and not, in fact, the definition of convention itself.)

Something in Nina deflated for a moment, more tired or humiliated than sad. She had thought of Fawn as a revolutionary, like Tessa. That belief lived central to the canon of their joining, inseverable from their first meeting (which, Nina realized, was also the result of Tessa). The more Nina searched her memory, replaying the last few weeks without the rosy veil of longing or things that Tessa had actually been the one to say, the only thing Fawn had explicitly gone to bat for was Caroline—which was either a strategy (depressing) or a personal favor (unbeneficial to The House as a whole; also depressing). What did Fawn actually want?

Nina shook herself. This wasn't doubt. It was mere . . . consideration.

"Fawn's made a lot of enemies over the course of her presidency," Tessa went on with a grimace. "She can be . . . opaque sometimes. It's hard to tell whether she'll be on your side or not when it comes down to it. And she's definitely had someone in mind for the ritual all year, so maybe this is her way of preempting it."

Nina realized there was one other thing aside from Caroline that Fawn had been adamant about—only one thing that she'd brought up multiple times. The ritual, and specifically Professor Villanueva as a candidate. But that was for *Nina's* benefit, was it not?

Of course it was. "Isn't that the whole point of the ritual?" Nina focused on Tessa's latter critique, having no means to combat the former. "I mean, you said it, right? Justice? It's not supposed to be just some random, spontaneous luck of the draw—"

"I explained it to you the way that I did because I knew you'd agree with me," Tessa cut in gently, maybe even regretfully. "But not everybody does. A lot of the girls want to focus on the first part Fawn talked about at chapter—the meal. *Enrichment.*" Tessa's face belied some level of repulsion. "There's a reason it's for the seniors. The meal is what's most important to them, because for them, it's their last chance to soak up as many nutrients as possible before they start the next phase of their lives. But to me, the whole concept of the dinner . . ." Tessa trailed off again. "It doesn't last forever. It can't, and it isn't meant to. Unless you're willing to risk everything like Caroline, I guess, but even so, it has to be about more than just the meal."

Nina frowned. "I don't understand. You're saying that—"

"I'm saying that philosophically speaking, half The House would prefer to eat someone young and hot like you than a crusty old white dude, even if he's actively more of a problem," joked Tessa. "To them, the point of the ritual is to take on some of the qualities you consume. Historical societies like the Tupi ate their enemies or even family members from a place of respect. And in terms of reaping a reward, a geriatric liver is less than ideal even if we *could* eat the Supreme Court. Though," Tessa continued, "I happen to think there has to be a balance. Ritual aside—assuming for a second this isn't about some flimsy concept of magic, but about real, actual power—then the decree of judgment needs to matter. Strategy counts for something. The only thing that changes the system is a threat to the system itself.

"And Fawn . . . agrees," Tessa said after a moment's pause, though she didn't sound like she'd profess to it in court. "Or seems to. The point is, it's not that the ritual is either wellness or violence. It can and should be both."

"But that wouldn't actually happen," Nina argued, stuck on the idea of eating someone to absorb their beauty or youth. It felt cartoonish, vaguely Victorian, distorting the righteous sanctity she'd associated with the hunt. "Right? Choosing someone young, or even a woman? Like, that's—" Nina broke off, flustered, and fell back on the sharpest weapon she had the language for, unable to conceive of a more viable string of words. "Like, deeply unfeminist, right?"

"Feminism is a matter of structure," came a voice behind them. "It's about institutional resources and opportunities. It's not some arcane throw pillow that says 'live, laugh, love.'"

It was Alina, whom Nina hadn't spoken to all that often since recruitment. She was looking at Nina with a wry, condescending expression. "Just wanted to check your vibes on something," said Alina, addressing Nina with a mere fleeting glance before turning more conclusively to Tessa. "I'd wait to catch you alone, but I'm pressed for time. How do you think Sister Serrano would feel about the presidency?"

"What?" said Nina.

"Slate wants to know," Alina said in apparent explanation. So then Alina was on the Slate committee—she was one of the girls tasked with selecting The House's new leadership, something Nina hadn't known until ten minutes ago was even relevant to her. She'd thought Fawn's second term as president was an obvious lock, a foregone conclusion.

"Alina. Are you serious?" Tessa shot Alina an odd glance. "You're not trying to humiliate her, are you?"

"Humiliate Dalil?" echoed Nina.

"Come on, Tess," said Alina, now negotiating with Tessa in some way that Nina couldn't follow. "You know I love Fawn— honestly, this is a compromise. It's still keeping Fawn's legacy intact. She can announce she's going abroad in the spring and use that as an excuse if she's worried about her reputation. And Dalil is a perfectly neutral candidate—"

To that, Tessa threw up her hands in apparent repulsion. "Come *on,* Alina! You know Dalil's the one person Fawn can't possibly run against—she's her *Big*. And it's not like Dalil can win against Summer—"

"That's assuming Summer decides to run if she's not Slated," Alina said, cutting Tessa off before her rant could escalate. "And even if she does run, who cares? If Summer runs against Dalil and wins, that's just democracy, baby." Alina's tone was grim.

"But I thought you guys weren't sure about Dalil," said Nina, glancing between Tessa and Alina with an utter absence of plot. "Right? I mean, during rush you said that thing about, you know, her social media or whatever—"

She broke off when she realized Alina and Tessa were busy having a wordless argument, one that seemed to have started long before Nina entered the conversation, or even The House.

"You've basically admitted that Summer's the heir apparent," Alina said flatly to Tessa, "and this shit with Fawn aside, I do think Summer's a solid choice. But what I do *not* want to do with my last days in office is start an unnecessary war."

"So then don't," Tessa insisted. "Slate Fawn because she's the incumbent and she's eligible, and then let *The House* vote Summer in—"

"Tessa." Alina gave Tessa a look that edged close to pity. "It's not going to be Fawn."

Tessa looked like she'd been slapped.

Nina felt it too, the thud of something. Significance.

"Alina," Tessa said hoarsely. "You'll *destroy* her."

Alina brushed this away. "Come on, she knows it's coming—"

"She knows she won't run unopposed, but to not even get Slated?" An insult, Nina pieced together contextually, or possibly worse. She herself was still shocked to some degree, as she could not imagine Fawn without the presidency, nor could she imagine someone else filling Fawn's hallowed shoes. (Fawn's feet didn't sweat—another otherworldly thing about her.)

"You of all people know Fawn turned out to be . . ." Alina hesitated, her attention slipping briefly to Nina before she shrugged in put-on indifference. "Look, Fawn does Fawn, end of story. And I get that, honestly, I do. I wish her luck with it. I just don't respect it." Alina's expression was stone. "If we're going to leave this house in someone's hands—this *ritual* in someone's hands—then it should be someone who comes to it with fresh eyes. That's the point of trying to pick someone like Dalil—someone without any baggage. But I promise you," she finished, "the only thing that room can agree on right now is that Fawn is definitively out."

Tessa looked stung. Then pained.

Then, within a matter of seconds, Nina watched Tessa run through a cycle of grief that resolved with a weary look of acceptance. Like a flower blossoming under accelerated time-lapse.

Then Tessa shook her head, exhaling, and looked square at Nina.

"Pick Sister Kaur instead," she said, and Alina and Nina both balked.

"What?" said Nina, at the same moment Alina let out a frustrated sigh.

"Tessa. Sister Kaur—" Alina cut herself off, potentially realizing that Nina was right there, and a person. "Nina is a great candidate," Alina said with an air of weighty deliberation, "but she hasn't shown any sign of interest in joining Exec. Dalil is more active and influential within their pledge class, and she shows more of an interest in the other members of The House—I mean, Nina is basically Fawn's acolyte. No offense," she added to Nina.

"None taken," said Nina faintly. It was, after all, true, although she hadn't previously known there was another option. She'd thought Fawn *was* The House, and vice versa. It hadn't occurred to her that Fawn's agenda could ever be separate from the rest of the hunt.

The House, Nina corrected herself.

"Exactly," said Tessa, with a grim air of necessary risk. "Then

Nina can say she learned from Fawn, or even that Fawn personally tapped her. Right?" Tessa looked at Nina again, imploringly, before turning back to Alina. "And if Nina loses to Summer, then fine, the other faction gets their pick. Democracy, baby," she added, echoing Alina with a similarly bitter laugh.

But this course of action did not seem as reasonable to Alina as it did to Tessa.

"Tessa, *why*—" Alina looked like she'd begun to say something more inflammatory, but stopped herself just in time. "Why are you still trying to protect her?" she said, with slightly more measured frustration that time. "She doesn't deserve it. You of *all* people know she doesn't deserve it."

Nina looked sharply at Tessa, who lifted her chin and refused to meet Nina's eye.

"It doesn't matter what she deserves," Tessa said after a moment. "She can fail me all she likes, that's her choice. Doesn't mean I have to do the same." She straightened, then said, "With Nina, Slate gets what they want: a fresh candidate. Summer probably knows she'll have to run either way, so does it matter which pawn you sacrifice to take Fawn off the board? Do it as a favor to me."

The expression on Alina's face said that she'd lost the argument. Nina couldn't imagine how—she agreed with Alina, frankly, that Dalil was a more compelling candidate. Nina didn't understand how Tessa could feel *she* was any more suitable a choice, or what possibly gave Nina the credentials to be president of something she'd only belonged to for a matter of weeks. But to Alina, Tessa's decision was obviously final.

"Fine. Say we play it your way and Slate Nina," Alina posed aloud. "There's no chance Summer sits it out."

"No," Tessa agreed. "If you pick Nina, Summer runs and she wins. That's your argument to convince Slate."

Nina tried to do this math in silence. It seemed like Tessa was implying that people might actually like Dalil enough not to run against her, whereas Nina was no such threat. Nina did not feel this observation like an injury; she felt it like awe. Like she was watching Tessa take the Western Front.

Everything Nina thought she knew had shifted. The person she'd thought was everyone's idol was only her own, and now her hero lay on the floor with twenty-three knives in her back, with only Nina left to praise her. It was Tessa everyone looked to all along. Was *that* power?

Alina, meanwhile, was still posturing. "Even if Fawn does decide to run, the best she could hope for is winning over the younger members, who'd more likely vote for Nina. Which would still split the vote in Summer's favor—"

"Fawn won't run against Nina," Tessa cut in loyally, with certainty. "She loves her."

"Yeah? She loves you, too." Alina arched a brow.

Tessa said nothing. Nina opened her mouth and then, finding nothing, closed it again.

Alina heaved a sigh before diving back into her calculations like a person performing surgery. "If Fawn does run against Nina, so will Summer, and then Nina and Fawn both lose. That's actually the easiest possible sell for Slate." Something in Alina's expression had changed. She looked at Nina for a long, invigorated moment, like seeing someone who wasn't actually there. "Okay, Sister Kaur. Congratulations." Alina's smile, unlike Tessa's, was bright with relief, and then she disappeared back inside the chapter room, leaving Tessa and Nina alone.

But having time to process derived no clarity for Nina. "What the fuck?" she finally said, after several seconds of silence. "Did you just orchestrate a coup against your best friend? And did I . . . *help*?"

Tessa sighed witheringly. "Look," she said, turning to Nina. "I did what I could for her. And I suggested you because I know you will, too. But as Fawn would say, you either eat or you're eaten. That's just what the world is."

It did sound like something Fawn would say. Was *that* power? Or was it just nihilism?

"Am I the one being eaten in this scenario?" demanded Nina, suddenly frustrated beyond belief.

Tessa's laugh was listless and dry. "Do you even want to be president?"

"Of course not." That much was obvious and accessible. "But I don't know, wasn't there more we should have done? Shouldn't we have defended her, or—?"

"Look, I meant what I said. Fawn loves you." Tessa rubbed her temple, looking tired. "And *because* she loves you, you being Slate's choice will spare her in a way Dalil wouldn't. This way, she stands a chance to walk away unscathed."

Unscathed. Well, fair enough. Fawn was never *scathed*, which was half the reason Nina couldn't envision anyone else in her place. Fawn said things like "you either eat or you're eaten" specifically because she was cool, so cool in the face of scarcity, so cool she always knew how to walk away with grace. Which Nina didn't understand, because Nina wasn't cool! Nina had never been cool because Nina was too fucking hungry—she wanted things too powerfully, too close to the surface.

She felt, then, the presence of two options: get over it, dummy! That was an easy one. Sometimes the person you were secretly fooling around with didn't get to be Lady Superior anymore and that wasn't a tragedy. It was just one person's bad day.

But then there was another, nearer option—the one always chanting FAWN FAWN FAWN at all hours of the night and day—which was, obviously, to go insane.

"Tessa," said Nina, "sincerely, no fucking joke, this is bullshit. I'm not even talking about one sorority election here. Or one dinner." What *was* she talking about? Everything seemed to blur, and everything hurt. "I just mean . . . Come *on*. 'Eat or be eaten'—is that really the world? Because you can't tell me what power is or what feminism isn't and still try to convince me that everything's just a zero-sum game." There! Abruptly, departing wildly from the matter of Fawn's displacement, Nina could finally diagnose it—the visceral problem her body seemed to have with The Country Wife. As if, with enough distance from the point, her internal organs could finally become the oracle making sense of the unknown.

It wasn't The Country Wife's mere existence or her popularity or even her embrace of the bizarre, pseudo-religious practice of traditional feminine roles that relied on the hegemony of white men. It was the fact that there was no objective measure of a woman, no simple framework by which to exist, and the only real danger was in the pretense that there was.

It was the performance again, Nina realized. The performance of respectability! The performance of womanhood! The fucking oxymoron that was the performance of an election designed to stab one woman gently in the back!

"I promise you, this is not about feminism," Tessa sighed, just as Nina felt a rush of adrenaline, another shock to the framework of what she could or couldn't accept. "I mean seriously, Nina, you think I don't know the world's fucked up? The only thing I'm 'Black enough' for is racism and I still wouldn't be here if I were about fifteen percent less hot. So honestly, this shit is just . . ." She waved a hand, and Nina thought again, helplessly, about what power wasn't. "It's politics. Okay? Someone loses. Someone wins. Believe it or not, this is the softest landing. I truly think this is the kindest thing I could have done."

"But it can't just be that, though!" Nina felt hysterical. "Like, if there are no other options, if there's no good or right choice—if everything is some stupid game we can never actually win—then what the fuck are we even doing here, you know?" Nina pleaded with Tessa, and then stopped. "What the fuck *are* we even doing here?" she registered aloud.

As if in answer, several things occurred to Nina at once. One, that she would have to tell Fawn about becoming part of a hostile takeover despite never answering the question as to whether or not she'd accept. Two, who the fuck was she going to bring to dinner. Three, this was what everything ultimately was, wasn't it? Just filthy compromise and little treats.

"What is any of it for?" asked Nina desperately, to which Tessa gave a dry laugh.

"No idea," she said, and then, "The economy?"

"What about me, though?" Nina demanded. "Can't I be, I don't know, different? Can't I just say no?"

"To what?" asked Tessa skeptically. "Slate? You could, but why? Fawn would rather have you than any of the alternatives, believe me."

"But what about devotion to the sisterhood?" Nina asked, or maybe begged. The hunt, her precious hunt. That sacred, innermost desire to devour, born from the innocence of girlhood, stoked by a lifetime's hunger to the point of righteous flame. Was it not holy after all? "What about the high ideals of friendship?" What about the power I was promised? What about The House's salvation that was supposed to be my grace?

"Oh god. Nina." Tessa cupped one of Nina's cheeks in her hand. "The dumbest part is that you'd make the perfect president. Alex would love you. The whole goddamn House would be better off."

"But *why*?" Nina's eyes had filled with tears.

"Because you still believe in it," Tessa said, and her voice was gentle, and her touch was kind. "Even though it lied to your fucking face."

35

"Where's your husband?" asked Sloane, stepping foot once more into The Country Wife's farmhouse. There was fresh paint on the walls, a new wall of built-in bookcases that had been decorated—that was the only word for it, more so than shelved or stocked—with an ombre pastel palette of coordinated spines.

"Oh, locked in the basement," said Caroline. "I mainly just go down there for sex or when I need the Wi-Fi unplugged and plugged in again."

"Oh," said Sloane faintly, and Caroline fixed her with a look of supreme condescension.

"I'm joking," said Caroline. "He's out to dinner with a client."

"What does he do?" Sloane wandered the living room, looking at the books. The titles were all familiar. She recognized some book club bestsellers, some mainstream nonfiction, a few sci-fi classics that Sloane remembered reading in school. She had the sense that despite the curated arrangement, Caroline had actually read them all.

"Internal audits," said Caroline. "It's dull as shit. He's funny, though." The last bit was faint, pulled from her like teeth, despite being unsolicited.

"You actually like your husband?" Sloane turned to look at Caroline as she asked, amused.

"I'm not just using him, if that's what you're implying." For the first time, Caroline seemed a little bit guarded, as if Sloane had uncovered something horrific or maybe even repulsive—*more* repulsive than being fed human heart. "He's got a great cock and he's nice to animals. All in all, I've got no complaints."

Sloane turned back to the books. "Is it really that shameful for you to admit you're in love with the man you married?"

With a jolt, she ran a finger down the spine of her first book. The name *Sloane Hartley* gleamed in tiny, unimportant letters.

"I don't find it shameful. I just don't expect it to last." Caroline gave a disaffected shrug.

"You know, I remember thinking that marriage was kind of scary at first," Sloane mused aloud. "It changes shape, and that can be alarming."

"Are you honestly trying to give me advice?" Caroline barked a laugh. "Your husband is cheating on you."

Sloane froze, her hand still curled in the air from where she'd been fondly stroking the ghost of herself, the spine of her work. Then she turned sharply. "How do you know that?"

"By looking at you." Caroline's aggressive, predatorial smirk was back. "You don't like your husband anymore. But for some reason, you're trying to teach *me* something. Why, because you're older? So you're supposed to know something I don't?"

Sloane shook her head. "I couldn't get comfortable at first," she said, unsure why she was disclosing any of this. Only that she felt too tired to play games. "For a long time, I didn't really believe he was going to love me forever. For years I was as happy as I could be while still half expecting him to leave." She stopped. "I think it's why I took things on that . . . I don't know. It seemed like maybe he'd love me more, I guess, if I just became everything he needed. If I took better care of him than me. I think that's what backfired on me in the end. I taught him exactly how to neglect me."

"Oh my god," said Caroline, wrinkling her nose. "Stop. This isn't even sad. It's just gross."

"I came here because I wanted to ask you about the ritual," Sloane said, rolling her eyes internally at this literal child, who would either learn one day to be grateful for what she had for the time that she had it or she would simply eat her husband, and either way it made no real difference to Sloane. "How does it work?"

"Like any form of hunting," said Caroline, her eyes big and deep when they looked at Sloane. Sloane was beginning to understand this was Caroline's face of interest, and the one she made when she was waiting for a reaction. "You don't want gunpowder residue in the meat. You don't want something that's been dead for a long time. You want the slaughter to be efficient and humane. We usually stun them first, then slit the throat. Oh, and a restraint system is critical. Don't want to waste the blood, that's valuable. Don't want to bruise the carcass either, that's bad for the meat."

"When you say 'we,'" Sloane began, and Caroline shrugged.

"I told you, I learned all this from Alex," she said. "She's the one who came up with the ritual."

As if by magic, there was a knock at the farmhouse's front door.

"Did you call her here tonight?" asked Sloane with a sigh.

"Yep," said Caroline, waltzing leisurely to the front door. "Like I'd speak to you without my lawyer present," she muttered, followed by an eye roll that Sloane already knew Isla would give her millions of one day.

Caroline opened the door, and Alex stepped inside the farmhouse with a tired expression on her face. "You're driving back this time," she said to Sloane without preamble, and to Caroline, she said, "What's for dinner?"

"Coq au vin," said Caroline.

Alex nodded approvingly. "A classic."

"Is it *actually* coq au vin?" asked Sloane.

"Dude, if you can't tell the difference between chicken stew and dismembered human, that's on you," said Caroline.

Alex sat down beside Sloane at the kitchen island. Caroline moved blithely around the kitchen, gathering iridescent wineglasses. There was a new lightness to her performance, like someone gladly showing off.

"This is beautiful glassware," murmured Alex.

"Thanks, I'll send you the link," said Caroline, pouring a bottle of glittery, sanguine Zinfandel first into Alex's glass, and then Sloane's.

Alex raised her glass to her lips, draining it. Then she turned to look at Sloane.

"I heard about your husband," she said.

"Mm," said Sloane, taking an extravagant pull from her own glass. It would be a long drive, but she suspected it would be a long meal, too. "It's just a sabbatical. To work on his book."

"That's good—that means they have no proof." Alex nodded approvingly, just as she had to the menu. "Unsubstantiated rumors."

"Yeah. It's great." Sloane took another drink. "I'm the wife of the man with unsubstantiated rumors and there's a house full of young women in my care."

"Could always serve him as a nice roast," said Caroline cheerily. "I've got a great rub for that."

"I don't think Dr. Hartley wants to talk about our little proclivities, Caro," murmured Alex.

"Actually, I was just asking Caroline about the ritual." Sloane turned to face Alex. "I want to know something. And honestly, I'd love to hear your answer."

Alex shrugged. "Hit me."

"Are you happy?" asked Sloane. "Like, does it work?"

"What, the ritual?"

"Yeah."

"Do you mean me specifically, or . . . ?"

"I mean all of you. The House," said Sloane. "Are you actually different from me? I guess I'm including you in that," she acknowledged to Caroline, who winked at her over her glass. "I want to know if it's real. Or if it's just another fucking VidStar trend."

Caroline refilled Alex's glass, and Alex swirled it contemplatively, twice, before looking back up at Sloane.

"Like I said, no member of The House has died of any illness since the ritual began," she said. "Nobody has ever gotten Botox or any other reconstructive surgery, either. Nobody wears glasses or has carpal tunnel and the pregnancies were all safely delivered and nausea-free. We all have the careers we wanted—including Caroline," said Alex with a toast in her direction, "who, as you know, is a serial killer with 4.5 million followers."

"My dream ever since I was a little girl," Caroline contributed wistfully.

"So then it works," said Sloane, breathing out. "It actually works."

Alex pinched the bridge of her nose as if to contemplate something, or to still her swimming thoughts. Her eyes darted to Sloane's, a look of concern passing over them. "Is this for your book? Because I think even the social sciences require a longer period of experimentation. Of course nobody has died of any illness; the oldest members who've completed the ritual are in their mid-thirties. I'd hardly call it conclusive."

"You do it anyway, though, right? You believe in it?"

Alex's knee jiggled apprehensively. Again she seemed to look warily at Sloane, as if she saw something on Sloane's face that worried her. "Wherever you're going with this, Sloane—"

"I have a daughter," said Sloane. "Someday she's going to be a woman."

Alex grimaced. "I know."

"I can't give her *this* world, you know?" Sloane felt like she was pleading, and maybe she was. Neither Alex nor Caroline seemed able to look at her. "The world where you fall in love but then he fucks teenagers. The world where the dean cuts your hours because he doesn't understand VidStar and then you die just to get out of your debts."

"World's fucked, Sloane," Alex confirmed with a shrug. "It's why I tell The Girls they have to go far, as far as possible. It's not about girlbossing or whatever the shit Fawn Carter thinks I'm trying to enforce. It's about being in the room where the decisions are made. It's about doing whatever it takes to break down that door and let others follow."

"You have so much time," Sloane said wistfully, looking at Caroline. "So much time."

Caroline's brow furrowed, her eyes darting to Alex with something that looked to be a wordless cry for help. Sloane understood, then, that Caroline was just a tiny little baby. Just a sweet little girl who happened to be clinically deranged. Why, then, was she looking at Sloane like *she* was the crazy one? "You shouldn't eat everyone you kill," Sloane said to her, gently. "You'll get some incurable brain disease."

"I don't," said Caroline, looking at Alex again. "I already know about kuru. And I don't eat human brains, I'm not a fucking zombie—"

"Calm down," Alex said to Caroline, her gaze flicking worriedly to Sloane's again. "Sloane's just a little upset."

"I'm not upset," said Sloane, laughing a little into her wine. Again, she felt Alex and Caroline exchange glances in her periphery, as if there was something inherently threatening about a woman who managed—despite great personal crisis!!!!!!!—to stay rational and calm. "I'm *curious*. I find I have a deep, intellectual curiosity about this. I want to know how it works, why it works, and how long it takes to *start* working."

"Scientific method," remarked Alex dully, with a slight frown.

"Exactly—I'm doing my research," said Sloane. "I don't doubt that whoever Caroline hunts deserves his comeuppance. Right? I'm not saying we shouldn't become violent. Ultimately all movements for liberation do." She was talking a little fast, she realized. A sweat had broken out on her brow, perhaps from all the gesticulating.

"Sloane," said Alex.

"Dude," whispered Caroline loudly to Alex. "Is she, like, okay?"

"Just get the stew, Caro—"

"The thing is." Sloane felt something inside her chest catch fire. "They're bad apples. Right? They spoil the bunch." Yes, she was definitely talking too fast.

"Are you talking about cops?" asked Caroline, who turned to Alex. "Is her husband a cop?"

"No, he's a professor. Sloane," said Alex, using the voice she used to placate toddlers. "Look, I'm sorry. I didn't mean to tease you. Yes, the ritual works, but you shouldn't use it on anyone you're close to."

"Because of cops," said Caroline.

"Yes, Caroline, thank you—"

"What you need is therapy," Caroline interjected again.

"No, I'm fine. I'm seriously fine." Sloane laughed and laughed. Like: AHHHHAHAHAHAHAHAAAAAHHHHHH!!!! "You can both stop looking at me like that, okay? I'm just trying to understand the benefits here, you know? Like, how magical is it? Is it actually *magical*, or just medicinal? Have you actually cured anyone of something, or is it more preventative? Just from your observation, obviously—I mean, look at the followers thing," she said to Caroline, who'd been trying to surreptitiously remove Sloane's knife. "Put that back, I'm fine. Is the followers thing because you're hot and crazy and have decent video editing skills or is it because you eat human hearts? Like, can you actually separate correlation from causation? Methodically speaking, is that something you can do? I just have to know," she said, and laughed again, though it sounded wrong. "Speaking as a sociologist, I have to know."

She could feel that she'd begun to rant a bit. Alex pushed a bowl of stew toward her and Sloane leaned forward with relief, using the serving spoon to take a bite. The broth was rich, laden with umami from the mushrooms. "Is there miso in here?"

"Yes!" Caroline said excitedly. "Wow, I definitely thought you were too white to notice—"

"Britt sent me a link to a miso carbonara." Sloane took a bite, then another bite. "Is there some bread?" The words got a bit lost. She was shoving bites in faster than she could chew. "Sorry, so rude, I said—bread?"

"Oh my god, of course," said Caroline, turning to cut a fresh piece. "I meant to offer you some but you were talking so crazy for a second there, I completely forgot what I was doing—"

"I made the carbonara, you know, thinking that Isla would eat it," Sloane told Alex, greedily tearing into the bread that Caroline handed her. "But she didn't, of course. Wouldn't even touch it. Just said 'no' and bounced. She asked me for ketchup and that's all she ate for dinner." Sloane swallowed thickly. "Guess how much iron is in ketchup?"

"It's just a phase," Alex said. Her eyes were filled with something now. Worry. Pity. It was familiar, Sloane realized.

It was *motherly*.

"She'll be okay," Alex said, and her voice was gentle, like a friend. Like a sister. "You're a great mom, Sloane. Lots of picky eaters have turned out okay. You're doing the best you can for her, and she'll be fine. I promise."

"Alex." No laughter now. Now Sloane's throat was thick with something. Lust. Love. Did it matter? "Don't leave me, okay? Don't leave me." She said it again and again. In her mind, she just kept going.

"Oh, Sloane." Alex's eyes were shiny and soft. "Why would you say that?"

"I need you. You're my best friend, and you're the only person—" Sloane broke off, choking. "You're the only person I trust. I know I called you an insane fucking cannibal and that's still true." She wiped thoughtlessly at her eyes. "But it doesn't matter. I love you so much."

Alex wrapped Sloane in her arms. "Oh, Sloane. I love you, too."

Sloane shuddered in Alex's arms, suddenly crying like her heart was breaking. "It's so hard," she said into Alex's baby-soft cashmere. "It's so hard. I'm trying *so hard*—"

"I know, Sloane, I know—"

"Oh! I've got a great waterproof mascara I can send you the link for. Or wait, I think I have some samples," said Caroline suddenly, scuttling off as she tossed over her shoulder, "It just came out. It's technically a celebrity brand but I'm like a *thousand* percent positive she never actually comes in—"

"There's no way to win," Sloane sobbed, and sobbed and sobbed. In her mind, on her cheeks, the dam had broken. "It doesn't matter how hard you try, how much you love, how smart you are. How am I supposed to do it? How am I supposed to tell her to love or to dream when I know goddamn well that it always ends like this?"

"How do you think I feel?" muttered Alex in her ear. "I'm raising a tiny man."

"The future *isn't* female!" Sloane screamed, pulling away from Alex in a sudden burst of pain. "I can't be expected to girlboss under these fucking conditions! And what the *fuck* is a She-E-O?"

"Whoa," said Caroline, who had just reentered the room. "I have some CBD gummies too, if that would help?"

"Sure, Caroline—Sloane." Alex's voice was prying now, trying to open a jar that wouldn't budge. "Here's what you do. Okay?

You have a nice meal with us. You cry a little. Then you get your fucking accounts in order. You write your book and let Skit help you publish it. You go on a book tour and you grow your brand. You use that money to put your daughter in the best schools you can, to give her all the resources she needs. You raise her to be strong. You catch her when she falls." She rested a hand on Sloane's shoulder. "That's all you can do. It's that simple."

"But that's not all *you* do." Sloane stared at her. "How do *you* do it?"

That time, when Caroline reentered the room, it was to loaded, sacrosanct silence.

Alex reached out, touching Sloane's cheek, running a finger comfortingly along her jaw. Caroline crept around the island to rest her own cheek on Alex's shoulder with the softness of a portrait.

"Well, as you know, I like a classic Bolognese," Alex said, and pushed the bowl of stew toward Sloane, encouraging her to take a bite.

And suddenly, Sloane felt much better. She really, really did.

36

"You traitor." Fawn's red-rimmed eyes shone cold from the dark of her bedroom. The clock on the nightstand now read 11:16 P.M., meaning they'd been at this for over an hour already. Nina had lost feeling in her toes. "You fucking traitor. You should have turned them down. You should have said no."

Nina felt numb, chilled to the bone from her time on the roof with Tessa, the subsequent minutes spent locked in indecipherable warfare now with Fawn. "I can still say no, Fawn. Obviously I can still say no. I don't have to run just because they nominated me."

But Fawn wasn't listening. "You should have let them slate Dalil. Nobody actually trusts her. She barely made the cut during rush."

"Why not?" asked Nina, realizing belatedly that while she'd brought it up, she'd never actually asked.

"Why?" Fawn nearly spat it back at Nina. "She's a fucking *mess*, that's why." She rose to her feet and started pacing. "Bad enough I had to take her as a Little because Nicole wasn't sure she'd buy in," she was muttering, half to herself. "I shouldn't have listened to you, or to Tessa. Alex was right. The House gets way too much scrutiny, we can't have someone with a record of a past—"

"Past? What does that—"

"There are sisters in this House who want to run for political office, *Nina*." Fawn had spun on her heel and speared it at her, like this was Nina's fault. "One bad association can take down a whole career—you're a woman, you fucking know that. We can't have members who aren't careful with their internet history. Revenge porn just floating around out there is leverage for someone to use."

"What?"

Nina felt a deep, profound sadness, a tenderness that made her wish she'd given Dalil an extra beat of kindness the last time they'd hugged. The last time she'd laughed with Dalil over a name as dumb as Yarden, Nina wished she'd taken the time to squeeze her hand, like a little doggie bag of softness for the road. "But Dalil's only eighteen, something like that couldn't have been legal—"

Fawn waved an impatient hand. "I'm not saying it's her fault, but you know how the world works. It's just stupid fucking optics, Nina, come on. Everyone always blames the woman."

"But *you* know that's horrific. Right?" Nina was staring at Fawn like she was watching her undress. Like Fawn was slowly but surely shedding her dignity, her humanity, everything Nina had so desperately wanted for herself. "You're, like, a vigilante. You're fucking . . . you're *punk*." She felt like she was doing calculus or landing a satellite on Mars. "You don't care about respectability or 'optics,' right? You *hate* the institution, you don't care about clout—"

All those followers, Nina suddenly heard Fawn say. *That's not nothing.*

Fawn wasn't looking at her. "Nina, please. I'm as liberal as anyone in this fucking generation but the fact is that right now, on about a dozen levels, Dalil is more of a liability than an asset. Unless she decides to—fucking, I don't know, use her story for a book deal or negotiate world peace." Fawn was obviously being sarcastic, but suddenly Nina couldn't breathe. The usual internal voice was starting to sound like this: FAWN FAWN FAWN ?

"But if that's what matters to you—" Nina's exhale was hard and swift. "If all you can think about is not getting *canceled*—"

She couldn't finish the sentence, it was too ridiculous. "I just—I mean come *on*, Fawn," Nina blurted suddenly, "how are you any different from Alex?"

"Oh, grow up." Fawn looked hard at Nina then, and Nina's eyes stung as if Fawn had slapped her. "You already know the world's shit, Nina. Seriously. You understand how this works. You're watching it now, in real time."

"What?" Nina blinked at her. "You mean the Slate thing? Because first of all, I only said yes because Tessa was the one who—"

"Jesus." Fawn's mouth tightened. "Don't get me started on Tessa."

"What did you do to Tessa?"

"What did *I* do—" Fawn stared hard at Nina. "Is she still not over that? It was a *closed vote,* Nina, and I was doing *my job*. Tessa was never supposed to know what was said in that meeting, and if Summer didn't have such a big fucking mouth—"

"What meeting? What vote?"

Fawn shook her head. "I'm sick of talking about this. Can you just leave, please? I can't deal with you right now."

"Can't deal with *me*?" Nina couldn't understand why she was having these sorts of feelings in The House—in the place that was so sacred, so safe. The place she'd sworn she'd die to protect out of the belief she could never get hurt here, never bleed like she had before.

"I get that you're upset, Fawn, and believe me, I understand why, but can you find a little perspective, please? I can still turn Slate's nomination down—that's what I came in here to ask you about, to see if you wanted me to just say no. This stuff isn't important to me," Nina added, "it's really just sorority politics—"

"*Just*—" Fawn gaped at her in disbelief. "You realize this is just *one more betrayal,* right? Just one in a long line of many. We can eat all the goddamn hearts we want and there's still men lining up outside our doors like fucking wolves. But you know who'll always betray us the worst? Not them, Nina!" Fawn sounded hysterical. "It won't be *them*. Their reasoning is selfish but at least it's logical. They can't stand us because we're a threat. So you know who the real problem is?"

Fawn's white canines were glittering in the dark. "It's our *friends,* Nina. Our fucking *sisters*." She looked like she would spit at Nina's feet, though she turned away instead, throwing herself onto her bed. "Because even people who say they love you are just lying through their teeth," Fawn muttered, turning her back to where Nina stood silently watching beside the door.

She was there again. Fawn Carter, the golden girl. Maybe she was right, her job involved hard choices—maybe Nina couldn't understand. Maybe it was easy for Nina to play the revolutionary because she didn't have to answer for the well-being of anyone else. Maybe the truth wasn't that Fawn was duplicitous, maybe she wasn't a hypocrite, maybe she was just lonely. Here in her single room with its single bed, the only member of The House without a group, without a partner. Did they really have to throw away so many weeks of gold on the revelations of a single night?

Ultimately: Nina was a believer, and she wanted to believe.

"Fawn." Nina softened then. "I'm not trying to betray you. I *do* love you, I—" She broke off. "I don't know if I . . . I don't want to spook you." She stepped forward, perching tentatively on the edge of Fawn's bed. "I love you, Fawn, I do. And if you want me to tell people that—if you want me to tell The House it should be you instead of me, I will absolutely—"

"Oh *god*." Fawn sat up to look at Nina with open disgust. "You thought I meant you? Jesus *Christ,* Nina. You really are a fucking idiot."

Fawn threw herself back down on the bed, turning away.

Nina stayed there for a moment, numbness creeping up her spine.

Then she got up without a word and returned to the Icebox,

falling into her desk chair with a sense that something horrible had just happened to her, and unlike all the other times she'd suffered some psychosexual atrocity, there was no chance she'd ever be able to put the specifics of this particular wound into words.

"Hey, there you are!" Dalil's voice was bright over Nina's shoulder. "Just grabbing a textbook, but then I'm heading back to the library if you want to come?"

"Oh, thanks," said Nina numbly, slumping down in her chair and texting Jas. **hey gurrl u up**

"You okay?" Dalil bent over Nina worriedly, one hand on her shoulder. "You look sad."

Nina's eyes filled again with unspilled tears. "Do I?"

"Oh, Nina." Dalil dropped her books on the floor and bent to give Nina a hug, crouching on her knees beside Nina's chair. "It's okay. It'll be okay."

Nina felt a sharp flood of embarrassment. She wanted to choose to sit up straighter, to claim her power, to achieve indifference, to dry her eyes.

But it was nice, this.

Being loved. Being comforted. Being cherished.

How many times had she asked for love like this and not received it?

Had it ever been this easy before? Fawn aside. Fawn, who was not The House. Fawn who was *of* The House, and who owed it better than she had given it. Who owed it more than lip service, the aesthetic of belief. Who could not make a mockery of Nina's vows—of Nina's entire hard-fought reinvention—not like this, in a single night.

Nina hadn't promised fidelity until cancelation. Until indignity or disagreement or betrayal.

She had promised *until death*.

"You believe in it, right?" Nina asked quietly, and Dalil pulled away, looking up at her from her knees with patient bemusement.

"What?"

"Sisterhood," whispered Nina. "I know . . . I know we both said it was stupid before." She exhaled sharply, casting off a weight. "But you believe in it now, though, right?"

"God, yeah." Dalil reached up to scratch idly at her brow—taking the question seriously, knowing it mattered, without Nina having to ask. "I mean, what else do we have, right? Everything else out there is totally heartbreaking."

Nina remembered the sense that she'd had before. That every woman in the chapter room had something painful in her past. A heartbreak from out there, outside of here.

It wasn't The House that had failed her. It wasn't broken. It wasn't false.

It just had a flaw. A thorn in the paw.

Nina felt the presence of a cool breeze, the refreshing promise of pursuit.

Just then, her phone rang. It was Alina Antwerp calling.

Nina raised the phone to her ear. "Hello?"

"Sister Kaur, this is the Slate committee. Will you accept our nomination for president?"

Alina's voice was loud enough over the receiver that Dalil could hear it. Nina looked down, swaying on the precipice of indecision just as Dalil's eyes widened excitedly, with unadulterated joy. Just like Nina's prior fantasies of Fawn, Dalil's lips mouthed an adoring *yes, Nina, yes!*

In a stroke of sudden certainty, Nina knew what she was going to do. She knew exactly who she was going to offer up for dinner, and she knew precisely how.

"Yes," Nina said after a moment. "Thanks, Sister Antwerp. I accept."

37

Before Sloane had left with Alex, Caroline had paused her beside the door.

"I lied a little," The Country Wife said in a quiet, hasty voice, eyes darting to Alex's back, obviously hoping Alex wouldn't overhear them. "It's true that you shouldn't choose someone close to you. You'll get caught that way for sure. But also, you shouldn't choose someone just because they're bad." Caroline's face looked young then, girlish. "I have my own moral code, sure, but it isn't all about vengeance—it can't be. You can't come to the meal from a place of hatred if you want it to give you something back. It has to be communion." She pressed her hand quickly, gently into Sloane's. "You have to love the food."

Love the food.

Love was something that had gotten very complicated since Isla was born. Sloane was constantly asking herself to love things, to love herself, to love her body, to love her mind—things she had hated in varying degrees and to little consequence before.

Love the world to which your daughter will one day belong.

Love humanity and all its ills.

Love your husband and all his sins.

Love your fellow man, your fellow woman.

Love your work. Love the food. Love is all you need.

"You okay?" asked Arya, jolting Sloane out of her thought spiral. She jumped, her heart beating double-time as he dropped his backpack beside his usual desk chair in her office. She hadn't even heard him come in.

"What?"

"You had a look." He gestured vaguely to his own face, in reference to hers. His was remarkable, truly. Sloane knew things about Arya now, about the way he looked when he came, the way his sweat smelled and tasted, the laundry detergent he used that was almost too good, stealthily suggesting the presence of a woman's training or an actual, living woman. (Possibly his mother? The thought depressed her, a heavy weight to the center of her chest.) All the intimate things that under other circumstances Sloane would have begun to take inventory of, distributing them into piles. Keep. Save. Throw away. Sloane recalled suddenly that before Max, she hadn't been an easily amorous person. (One occasionally had to do this: view oneself in retrospect, as a person that one once knew, who was no longer familiar or even capable of existence.) She had not loved easily or hard. Max had changed that, rewritten the part of Sloane that could see things like the future.

The fucking bastard. He had made her see a future; he had made her chase one down. And now look where she was, exhausted.

"I'm fine." She blinked. Blink. Blink. "You're late today."

"Missed me?" Arya grinned at her, though thankfully did not wait for her to answer, too adept was he at flirtation, never leaning too far in. "I ran into my cousin outside."

His cousin, Nina Kaur. Nina Kaur with those legs and those tits. Nina Kaur with her zest for life and her dry sense of humor. Nina Kaur with her youth. Nina Kaur, whom Sloane did not hate, *could* not hate, for knowing her as fully as Sloane knew her own heart. For knowing the beat of it, the craving. Because what did Sloane want? What any woman wanted! To scream, to tear open human flesh. To suffer a love that was carnivorous and devouring, resting on the thinnest edge of peril, a blade to kiss the throat. To be handled gently, sweetly. To cry, to drown, to eat.

To be fucked, goddamnit, really fucked, lacerated by pleasure. To know what it was to feel worthy, to be cradled and cherished. To know you could crush a man's head between your thighs.

"What's she like? Your cousin," said Sloane, suddenly feeling like she was entering a trance. A fugue state. Like the ground beneath her was starting to shift.

(What is a Good Woman? One that is worthy.)

(Not of academic validation. Not of power.)

(One that is worthy of honest, unfailing love.)

Love.

Love the food.

"Oh, well, don't let her hear you call her that," said Arya, with an air of fondness. "She's . . . I don't know, sensitive, really. She'd kill me for saying it, but she is. She wants everyone to be different—she wants every*thing* to be different, and she has some really strong opinions about what falls within the constraints of right and wrong. She comes off tough as nails, totally confrontational. Bull-in-a-china-shop kind of recklessness. The kind of energy that makes you think wow, I need a nap just looking at you." He smiled, or grimaced. It was a look that was admiring, but shadowed with doubt.

"But?" Sloane prompted.

"But," Arya agreed. "Underneath it all, you kind of know she's one of the people the world is going to hurt."

"What?"

Sloane felt a sudden hammer of alarm. It wasn't what she expected—though, what *had* she expected? What had she wanted to hear? She didn't understand this reaction she was having, this abrupt sense of . . . pain. Yes, pain. Over the future belonging to some other idealistic girl, inevitable injury that was so completely irrelevant to hers. And yet not fully cleaved.

"I mean . . . maybe that's not true. I hope it's not true." Arya ruffled a hand through his hair with a shrug. "But do you know what I mean? There are some people who are just . . . innocent. Who only want good things for others. It's this, I don't know, this earnestness, this energy that you just *know* people are going to misuse." He fell into his desk chair, staring idly into nothing. "I don't know, she seemed off. I think something happened to her recently. She seems a little depressed."

"Yeah?" Sloane was holding her breath.

"She just doesn't seem . . . *light,* I guess, anymore. There's a heaviness to her now." Arya stared into space again, then shook himself. "I'm probably overreacting, or, I don't know. It's not like I really *know* her, I just—"

"It's her age," Sloane said quietly. "I was idealistic at that age, too."

"But you're not burned out, though," Arya said. "Are you?"

"Burned out?" Sloane had to consider it for a moment. "I mean, no, I don't think so. But I'm also not sure I was ever trying that hard to change the world."

"Why go into sociology if not to change the world?" Arya was doing it again, expressing an avid interest in her thoughts. Poor thing, Sloane thought. Don't waste this goodness on me, not when there are so many young ones left untainted, still intact. Not some purity bullshit, but a light—exactly as Arya had said, a lightness.

"I was trying to understand the world, I think," Sloane explained. "I guess in some sense to explain it, first to myself and then to others. And then try to get other people to see it the way I saw it."

"In order to . . . ?" prompted Arya expectantly.

"Change it, I guess. Sure, if you want to call it that." But Sloane didn't remember a lightness. "I just don't think I was ever that person. The kind of person with that kind of fragility, I guess, or that the world would try to hurt." As soon as she said it, she knew it rang false.

"Of course you were," said Arya, with certainty he couldn't possibly possess, but still Sloane wanted to believe it. "How could you not have been?"

"I just don't think I inspired this kind of protectiveness," she said, gesturing to Arya, who shook his head, rising to his feet.

"I would have wanted to protect you then," he said. "I still do now."

His eyes were dangerously soft, a reminder of Sloane's moral hazards.

A Good Woman didn't devour. A Good Woman left things intact.

No, not intact. A Good Woman was a nurturer. A Good Woman didn't leave things as she found them, she made them better. She simmered the sauces until the flavors melded. She made the home gleam again with airiness and health. She was deserving of love not because she was beautiful—she was beautiful because she shone with worth. It came from inside. Love that love had begotten. You had to treat the self with tenderness. You had to love the food.

"How can I help you?" Sloane abruptly asked Arya, who frowned. "What's something that will actually *help* you, Arya? Recommendations, of course. Anything else? Would you like any of my publishing contacts?"

Arya frowned at her, puzzled. "What?"

"Sex with me will get you nowhere, Arya," Sloane said matter-of-factly. "You're the garden. I'm not here to uproot what you're growing. Let me tend."

"That cult is really getting to you, huh?" Arya's eyes were laughing, confused, hurt.

"I really enjoy fucking you, Arya," Sloane said seriously. "If I didn't have a daughter, I'd be fucking you right now."

Arya blinked, his expression only barely faltering. "I'm not totally understanding what Isla has to do with it—"

"It's her girlhood, Arya," said Sloane. "I can't rob it from her, okay? I can't let her see the ways I fail her. I can't *fail* her, don't you understand?"

"Sloane." Arya's confusion blended into concern. "Are you okay?"

She was talking too fast again, too passionately. "Your cousin, it's not that she doesn't know," Sloane tried to explain. "It's not like she doesn't understand that the world is going to hurt her. She knows the game is rigged. She knows she's playing to lose. She already crossed that bridge, you know? There's no going back now. That's the heaviness you saw in her." Sloane's certainty came from a place of experience. It came from history. It came from knowledge that was developed over time, from catcalls at twelve to a life built on the razor-edge of predation and exploitation. Confusion about whether the desire of others was good or bad. A reward or a punishment. Wanting without understanding. Catching glimpses, the way you could brace yourself instinctively, the way you knew from the shared history of your kind to reach for protection, but—god, how dark things could get!

Sloane ached for her—a version of herself that was dead now, long gone. A version of her that didn't exist.

No, Sloane realized abruptly, she *did* exist. She couldn't *stop* existing, doomed but unformed. She existed in all the bodies of all the girls who didn't yet see that they could no longer trust the intentions of their teachers. She was real in the heart of the girl who was only just beginning to understand that she wanted justice she could never achieve. She existed on the precipice, in the beauty that was desirable because it was unaltered by the knowledge to want better, to ask for more. She lived inside the value of youth, which wasn't value, not really, because it was mythological, empty—just a vessel waiting to be filled. She was the vacancy of potential, which was a shape constrained by nothing, which was the very same thing as being shapeless.

She existed—smarter, prettier, boundless, and younger—still ultimately destined to find her way here, to this place of endless failure—in the form of Nina Kaur.

Sloane rose to her feet then, kissing Arya's forehead. "I have to go," she said.

"Sloane," Arya called after her. "Are you okay? You look a little bit—"

She didn't hear him. Time, time was slipping away from her. With every moment that passed, Isla became a person that was further and further from the safety of Sloane's body. Closer to being injured, closer to being hurt. To being molded like clay into something that this disappointing world had made her. This world that wanted her to suffer, all because a woman in a story ate an apple in a garden—because a woman somewhere got hungry.

Because a girl could still starve and nobody would care, but a woman had to eat.

38

The day of the solstice dinner was a cold one. The sisters spent all morning huddled together instinctively under blankets, weighted down, waiting. Nobody touched their breakfast. There was an unresolved energy in the air, an active and prevailing wind, a distant hint of smoke. Tension knitted their shoulder blades as usual, this time shielding the collective heart rate of a conserving humpback whale.

It wasn't time; not yet. Patiently, enduringly, they waited. Time at half speed, they rested. The branches outside their windows rattled. The residents of the Icebox descended to the lower floors, where there was heat.

Then the guests started to arrive.

It was interesting, Nina observed, to see what each sister had felt was appropriate for the occasion, best suited for a meal. The room was entirely occupied by men. Dalil had brought someone Nina didn't recognize; someone she didn't think was even a student. A boy, not much older than the rest of them. Someone who looked like he had access to the internet, to ruining a life with the push of a button. He swayed a little on the stairs, like maybe he'd needed some early convincing. Wordlessly, Nina came over to help Dalil prop him up.

Alina arrived with her boyfriend, the knockoff Kennedy named Tripp. Nina blinked with surprise, and Alina lifted a brow as if to say, *We all make sacrifices.* Nina nodded. She already understood that was the truth.

Tessa arrived with someone in military uniform, early thirties.

Nina didn't ask. Similarly, though she had considered seeking out answers to whatever passed between Tessa and Fawn in the past, she dismissed the impulse almost immediately—it wasn't her pain or her story, and if Tessa didn't want to exhume it, then Nina wouldn't unearth it, out of respect.

There were two cops. A handful of what looked like service workers. Some athletes. Some frat bros. None too old. Perhaps among the oldest was Fawn's guest.

"Oh, hi, Nina," said Professor Villanueva. "Your term paper was excellent, I just finished grading it. Really strong analysis."

"Oh, thank you."

"Miss Carter told me this was a scholarship dinner?" Professor Villanueva was surveying the sea of guests, observing them with a brittle sense of suspicion, perhaps, that all was not quite right. Maybe he could feel it, the frequency, the thing Nina had first noticed; or maybe it was the girls who were licking their lips, baring their teeth, panting quietly. The occasional glint of canines flashing beneath the dining room's chandelier.

"Yes, sort of. More of a congratulations on the end of the semester dinner. Happy solstice and all that." Nina cleared her throat and held out a hand that was only slightly shaky with anticipation. She blinked away lightheadedness, a passing dizzy spell. "Can I take your coat?"

"Oh, I can't let you do that," said Professor Villanueva, and Nina wondered for a second if she'd imagined it, the certainty she'd felt that he wanted to fuck her. He seemed suddenly very paternal toward her, like his concern was that she hadn't eaten enough vegetables in recent days. He seemed frailer than she'd imagined, still healthy and active but not incapable of being taken down by sixty starving girls.

"There you are, Max."

Nina's eyes strayed to Fawn, who came over without acknowledging Nina. Professor Villanueva's cheeks grew flushed. "Sorry,

I suppose I hadn't mentioned to you that I had Miss Carter last semester," he explained to Nina. "She was one of my most promising students."

"Oh, Max, you really don't need to pretend around Nina," said Fawn with an air of dismissal. "I told you, she understands."

"Fawn." Professor Villanueva's mouth grew thin, his voice dropping. "We talked about this."

"Yes, you mentioned several times that it was a mistake. An accident!" Fawn laughed loudly, as if one of them had told a joke over cocktails. "You *accidentally* kissed me, of course, how could I forget. And the worst part," Fawn added to Nina in a performative aside, "is that I didn't even get the highest grade in the class. He gave it to some dude named Brody."

"Maybe I should go." Professor Villanueva looked uneasy. Next to him, one of the seniors—the one who'd first assured Nina about her uterus—touched the side of her dinner guest's neck like she knew exactly where to slice it open. "I—I think I should leave. I'm so sorry, Miss Kaur—"

"You can call me Nina," offered Nina. "I mean, we haven't done anything, so. There's no need to be so formal."

Fawn gave another high, distinct laugh. Professor Villanueva glanced hastily around the room.

"Oh god," said Fawn. "Nobody cares, Max. Literally *nobody* cares. That's the fucked-up part of the whole thing. It's not like fucking your students is new or creative. You're an evergreen cliché." She leaned over as if to kiss him, covertly removing something from her pocket, and Professor Villanueva shrank instantly away.

"Coward," snarled Fawn, and pressed a pink stun gun into his neck.

Professor Villanueva shuddered and fell, seizing as he went. There was a slight commotion as the other guests turned to look.

"Oh, no," Fawn cried out, bending as if to check Professor Villanueva's pulse.

Nina bent, too.

Across the room, the latch on the dining room turned audibly. At least three girls let out a soft, pleading moan.

"Why didn't you tell me?" Nina murmured to Fawn. Her finger did fit perfectly into the dimple of Professor Villanueva's unmoving cheek.

"I did. But apparently you weren't listening." Fawn's eyes met Nina's then, hard, angry. An unmistakable *fuck you*.

Nina understood, finally, that she had been wrong and she had been right. Fawn was honest, Fawn was fake, she was both the friend that Tessa loved and she wasn't—Fawn was a coin that would fall wherever it needed to for Fawn to wind up on top.

Fawn had never contradicted Tessa or renounced Tessa's approach to the ritual because it was closest to her own. But it wasn't exact, because justice wasn't necessarily altruistic. It wasn't *always* systemic. The violence in Fawn's justice was personal, singular. With a subtle hint of vengeful smoke—that feminine mesquite.

Then, a secondary epiphany, via the usual am-I-a-narcissist internal reckoning: it was never about Nina. Not the sex or whatever it was—that was probably just lust and convenience—and not the betrayal, either, because Nina never meant enough to Fawn to leave a mark. That was the truth, and the truth fucking hurt. Nina could admit that. Her heart shattered because she still fucking had one, thank you very much. It was the end of something. The end.

"I really did love you," Nina said.

Fawn looked up at her, expression contorted with something that was guilt and envy and the loathing you could have for a person whose pleasure you once craved.

"Bummer," said Fawn.

It was everything Nina needed to hear.

39

What do I use?

A stun gun works. Hang on, I'll send you a link.

40

"Sister Kaur? Your candidate?"

Nina rose to her feet, exhaling. This was her moment. This was what she had known would have to happen the moment Slate said her name. The one choice she could make that would finally make sense of everything. She would stitch up the wound, mend the hypocrisy; she would make two contradictory things equally true.

The House was holy. The House was violent.

It was possible to win, but only if you were willing to lose.

"My candidate," said Nina, rising to her feet, "is myself."

There was a collective gasp around the dining room. Beside the unmoving bodies of their recently incapacitated guests, The House was filled with sudden motion as girls turned to each other to whisper, to throw uneasy glances across the room.

"I believe in this sisterhood," Nina explained simply. "I believe in it so much and so fully that I mean to prove every word I said to you the night of my initiation. I love The House unconditionally. I want every sister in this House to eat well."

She looked around the room, her hands spread wide in saintliness, in invitation.

"I love you," she said to her sisters. "This much."

For a moment, it was deathly silent.

"*Nina,*" whispered Dalil, in reverence. In awe.

Beside her, Tessa's eyes had filled with tears. Summer's lips parted with a quiet sigh.

Across the room, Fawn swallowed hard, her jaw visibly tensing. Nina understood the hand she'd played, the way an ax was falling. Because who could beat it?

What had any of them ever wanted but love?

41

There was a hardware store about three miles from campus that sold everything Sloane would need. She just had to drop off Isla first at Britt's.

"We're having a group playdate," Britt's husband Finn announced merrily, revealing that Theo was already there when he opened the door to let Sloane in. "Are you headed to The House for elections tonight? Tell Alex we're all doing great. The girls are being unusually docile—I'd be concerned if I weren't so impressed."

"Oh no, no House business for me, I just have to pick something up at the store and run an errand before dinner," said Sloane, and bent to kiss Isla's head. "I'll be back in a couple of hours. Thanks so much for doing this."

"Oh, it's really no trouble—"

"Hey, Finn?" asked Sloane on second thought. "Do you know about . . . you know."

Finn, who had bent to remove Isla's coat, looked quizzically up at her. "Hm?"

"Nothing. Never mind." Of course he wouldn't. It wasn't for him. Sloane knelt beside Isla, taking her pudgy hands to her lips. "Be back soon, sweet girl."

Isla smiled, and Sloane's heart filled.

(With tenderness. With certainty.)

(With the sudden reappearance of a forgone beacon of light.)

42

Of course they wouldn't *eat* Nina. For fuck's sake, she was the only one who really loved them. That kind of unselfishness, that kind of devotion . . . it wouldn't be wasted.

So it came down to two final candidates. One was Tripp, Alina's boyfriend. It turned out he wasn't a Kennedy, but he *was* a Carnegie. His organs were maybe a little compromised by alcohol consumption, but there was no discounting that kind of privilege. That blinding sweetness of youth.

And then there was Max Villanueva. "Too high profile," said Summer. "Didn't you hear he's on forced sabbatical next semester? If something happens to him, they'll definitely look into it. We don't want that kind of exposure."

"Come on." Fawn looked to Alina in frustration. "You seriously want to eat your own boyfriend over some deadbeat dad who cheats on his wife?"

"Fawn, what I *want* is a Nobel Prize," snapped Alina, her voice stiff. "I don't give a fuck what some guy does in his spare time. I want this dinner to mean something."

"How could this not *mean something*—"

"Do you really care more about your personal vendetta than this sisterhood, Sister Carter?" Leonie asked Fawn.

Fawn looked at Tessa, who said nothing. Then she looked at Nina.

"He would've done it," Fawn hurled at her in a low voice. "Used you."

"I know," said Nina.

"They all will." Fawn's voice sounded broken. "Everyone does."

Something in Fawn went out. It flickered, then extinguished.

"You taught me that," Nina agreed.

Even from across the room, Nina could see Fawn's nails biting white crescents into her palm.

"Sister Carter," interjected Leonie. "We need to get on with the vote."

"It's Lady Superior," Fawn spat.

"For now," muttered Summer, under her breath.

"The point is it's already been over forty minutes—"

"Nina?" came a quiet voice on Nina's right.

Tessa was looking at her. The House was looking at her.

Their one true savior. Their one honest martyr.

"What do you think?" asked Tessa.

Nina looked at Fawn. She looked at Dalil. She looked at the dreams of her sisters and inspected each of them closely in the light. The one she wouldn't let fade.

"I think Tripp would be more filling," she said.

And yes, maybe Fawn would be disappointed. But it was really about the quality of the meal.

43

"What do you need this for, little lady?" asked the cashier at the hardware store.

"Good question," said Sloane. "Content."

"Ha ha," the cashier said.

44

It was an incredibly satiating meal. Nina chewed slowly, each bite a tender kiss. After dinner, she would choose to briefly walk outside, to get some fresh air, a moment of quiet contemplation. She would stand for a moment outside The House gazing up at the pillars, the way its windows faced the street like watchful, vigilant eyes. She would feel the tension leave her, the hunger that seemed so limitless and eternal finding rest for the time being, the magic or whatever it was that so readily absolved her of her body's aches and pains now coursing steadily through her. Making her someone worthy, someone protected, someone new.

But that was later. In the moments before Nina reached the front door, Tessa caught her by the elbow, holding her back for the briefest, quietest exchange. "I didn't expect you to fight like that." Her expression was laden with accusation, with meaning. "I didn't think . . ."

"That I was like that?" Nina guessed.

Tessa's mouth was a thin line of conflict. "I just thought—"

"The problem with Fawn is that she couldn't pick a side," said Nina. "But I can."

Tessa's eyes fixed on hers intently.

Then she nodded with understanding, or acceptance.

In the end, it didn't matter which. Nina knew she'd come around.

45

The gray sky parted, a patch of sun slipping through the clouds before disappearing in a haze of red. A tendril of light fell upon a head of thick raven hair like a weight, a slipping halo.

The girl stood outside The House looking up, her gaze casting solemnly across the noble pillars.

Then the clouds shifted, and the shadow of The House was like a blanket, a heavy cloak.

Sloane got out of the car and walked toward The House quickly, very quickly, her knuckles white around the newly purchased stun gun.

She was in a hurry. It would be time for dinner soon.

46

"Lady Superior," called a voice. Summer Toft.
Nina looked up from her phone. "Yes?"
"Would you like to be the one to serve dessert?"
"Oh. Sure, Sister Toft. Just a second."
Nina reread the texts she'd just exchanged with Arya.

Arya: did you and jas forget about me???

Nina: what?

Arya: i asked her if you two wanted to get dinner tonight but she hasn't replied

Nina: why would jas get dinner with us???? she lives in ohio

Arya: ?? she didn't tell you she was visiting? i ran into her on campus earlier

Arya: she said she flew out to surprise you bc she's "depressed out west," i believe. u know jasleen's got bars. she's on lexapro now lmao long time coming ig

Nina: literally what are you saying to me right now arya

Arya: ???? jas said she was on her way to your house, like, hours ago. has she not gotten there yet?

47

Alex's Bolognese recipe had to simmer for three hours. Sloane put everything on the stove, dropped the disemboweled body off at Caroline's, then picked Isla up from Britt and Finn's. She let Isla watch the movie she loved. She showered her with kisses, let her stir the pot. The car's plastic lining had been moved; not yet disposed of, but that could wait until tomorrow. In the meantime, Sloane sat with her baby, tickling her feet, pretending to eat her toes. Isla laughed and laughed.

When the sauce was done, Sloane ladled it generously over fusilli, the meat clinging to the twisted grooves. Fresh liver was rich in iron, something Isla sorely needed. Sloane blew on the pasta to make sure it wasn't too hot; that it wouldn't burn her precious daughter's tiny mouth.

"Have a bite," whispered Sloane, bracing for refusal. The smell in the air was heavy, coppery and rich.

Isla opened her mouth. Sloane slid the pasta carefully inside. Isla chewed and swallowed.

Her eyebrows rose. "Mmmm," she said. *Yum.*

Sloane exhaled. "More?"

"Mmmm," Isla repeated. She held out a chubby hand and Sloane gave her the tiny fork. Frankie the dog was uncharacteristically devout, still glowing with gratitude over his opportunity to lick the spoon.

Isla punctured another noodle, then raised it to her mouth. "Mama," said Isla. "Mama, mmmmm!"

"Yes, baby." Sloane's heart pounded in her chest. "Yes, isn't it yummy?"

"Mama, mmm!" Isla repeated.

A good meal. Finally.

Finally, Sloane had done it. She was a Good Mother, at last.

There was a sound from the front door then, a scratching. Like someone couldn't quite fit their key into the latch. Sloane looked up with a frown, waiting, until Max staggered in.

"Sloane." His voice was hoarse, his pallor near translucent. "I have to tell you something."

She could read it on his face. She already knew. And they would deal with it.

Tomorrow.

"Later," said Sloane.

Max looked at her then with adoration. With relief. He took her face in his hands and kissed her hard, almost toppling into her. As if she held in her hands his salvation. A Good Woman. Her future at the price of the girl she'd once been.

Caroline was right. You had to love the food.

"Eat," said Sloane.

Max pressed his forehead to hers, grateful and unfailing. Saved.

From the sidewalk outside The House, a mislaid cell phone buzzed again, tumbled from the hand of a girl whose abduction no one had witnessed. The name *Nina Kaur* lit up across a picture of twin faces laughing, a seventh missed call. An incoming text sluiced across a black screen: **jasleen i'm serious where the fuck ar** . . .

Some games you couldn't win. That was the thing! You just couldn't save everyone. It was pointless even to try.

What mattered was dinner, and that everyone was finally eating well.

CREDITS

The book you've just read would not have been possible without the effort and expertise devoted by every member of my unparalleled publishing teams. I am honored to have worked with each one of them, and they all deserve proper recognition for the time and talent they brought to this book.

UK
Publisher Bella Pagan
Editorial Assistant Abbie Gibb
Senior Marketing Manager Becky Lushey
Senior Communications Executive Olivia-Savannah Roach
Communications Assistant Grace Rhodes
Publicity Assistant Emelie Gerdin
Senior Influencer Marketing Manager Emma Oulton
Content Manager Carol-Anne Royer
Video & Influencer Marketing Executive Dais Whitfield
Audience Development Director Andy Joannou
Digital Marketing Manager Will Upcott
Email Marketing Manager Katie Jarvis
Senior Production Controller Bryony Croft
Editorial Manager Rebecca Needes
Cover Designer (UK) Neil Lang
Sales Director Stuart Dwyer
Head of Independent Bookshops & Wholesale Richard Green
Sales Manager Rory O'Brien
Sales Manager Ellie Kyrke-Smith

Key Account Manager Heather Ascroft
International Sales Director Leanne Williams
International Communications Manager Lucy Grainger
International Sales Manager Poppy Morris
Special Sales Director Kadie McGinley
Special Sales Administrator Molly Jamshidian
Head of Trade Marketing Ruth Brooks
Trade Marketing Manager Helena Short
Trade Marketing Executive Liv Scott
Senior Trade Marketing Designer Katie Bradburn
Metadata Executive Kieran Devlin
Audio Editorial Assistant Mia Lioni
Postroom Staff Chris Josephs

US
Executive Editor Lindsey Hall
Associate Editor Aislyn Fredsall
Editorial Assistant Hannah Smoot
Agent Amelia Appel
Publisher Devi Pillai
Associate Publisher Lucille Rettino
Publicity Manager Desirae Friesen
Assistant Publicist Lauren Abesames
Executive Director of Publicity Sarah Reidy
Executive Director of Marketing Eileen Lawrence
Marketing Director Emily Mlynek
Senior Marketing Manager Rachel Taylor
Jacket Designer Jamie Stafford-Hill
Interior Designer Heather Saunders
Production Editor Dakota Griffin
Managing Editor Rafal Gibek
Production Manager Jacqueline Huber-Rodriguez
Sensitivity Reader Lynn Brown

Copyeditor NaNá V. Stoelzle
Proofreader Jaime Herbeck
Cold Reader Sara Thwaite
Associate Director of Publishing Operations Michelle Foytek
Associate Director of Publishing Strategy Alex Cameron
Director of Subrights Chris Scheina
Associate Director of Sales Cristina Cushing
Senior Audio Producer Steve Wagner
Voice Talent Stephanie Németh-Parker and Rita Amparita

ACKNOWLEDGMENTS

This book is a satire—the focus on white, cisgender, able, attractive, upwardly mobile, and university-educated women is intentional, and many of the views expressed herein are ironic and/or aggressively limited in scope in service to the narrative. I was not specifically writing with the goal to educate. If you are looking to reconsider the lens through which you view feminism and intersectional politics, there are countless better resources, one seminal title and personal favorite being *Hood Feminism* by Mikki Kendall. Read diversely and do it on purpose—publishing as an industry does not necessarily create the circumstances for incidental exposure. The arguments presented in this book are just theoretical starting points, if you, like me, like to ponder things.

I continue to not be totally sure if anyone even needs this book. When I had the idea for it, I had just finished the first draft of my previous book, *Gifted & Talented*, and did not, strictly speaking, have time to start another one. But three things coalesced for me in 2023: the ubiquity of the *Barbie* movie; the books *Fleishman Is in Trouble* by Taffy Brodesser-Akner (2019) and *The Best of Everything* by Rona Jaffe (1958), which I read back-to-back by pure coincidence; and the prevalence of the "girl dinner" meme, a social trend that began with Olivia Maher (@liviemaher) on TikTok and eventually trickled down to me, a la Anne Hathaway's cerulean sweater. Which also coincided with the rise of "clean girl" makeup, coquette-core, trad wife content . . . trends that were aesthetically pleasing but also insidiously aligned with far-right ideologies of female purity and "traditional" feminine roles. It seemed to me that a classic Scooby-Doo "ruh-roh" would not be misplaced, especially considering that the media I referenced share the overall conclusion that it is not possible for women to have it all, unless the "all" in question are small treats.

Perhaps this was precisely the reason for the celebration of girlhood—but then, was there really a universal girlhood? Was it sinister to uphold the monolith of The Girl at the cost of necessary intersectionality? What *was* feminism now, post-girlboss? Were our goals being muddled? Had feminism revealed a tendency to cannibalize itself? Should I maybe write this down? But cannibalism is so overdone this year, I argued.

Shut up, no it's not, my editor Lindsey argued back.

At the time I'm writing this, the feminist deliverables (reproductive rights, equal representation, equal pay, the ability to occupy our bodies with dignity and safety) feel farther away than I can remember them seeming in my lifetime, which is a hard thing to sit with. I don't know how to fix it. Pause for primal scream—FUCK! I just don't! This conversation preceded me and will continue long after I'm gone. But experience has taught me that art can be transformative. Art speaks, and it motivates and unites, in a way that endless posturing (and doomscrolling) does not. I hope you took something away from this, but in the end, I'm just a storyteller, and it's really just a story. Whether it can be anything else is out of my hands. Hot potato. Bon appétit.

Massive thanks (or perhaps blame?) to my editor, Lindsey Hall, whose enthusiasm for the idea was the primary difference between me writing this book or not. Every time we do this together, Lindsey, I am reminded how lucky I am to have you. Thanks as well to Alex Cameron and Rachel Taylor for being there at San Diego Comic-Con when I delivered my initial pitch, and to TJ Klune for his proximity, and his jealousy. Hi, TJ, love you. Huge thanks to Aislyn and Hannah for their editorial work and for being on the receiving end of all my emails. Amelia, my

ACKNOWLEDGMENTS ♀ 357

agent, my partner in books. If you think I'm done thanking you for the chance you took on me, you are a fool. Are you having fun??? I'm having so much fun with you, it's honestly the best.

Thank you to the translators who work on my books in other languages. Wild! I don't bring this up often enough, but when someone who read my book in another language says they loved it, I know they're not just talking about my work—by necessity they're talking about the book you and I wrote together, and the craft and time you spent interpreting my meaning and being the vessel for story from one form to the next. What an incredible gift.

Massive thank you to Amy Lauer, PhD, for her help with the bureaucratic intricacies of academia. Thank you to Dalil Miranda, of Ediciones Urano, for being such a wonderful person I had to borrow her name. Thanks and apologies to my friend, fellow artist, and favorite poet Arya Shahi for the use of *his* name (I thought I would just swap it out but oops, I didn't). To my sorority sisters, especially Jen. Cannibalism aside, the full scope of my love is here in these pages. More thanks and much love to my friends: David and Stacie and Angela and Lauren and Lauren and Tracy and Veronica and Alix and Cat and M. To the crew of minis: Theo, Mateo, Harry, Miles, Eve, Clayton, Andi, Kally, Eli, and Harvey, and all their parents. To my family, especially my mom.

To Henry, my god!! How you changed me, how you continue to change me, how you've totally rewritten me. How unrecognizable my heart has become and how hysterical I've been in trying to record it—how much I hope I continue to change, how senselessly I want to do everything right for you (to unavoidable failure, of course). I felt this kind of violence only once before and it was for your father. Garrett, I love you and this life with you is the easiest choice I make every day. My feelings on this have been recorded somewhere. (See also: *Alone with You in the Ether* by some degenerate hack.)

Finally, to you, Reader. Forget about the audience who wants you to fail. So many people are here to watch you succeed. Scarcity is a myth, self-interest is a choice. Be generous and dauntless. Don't be afraid to lose. As always, it was an honor to put down these words for you. I hope you enjoyed the story.

xx, Olivie

ABOUT THE AUTHOR

OLIVIE BLAKE is the internationally bestselling author of sci-fi and fantasy for adults, including the Atlas Six trilogy, *Alone With You in the Ether*, *Gifted & Talented*, the short story collection *Januaries* and her most recent novel, *Girl Dinner*. With Little Chmura, she is the co-creator of the graphic series *Clara and the Devil*. As Alexene Farol Follmuth, she is also the author of the young adult novels *My Mechanical Romance* and *Twelfth Knight*. She lives in Los Angeles with her husband and son.